JANET:

Storm Witch

by

Christopher J. Reeve

JANET: Storm Witch

ISBN: 9798596296518

Cover design by Christopher J. Reeve

For Mum;
Thanks for the story

Prologue

She was twenty-one, her face streaked with tears, her disbelief
suspended only by the knowledge of what *they* thought, how she'd
been treated these last days; what they blamed her for.

The judgement had been made. Tomorrow she would die; one night
alone in Marwick's Hole, then processed through the streets of
Kirkwall all the way to Gallow Ha, where she would be strangled and
burned as a witch.

Forcibly the guard took her by an arm already black with the bruises
of those violent days. She screamed, 'Save me Ben!' but the clamour
drowned her calls, and the briefest glimpse of him amongst the jostling
shadows, seemed only to confirm his indifference, his face twisted in
contempt.

Forced away towards the pit Janet's eyes sought out Bess and found
her mocking face. For a moment, their eyes were locked in mutual
venom as the guard cut her bindings and pushed her down into the
Cathedral's notorious cell.

The hole reeked of stale urine, the walls slippery and cold beneath
her searching, recoiling fingers. The floor littered with tattered rags -
the torn cloth of garments once worn by other tortured minds faced
with a night to contemplate impending death. A voice above her, most
likely that of the guard, said something she did not catch. Something
like spital spattered down the wall beside her, she shrank from it,
crouching fearfully against the opposite wall. A heavy grate rang
closed across the opening, all hope… gone.

Chapter one

Carl turned the key and pushed the door with his shoulder to open it. He stepped inside. 'I'm home!' All was silent. He glanced back through the window as he attempted to close the door a second time. His wife's old, silver Polo sat on the driveway, its front tyre sitting in a hollow where the day's rain had produced a swollen puddle. Carl sighed, succeeding in closing the door on his third attempt.

Last night's dinner plates were sitting beside the sink, the remnants upon them now firmly part of the pattern. 'Sally, are you home?'

'Up here.'

Carl made his way from the kitchen, through the lounge and up the stairs, finding Sally sitting at her laptop in the spare room.

'Nearly done, Carl love. Good day at the office?'

'Not really...'

Sally glanced up with a "poor dear" expression, then returned to her typing.

'Chambers is getting offish about the column again.'

Sally didn't respond.

'I know for a fact that what the boys and I write, sells that blasted rag...'

Sally looked up quizzically, 'What's that dear?'

Carl turned in the doorway, 'Just gonna do the washing up.'

'Thanks. Assignment's due in the week we get back. Will you read it later, check on my spelling?'

Carl turned, smiling affirmation before heading back downstairs. "...The week we get back." Carl allowed himself a little skip at the bottom of the stairs. It may have been a bad day at work, but a week of escape now loomed. He paused thoughtfully at the kitchen sink; part of the break was to get new material for the column. He shrugged and turned on the tap. 'It fascinates me. So, stuff what Mr. Alfred B. Chambers thinks, whatever the "B" stands for... Ha! Brat! Alfie Brat Chambers!' He'd amused himself. 'I'm just gonna enjoy the island, immerse myself in the folklore...' Carl stood still, letting the tap water run over his hand. 'Crap! No hot water!' He flicked on the kettle and opened the freezer, retrieving a thin, crispy, Italian pizza. 'Pizza Sal?'

A positive sounding noise echoed down the stairs.

Carl freed the meal from its packaging, placed it in the oven and set the timer. The kettle clicked off. Carl added some hot water to the sink and started washing up.

Later, Sally laughed at Carl's failure to turn the oven on and Carl laughed at Sally's failure to notice that her laptop's spell-checker had changed a misspelt reflection into erection. The evening was spent getting the bags and tent ready for when the taxi arrived for the airport run, the late hours concluded with a little wine and tender petting in front of a favourite movie. The start of the holiday would mark the anniversary of their wedding, one year to the day, probably the only time in marriage when camping on the Orkney Islands so early in the season seems a bright idea.

~

Carl Ree worked for Mr. Alfred Bartholomew Chambers, owner and editor of the Wymondham Herald, a young man with big ideas. Under his father's management the paper had grown beyond its local boundaries and gained cult status throughout the county. Alfred's plan was to bring it into the twenty first century, go online, change the name, go national, perhaps international... Carl wasn't at all bothered with the digital concepts, these had to take place - if anything they were overdue. What agitated him was Alfred's other requirements.

Carl's column was called "Mr. Ree's Mysteries", a cheesy name sure, but his writing had earned him the annual readers award more times than any of his colleagues. By definition he felt it defied modernization, but Alfred wanted new - new myths, urban legends, a hat tipped to the contemporary lust for occult, supernatural and conspiratorial themes - Carl felt hassled. The mysteries he loved weren't things that reminded him of recent film releases - as if some individual, influenced by the old amber nectar, had mistaken the sound of cats fighting for the invasion of flesh-eating-zombie-vampires-from-Mars - no, he wanted to write about ghostly Roman legions, the Devil's footprints and headless horsemen! Carl liked the tendency of

3

the past to resist investigation, he could pick holes in contemporary testimonies; history had its own fog. That was where he felt he fitted in. He was a man comfortable in his own stubble, his goatee caught the breeze shy of his sternum and boasted two or three white strands that, in his eyes, confirmed wisdom, or the dawn of it, and his eyes sparkled with a wildness born of excitement.

There *were* modern phantoms and conspiracies of course, and Carl knew he'd have to give them page space if he wanted to keep his job - This he begrudgingly accepted. What had finally stripped his cool was Alfred's visit just minutes before the close of day. He had insisted that Carl return from his "Highland fling" clean shaven, with shirt, tie and a more business-like attitude. Carl's incredulous stare had sent Alfred scurrying away with no further demands. The last Carl had heard as he left for home, was the grilling Henry was getting regarding Chris's whereabouts.

Carl had fumed all the way home. His wife loved his beard, it was as much a part of his character as it was a part of his face. It was right there alongside his cracking sense of humour and instinctive feel for the weather. Alfred, in Carl's mind, was a prick.

Sally comforted her man that evening; she didn't really mind if the goatee had a little trim, it tickled an awful lot when they were close anyway, and sometimes she got a mouthful of it when they kissed, which she disliked. He'd had shorter hair when they'd met six years ago. He'd looked so much more dashing back then. That said, she adored his passionate enthusiasm and didn't want to knock it whilst things were unsettled, and it all seemed inextricably bound to his perceived public image anyway.

Sally studied. Carl's wage paid for what they had, but it would never afford them a place of their own. Their rental was cheap by choice in order to set a little by, but Sally's earning potential after Uni would see them happily into family ready living. Carl could probably leave the old rag once she was qualified; freelance whilst looking after the children.

Sally loved that Carl wasn't a fitness freak or football fan. He wore his little excess tyre quite well, and she felt slimmer on his arm than she felt with her "skinny" friends.

Carl liked that his friends double-took Sally before he introduced her to them. It was safe to say he loved her more than words.

Chapter two

Carl and Sally woke a little later than they'd planned, but a half hour of clawing around in order to be ready for the taxi, proved unjustified. It didn't arrive.

Carl called the taxi firm.

'Sorry Mr. Ree. Our driver is on his way but he's caught in traffic; a lorry's shed its load on the bypass.'

'A lorry, huh?'

'Afraid so Mr. Ree...'

'It's never anything more exciting, is it? It's never an escaped Rhino.'

'Er, no - one moment...' The phone line was muted for a few seconds, Carl looked at his watch. 'The driver just rang in; reckons he can get to you for nine...'

'No, that's gonna be too late, the flight is at nine fifteen, er, OK, we'll make our own way...'

'OK Sir, sorry about that...'

Carl sighed, and put his phone down on the kitchen table. 'Sal...'

Sally came downstairs at a gallop. 'Taxi?'

'No, they can't get here, lorry over on the bypass.'

'Oh no! What are we going to do?'

'Grab your bag, Eddie owes me a favour...' Carl slung his rucksack over his shoulders - cooking utensils clattering loudly - grabbed up the cool box in his left hand, and wrestled with the back door. Outside he called back to Sally, 'Slam the door and lock it behind you love.'

~

Carl thumped on his neighbour's door, 'Ed... you in mate?'

Eddie appeared from the back garden and chuckled at Carl's backpack. 'Ya emigratin' Carl?'

'No, but we're late for our flight and the taxi's stuck in traffic on the bypass, some lorry's shed its load. You couldn't whip us up to the airport by the old road, could you?'

Sally appeared with a neatly packed tent under her arm and a large canvas bag in each hand. Eddie laughed, 'Best load up the van. I'll let the missus know where I'm off to.' He freed some keys from his pocket, unlocked his Transit and disappeared into his house. Carl and Sally loaded their bags and camping gear, and climbed into the cab.

~

It was only as the plane reached an altitude of thirty metres, that Carl recalled placing his mobile phone on the kitchen table. Sally assured him that he could probably survive without it for a week and that it would probably be good for him. 'It's only work stress when it goes off...'

'Nothing I can do about it now anyway.' He sat back and gazed out the window. Norwich fell away. In one hour and twenty-three minutes they'd arrive in Edinburgh with two hours to kill before the connecting flight to Kirkwall. At two forty they'd touch down, the mysteries of the islands at their feet, and he could finally place a long-awaited tick on his bucket list - visit the place his mother lived as a child.

Sally squeezed his arm and snuggled up to him. 'You'll be able to chat to me a bit more.'

'If I must.'

Sally thumped his arm and snuggled closer, 'Meanie.'

Carl kissed her forehead, 'Let's have fun.'

~

Due to their haste that morning neither had switched on the

television. Had they watched they would have seen the weather girl chirpily warn viewers to keep up to date with the track of a storm. Where it would hit was under debate but it was predicted to trouble the UK towards the end of the week.

Had Carl remembered his phone, the weather App he ran would have flagged up the weather warning for the Orkney's as early as Tuesday, but everything was as it was, and, as they glided down, Carl and Sally felt nothing but excitement watching South Ronaldsay, Hoy and Mainland Orkney passing slowly beneath them.

~

The decision to go camping on Orkney had come some three months before. Carl had met a native Orcadian, a man of about sixty-five called John Tulloch, whose daughter worked in London. He had moved to Wymondham to be closer to her. On reading Carl's column in the Herald, John decided to make contact. He intended to talk about the many stories of the islands that he had heard as a boy.

A meeting was arranged at The Green Dragon pub, but for all of John's email enthusiasm, Carl found him timider socially, and the conversation started in a strained, somewhat forced manner. Carl, a self-styled champion of the people, and always one for finding common ground, brought up his own links with Mr. Tulloch's homeland.

'My mother spent some of her youth on Orkney you know.'

'Oh?' John looked up from his Woodforde's real ale.

'Coastguard's daughter.'

John stared back.

'The name was Hunt, they would have been there in '53, I'm afraid I've never researched much deeper to find when they arrived and when they left.'

'Hmm '53 hey? Year of the great storm.' John's confidence was growing. 'Et would have ben Arthur, en '53...'

'That's right! You knew him?'

'Strong man that one, his wife got poorly ef I recall...'

'Yes, they moved south, ended up in Aldeburgh in the end. That's where my father and mother met.'

'Had four children…'

'My mother; her two sisters and a brother…'

'Caught the boy scrumpin' from the Apple tree en my farm yard.'

'Really! Ha! Not many trees on the island I heard…'

John nodded, 'There's some, where et's sheltered. We're no' so barren as the Shetlands…' He paused thoughtfully. 'Yoo ben to the Islands much?'

'Always wanted to, but there's no family up there now, and what with cost and distance…'

'Yoo ken use my farmhoose, do a bit o' research?'

'Actually…' John could almost hear Carl's brain working. '…my wife and I love camping. Could we put a tent up on your land?'

John laughed out loud, 'Ha! Yoo havne ben before!'

'No, really, we love camping…'

'Ha! Well, ya welcome. There's ample space on the lawn where the Apple tree grows, an' the wall'll afford ye some shelter, aye, et'll be cosy enough later en the year.'

'Wow, sounds great!'

At ease now, and with another ale half consumed, the evening was spent to Carl's great benefit. He learnt a little more about his family and the place where they'd lived, and enjoyed talk of Selkies, Trows and Finmen until last orders.

Sally wasn't impressed with his late return home, although news of a Scottish holiday did a great deal to cheer her up again.

Chapter three

It had taken them just five minutes to walk from the airport to Tulloch's farm. Carl had the big rucksack now with the tent properly attached, and a canvas bag in each hand. Sally had the cool box. Both were pretty red as they stood in the gateway of the farmyard in brilliant sunshine, a mild but assertive breeze dancing up from the nearby beach with its little wreck just visible above the high tide. A SAAB 340 aircraft growled its departure from the Island, arcing smoothly away in the sky above them as it headed back to Edinburgh.

'Oh Carl it's lovely. Look at the apple tree!'

From the gateway a tall, stone wall encircled the yard, the only other gap a wide gate that gave access to ramshackle barns beyond. The farmhouse overlooked a largely gravelled area with little, tufts of wiry grass dotted about it. To one corner was a triangle of rough lawn where the apple tree stood, its May-blossom-coated branches demonstrating the sculptural prowess of the prevailing wind. The farmhouse also looked weather beaten; the windows hadn't been cleaned, and the paint on the sills was flaking away. That said, it had a homely feel, and a solid, dominant position in the landscape.

Carl lay down the canvas bags and swept Sally into his arms; the cool box clattered to the ground. Sally laughed.

'This is magical!' Carl grinned. 'Hey!' He held Sally at arms-length, gazing wildly into her eyes. She nodded expectantly. 'I should write all this down it's such a great setting for...'

Sally's face stopped him dead; she wasn't smiling anymore - she was frowning. 'They owe you nothing Carl! Since Alfred's dad left, it's been nothing but demands. Clive let you do your thing, his son...' Sally calmed in response to Carl's concerned face. 'This is *our* week, get away from writing, enjoy yourself.'

'It was part of the reason for...'

'May wedding, a year ago... let's be us.' She tugged on his arm pulling him towards the lawn. 'Let's get the tent up!'

Carl's immediate inclination was to protest, but Sally was changing the subject and was already unclipping the tent from the rucksack. Tent away, Carl hitched the rucksack from his back and placed it down. He shrugged to himself, the folklore was probably everywhere, they'd be immersed in it before too long. He'd make a mental note of it all and write it down later. Sally's sweetly curved figure was enticing; she was right, of course, this *was* a holiday.

It didn't take long to get the tent up; it was one of those three-man

9

domes, with two collapsible poles that you thread through to give it its shape. Six guy ropes fixed down with corkscrew tent pegs and it was up.

Carl retrieved the bed roll from the rucksack outside. Upon returning he found Sally waiting, her blouse loosened and glancing off one shoulder. He pretended to ignore her, rolling the foam layer over the groundsheet. He rested back, 'Mmm, with the grass beneath, this is really comfy...'

Sally pounced.

'Ha! You really are keen on having fun!' Carl pretended to fend Sally off, but with every move he ensured she couldn't get away.

~

The couple lay back, giggling like school children.

Carl chuckled 'I don't think Mr. Tulloch had this in mind when he said we could park our tent beside his apple tree.'

'No...' Sally laughed, then, sobering a little, continued, 'No, he meant you to take in the folklore and do a little research. I'm sorry; I'm sure there'll be moments when we can explore a little of the myths of Orkney together...'

Carl propped himself up on one elbow. 'That's what I want Sal, both of us to enjoy this together.'

Sally smiled.

'There's still some things to unpack.' Carl reached for his shirt. Sally wasn't going to let him escape so easily and again they were wrapped in each other's arms. Suddenly Carl froze.

'What's wrong?' She attempted to kiss him.

'Didn't you hear it?'

'Hear what?' Sally tried to kiss him again.

'Giggling! Someone's outside!'

Sally sat up and started doing up her blouse. Carl, quickly decent in an unbuttoned shirt and jeans, peered out through the entrance of the tent.

The giggle matched the giggler. Carl could see a little girl with jet black hair and pale skin, rummaging through the now open cool box; her long skirt was scrunched up around her where she crouched, and a little woven shawl, held tightly, gave her form definition. She was a slight creature; her clothes reminding Carl of some period drama that Sally might watch.

Instinctively, Carl called out. 'Oi! Get out of my cool box!'

The girl looked up, startled. Her wide, mesmerizingly green eyes, momentarily stole Carl's words. Her face was gaunt but pretty; she could be no more than seven or eight years old. Carl felt a wave of compassion. 'It's OK. Are you hungry?'

'What's happening?' Sally's view was blocked by Carl's ample bottom. 'Who's there?'

Carl turned to her. 'It's a little girl. I think she's raiding our cool box.' He turned back to see the girl climbing over the farm gate and heading towards the barns. 'Here! Hold up! It's OK!' Carl shot out of the tent in pursuit. Sally watched him run to the gate and attempt to climb it too quickly.

'Careful!' She squinted as he stepped wrongly, stubbed his toe and tumbled over the top bar.

'I'm fine!' He scrambled back to his feet and headed off towards the old farm buildings.

Sally surveyed the scene, the contents of the cool box were mostly still in place, but several bottles of Carl's favourite yoghurt drink were scattered around it. Sally looked at the smiling cow on the labels. 'So that's what you were giggling at.' Sally was well aware of how commonplace cows were on the islands. She placed them back in the box, and wandered to the farm gate.

The gate latch was a simple bar, the sort you push like a lever and the gate is instantly freed. She laughed that Carl had climbed it, but seeing now that he was well up the track towards the barns she returned to the tent.

Carl searched frantically around the barns, calling, and peering behind and under things, but he found no-one.

Caught on the breeze was a piece of paper. Had he not briefly seen something interesting on it, Carl might have let it blow away, but he did see something. He abandoned his search for the girl and pursued the tumbling sheet; finally, pinning it down with his foot.

There was a child-like drawing on it and a loosely defined name, "Janet" Carl flipped the paper over. The sheet was actually a small poster, advertising a local band "Ceilidh Girl" at the Auld Motor Hoose, Kirkwall. It was that very night, wasn't far, and perhaps someone might know the cool box raider. Carl felt sure the drawing and name were hers, and that she must have dropped the poster as she'd fled. Sally would want a local night out, and he could do a little investigating - perhaps not the sort he'd wanted, but a little mystery none-the-less.

Chapter four

Sally had finished setting up camp by the time Carl returned, she'd even placed homemade bunting through the blossom laden branches of the Apple tree; giving an unmistakable glamping feel to the plot. The Whistling Jenny was growing warm on the camp stove.

'No joy?'

'Vanished.' He held up the poster. 'Live music in Kirkwall tonight though, if you like? Ha! Didn't see you pack the bunting, nice touch!'

Sally took the poster. 'Looks good...' She flicked the sheet over and saw the drawings. 'Where did you get this?'

'It was blowing in the breeze. I reckon the girl dropped it; not sure what she's drawn though.'

Sally laughed. 'It's the cow from your yoghurt drink bottles.'

Carl glanced down, 'Oh yeah. So that's what she was doing...'

'You thought she was stealing food?'

'She was ever so skinny; I thought she must have been.'

Sally shrugged, 'I didn't actually see her.'

'Maybe we'll get some answers at the Auld Motor Hoose. If the poster came from there, they might know who she is.'

'Not your usual mystery, Mr. Ree.'

'Same investigative skills, my dear.'

'Ooh, should have packed your pipe and dear-stalker!'

'Cheeky…' Carl drew her close.

'I'm your "Cheeky" though.' She let Carl wrap his arms around her. A whistle came from the kettle. Sally smirked, 'Cup of tea?'

Carl bent down and switched off the stove, 'Maybe after.'

~

By the time they re-emerged from the tent, the water had cooled too much for tea. Both opted for a carton of apple juice, and decided it was time to head towards Kirkwall. Carl was rummaging around in the rucksack.

'What are you looking for?'

'I packed a torch; it'll be dark when we come out later.'

'You're going to walk back?'

Sally was right of course; Carl liked his beer… He put down the rucksack. 'We'll get a taxi back. Come on, let's go.'

It was soon apparent that the wall around the farmyard had deceived them. It was rather cool outside of it. That said, walking was warm work, and as long as they didn't loiter too long admiring the sweeping views across fields of black cows, or bending down for a closer inspection of the roadside wildflowers, they felt quite comfortable.

Sally clung closely to Carl's left arm, and Carl walked with a lightness that he could only attribute to a deep sense of happiness, gazing down into Sally's bright eyes.

That was when it happened.

They'd passed a gentle curve in the narrow road. On their left was a post and wire fence leading down to a farm entrance, and on the right was a low stone wall. They could see the top of a car approaching quickly from behind. Doubting that the driver could see them for the height of roadside grasses, and aware they'd never make it to the wider, farm gateway, the couple quickly split, heading for their nearest verge; Sally by the wire, Carl by the wall as a little, orange car whizzed by.

Carl shot his hands into the air, 'Hey!'

The car was gone by the time Sally got over her shock, her call echoing up the empty road, 'Bloody idiot!' Attempting to return to Carl there was a tug at her side and a sound of tearing. 'Oh no!'

'What's up?'

Sally was craning around to see for herself. There was a small hole in her blouse. 'Damn it! The wire snagged on my blouse; it's torn a hole.' Sally had gone to the effort of changing into a pretty floral blouse that she'd purposefully packed for socialising. 'It's ruined.'

Carl peered down at the damage. Sally's eyes looked a little watery, so he gave her a hug. 'Do you want to go back and get changed; we've got a bit of time…'

'I've nothing else to change into.' She took Carl's hand and resiliently headed onwards. 'It's not flashing my bra. You can pop your hand over it when we're dancing. I just hope for his sake we don't catch up with him.'

Carl smiled; he wasn't any kind of dancer but he loved Sally's determination when unforeseen circumstances required it. There was no real hope they'd catch up with a speeding car, but he couldn't help but feel the driver would get a sound piece of Sally's mind had he pulled up around the next bend.

~

Ten minutes later Sally and Carl had reached the outskirts of Kirkwall, a footpath serving outlying bungalows made their journey easier, and it wasn't long before they arrived amongst buildings with a more classic, architectural feel.

The impressive bulk of an ecclesiastical building began to appear as they followed the curve of the road. Constructed of red sandstone it stood out boldly against the surrounding grey masonry and pebbledash.

Sally was impressed.

Carl saw the need for interpretation, 'St Magnus Cathedral, and the ruin over there is the Earl's Palace, and further down, the Bishop's Palace.'

'Tour guide.'

'I don't know anything about them…'

Sally gave Carl a gentle shove. 'You had me going there!'

They both laughed and walked on. They skirted the Cathedral, passed some shops and a Masonic Hall, before sighting their destination. Carl sighed, 'Doesn't look very big.' A red "Theme-Bar" sign jutted out from the white painted wall of a diminutive building.

'Perhaps it goes back from the street, or uses part of the building attached that isn't painted?' Sally stopped walking; her eyes fixed on the other side of the road.

'You OK? We don't have to go in if you're not keen…' Carl looked across the road. There, in the small carpark opposite, was a familiar, orange car. 'Oh.'

'Do you think *he's* in there?'

Carl shrugged, 'Dunno, could be. Although it looks like a general carpark, pubs don't usually have pay and display signs.'

Sally tugged him towards the door. 'Come on, let's see if there's anyone inside who it might be.'

'Guess Who?'

Sally swung around, still pulling him towards the door. She giggled, 'I won't challenge anyone, promise.'

Carl stopped resisting and they plunged through the door. A barmaid flashed a friendly smile but Carl's attention was immediately taken by a large Juke Box. Sally had already surveyed the room but on failing to immediately find anyone resembling Dennis the Menace (the mental picture she had of her adversary), she'd begun to allow her eye to traverse the décor of the room.

A large, illuminated SAAB logo hung from the ceiling, Shell, ESSO and Texaco pumps were dotted around the room. The band were setting up by the Shell pump, and there were signs for Pirelli Tyres, Reliant, Ford and Leyland, amongst car badges, grills and headlamps, covering every available space on wall or shelf or bar top around them.

Sally pulled Carl's sleeve.

'Wassup? Oh... Nice.'

The Barmaid smiled, 'Yoo like et?'

Carl nodded, 'Pretty cool.'

'Et'll liven up later, we've got a band t'night. Ya English, aye?'

'Aye, I mean yes.' Carl pulled out the poster from his pocket and approached the woman. 'A week on your islands. Do you know the Tulloch farm?'

The Barmaid smiled affirmatively.

'We saw the poster for the band, are they good?'

'Aye, they're great.'

Carl leant forwards over the bar and turned the poster over, 'Just wondering...' He pointed to the name. '...whether you know of a child called Janet?'

Chapter five

The Barmaid looked at the drawing then thoughtfully shook her head, calling to a back room, 'Kirsty!'

Another girl appeared, 'Hello?'

'Do yoo know a Janet locally?'

'There's Janet Sinclair...' She smiled at Carl, '...She's juss had a wee baby.'

Carl shook his head, 'The Janet I'm looking for is a child.' He held up the drawing. 'She appeared where we're staying at the Tulloch farm; no adults about. We were concerned, she looked... a little wild.'

Kirsty frowned at the picture. 'No... sorry... Would yoo like somethin' to drink?'

16

This wasn't what Carl was seeking but he certainly liked the suggestion, 'A local beer perhaps?'

'We've got Swannay Scapa Special…'

Carl nodded, glancing back at Sally, who was reading the Juke Box lists. 'And a white wine too, please.'

The Barmaid busied herself with the order.

'Up at the old Tulloch place, huh?' The enquiry had come from a woman around her mid-twenties, not unattractive, with wild, auburn hair. she'd been waiting patiently to order drinks for the band whilst Carl had been talking.

'Er, yes.' Carl was a little flustered by her friendly advance.

'Are yoo here all night?' She tapped the drawing. 'I havne the time now, but I do know a Janet that way…'

The Barmaid interrupted, 'Six eighty please, love.'

Carl sought his card as the woman from the band made her order. Having done so she started back towards the band, leaving Kirsty to get the drinks ready on a tray. 'I'll chat to yoo later maybe?'

Sally appeared. 'Making friends?'

Carl paid the Barmaid. 'She overheard me talking to the bar staff, She may know Janet.'

'That was quick work! So, who *is* Janet?'

'I don't know yet; she's busy with the band, said she'd be able to chat later.'

Kirsty passed them with the band's drinks, 'Tha's Kayleigh, the singer.'

Sally grinned, 'Oh, that's clever.'

'What's that?'

Sally turned the poster over, and pointed at the name of the band. 'Kayleigh, Ceilidh…'

'Oh, oh yes. It's pronounced *Kayleigh*.'

Sally laughed out loud.

Kirsty glanced back at them, 'Yoo'll like 'em, I'm sure. A lettle feel o' the Island's folklore.'

Carl shot a glance at Sally.

Sally rolled her eyes. 'There, you don't have to look for it, it finds you!'

The couple found a seat and settled in. The Bar began to fill up steadily and was soon a sea of loud conversation and laughter.

With just a few words Kayleigh swept up their attention. 'Et's great to be back at Moho, ya my favourite crowd. I'm gonna kick off with the first song I e'er sang here. Thess es "The Brodgar Stones", thank yoo…'

The customers cheered their approval, and the song began.

> 'Days now lost en mists o' time
> Saw the Giants marchin',
> All the fears o' mortal men
> Would soon sure be descendin'.
> 'Til one soul, brave, an' skilful still,
> Although his hands ded judder,
> Ded take his strings upon the way
> To play a merry banter.
>
> Comin' to chomp on Kirkwall's young,
> Felt sure none strong to stop 'em,
> They trampled doon the purple heath
> Where'd stand the Stones o' Brodgar.
>
> Giants spied hem from afar,
> First blood warm an' tasty,
> Came a chasin' 'long the Ness,
> Progress grim an' hasty
> But bold, he drew his bow to gut
> (A magic he was weavin')
> Flourished fiddle high an' played
> Enchantment 'gainst the droolin'.
>
> The Giants charmed, they danced all night,
> One great ring an awesome sight!
> They tallied, an' at dawns first light
> Became the Stones o' Brodgar.

Fearin' foes return to flesh
Our hero's resolution,
Turn the tune upon hemself,
A sacrificial guardian.
The rhythm teased upon his flesh,
Muse chillin' to the bone,
He gave his life to save the town
Became the Comet Stone.

An' to thess day yoo'll see 'em there,
Firm strong still 'gainst the weather;
The Comet an' the circle wide,
We call the Stones o' Brodgar.'

Carl found that he'd been undeniably impressed by the song and the reaction of those that had come to the Bar to hear it. The song, because it outlined a fascinating piece of Orkney mythology; the fans, because they sang along and froze like musical statues every time the Stones were mentioned. The singer had the love and admiration of her audience.

Carl felt his eye drawn to Kayleigh, and found her staring straight back at him. She smiled warmly. He nodded back and raised his glass.

Sally leant forward speaking directly into Carl's ear over the appreciative noise of the crowd 'I'm beginning to think you organised this with John Tulloch.'

'Huh?'

'The little girl, the poster, a band that sings about folklore.'

Carl felt stung but he didn't want to spoil the evening, he was gaining so much from it after all. He glanced down at Sally's glass. 'You should have said, I'll get you a top up.'

Sally was left bemused, had Carl misheard her? The band began another tune. Sally's foot began to tap, she shrugged, setup or not this band *was* fab.

Carl had found it difficult to move across the room; "Ceilidh Girl" was certainly very popular. He wondered how many more people would be allowed to squeeze in, though he marveled at the fact that everyone seemed so friendly. If "orange car guy" was here, he was just a bad driver, not a bad person, he concluded.

Kayleigh was singing about the "Dweller O' The Mound" as Carl returned to Sally. Sally, seemingly enchanted by the songs, stood, took the drinks and placed them on the table, then swung Carl back to the already packed area of floor that folk were using to dance in. Everyone was clapping to this part of the tune, so they joined in, jigged about and laughed. Many times, Carl's eyes found Kayleigh's smiles and the evening went by with a tangible, carefree happiness. Sally seemed to have forgotten about the tear in her blouse completely.

The end of the band's set was a stirring reel of Selkie stories; Carl was unsurprised, most of his research before their trip had centred around these creatures who were seals in the water and, on casting off their skins, able to walk as people on the land. Some of the song's verses were from the tales Carl had read, and he quickly relayed them to Sally before they were fully sung. Sally seemed beyond any disappointment now, she glowed and her eyes told Carl that he had her complete attention.

Song over, they returned to their seats. Some customers left, but enough remained to keep the venue vibrant; the evening keeping time with the beats of the Juke Box.

Kayleigh, concluding her business with the musicians and accepting the passing praise of her fans, cut across the room to Carl and Sally. Carl stood and shook her hand as she arrived. 'That was marvellous.'

Sally nodded enthusiastically. 'Can we get you a drink?'

'Auch no, I've got a bottle o' water. I'll be drivin' shortly, thank you.' She borrowed a stool from the neighbouring table. 'I didne introduce myself earlier…'

'You're Kayleigh, I'm Carl and this is my wife Sally.'

Sally almost convinced herself that Kayleigh looked disappointed but found her hand swept up by Kayleigh's enthusiastic shake.

Kayleigh got straight to the point, 'Tell me what yoo know o' Janet.'

Carl puffed his cheeks, 'Very little, really. She was outside as we were, um…' He remembered what they were doing. '…getting unpacked.'

'Up at Ole Tulloch's place, aye?'

'Yes.'

Kayleigh looked at Sally, 'What ded she look like?'

Sally shrugged, 'I didn't see her, Carl…'

Carl took over, 'About eight years old, black hair, very slim. Her clothing looked like something out of the history books.'

'Ded she say anythin'?'

'No, she shot off and I couldn't find her.'

Sally didn't wish to be excluded from the conversation, 'He was looking for ages.'

Carl smiled, 'I take it she's some local farmer's daughter?'

'She was.'

'Go on.' Carl leaned towards Kayleigh so as not to miss her answer in the "Red-Hot-Chilli-Peppers" song playing on the Juke Box.

'She was the daughter o' Edward Forsyth, a farmer from Westray, Story goes that she was brought to Mainland fer correction, that she was a wayward bearin'; but et didne help, she was found guilty o' witchcraft an' sentenced to be burned at Gallow Ha.'

Carl frowned, 'I didn't know children could be accused of witchcraft.'

'Witchcraft trials were centuries ago, are you saying Carl saw a ghost?'

Kayleigh addressed Carl first, 'Nay, she was a young woman when she was sentenced.' She turned to Sally smiling warmly, 'No, no' a ghost…'

Carl interrupted again, laughing, 'We've been talking at cross purposes. No, we saw a little girl.'

'Aye,' Kayleigh placed a reassuring hand on Carl. 'Tha's how she appears…'

Sally couldn't take her eyes off Kayleigh's hand. 'But you said she was executed…'

'Nay, she disappeared from Marwick's Hole before her execution en 1627…'

Sally laughed, '1627! Ha! It doesn't matter who she was, child, young woman or old lady, she'll be a ghost by now!'

'What's Marwick's hole?' Carl's genuine interest killed Sally's mirth.

Kayleigh noticed that Sally was looking at her hand and promptly removed it from Carl's arm. 'The St. Magnus Cathedral dungeon.'

Sally's eyes followed the hand, 'A dungeon in a Cathedral?' Her tone was loaded with doubt.

'Aye, all matters relatin' to the islands laws were dealt with there. The hole stell exists.'

'You can see it?'

'Aye, right there en the wall.'

Carl looked at Sally. Sally rolled her eyes. 'Fine, the place isn't far away. We'll pop in and have a look at a hole.' She wasn't finished, she smiled at Kayleigh. 'People don't disappear and return hundreds of years later, younger than they were. So, if you'll please excuse us...' She put down her empty glass. 'It's time we got a taxi and headed back to the farm.'

Carl glanced at his watch. 'We probably should be heading back. I'll see if they've got a number for a taxi firm at the bar...'

Kayleigh's face filled with revelation, 'There's relly no need fer yoo to call a taxi. I ken easy drop yoo back at the Tulloch place. Es no' oot o' my way.'

Again, Carl looked at Sally. Sally nodded, sure this woman was a little over-friendly, but she'd given them an entertaining evening. 'Are you Ok to go? Your band are still sorting equipment.'

'Oh yes. The boys sort all the gear an' Danny handles the cash; all I do es show up an' open my mouth!'

Chapter six

The little group laughed together and headed for the door. Kayleigh gave some parting goodbyes and they were outside. 'Thass the Cathedral.' She pointing out over the car park. The building was lit up and seemed to glow with a welcoming warmth.

'Yes, we walked by it as we came into town. When is it open?'

'Well, thess time o' year et's open at nine, there's a service tomorrow though, et bein' Sunday, at eleven… I think.'

They had already crossed the road heading for the car park, when Sally froze.

'What's up Sal?'

'Please tell me that's not your car, Kayleigh.'

'Mine's the orange Micra.'

Carl grimaced, 'Oh.' He collected Sally in his arms.

Kayleigh laughed nervously, 'Wha's wrong?' Having made ground on the couple she began to return.

Carl raised a hand and she halted.

Sally seemed very upset. 'You ruined my blouse!'

Carl took over, trying to keep the peace. 'You forced us off the road earlier this evening as we were heading into Kirkwall; Sal's blouse caught on some wire and got ripped.'

Kayleigh raised her hands to her face in genuine shock. 'I'm so sorry, Sally. I saw ya either side o' the rood. I hadne realised I'd caused yoo to get caught on the fence…'

'YOU WERE TEARING DOWN A SINGLE-TRACK ROAD!' Sally's outburst was unexpected and Kayleigh stepped back.

Sally was torn, earlier in the evening she had convinced herself that she'd never meet the driver, and that the tear wasn't so very big. Now it would have been easier to chastise Kayleigh if she *were* an inexperienced, young, male driver; not a likable woman who had just entertained them all evening. She huffed loudly and rubbed her arms for warmth as she stared intently at the pavement.

'Please, let me drive yoo back, es the least I ken do, aye?'

Carl tipped his head down until he could see Sally's face. 'Sal?'

Sally nodded indifferently and Carl edged her towards the car.

~

The journey was very short on four wheels. This seemed a mercy to Carl as they'd sat in silence all the way. Kayleigh pulled up close to the gate. 'Well yoo be able to see ya way?'

'Moon's quite bright, we'll be fine. Thank you.'

Sally was already out of the car and heading through the farm gate.

Kayleigh took Carl's arm as he moved to open his door. 'Look, ef there's anythin' I ken do, juss let me know. My kin run the guesthoose doon by the airfield.'

'Thanks Kayleigh, I think she'll be fine. Although I've not seen her quite so rattled before.' He shook Kayleigh's hand. 'Loved your songs. It was really nice to have met you, and thanks for the lift.'

'Thanks Carl, I hope yoo enjoy the rest o' ya holiday.'

Carl slipped out of the car, 'Thanks Kayleigh. Bye now.'

The vehicle rolled away. Carl could hear Sally unzipping and entering the tent. He looked out over the bay, the wreck was silhouetted against waves that reflected the moon like a million dancing lights and up above the sky shone with stars, clearer than he'd ever seen them before. He approached the tent, 'Sal, did you see the stars?'

There was a subtle noise within, 'I just want to get some rest.'

'OK, Sal. I'll be in shortly.' Carl stepped quietly back to the gate and looked out over the bay. It was beautiful. Then, on the breeze, Carl noticed something. It sounded like someone singing down on the beach. Was it Kayleigh so quickly? Had she stopped down there on her way home? No, it was a younger voice. Carl listened hard, trying to make out the words, but all he could discern was the sorrow of the tune. He shivered and headed for the relative warmth of the sleeping bag. He was just about to tell Sally he'd heard something, when he suddenly convinced himself that she didn't want to hear it. He got undressed and slipped in beside her. 'Goodnight love.'

Sally turned, gently stoked the side of his face and kissed him softly. 'Goodnight.'

~

Carl did get a little sleep, but he'd hardly noticed it. Sally's upset played on his mind, her accusation that he'd somehow orchestrated the evening bothered him and many times during the night he felt he could hear that sweet, melancholy voice pricking at the edge of his sought-for sleep. He gazed at the still, sleeping Sally, eased himself out of the sleeping bag, dressed quietly and gently unzipped the tent.

It was just five in the morning but the sun was already round on the horizon, the air crystal clear and fresh, and the tide out almost as far as the rusty, red hulk in the bay. A worn track led down the hill towards the beach. Carl looked back at the tent, then down the track. He quickly reasoned it didn't look far, and headed - at an appreciable pace - down the path.

Within a few minutes he was standing on sand punctuated by sharp little rocks that jutted up from something more solid beneath. Sea gulls called overhead, little, choppy waves splashed rhythmically and Carl felt sad for not waiting until Sally was awake to share the moment. His eyes downcast, he noticed something in the sand. Children's footprints, either those of many children or one child pacing around and around. He bent down, placing his fingers into one particularly sharp print. 'They could be hers.'

He shook his head and looked back up the path towards the farm. He had to leave this mystery alone. Sally wanted an "Us" holiday; he would give her an "Us" holiday. It had been a little disappointing for her already, and he didn't want her to be unhappy. He'd write about the band when he got home; that alone would make a good read - his work part of the holiday was done.

Carl returned to the farmyard. Finding that Sally was stirring he set up the little stove, topped up the whistling Jenny from the outside tap, and arranged some bacon in the pan. The smell and sizzling drew a tired looking face to the entrance of the tent.

'Ooh, bacon.'

'Ready when you are.'

Carl was relieved that Sally seemed happier, and they enjoyed their breakfast in the warm, early morning sunshine.

'What shall we do today?'

Carl had a little think. It was Sunday, few places would be open. He didn't want to suggest visiting the Cathedral in case it upset Sally again. He looked up at the gate. 'There's a footpath leading down along the coast. We could go exploring?'

'Sounds good.' Sally smiled, edging closer and cuddling up to him.

Carl felt guilty, he just wanted to see if the footprints on the beach led anywhere. He was pretty sure they didn't - as soon as the tracks left the beach they'd disappear - but his curiosity had been pricked. All things said, the sad voice wafting up from the shore that night had moved him somewhere deep down. He wanted to understand it. His intuition linked it to the child, and Kayleigh's story gave fuel to his interest. He knew there'd probably be information online for such a local legend, so he could pursue it after their break, but if further material became evident whilst they were here, well, that was fine by him.

~

Ten minutes later they were making their way down onto the beach, a light canvas bag slung over Carl's shoulder, containing sandwiches and a map. The wreck could probably be reached now wearing waders, and Sally's interest in it took them out towards the water's edge, Carl gazing back at the footprints.

'You OK?'

'Did you see the footprints?'

Sally laughed, 'No. What were they? Dinosaurs?'

Carl knew she was teasing him at the expense of his interest in the unexplained. He poked her in the ribs. She squealed and started to run away. He knew he had to give chase, that was what young love did, it frolicked on beaches, rolled in the sand, it caught and it held and it kissed and grew stronger. In a moment he was after her, she screamed at his rapid approach, he was so much faster than her. She spun around, giggling and holding her hands out as a last ineffective defence. 'Sorry.'

Carl grabbed her up and swung her into the air. On touching the sand again, Sally was clinging to him, panting loudly. He kissed her. 'I love you Sally Ree.'

'Of course, I'm above your game.' She wobbled his belly.

'Oi!' Carl protested, pulling her closer.

They both laughed. 'What was so special about your footprints?'

Carl thought, 'Nothing really, just kids prints.'

'Well, it is a beach, that's their natural habitat.'

Carl nodded, but he couldn't explain how they'd appear below the tideline overnight, and the voice he'd heard still played on his mind.

'Hello? Cute wife trapped in a bear hug!'

Carl released her and they strolled on towards the lapping water.

They gazed up at the rusty hull of the wreck. 'I wonder if the footprints belong to that girl you saw?'

Carl smiled, Sally *was* interested, this was good news.

But Sally wasn't finished, 'She probably is just a local girl exploring her small area of the island. Ghosts don't make footprints.'

Carl's heart sank, he knew he had to leave it alone. The ghost idea was Sally's assumption; Kayleigh had hinted at something more mysterious.

'We're being watched.'

Carl turned to see what Sally meant. They hadn't noticed his approach, but there on the wet sand behind them stood an elderly man. He was dressed for cooler weather in clothes that, despite being well made, seemed to testify to long use. His shock of white hair stood, of its own accord, upon his head. A small, odd-looking dog stood close to his ankle and an old stick, smooth at the hand, served him as a cane.

Carl gathered his wits, 'Oh, hello.' He wondered how someone might appear out of the blue like that, but he hadn't of course, for behind the man, stretching back to the tideline and up to the road beyond, were a set of footprints, man and dog.

The man nodded.

Sally assumed he had approached them purposefully. 'Can we help you?'

He smiled, clearly understanding Sally's misinterpretation, 'Nay, lass, juss walkin' the dog.'

Sally blushed.

The man started to walk away, his dog bounding ahead along the water's edge.

Sally rallied. 'Er, excuse me.'

He stopped, and gazed back at the couple. Carl wondered what she was going to ask.

'Are you local?'

The man pointed at a stone house along the cliff with his stick. Carl and Sally had assumed earlier that it was a ruin, it didn't even look like it had a roof. It still looked like a ruin from where they were. The man looked ready to move away again.

Sally called after him, 'Do you know a little girl called Janet?'

Carl noticed the reaction of the old man; he was frowning - was it a frown of concern and protectiveness, or one that asked why a stranger was asking about someone he didn't know? Carl attempted to clarify, 'Young, black hair, slim, pale, with green eyes…'

The man looked out to sea, rubbing his bristly chin. He looked up at the sky, then inland. It was as if he were remembering something, then, with urgency, he gave a sharp whistle and his dog started to return to him. 'Young yoo say?'

'Seven or eight I guess.'

'Hmm, There's time.' The old man bent down and whispered something to his dog, then, rather abruptly, started back over his own footprints, declaring that there was a storm coming.

Sally didn't seem willing to let it go. 'Do you know her?'

'Aye.'

Carl and Sally stood dumbfounded on the beach as the old man reached the road and disappeared from sight.

Sally huffed, 'Well, that was weird.'

'Yep.'

'He seemed more interested in the weather than the girl.'

Carl scratched his head, 'Unless she's got something to do *with* the weather.'

Now Sally frowned.

'Kayleigh said she was sentenced to death for witchcraft. Maybe…'

Sally was back to rolling-eyes-mode. 'Back in the 1600's a young woman was sentenced to death, not a girl; anyway, he knew her - local girl, mystery solved. Let's get back to our holiday.' Sally took his hand and led him on. 'Do you think there's going to be a storm?'

Carl prided himself on his meteorological knowledge. He looked up at the sky, it was blue and cloudless, and the air was warm; he looked out to sea, if anything it was calmer than earlier. He nodded, 'Might get a shower later this evening.'

Sally looked back up the beach. 'What a funny old man - I still think he crept up on us.'

~

They joined the wiry coastal path that had brought them to the farm from the airport. Their load lighter than on arrival, they had soon travelled beyond the runways, following the track as it wound its way along low cliff tops and around pretty sandy bays. Dwellings were few and far between, and both felt that they'd found a place of peaceful retreat.

They ate their sandwiches when they felt peckish in the afternoon; sitting for a while to soak up the sunshine. To Carl's disappointment there was something wrong with the flask he'd prepared tea in, at best it was tepid. They'd laughed about it but Carl loved a nice, hot tea. They lay back and attempted to find shapes in the fair-weather clouds above them, but they were moving so slowly and in such few numbers that they soon exhausted the possibilities. Out of mischief Sally began tickling Carl's ear, and they ended up rolling around in the soft dry grass.

Carl consulted the footpath map he'd packed. 'Crikey.'

'What's up?'

'We're over here…' He pointed at their location. 'Hangie Bay.'

'We'd better start heading back then.'

'Yep.' Carl stood up.

'It's been a really lovely time, thank you.'

Carl helped Sally to her feet a manoeuvre that positioned her nicely in his arms, 'What for?'

'For us being us.' She kissed him. Then started to lead him back the way they'd come.

Carl resisted pulled her back and kissed her again, 'Actually we've worked our way around part of the island...' He pointed in the opposite direction. '...carrying on this way will be a shorter journey than turning back...'

'Getting tired, old man?'

'Not really, it's just a chance to see something different. The map says there's an old mill.'

'Sounds exciting!' Sally mocked. 'It isn't the way to another of your organised mystery meetings then?'

'Huh?'

'Like the band; *find* a flyer...'

'I didn't plan that in advance you know. The poster was blowing around the barns in the wind.' Carl remembered Sally suggesting this the other night, and he felt a bit hurt again.

Sally could see she'd upset Carl, perhaps the band wasn't a deliberate, prearranged dose of folklore after all. 'Sorry map bearer; lead the way.'

'Had I known their songs, and that they were playing at that bar that night, I would have arranged to be there; that much is true - you've got what I like bang on. But I had no idea.'

'It *was* a good night, despite my blouse. I'm sorry. Pretty weird that your mystery girl should scribble on a poster for that band on that night.'

Carl looked at Sally, she seemed serious. 'It *was* pretty strange, wasn't it?'

Sally laughed and ran off along the footpath, she glanced back to see how quickly Carl was catching up, only to see him lying on the path. She quickly ran back. 'Carl! Carl!' She crouched down beside him; remembering her first aid module at Uni she called out for help, then rested her head on Carl's chest to assess his breathing.

Carl pounced. Before she knew it, it was no longer Carl on his back but her! She let out a startled scream, though in all honesty she liked his strength.

'That'll teach you for making me think you're remotely interested in strange happenings…' Carl straddled her and plucked a long grass stem from the side of the track, repeatedly teasing her nose with it as he held her hands down.

'Hey yoo!' A young, solid looking farmer had appeared on the other side of a drystone wall. He'd clearly responded hurriedly to Sally's call for help, and seemed ready to muscle in with a rescue. To his absolute bemusement Sally and Carl burst into embarrassed laughter, hobbled to their feet and headed off down the path at a fair pace.

Unimpressed the farmer headed back to his work, 'Tourists!'

It wasn't long before the couple reached a wide sandy bay, through which a stream babbled toward the near-returned tide. At the head of the stream was a long, grey stone building, partly ruined at one end. 'Is that your mill?'

'I guess so.'

They approached it, leaving the footpath and crossing the road for a closer look. A low curving wall protected the mill stream which passed under the road to the beach beyond.

'Look.' Sally pointed. 'The wheel!' A large, wooden water wheel still stood at the far end, although the stream had found its way around it rather than through.

'In its heyday, the water would have travelled along that stone gully.'

Sally acknowledged the feature, 'Do you think that Janet would have worked somewhere like this?'

'Only if there was an older mill here, this is nineteenth century not seventeenth.'

'Careful,' Sally warned. 'You'll turn me on again with your sweet talk!'

Chapter seven

After exploring around the mill, Carl and Sally headed in the direction of the farm; Carl gagging for a fresh mug of hot tea.

As they approached the farm yard Sally tutted loudly, 'Looks like your new friend is back.' Parked outside the gate was an orange Micra.

The couple rounded the wall to find Kayleigh stooping down at the entrance of the tent.

Sally challenged her immediately, 'Hey! What are you doing?'

Kayleigh spun around. 'Oh! There yoo are.' She smiled in a sort of relieved way. 'I didne know yoo were campin'!'

'Yes, we're camping!' Sally pushed by to check the entrance of the tent and picked up a shopping bag. 'What's this?'

'A couple o' blouses, I fel so bad aboot bein' the cause o' yours gettin' damaged...'

'That you thought I'd like your cast offs.' Sally interrupted.

'Sal!' Carl protested.

'They're my best, relly.'

Sally swallowed her pride. 'I'm sorry Kayleigh, it's a really nice gesture but I'm sure they will look best on you. Fifty pounds would probably replace mine...'

'Sally!' Carl barked.

Sally smiled. 'I'm kidding!'

'Wow, phew!' Kayleigh gasped.

'Thirty would be ample...'

Glances were exchanged and they laughed. Kayleigh warned them that rain was forecast overnight. Sally boasted that Carl had already predicted that, and that Kayleigh shouldn't be surprised if it didn't turn out a bit thundery. Kayleigh agreed that it was rather mild for the time of year, and Carl noticed that Sally was easing Kayleigh in the direction of her car. He chuckled to himself.

Before she left, Carl managed to learn that there was a half-hourly bus service on the main road, reached by crossing the neighbour's field at the end of the farm track. He knew they could happily walk all day, but they wouldn't see much without other options.

Kayleigh headed off with a friendly wave, Carl turned to get his kettle ready for that mug of tea, but Sally remained at the gate.

'Look.'

Carl peered in Sally's direction, she wasn't looking at Kayleigh's departing car, she was looking out towards the bay. Heading along the cliff edge with his odd little dog and a wheelbarrow was the old man they'd met in the morning. 'What's he doing?'

'Dunno, looks like a barrow of firewood.'

'But it's so warm, and that cottage still looks like a ruin, there's no roof, for crying out loud!'

Carl headed back to the tent, 'Shouldn't let it worry you; old folk feel the cold more. I expect he's lived up there all his life and it's quite ample for him and his... er... terrier. I expect the roof pitches away from the wall, or it's flat or something.'

Sally came away from the gate, and lay on a blanket beside the industrious Carl.

'Brew?' He enquired.

'Mmm, yes please. We can get a new flask in town, tomorrow.' Sally closed her eyes. With the warmth of the sun on her face, she felt she could be anywhere, the south of France, Gran Canaria. She smiled contently; she hadn't expected it to be so summery. She turned to Carl, 'If we're going to town tomorrow anyway... did you want to go and find that dungeon in the Cathedral?'

Carl was delighted that she'd suggested it herself, he was going to let it slide and contact the Cathedral for more details when they returned home, he was actually desperate to see the unusual feature with his own eyes, but he'd made other arrangements. 'I've got plans tomorrow, perhaps Tuesday?'

Sally propped herself up on her elbows. 'Plans?'

'You'll see.'

Carl ended up wishing that he'd just agreed to visit the Cathedral; Sally wouldn't let it go, she kept guessing and prying, asking for clues and offering incentives for disclosure. Carl remained steadfast throughout their evening meal of sausage rolls, washed down with some wine, and didn't give in once through the evening.

'You're no fun.' Sally accused, finally.

'You'll eat those words tomorrow...' Carl began, but a rumble of thunder cut him short. 'Better get our gear under cover.'

Sally nodded. 'How do you do that?'

'You pick it up and put it in the tent...' Carl jested.

'No, silly. How do you know what the weather will do?'

Carl waved a hand dismissively, 'Family gift.' He picked up the warm stove and stowed it in the awning.

The thunderstorm was unremarkable, some heavy rain but Carl and Sally were warm and snug in their big sleeping bag.

With the day's exertions, both were soon fast asleep in each-other's arms.

~

Next morning Carl awoke to Sally's quiet humming. The tune was familiar to him. He rolled on his side facing her. She smiled up at him.

'Good morning.'

'Good morning... tell me, what's that tune you're humming? It sounds familiar.'

'I don't know; I woke up with it in my head. It's a lovely melody, but a little sad I think.' Sally hummed it some more.

Carl listened; he'd definitely heard it before. 'It's not one of Ceilidh Girl's songs, is it?'

'I don't think so; they were more upbeat. Does sound folky though, now you mention it.' She started to get out of the sleeping bag. 'Just popping to the loo, keep my spot warm.' She disappeared out of the tent and Carl heard the latch click on the outside toilet in the farm yard. On the edge of his discernment, he could still hear her humming, and he suddenly knew where he'd heard it before. It was the song that had drifted up from the beach. Had it happened again last night as they slept? Was that why Sally had it in her head this morning?

Click went the latch, and Sally returned. 'Fresher out there this morning! Clear blue sky again though.' She grabbed the edge of the sleeping bag and dived back in.

'Argh!' Carl protested. 'Your hands are freezing!'

'And my feet.'

'WHOA! Quit it!' There was a good deal of thrashing about for a few minutes, before the sleeping bag settled down into a gentler rhythm.

~

A little later Carl prepared some bacon butties, and was outlining his plan for the day. 'I've made some arrangements, and we'll have to set off at ten if we're to get there on time.'

'Get where?'

'You'll see.'

'Well, what do I need? Walking boots? Jeans or skirt?'

Carl winked, 'You know I like it when you wear jeans.'

'Yes, but would it be appropriate for what you've planned?'

'Can't see why not.'

'If you told me what we were doing…'

Carl laughed.

'Carl…' Sally pointed at the gate.

Carl looked. The odd little dog was standing there, quietly watching them. 'Oh! It's the old man's dog again. Want a bit of bacon boy?'

Its stumpy tail wagged.

'Don't encourage it!'

The old man appeared from the direction of the beach path. He looked like he'd pass by without a word, just a short, throaty click that sent the dog bounding to heel.

'Hello again.' Carl called.

The man stopped, almost out of view, he seemed amused. 'Campin', Aye?'

'Yes.' Carl stood and approached the gate. 'I'm Carl and this is Sally, we're your neighbours this week.'

The man seemed to acknowledge the introduction then asked, 'A good strong tent, Aye?'

'Yes, it's a…'

'Fel yoo'll be needin' et to be. Now ef yoo Dinny mind. Good day.'

35

With that he headed off.

Carl shrugged and returned to Sally. 'Odd.' They both agreed.

'Come on.' Carl urged. 'We may as well get going.'

'Walking boots or sandles?' Sally asked.

'Tell you what.' Carl grinned, placing the sandles in his shoulder bag. 'Let's take both!'

Sally pulled her boots on, shaking her head in amused frustration.

Chapter eight

When all became clear, Sally was thrilled. John Tulloch had a Nephew, Kenny, who flew helicopter tours, and arrangements had been made to fly a circuit of the islands.

They were soon away too; Kenny had performed all his pre-flight checks and was ready for the off. He handed them protective headphones that would allow them to chat through the aircraft's intercom, and gently put Sally's in place. Carl had expected Kenny's help too, but found himself left to do it as the charismatic pilot helped Sally board the aircraft.

Sally became quite giggly; she'd never flown in a helicopter before and Carl became the recipient of an enthusiastic hug as he reached his seat. 'Thank you.' She kissed him; their microphone stems becoming momentarily tangled.

Kenny, who'd been speaking to the Control Tower, glanced over his shoulder at his passengers. 'Here we go.' He increased the power, and they were up.

Sally gave a scream of delight, Kenny smiled back at her and Carl noticed just how good-looking the man was. Chiseled features, full, dark hair, hazel eyes and his voice was calm, assertive and lacking any trace of a local accent. He felt a little, unexpected angst about Kenny's focus on assisting Sally. He shook his head, chastising himself. Sally was sitting in the back with him nervously rubbing *his* leg, not the Pilot's.

Sally was like an excited child, 'We're going up so quickly!'

'Look! I can already see the farm.' Carl pointed, then clicked a photo.

The farm passed beneath them, the glorious blossom on the apple tree seeming to glow; the tent dwarfed by the farmhouse and outbuildings.

Kenny laughed, 'I won't fly too close. Reckon my downdraught would unsettle my uncle's barns!'

The farm became less and less discernible as Kirkwall loomed; the great bulk of St. Magnus Cathedral dominating the view. The Bishop's, and Earl's Palaces looked more extensive than they did from the ground, and the bay yawned widely, its stone armed harbour cradling an eclectic collection of yachts and fishing boats.

A large circle caught Sally's attention. 'What's that?'

'That's the Peedie Sea and the Model Boat lake…'

Carl took a photo, 'That's huge!'

'Aye, popular too.' Kenny informed air-traffic control of his intentions and positioned the aircraft for a better look. As they flew overhead the couple could see several tiny models, some with sails some clearly controlled, bobbing and darting across the surface of the lake. They were close enough to see that some of the people on the lake's circular footpath were waving. They waved back.

Sally seemed to glow, 'I feel like a V.I.P.'

'You are one when you're in my helicopter.' Kenny grinned, throwing the machine away from the town and out across the island.

Carl eyed Kenny up and down, again perturbed by his charm towards Sally. 'Everyone seems very friendly around here.' He remarked, barely able to mask that the comment was focused rather than general.

Sally seemed too enthralled by the landscape below to have noticed. Kenny nodded and smiled. 'The good weather's making us pretty cheery at the moment.'

Carl quietly sighed relief, the last thing he wanted to do was upset the pilot. He was probably like this with all the ladies. 'We bought the weather with us.'

'Far from normal.' Kenny added. 'Last night's storm was sparked off by it I reckon. Supposed to get more unsettled as the week goes on…'

Sally tutted, 'Let's not talk about the weather!'

Everyone laughed. The weather wasn't mentioned again and it soon became apparent to Sally that the main topic of Kenny's tour would be the folklore of the islands. Carl had definitely organised *that*. Sally was a little annoyed, but Kenny was quite dashing and the ride was fabulous. The sandy bays, the rise and fall of the landscape, the untarnished blue above them; it was bliss.

Kenny showed them the Stenness and Brodgar standing stones, and it soon became apparent that Kenny had also been at the Auld Motor Hoose, listening to the band. Carl's comment of it being "a small world" was met with a laugh, 'It *is* Orkney.'

The flight took them to the coast; Kenny conversing frequently with the ground to keep his course known. Sally was the first to see a sea stack off the cliff face.

'Is *that* the Old Man of Hoy?'

Kenny pointed out that the 'Old Man' was on the coast of Hoy, not Mainland. Sally had blushed, but Kenny went on to explain that this stack was known as Yesnaby Castle, and he hovered so that they could see the gap at its base. He then related some information on the Yesnaby Healer, an old woman who had lived nearby. In her day she'd gained a reputation for being able to stop wounds from bleeding, even when the injury was many miles away.

Sally had switched off as Kenny and Carl discussed Orkney's reputation for witchcraft, especially when Kenny repeated what they'd already heard about Janet's story. She just watched the impressive cliffs and wheeling seabirds.

Kenny paused briefly over Skara Brae and the Brough of Birsay, pointing out the ruins and declaring 'If you scratch Orkney, it bleeds archaeology.'

Sally was impressed by the observation but Carl had heard the saying before. Seeing Skara Brae was a treat however, as his mother had often talked of it; it was a big tick on his bucket list. They'd have to come back and explore later in the week.

The journey took them to Rousay where the cliffs were just as impressive and they saw some seals, sunbathing on the rocky shore. Kenny didn't miss his opportunity to talk of the Selkie folk, but Sally was beginning to think of him as a bit of a myth nerd, like Carl, and found herself gazing inland at the stone-built farms.

Westray was next, apparently the birthplace of Janet, and Sally didn't tune into the conversation again until something was said about the shortest scheduled flight in the world, that linked Westray to Papa Westray, a trip that - even taken leisurely - lasted little over two minutes.

The islands fractured away now, Eday, Sanday, Stronsay. Kenny invited them to lunch, flying over Stronsay airfield and putting the helicopter down behind the village of Whitehall. The field belonged to his father, and was a stone's throw away from the Fish Mart Café.

By the end of lunch Sally was quite bored. Carl, on the other hand, was much happier, he'd engaged Kenny in much chat about Trows. He knew the diminutive, troll-like creatures were an integral part of local stories, he knew Kenny would relate the stories he'd already found online, and he knew Sally wouldn't find him at all interesting. Carl thought himself quite the victor as the helicopter took to the air again. 'Blooming cheek, inviting my wife to lunch.'

Kenny took them over Shapinsay and Balfour Castle, then, again crossing the water, Sally recognised something. 'The Cathedral! Is our flight almost over?'

Kenny responded that it wasn't, taking them out over Scapa Flow and relating the demise of HMS Royal Oak, victim of a daring U-boat raid during the Second World War.

He carried on down the coast to Hoy, locating the Old Man stack as a thank you for being such great passengers. Both Carl and Sally agreed, Kenny had saved the best for last; Hoy was far more mountainous than the other islands, its hills rolling down into precipitous cliffs.

Finally, Kenny headed up; soaring high and wide over South Ronaldsay, to give an impressive birds-eye-view of all they had seen, before flying a fast, straight approach to Kirkwall Airport.

Chapter nine

On learning that Carl and Sally intended to do some food shopping, Kenny offered to drive them into Kirkwall. Sally noticed that Carl was reluctant to accept, but it was already nearly four in the afternoon - and it would take at over thirty minutes to walk.

'I thought we might try out the local bus service.' Carl offered.

Sally took Kenny's arm, 'After a flight like that? Come on Carl, Kenny's offering to be our pilot a little longer.'

'Really is no trouble.' Kenny smiled, placing an arm around Sally's shoulder and leading her off towards his car.

Carl followed closely.

Kenny's car was an American classic. 'Carl, look. Even his car has wings!'

Carl laughed, 'A Cadillac!'

'1956 Chevrolet Belair, actually.' Kenny corrected. 'Isn't she gorgeous?'

'She's red.' Sally clapped her hands, and seemed almost as excited as when she'd discovered she was going to have a ride in a helicopter. Carl felt that Kenny was a real cad.

'Bagsy the front seat!' It was a call Sally regretted on discovering the lack of seatbelts.

Carl slid around on the rear bench seat, wishing that Kenny would stop talking about the provenance of his car. Sally looked to be hanging on his every word. If he could find a way to get Kenny talking about the Orcadian fairy folk, he knew Sally would soon lose interest. Try as he might, Carl couldn't find a way into Kenny's monologue.

'Oh, there's Ole Garrie.' Kenny exclaimed, as they passed the Tulloch farm. The Old man was striding down the farm track with his dog and a bundle under his arm, heading towards the stone house near the cliff.

'We met him on the beach yesterday.'

'He's a funny old boy.' Kenny laughed. 'He was ancient when I was a boy.' He peeped his horn. Garrie turned and stared, not reacting to Kenny's friendly wave. 'Us kids used to tease him a bit. Not that we saw him that often. Ha! Uncle John always used to blame Ole Garrie for bad weather…'

'Can't do that today.' Carl slipped in.

Kenny glanced over his shoulder at Carl. 'Perhaps later in the week though, eh?'

Carl wasn't listening, he just watched Garrie through the back window of the car, until he disappeared from sight. The old man hadn't stopped staring at all.

It wasn't long before Kenny pulled up outside the food store.

'Tesco!' Sally laughed. 'I was expecting some local grocery!'

'I could take you somewhere more select if you'd like.'

Carl saw his opportunity to offload Sally's eye-candy. 'Here's fine Kenny. All we really need are the basics, you've been an absolute star.' He opened his door. 'Perhaps we'll see you around? Can't miss this beauty.' Carl slapped the rear seat playfully, and in the blink of an eye he was out and opening Sally's door.

Sally turned to shake Kenny's hand but found it swept up by Kenny, who gave it a quick kiss. 'The pleasure has been mine.'

Sally pulled her hand away and slid out of the car in a graceful, fluid movement, closing the door behind her and wiping her hand on her jeans.

Carl leant in through the open window. 'Thanks again for the flight, it really was marvellous.' Both stood back, waving, and Kenny - left with no other option - pulled away. 'Oh, that's interesting.' Carl pointed.

'What is?'

'Isn't that the Peedie lake and the boating pond we saw from the air?'

'Peedie Sea.' Sally corrected. 'Yes. It looks even bigger from here. Fancy a short stroll before we get our eggs and milk? We've plenty of time.'

Carl, glad to finally have Sally to himself, offered her his arm and they set off over the crossing towards the water park.

A couple of children were playing in canoes on the "Sea" - which was really a long lake, cut off from the actual sea by a causeway. The footpath angled down to the boating lake, where quite a few families and individuals were still gathered.

Carl and Sally walked right around the great circular path, stopping frequently to admire all manner of miniature yachts and scale replicas. There was even a little fireboat that squirted water. They had to run from that, as its owner had targeted them for a cheeky wetting. The pair ran and laughed, acknowledging the joke with a smile and raised hands of surrender. The locals were far friendlier than folks back home and the couple agreed that Orkney was proving to be a very attractive place indeed.

They sat for a while, away from the water's edge on an area of grass that jutted into the Peedie Sea behind them, watching the locals and listening to the laughter and excitement of the children.

Sally sighed deeply, 'Am I doing the right thing?'

'If you mean sitting, using your husband as a backrest... yes...'

'No. I mean...' Sally paused, reflectively. 'I mean, studying now and waiting to have a family?'

'Wow, that's out of the blue.'

Sally looked at him with big concerned eyes. 'You don't think I'm doing the right thing?'

'I didn't say that. I just didn't expect the question.'

They sat in silence for a moment.

'Are you unhappy with your course?'

'No...'

Carl continued. 'It's a means to an end. We'll be in a better position to have a family when we've got a place of our own.' He could see that Sally was gazing at a particular group of smiling children. 'I bet they're terrors when they're not distracted by models and ice-cream.'

Sally smiled awkwardly.

'The one in the blue T-shirt... I bet he's a total menace.'

Sally slapped his leg and stood up.

'Ow! What was that for?'

'Mocking me. Come on…' She offered Carl her hand. '…let's get our food.'

~

Sally seemed subdued as they selected the few items they required, Carl suggested they get some wine, but Sally wasn't so keen, so Carl insisted on getting some chocolate. Outside the store they found a bus at the bus stop.

Carl took the opportunity, 'Excuse me. Can you tell me which service goes to the Airport?' He knew the route would take the main road near to Tulloch's Farm and that they would be able to cross the field as Kayleigh had told them.

'That would be thess service, Sir. Number four.' The driver pointed at the screen above the window, Carl looked out at Sally, she seemed happier again.

Giggling she got onto the bus saying, 'It says Airport on the front of the bus.'

'Gotta flight t'catch?'

'Er, no, we're staying up at John Tulloch's Farm and there's a footpath from the main road…'

'Oh, aye, I know et. I'll drop yoo there.'

'That would be great, thank you.'

The bus soon departed and it wasn't long before Carl and Sally were striding across the field towards the farmhouse, waving goodbye to the Bus Driver.

'Oh, bother…' Carl exclaimed.

'What?'

'We didn't get a flask!'

Sally giggled, 'I'd just spotted them when you said 'chocolate'!'

Carl laughed, then sobered, 'Evening's got a stormy feel to it again.' The air was warm, heavy and still. 'Look… the Old Man's place can't be as bad as it looks.'

From their position near the farm gate a thin ribbon of smoke could be seen rising from Old Garrie's chimney. Sally gasped, 'What on earth does he want a fire for tonight? I'm sweating!'

'Maybe he's got an old stove for cooking?'

Sally nodded her acceptance of Carl's theory.

'Shame he's not friendlier.' Carl said as they unpacked the shopping into the cool-box. 'I'd ask him over for a bite to eat. I reckon he's got some stories to tell…'

Sally huffed, 'And have a whole evening of fairy-tales as well. No thanks, I'm glad he's grumpy.'

'What do you mean?'

'That's all you and Kenny talked about the whole time we were up in the helicopter!' Sally put some scones on a plate and settled down on a blanket under the apple tree.

'It wasn't *all* the time.' Carl protested. 'Anyway, it stopped you eyeing him up and down.' He sat next to her.

'I beg your pardon?'

'You thought he was good-looking…'

Sally snorted amusement, Carl was surprised. 'He was a total letch!' She chuckled, then paused, 'Was Mr. Ree feeling insecure?' Sally put her plate down on the blanket and crawled onto him. Carl quickly accepted her advance, embarrassed by his accusation, and in the following few moments a number of scones were brutally knocked from their plates.

~

Later, with night setting in, Carl sought his backpack and retrieved his camera from it. He gazed studiously at the picture of the Farm that he'd taken from the helicopter, at the edge of the image was Garrie's cottage, and Carl's suspicions about it seemed to be correct. He pointed, drawing Sally's attention to what he'd discovered.

'That *is* odd.' Sally admitted.

The image seemed to confirm their original thought that there was no roof.

Carl shook his head. 'I don't get it.'

'Hey, maybe he's all eco. You know. You thought it might be a flat roof. Maybe it's one of those green roofs, with the plants on.'

'I suppose so.' But Carl was still intrigued. Perhaps he'd visit the old place tomorrow for a closer look.

Chapter ten

After the excitement of the day Sally and Carl had quickly fallen asleep. Both, however, were now awake. Sally sat upright.

'Are you alright?' Carl asked.

'Shhh. Listen.'

There was a rumble in the distance. 'Oh, another storm, I thought it...'

'Shhh. It's the tune I was humming this morning.'

'I heard it the evening we came back from the Band; it was coming from the bay. The little girl's voice...'

'That's not a little girl.'

Carl listened; Sally was right. It wasn't a mature voice, but it lacked the child-like tone he'd heard before. 'It's getting closer.'

It was true; the voice seemed to be coming slowly up the footpath from the beach. Neither Carl nor Sally felt perturbed by this, the voice was lovely, and although the song was sad there was nothing threatening about it. Carl grabbed his jacket.

'What are you doing?'

'What do you think. It's an opportunity to solve the mystery.'

'Don't scare her; she won't be expecting someone to leap out of the farmyard.'

Carl nodded, 'Are you coming?'

Sally took up her coat and wrapped it around her. 'Ok, we'll wait for her to reach the gate.'

They climbed out of the tent and stood in the yard staring intently at the gate. The moon lit the night around them but small clouds at the leading edge of the approaching storm, dimmed then restored the light with little warning. Carl grabbed up his torch. Now they could hear the words of the song…

'Where are my lover's arms
That dedst hold me an' wrap me aboot weth their protection?
Thess strength now gone I'm flailin',
And fet to faint I'm feelin'.

Where are my lover's eyes?
Those eyes that ded first catch me an' confirm their desirin'.
No longer seen thro' love's filter,
I've no wey to warmth or shelter.

Where es my lover's tongue?
Those words he spake cross fine teeth, thengs that charmed me to my heart.
All that wes spaken has gone; flown
I'm left cold, en silence; aloon.'

The voice grew louder. Carl and Sally could hear the scrunch of footsteps on the rough path. There was a flash of distant lightening and the despair in the voice grew; playing on Carl and Sally's emotions…

'Where es my lover's kiss?
So sure an' confident to light me; so firm to assure.
Inside I long to feel thee,
Now only breeze to brush the lips o' me.'

It was clear to Carl and Sally that they would soon see her. The thunder rumbled; the light of the moon suddenly lost to the leading edge of the storm. Carl fumbled with his torch.

'Where es my…'

The light from Carl's torch shot out across the yard then swung towards the gate illuminating the owner of the voice. The figure stood silent and wide-eyed, stunned by the glare; a girl of about fourteen.

'Hello.' Carl ventured.

A flash of lightening made night briefly into day.

'GO! Flee!' Cried the girl, breaking into a run back down towards the bay.

'Wait!' Carl ran towards the gate.

'What are you doing? It's about to pour with rain.' Sally called.

Carl ran out onto the track, Sally started to follow. Carl stopped dead, flashing the torch up the path and across the fields.

Sally reached him, 'What's up?'

'She... she's gone!'

The sound of barking came from the direction of Garrie's cottage. Carl started to head towards it.

'Carl! Stop!'

Carl stopped, and turned back to Sally. 'She's gone that way; she's upset Old Garrie's dog.'

'Let her go. She was terrified. It's going to rain.'

Carl looked torn.

'Come back to the tent.'

There was a flash of lightening, illuminating a figure behind Carl. Sally screamed. Carl turned.

'What yoo doin', upsetin' my dog?' Old Garrie barked.

Carl quickly stated his defense 'It was the girl again. She was singing this sad song, it woke us, but she vanished...'

Thunder rumbled overhead, but Old Garrie, partially lit by the downcast torch, looked satisfied with Carl's explanation. 'How old?' He asked.

Carl frowned. 'She was older...'

'Perhaps her older sister,' Sally suggested. 'Black hair and green eyes, About thirteen or fourteen.'

Garrie looked up at the sky. 'Cupla days...' He murmured, turning to return to his house.

Carl challenged him, 'She's up at your house.'

'Nay yet.' Garrie replied, walking away.

Carl stood, speechless, staring at Garrie as he vanished into the darkness. A heavy drop of rain hit the back of his neck, then a flash of lightening lit the field. Carl couldn't believe his eyes, for Garrie was already gone, despite the distance.

There was a loud peel of thunder. Carl quickly returned to Sally, took her hand and led her back to the tent as great drops of rain began to fall.

Both sat without comment for a while, listening to the pounding raindrops on the canvas around them. Sally holding Carl tight.

'Storms don't usually bother you.' Carl pointed out.

'It's not the storm.'

'The girl?'

'I think she's an older sister, but you don't.'

'Same girl.' Carl nodded.

'But you said she was seven...'

'Garrie seemed to relate her age to something coming. On the beach he said that there was still time, now it's a couple of days, and that she wasn't at his house *yet*.'

'What do you think she meant by 'Go! Flee!'?' Sally's heart was racing.

'I'm not even sure that was directed at us.'

'She was staring right at us; you'd shone the torch right in her face!'

'She's a manifestation of Janet.' Carl sought a hint of understanding in Sally's face, but there was none. 'She's growing older in the lead up to some event...'

'People don't put on seven years in two days, Carl.'

'She's not "people".'

'She looked peopley. What do you mean by event?'

Carl smiled; this was his territory. 'Well, certain ghosts are said to appear on a specific night...'

'Kayleigh said she wasn't a ghost.'

'I didn't mean *she* was a ghost, I just wanted to make a point about 'events'; I've touched on them in my column in the paper.'

Sally flopped onto her back.

Carl continued. 'The appearance of some ghosts, or in Janet's case "manifestations", can often be linked to some event that occurred as a

48

cause of their being a ghost or manifestation.'

'So, there's something happening in a couple of days that links to this person's disappearance and why she's appearing now.' Sally proposed.

'Yep.'

Sally shook her head, 'So, what's happening on Orkney in a couple of days?'

Carl stroked his goatee, 'I don't know, maybe there's some festival?'

'Old Garrie keeps asking about her age; why's that? If it were a festival he'd know when she was coming.'

'Easter jumps about.' Carl defended.

'We're nowhere near Easter.'

'Well, I know *that*. Perhaps some old Orcadian Eastery thing; I don't know. I'll ask someone tomorrow.'

Both sat quietly, listening to the rain on the canvas and the rumbles of thunder. 'Bigger storm than last night.' Sally said after a while.

'It's closer. I think last night's one was further south.'

'Tonight's really freaked me out.'

'You're Ok, I'll look after you. I don't think Janet means any harm...'

'Did you hear the words of her song?'

Carl nodded.

Sally juddered, 'She's so sad; she's lost someone. Could that be the event?'

Carl shrugged. 'Waiting for someone to return?'

'Hold me.' Sally requested.

Carl happily obliged.

Chapter eleven

Sally rose early the next day, Carl found her sitting on a rock on the beach, wrapped tightly in her jacket, her legs folded within for warmth.

49

'Hey.' He greeted.

'Hi, I didn't want to wake you… It's cooler this morning'

Carl sat beside her and held her tightly. He looked out at the waves. 'Last night's storm has cleared the air. You Ok?'

'I want to see that Dungeon in the Cathedral, the hole.'

'Marwick's Hole?

'Yes. I want to see where she was.'

'You're not teasing me again are you?'

Sally smiled. 'No. I thought, if I saw the place she'd been imprisoned, perhaps I'd… I don't know… feel closer to her.'

'You don't think it's all an elaborate hoax I whipped up before we came anymore then?'

'No… you're not that clever.'

Carl almost objected, then, nodded in agreement.

'There probably is an explanation, don't get me wrong, I just want to see the place with my own eyes. Even if it has nothing to do with what's been happening.'

To Carl, all that had occurred pointed to some supernatural cause. He saw no naturalistic explanation: the girl growing older, the fact it was a well-established story; elements of which had been corroborated by more than one testimony. He wasn't going to attempt to sway Sally though; it was enough that she genuinely wished to investigate. 'I picked up a timetable on the bus. First bus from the main road into Kirkwall is soon after six thirty…' Carl paused. 'But that's pointless, the Cathedral isn't open until nine…'

'Let's have breakfast; we can walk in again. If we're still too early we can wander around a bit, explore.' Sally's legs appeared from her jacket.

'Are you wearing anything under that?'

'Just my jim-jams.' Sally giggled, giving Carl a quick flash.

'No wonder you're so cold. Come on.' They wandered up the path back to the tent and Carl prepared some scrambled eggs whilst Sally dressed.

~

By eight o'clock they were standing outside the Cathedral. Sally took Carl's hand and they wandered off down a narrow, one-way street. Beneath their feet were flagstones, and the buildings, rising either side of them were an eclectic mix of styles, new and old. Carl stopped briefly at a cash point then they headed on. Narrow alleyways split off the road between buildings and the couple found themselves weaving up and down them. In one alley was a tiny shop, the stone step at the door was worn into a soft curve and the subtly bayed window, no more than three feet wide, bore on display a multitude of artefacts.

Sally beamed, 'An antique shop.' She loved rummaging in places like that, especially places like that that were off the beaten track. She tried the door then noticed the handwritten opening times notice. 'Nine-thirty.' She looked at Carl.

'We'll come back later. I won't keep you from treasure like that.'

The couple headed down to the Harbour, they looked at the boats, admired the stubby lighthouse on the west pier and wilfully disturbed some resting gulls.

Taking a different route back to the Cathedral they rediscovered The Auld Motor Hoose bar. Sally snuggled into Carl's embracing arm. 'I'm having a great holiday.'

'That's good, Me too.'

As they approached the Cathedral, with its richly hued, red masonry, one of its ornately hinged wooden doors swung open. They ascended the few steps, entered and were Immediately greeted by the diminutive, wizened man who'd just opened the door.

The couple returned the pleasantry and were directed through the entrance into the nave.

Carl's eyes filled with the architecture, 'Wow.' Robust cylindrical columns stretched up to strong, brightly lit, beautifully hewn archways that supported further arches and a great vaulted ceiling high above them. Their footsteps echoed as they walked up the aisle; either side of them were row upon row of neat, wooden chairs with woven seats.

'The singing must be lovely, if they fill all these.' Sally remarked.

Carl was looking at the walls, he grunted acknowledgement but he was searching for the prison. The walls were certainly thick enough to hide a cell. He noticed some carved skulls but they turned out to be tombs of some sort. Then Sally noticed a large opening from the ground to chest height. 'Is that the hole?'

'I don't think so, let's keep looking, we can always ask someone if we can't find it. Oh, hold on, what's this?' Carl walked a few paces forward and pointed at a feature in the wall.

Sally looked. 'That's less convincing than the last opening.'

'I don't know.' Carl replied. 'The wall is thick here, and these look like bricked up openings…'

'Are yoo lookin' fer a particular crypt?' The voice came from the man who had opened the door.

'Er, no, we were told that the Cathedral had a dungeon.'

'Oh, aye, stell has et; quite unique. Et's thess way.'

The man hurried off ahead and the couple followed. Sally nudged Carl, 'I didn't think *that* was it.'

'Ok, smarty pants.'

The little man glanced back at them, looked up then stopped, 'Here et es. Marwick's Hole. Most walk by withoot any idea o' et's significance, or e'en what exists beyond the openin'.'

Carl noticed that the man was staring intently at them. Carl assumed that he was waiting for a reason for their interest in the Cathedral's unusual feature.

'I write for a newspaper, back home in Norfolk.'

The man smiled back at him.

'He writes about mysteries, unusual events and places.'

'Do you know much about the story of Janet Forsyth?' Carl asked.

'Ya seem to know a deal already ef ya seekin' oot Marwick's Hole.'

'All we know is…' Carl looked at Sally. '…she was tried for witchcraft, born on Westray…'

'She disappeared from there.' Sally said abruptly, pointing at the opening.

'Aye, tha's what they say. Though I believe et es quite inescapable. James es who yoo need.'

'James?'

'He does the tours…' He became reflective. 'Oh, but I donny think he does Tuesdays.' He frowned and scratched his head, staring down at the floor. 'Yet I'm fair sure he was here last Tuesday…' He looked up at the couple, gesturing with his hand that they stay put. 'Hold on here, I'll juss check. What he doesne know, ha, yoo understand, aye?' With that Carl and Sally were left alone, the Cathedral echoing to the man's hurried footsteps.

Carl looked up. 'It's awfully high.'

'Forget about it being inescapable.' Sally laughed. 'How on earth did they get the prisoner in?'

'Kenny said the accused would be dropped down a chute into the chamber below. So, there must have been a floor above; like a court room. Bother…'

'What is it?'

'It's just, well, I kind of hoped I could look inside.'

Sally tugged on his sleeve, and drew him back in the direction they'd approached from.

'Where are we going?'

'Not far.' She pointed into the south transept.

It was obvious to Carl that some workmen had been busy in the great building. Some buckets and masonry tools sat neatly beside some scaffolding boards and an extending ladder. Carl looked with surprise at Sally as he realised what she meant by pointing out the equipment.

'You want me to put a ladder up?'

'How do you get your journalistic scoops without investigating the facts?'

Carl looked up at the arched hole, he looked in the direction that the man had headed off in. Suddenly, moving quickly, he grabbed the ladder. 'You're going to get us into trouble Mrs. Ree.'

Sally giggled excitedly.

Carl pulled his torch out of his pocket and began to ascend the ladder.

'Look at you, all prepared!'

'Well, I just thought, you know? Dungeon, hole, probably dark. So, I brought my torch.' His head disappeared into the opening of the dungeon, closely followed by his hand and the lit torch.

'No, no, no, come doon!' The man had returned, and he seemed rightly vexed.

Carl half stepped, half slipped down the ladder. 'Sorry. She made me do it…'

Sally almost protested.

'That wus Adam's excuse young man. What were yoo thinkin'? Yoo could have damaged the masonry.'

Carl understood the man's comment as relating to the blame Adam had placed on Eve in the garden of Eden, and he now looked like a scolded schoolboy.

'Ha, hah!' The man became quite amused. 'Yera determined man; I've got to credit yoo that.' He lowered the ladder. 'Aye, no damage done, but I'm afraid James isne here. Hmm, look, as ya so keen fer answers, I'll take ya number an' contact yoo weth any further information on the Janet Forsyth matter. Yoo ken discuss emails or addresses weth James, I'm no computer fan. Now ef yoo Dinny mind replacin' thess ladder where 'twas yoo took et from, I'll get ya number from Eve here.'

Sally blushed, she wasn't a church goer, at least not regularly, but she also understood the comparison between Eve persuading Adam to share in the forbidden fruit, and her part in encouraging Carl to use the ladder. She told the man Carl's number, then quickly asked, 'He's not in any trouble is he… for climbing?'

'Ah, no, we'll have a good laff at ya expense o'er coffee. James'll be en touch, I'm sure. Et's his domain relly. Please enjoy ya visit, oh, an' nay more climbin', Aye?'

Sally nodded and Carl, quickly returning, shook the man's hand and thanked him for not having them kicked out.

'God's hoose es a place fer forgiveness, son.' He smiled, and headed in the direction of some newly arrived visitors.

Carl looked at Sally, 'Phew! If that had happened back home…'

'Excommunicated.' Sally chuckled. 'OK, so it wasn't my best idea, but did you see anything?'

'Before I nearly toppled in with shock you mean? Well, deep, square hole, cramped. The old boy was right; you'd have to be an expert freeclimber to get out. Looks like it had some sort of lid at some point too, there are marks around the opening.'

'Poor Janet. She was so sad already. I can't imagine how alone she felt in there.'

Carl too seemed touched by this idea. He hadn't really allowed himself to think too personally of Janet, but now, having seen that suffocating void, the horror of her situation really began to sink in.

Chapter twelve

The couple had continued to explore the building, Sally being particularly impressed with the level of craftsmanship almost everywhere the eye fell, but they had seen what they'd come to see and it had left each of them with an uneasy feeling, a feeling that seemed to surpass the ordinary sensations of being caught doing something that wasn't clever.

'Let's go back to that antique shop.' Carl suggested.

Sally had agreed, but try as they might the shop eluded them.

'I don't get it.' Carl huffed with frustration as he stood in the alley, 'I made a mental note. That lamp post and that blue shopfront.'

'It's just an old, crumbly, stone wall… It can't be this alley. There's probably another blue shop.'

Carl approached the wall, it made the alley seem narrower, and at two and a half metres tall it was the sort of wall you built around a garden, not against an existing wall.

'Come on.' Sally urged.

After almost an hour they found themselves back at the Cathedral and conceded defeat.

Across the road was an archway with a sign above it "The Orkney Museum". Sally looked at Carl. 'If I can't browse antiques, I'll be satisfied with looking and not touching.'

Carl nodded and they crossed the road.

Passing through the arch they found themselves in a little courtyard with sundry objects, a couple of small wooden boats, a cannon. 'Hmm, maritime history.' Carl stated flatly. 'I suppose that's to be expected on an archipelago.'

Sally, sensing a lack of enthusiasm on Carl's part, urged him on, 'There's bound to be some interesting stories in there. You know, like some of the things you and Kenny were chatting about yesterday.'

Carl had visited museums before when researching local mysteries. Many of these visits had revealed dusty collections of out-of-context objects with subjective just-so descriptive stories to explain them. He knew however, that Sally loved period "stuff", so he smiled obligingly.

By the door was a noticeboard indicating that there was an exhibition running, called "1914: The Calm Before the Storm". The sun had broken out now and shone pleasantly into the museum courtyard. 'More like the calm *after* the storm.' Carl chuckled.

Sally wanted to say that it was about the lead up to world war one, but realised that he was referring to the storm the night before, was attempting to make a joke, and simply nodded graciously.

They entered.

A man beside a till in the entrance hall, greeted them exuberantly, 'Welcome. Welcome.'

'Hi!' Carl responded, somewhat surprised by the greeter's friendly enthusiasm. 'Er, how much for entry, I didn't see any signs…'

'Free entry, come on en. Totally voluntary donation ef yoo feel yoo'd like to support the werk here.' He indicated a collection box. 'Clearly ya first visit, so I'll juss give yoo some info. The museum es set up like a timeline, from prehistoric Orkney right up to ets involvement en the second world war. There are files dotted aroond that give further interpretation, newspaper cuttin's, that sort o' thing. There are also some hands-on exhibits…'

'Ooh.' Sally remarked, positively.

'Ef there's anythin' yoo need, I'm happy t'help. Oh, an' there's a lovely garden oot back.'

The couple thanked the man and headed further into the museum. It quickly became clear to Carl that this was a very well-presented space; the exhibits neatly displayed and informatively explained. Yes, there were the obligatory model boats, oil paintings, broken pottery and local rocks, but there were also rooms that had been restored to how they would have looked in the days that the museum was a town house, owned by the wealthy Baikie family. Sally seemed particularly keen on these.

Carl tried his hand at piecing together some fragments of pottery in one of the hands-on exhibits, and had to admit it was more difficult than he'd assumed.

It was then that Sally spotted it, 'Carl…'

He turned from his efforts to see Sally standing, transfixed by the interpretation board in front of her. 'What have you found?' He put down the unfinished ceramic.

Sally beckoned with her hand urgently.

Carl approached. 'What is it?'

Sally pointed to a paragraph on a board entitled "Orkney Witch Trials".

'Oh! Well done.' Carl's eye fell on Janet Forsyth's name. He read the charge. 'Accused of witchcraft, devilry, and of inciting the elements. Storm Witch, murderer, summoner of foul beasts...' Carl's voice trailed off and they both stood in silence, Carl no longer reading aloud. Finally, he turned to Sally, she was staring straight at him; she looked pale.

'Oh Carl, I don't understand. That song she sang; it wasn't the song of the person described here…'

Carl, although thoroughly convinced that the girl they'd seen was a supernatural manifestation of Janet, decided it was best to play down the whole thing. 'This is just a museum display.' He offered. 'As for the girl and the song, well, like you said, probably a local kid singing something she's learnt somewhere.'

'*You* said she was younger before!' Sally retorted.

Carl wasn't expecting Sally to get angry. 'Hey, calm down. I'm sure there's a perfectly reasonable explanation for everything. No-one else has been with us when we've seen her. They've just related some local legend in response to our enquiries. That old boy living next to the

Tulloch farm, for example, well… he could be having a game with us; mess with the tourists, you know. As for the younger girl… Maybe you're right, a younger sister. This…' He pointed at the display. 'This happened nearly four hundred years ago.'

They stood in silence again.

'I got a bit drawn in.' Sally said at last.

'It's what makes mysteries alluring.' Carl pointed to the line of text that reiterated what they'd already known; Janet's disappearance from Marwick's hole. 'I bet the story's true…' His finger moved down a line. 'Here it's suggested that her lover may have rescued her. I bet he did. I bet he found a boat and they fled Orkney forever.'

'But the storms!' Sally said.

'Natural… Coincidental.'

Sally shivered, 'It's still a bit freaky. I don't think I'm going to sleep tonight.'

'We could use the farmhouse. John told me where to find the spare key. It's in one of the barns…'

Sally started to giggle.

Carl frowned, 'What now?' He couldn't keep pace with Sally's mood changes.

'You're supposed to be my big strong man, are you scared of a little girl and a fourteen-year-old?'

Carl grinned broadly, 'Supernatural manifestation.' He pointed at the display and put on a scary voice, 'Murderer, summoner of monsters, wooooo.' Carl chased Sally around the room.

'Stop it!' She squealed, laughing anxiously and swiping at him. The merriment ending with notable embarrassment, as an elderly couple entered the room with disapproving expressions.

~

Carl and Sally ended their museum visit enjoying the garden, the Tulips were still in bloom, accompanied by some small cherry trees that - although not old - already showed signs of being subject to the prevailing wind. Both stood looking at an unusual building when the man who had greeted them on arrival, appeared with a cup of tea.

'Tea break.' He announced. 'Suzie's coverin'. Do yoo like the Groatie Hoose?'

'Eh?' Carl replied.

'The Summer hoose yoo are lookin' at, et's called the Groatie Hoose.'

'Oh.' The couple acknowledged.

It was a square, stone building with a conical spire that ended with a weathervane, four tall ships marking north, south, east and west. On each corner of the roof another, much smaller spire filled the space created by the main spire's circular footprint.

'I like the little arched windows and door.' Sally said.

'It's the shells for me.' Carl pointed. 'Are they local?'

'They're European Cowries, known on the islands as Groatie Buckies. They're how the buildin' gets ets name. I'm Philly, by the way.' He offered his hand. Carl shook it.

'I'm Carl and this is my wife, Sally.'

'How old is it?' Sally asked.

'Ooh, aboot 1730ish I believe.'

Sally looked disappointed; Philly noticed. 'Es that too old fer yoo or too young?'

'Oh, no, it's just... oh it's silly.' She looked at Carl. 'I just wondered if it was somewhere else that Janet would have been?'

'A bit o' family history?' Philly asked.

The couple laughed and he joined them.

'No.' Carl responded.

'We're researching a young woman who lived on the islands in early sixteen-hundred; Janet Forsyth?' Sally informed, with an air of enquiry.

'Aha! The Storm Wetch.' Philly acknowledged.

Carl was just pleased that Sally had said "We're researching..." He smiled happily.

'Can you tell us much about her?' Sally pressed.

Philly seemed enthusiastic, 'We have an exhibit on the Orkney Wetch Trials; et's upstairs en...'

'Yes, we saw it.' Sally interrupted.

Philly's enthusiasm faltered. 'Tha's all I relly know.' He briefly slouched to exaggerate his own sorrow, then his friendliness returned with bright revelation. 'My Dad would know. He does tours en the Cathedral…'

'James?' Carl offered.

'Wow, aye, yoo two are good researchers! Yoo've met hem?'

'No,' Sally said. 'A little old guy in the Cathedral said he'd pass on our number…'

'Gerald.' Philly nodded. 'He *es* a tiny man! Pictish blood fer sure. Hey! He willne see Dad untel late tomorrow, what say I take ya number too? I'll see hem tonight.'

Carl saw no harm in this and gave his number, only later remembering that it didn't really matter; his phone was at home, he would receive any messages at the same time when he got back, whether they were made tonight or tomorrow.

After some more chat about the Groatie Hoose, and Orkney pirates, Carl found a little book in the museum shop that covered all the folklore Kenny had been talking about during their flight. Carl had thought the man was knowledgeable on the subject, but this was nearly word for word! Visit over, they headed off to find somewhere to eat.

~

The afternoon was spent visiting the archaeological site on the Ness of Brodgar, it seemed to ground Sally again after her anxiety in the museum. On returning to Kirkwall, the couple visited the building that was the Coastguard station; Carl's grandfather having worked there so many years before.

On return to the farm and with the evening so mild, the couple prepared a picnic and wandered down to the beach. Sally again expressed her unease about the witch. Carl comforted her and pointed out that, in all their sightings so far, the child they've been told is Janet has fled from them. 'She's more scared of us.' He pulled something from his pocket.

Sally laughed as Carl pushed the two candles into the sand and lit them. 'I didn't know you'd packed *them*.'

Carl chuckled, 'Just thought using them might reduce the weight of the rucksack.'

'Oh, you spoilt the moment!' Sally thumped him.

Carl took her hand and kissed it.

'That's better.' She purred.

Chapter thirteen

The evening was more pleasant than Sally had expected, and she had none of the trouble getting to sleep that she had assumed. Carl's observation that the child always fled from them had put her mind at ease. She scolded herself for getting so easily spooked, and drifted happily into her dreams.

Carl couldn't settle. Three things went around and around in his head like a constant buzz. He was convinced that what they'd experienced of Janet was a real supernatural phenomenon, and that her appearance had some unresolved factor. He was sure that she was like a wronged and restless spirit, although he had never heard of ghosts that copied pictures of cows from yoghurt drink bottles.

The missing shop seriously bothered him. It *had* been in the alley adjacent to the blue shop - of that he was sure.

He had almost slipped into a light doze, when thought number three robbed him of it. The candles, what was going on with the candles on the beach? He'd been staring at them in the warm evening, Sally's head rested on his chest, the stars in profusion in the sky above them, and yet his eyes were arrested by those tiny flames. Was it the way they moved? They seemed to flicker frequently towards the land, despite the stillness of the air. Was that it, or was there something else?

He pondered what it was that bugged him for almost half an hour, before something came. After a warm day, there should be an offshore breeze. The flames kept pointing inland. He shrugged, maybe that was a local phenomenon, maybe the islands were just too small to produce this effect? He pictured the flames again, no; he caught himself imagining a generic candle flame. Quickly he compared the generic thought to what he'd seen.

Why were the candle flames so bright? They'd seemed to have an aura. Was that how candles burnt this far north of Norfolk? He couldn't entertain that wax and wick would behave any differently in Orkney than Wymondham. So, what *was* that? And what explains Janet's presence, and where *did* that shop go? Why were the candles so bright? What's Janet here for…?

Finally, Carl got up. Flicking his jacket on, he wandered down to the beach with his torch. He stood drinking in the cool sea air. 'No singing tonight.'

'Aye, but where es she?'

Startled, Carl looked up to see Old Garrie standing on a low part of the nearby cliff.

'Oh, sorry, ded I make yoo jump?'

Carl found himself unable to speak.

'Ah, well, I've a ken she's buyen yoo time.'

'Wh… What?' Carl stammered.

Garrie looked along the beach and pointed. 'Now tha's a fine sight.'

Carl, intending only a glance before asking the old man to repeat what he'd just said, found himself transfixed by the luminescence of the gently rippling waves. They flickered and glowed with a deep, blue light. By the time Carl could tear his attention back to Garrie, the man was gone, *again*.

Carl returned to the tent, 'Sally, there's a beautiful glow to the waves as they break on the beach, I think it's caused by bioluminescent plankton.'

'That's nice darling.' Sally replied and rolled over producing a gentle purring snore.

Carl stretched out beside her; he was more awake than earlier. What had Old Garrie meant when he'd suggested that Janet was buying them time? Time for what? Why? How?

~

Carl had finally managed a couple of hours sleep before the first grey light of dawn. Judgement impaired, he resolved to seek answers, and in his mind there seemed no better time than now.

A heavy moistness trickled off the canvas, the grass was thick with dew, and webs showed up distinctly like ornate diamond encrusted necklaces. The morning felt chilly and a light mist held the air static, like a soft-focus photograph. The sun wasn't yet up, but it wouldn't be long now; the thin, high clouds glowed with a pinky-red hue. Carl turned around, 'Sal, Sal, you should see this sky.'

Sally responded with a don't-wake-me-yet grunt.

Carl zipped up his jacket and headed determinedly towards the old cottage on the cliff.

Disbelief rose within him the closer he got. The building *was* a ruin. The walls looked ready to tumble down. He reached the building and attempted to peer in through the window. Thick, dirt-laden cobwebs obscured his view, although he believed he could see daylight permeating through, as it would if there was no roof!

It seemed pointless, no-one could possibly live here, but Carl knocked on the door anyway. The door rattled in its frame. There was no response, no answer, not the slightest noise from within.

Carl shook his head, 'What's going on?' He walked around the building, discovering a great hole in the further end wall. He called in, 'Hello?' No response. He peered inside.

The whole place was a wreck, the roof must have fallen years ago. Moss and tufts of grass now grew on the slates and rubble. Carl purposefully checked the fireplace; he had seen smoke coming from the chimney earlier in the week. No, no ash in the hearth. No sign of habitation at all!

Carl's ears pricked up; was that barking? It sounded like the old man's dog. Maybe there *was* somewhere else along the cliff. Carl made his way outside.

There were no other buildings on the cliff top. 'They must be in

some cave or something!' Carl approached the cliff edge to look…
The only life visible was a seal and its pup. They were resting on some
flat rocks that dipped gently into the sea below. Carl sighed. Both seal
and pup seemed to be staring right at him. 'You're noisy.' As Carl
called a deeply yellow sun pricked above the horizon, staining the
morning mist with a dazzling gold.

Carl stroked his beard, thinking, 'What was it that Old Garrie had
said last night? Where es she?'

Although it didn't explain where Garrie was, or where he'd been
living, Carl knew that somehow, Garrie and Janet were linked. Garrie
knew more than he told. Perhaps they *were* related after all? Perhaps
all this *was* some tourist stunt. Perhaps John Tulloch was the
organiser? It was he who offered the use of his property, Kayleigh
knew him, Kenny was his nephew and Garrie had lived here for at
least as long as Kenny could remember. Carl nodded to himself with
satisfaction. 'I'll bet I'm right.' He smiled. 'Tulloch just wanted a
piece in the magazine to bolster tourism.' He nodded respectfully,
'Clever ruse.'

Now Carl had solved the mystery of Janet, there remained the puzzle
of the antique shop. John Tulloch couldn't possibly have arranged *its*
disappearance. To Carl, this was the real mystery now. He headed
back to the tent, the early morning mist lifting into steamy ribbons in
the warmth of the sun.

He found Sally propped up on her elbows as he entered the tent.

'You're up early. Everything OK?' She sat and started to get
dressed.

'Didn't sleep that well, I was just getting some fresh air, but you
won't believe what I discovered at Old Garrie's place. It's no-one's
place at all…' Carl told Sally what he'd found, and what he assumed it
meant.

'What a well-conceived plan. Your new friend certainly pulled the
stops out to get Orkney into your column!'

'Sad thing is, there's plenty here to fill my column anyway, without
resorting to such a performance.'

Sally nodded. 'So, what are we doing today?'

'Thought we'd find that antique shop again.'

'Oh, yes, we don't want *that* to remain a mystery.'

Carl wholeheartedly agreed.

Sally pulled a cardigan over her blouse to counter the freshness of the morning air. 'We'll probably walk straight up to it!'

~

With a fried breakfast inside, and a determined march into Kirkwall behind them, Carl and Sally now stood victorious at the door of the Antique shop.

Sally seemed quite amused, 'That was too easy.'

Carl stroked his goatee. He pointed back down the alley to the street, 'Blue shop.'

'It's got to be a different blue shop; walls don't appear and disappear. It does feel like it after yesterday's searching though, I must admit. Ha! Early again!'

Carl looked at his watch. 'Hmm, ten minutes. Well, I'm not leaving until we've been in the shop.' He looked around, and, finding a low window sill, perched.

Sally grinned.

'What?'

'You're funny.'

He smiled. Sally drew close to him. She stroked his face and kissed him. 'Where do you think folk are heading?'

'Huh?'

Sally pointed to the blue shop, there was a steady flow of people heading in the direction of the Cathedral.

Carl looked, 'Dunno, wedding?'

'Bit early…'

'Mmm, we'll check it out after the antiques…'

'Are yoo waitin' to come en?'

Carl and Sally, still partially locked in their embrace, looked. There in the doorway of the shop smiling broadly, stood a wiry, wrinkled old lady. The skin of her face, like the finest tissue paper, drooped around her friendly, open mouth in multiple folds. 'Please do come en. I saw

65

yoo yesterday, but yoo were gone before I got to the door.' She stepped back into the shop to allow access.

Sally stepped towards the door, closely followed by Carl. She was fascinated by the old lady's clothing; she was like some living history exhibit.

The old lady smiled wider, showing her crooked teeth. 'Tha's et my dears, come en, quickly now.'

The shop had an flagstone floor, the walls were entirely lost to lines of shelves, packed to breaking with artefacts displayed more like some ancient concept of a convenience store than a small, back street antique shop. There were neatly stacked baskets, woven in some uniquely Orcadian style. There were tools - from some more hands-on era - arranged in tidy, sized order, some of which Carl couldn't guess the use of. And there were more familiar things, sinkers and hooks for sea fishing, tools for tilling the earth. The scene was so absorbing for Carl that he found himself drawn right in; Sally, however, remained transfixed by the old lady, as if held by some enchantment.

'Yoo've seen her, aye?' The old woman's tone assured goodwill.

'Who?' Sally heard herself say.

The old dear seemed amused.

Sally had a sudden thought, 'Janet?'

The woman's eyes widened in delight. 'How long she's waited.'

'What for?' Sally asked quickly.

'What was taken from her, o' course. What, en absence, holds her to her restlessness; binds her to hold back what canny be held.'

Sally didn't understand.

The Lady started to rummage around in some draws behind a table, and for the first time Sally noticed the absence of a till, or a card reader. 'Is this a shop or some sort of museum?'

The old woman looked up briefly from her search. 'Many thengs are different now, aye, t'would be time fer me to rest soon too. Ah! Here 'tis.' She'd delved deeply into a particularly large draw, pulling out a long, thin strip of leather with something attached about mid-way. It was a simple necklace.

'Oh!' Sally's eyes met a tiny, exquisite object attached to a leather

66

cord. She stepped closer for a better look.

'Love's geft 'twas.' The room grew dark. Sally's eyes drawn to the window to witness a stone wall appearing. Sally felt a profound terror rising inside, barely hearing the old lady's next words.

'Ah! Yoo an' he, yoo'll help to break the curse at last. Aye, yoo well.'

Sally looked back at the old lady; eyes wider than they'd ever been.

Oil lamps flickered into life around the shop. Carl called from the back room, 'What's going on?' He hurried back to Sally and found her alone. 'Where's the shopkeeper?'

Sally turned to look at him, her face pale. 'She, She…'

Carl stepped quickly to Sally's side, full of concern. 'What happened?'

Sally pointed at the vacant space at the counter. 'She just… vanished…'

At that very moment the floor began to tremble beneath them, objects on the shelves began to crumble, as if countless years of rot were reclaiming time. Things began to topple.

'We'd better get out of here.' Carl tried the front door, but was confronted by the stone wall instead of an alley, the door swinging wildly off its worn, worm powdered hinges.

'I saw the wall appear…' Sally cried. '…it just seemed to build itself! What's going on?'

Chapter fourteen

Carl took control, 'There's another door at the back of the shop.' He seized Sally's hand firmly and lead her through as shelves, fittings and ceiling began to collapse around them.

As they approached the door it swung wide and they sprinted into the open air, a voice in their ears, the shopkeeper's voice, 'God speed.'

Sally stared back at the door. She'd just seen the woman disappear before her eyes! Suddenly it was all too much. 'I want to go home!'

'That's all good and well.' Carl replied flatly. 'But we're going to have to get our bearings first…'

Sally spun around to face Carl. He was still holding her hand but he was motionless, surveying their surroundings. It was overcast. They were standing on a rough, grass field. The landscape rose smoothly behind them to a ridge. The slope fell gently down to coastal cliffs, and a squat, castellated lighthouse stood to their left. This was not Kirkwall.

Carl was silent, staring out towards the cliff. Sally looked back at the door they'd run through. It was attached to a little, rundown outbuilding; a stone hut with a turf roof, on the edge of a field. Sally fainted.

~

'Sal, Sal, come back darling.' She looked up at him, he'd clearly caught her, her head was cushioned by his lap and he was leaning over her stroking her hair. 'There you are. It's Ok. I'll look after you.'

Sally flung her arms around him, 'I'm scared.'

Carl held her tightly. 'I know…'

'What just happened?'

'I don't know…'

'The shop went dark… the old shopkeeper said something about a curse; about us breaking it!'

Carl was listening intently.

'She knew Janet, said she was restless, holding back what she cannot hold? Oh Carl! She just went... just… evaporated!'

Carl nodded. 'A witch's curse.'

Sally clung to him more tightly.

'I begin to believe that John Tulloch is innocent. I think there's much more to the story than we've heard.'

'She *is* a witch then. Oh Carl!'

Carl could feel Sally's fear. 'It's Ok, Janet is the one who's been wronged… the one who's been cursed; the woman in the shop too. If

Janet's story goes back hundreds of years, so could the shopkeeper's. The shop was like, frozen in time or something. You should have seen what was in the back room; it was like a museum. Do you remember what happened before everything crumbled?'

'She pulled a necklace from a draw - the shop went dark; she said we'd break it…'

'The necklace?'

'No, the curse.' Sally frowned, 'She said the necklace was a love gift.'

'What happened to it?'

'That's when the wall appeared and she disappeared! Oh Carl! I don't know what happened to it.'

Carl rubbed her back, he understood that the necklace had to be found, that it held the key to ending the curse that must have been endured all these many years. Their priority was to get back to the shop - whatever remained of it.

Suddenly Sally froze again. 'Carl! Look.'

Carl eased back from Sally's arms; she was looking over his shoulder at the cliff edge. Carl's eye followed her trembling, pointed finger. 'Yes. She's been there all the time. I noticed her as we ran out through the door.'

Sally swooned. Carl supported her. She buried her head in his shoulder, 'Oh Carl, let's get away, I can't bear it!'

'She's not the threat, look, tell me what you see.'

Sally emerged slowly from Carl's embrace. Peering down the slope, she could see the figure of a young woman looking out to sea, hands raised, fingers spread as if holding back something invisible. She was leaning into this effort in such a way that she should have toppled over the cliff edge. Her raven black hair and dirty linen dress flicking this way and that in the strong sea breeze. 'It's her again, what is she doing?'

Carl pointed out to sea.

Sally gasped. The horizon was near black, fractured racks of cloud were being dragged off towards the darkness, they could feel the pull of the storm on the breeze around them but Janet seemed lashed about by a gale that roared off the ocean, a gale neither Carl nor Sally could feel.

'I know where we are.' Carl said. 'That's the lighthouse Kenny drew our attention to as we flew passed in the helicopter.'

'We saw a lot of lighthouses…'

'We're on the Brough of Birsay.'

Sally had been staring at the lone figure on the cliff edge. 'I'm worried about her Carl.'

Carl looked, he felt sure it was Janet, but again she was older than before. 'I don't think we can do anything for her. I think she's bound to a vain attempt to hold back…'

Suddenly there was a great gust that hit them all. First Janet's feet seemed to slide backwards shrieking in anguish and struggling for balance, then, gaining it, reasserted her efforts to hold back the storm. Carl was knocked clean off his feet, and Sally stumbled to the turf. 'We've got to help her; I think we're meant to.'

The sky churned; the racked clouds seemed to find their limit of approach to the encroaching tempest. Carl looked at Sally, then Janet. 'You say the old lady in the shop called Janet's efforts futile?'

'Yes.'

'I didn't predict this. Makes sense of the candles the other night though.'

'What have candles got to do with it?'

'The flames were being drawn inland, only not actually inland, but west. The storm was drawing the air towards it. Stay there.' Carl ran towards Janet, slowing only as he reached her. The gust had driven her far enough from the edge of the cliff now for Carl to see her face; he felt she must be about seventeen - but the cares of life were all too apparent. She looked pale and hungry, her tear-streaked face marked with toil and dirt.

The waves churned on the rocks below the cliff, giving Carl a giddy dizzy feeling. 'Please.' Carl ventured, 'Can we help you?'

'Get awey! Go!' Janet cried, and Carl felt the storm's power buffeting him as Janet's concentration faltered. He could see Janet's feet sliding slowly away from the cliff edge, as if she were being physically pushed. She gave a despairing gasp. 'There es a storm tide comin', yoo *must* go. Cross the causeway before et's too late. Follow the coast path, cross the stream beyond the Earl's Palace…'

'There's nothing you can do here, Janet. Your efforts are in vain. Come with us.'

Her eyes snapped onto Carl, 'En vain?' she hissed, dropping her hands.

Suddenly, all around was bathed in a ferocious wind, the whole sky out to sea seemed to approach them ominously. Janet raised her hands again and a tense, still pressure returned. Janet's eyes remained on Carl. 'Go! Get ya wife to safety.'

Carl backed away.

'Ef the causeway es lost, look to the seals.' Janet called, returning her gaze to the sky.

Carl turned, and with one last, bewildered glance at Janet, ran back to Sally.

'Won't she come?'

'Don't ask me how,' Carl panted. 'But… but she really is holding back that storm!'

'The old lady said…'

'Yes, holding back what she cannot hold.' Carl interrupted. 'I guess she'll fail in the end, but for now she *is* holding it back. She wants me to get you to safety.' Carl offered his hand. Sally looked down at Janet. 'Come on Sal…'

'But…'

'The curse binds her to her efforts. The old lady seemed to suggest that the necklace was the key to breaking the curse. We can only help Janet if we have it.'

Almost vacantly Sally took Carl's hand. Eyes still fixed on Janet, she let him lead her away.

Chapter fifteen

Reaching the top of the ridge, and with Sally fully committed to the run, the couple saw the causeway that linked the Brough to Mainland.

'There's still time! Quickly!'

They descended the gentle but uneven slope, stumbling as they went, barely aware of the low ruined walls of an old settlement as they picked their way down the path to the causeway.

Now, eyes level with their only route back to Mainland, both Carl and Sally quailed. The causeway dog-legged and looked slippery, the waves to left and right of it seemed to froth and bubble hungrily towards it before faltering and pulling back, then, as if bolstered by some unseen monster thrashing in the surf, they thrust forth with renewed but brief violence.

Sally wheezed, 'We'll never make it.'

'Not looking at it we won't.' Carl replied, physically urging her on.

They ran cautiously onto the concrete pathway. Their viewpoint lower still, it seemed as if the waves might engulf the path at any moment. Sally slipped, and screamed, Carl steadied her with an assertive pull. Their lips already tasted of salt. 'Blimey, this is intense!'

'Look!' Sally called, despairingly. Up ahead the causeway must have been lower, for the waves spilled readily across it. 'We can't get through!'

Carl swept her up in his arms and strode forwards. 'We've got to.' The water splashed at his ankles, then his knees, invisible forces threatened to take his feet, he stumbled, then he was made to stop by something blocking his stride 'What the!' It was firm, resistant and soft but then it was gone. He tried to step again, but the swell dropped, briefly showing the edge of the causeway; had something not resisted him they would have been straight into swirling, deep water. Waves and foam disoriented him, 'I'm not sure which way the path goes!' Carl exclaimed.

'Look!' Sally pointed. Two rows of seals marked the edge of the route; it had struck abruptly to the right. 'We're going to make it!' Sally marvelled at the bobbing mammals.

Something else was in the water too, something bigger, something that made the seals nervous, something in the deeper breakers.

Carl didn't hesitate a moment longer, some waves were reaching places that didn't like how cold the water was.

He splashed out onto a narrow strip of sand, gently lowered Sally and looked back at the seals. Gradually they disappeared beneath the waves.

'Which way now?' Sally asked.

'Janet said to follow the coast path.'

A path led off the beach, but quickly became a car park with a road leading away from it. 'There's no other way to go, but I suppose it was a path in Janet's day.' Carl took Sally's hand again, and they headed off urgently. The car park was empty. Carl shook his head, 'It's as if everyone knew this weather was coming.'

'Everyone but us!'

'It's what Old Garrie was counting down to, a weather event not a cultural one'

'As the storm grew closer so Janet grew older?' Sally offered.

'Yes.'

They came to a sweeping bay with a few small fishing boats pulled high up the beach.

'That must be the place Janet meant.' Carl pointed towards a ruined but imposing structure. 'The Earl's Palace…'

Before long they'd reached it. 'What now?'

'She said to cross the stream.' Carl looked around and frowned, 'Only I can't see one.'

At that moment there came a strange wailing sound from behind them. Both looked back and Sally drew closer to Carl. 'What was that?'

'We donny talk aboot et.'

Carl and Sally spun around. There before them was Old Garrie with a bundle on his back, and his dog standing obediently at his side, gazing loyally up at him. In that moment Carl thought the weird little dog had a similarity to a seal pup with gangly legs, his mind flitted to the seal and pup on the shore below Garrie's house, and then the thought was dashed by Garrie's urgent words.

'Ya route home es that way. Ya pursuer wellne cross fresh water.' Garrie pointed up the road that ran adjacent to the palace wall. 'Cross the stream, then follow et up to the main rood. Head fer Dounby an' Finstown. Weth luck yoo'll get a lift back to the farm. There's a spare key en the far barn…'

'John told me where to find the spare key, if we needed…'

'All's good then. Yoo'll be safe enside. Now get goin'.'

There was another screeching wail, closer this time. Carl, still holding Sally's hand, headed off. Sally's eyes remained fixed on the Scotsman and his dog, as she was dragged away. He bent down to the animal, whispered something in its ear and it headed off towards the wailing. At that moment Sally was convinced that the dog's size increased with each bound until it was more like a wolf, then it was out of sight. 'What's happening?' She asked, matching Carl's speed to counter the drag.

'I read about it on the Orkneyjar website. The tales have persisted until relatively recent times.'

'Tales about what?'

Behind them, but still out of sight around the bend in the road, came a wild cacophony of chilling howls, then an awful yelp. Carl saw a bridge on the road ahead. 'Fast as you can Sal; a Nuckelavee is hunting us.'

Sally felt an inexplicable fear rise within her, 'What's a Nuckelavee?'

'A beast of the sea,' Carl puffed. 'Orcadians tell of it coming ashore to spread blight and disease amongst crops, livestock and people…'

 Allowing Carl to lead her, Sally glanced back. Her eyes widened with horror. Garrie had disappeared; a red form, like a bloodied horse, was peering at them from the bend in the road. Seeing the couple, it began to gallop towards them. Sally screamed. Carl also screamed, but his goal was in reach. They stomped over a stone bridge, over the stream that ran beneath it, and Carl spun them around to face the creature. Sally wanted to keep running. She pulled against him. 'What are you stopping for?'

'The stories say that it can't cross fresh water.'

'Stories are stories, Carl!' Sally cried. 'This is no time for experiments! That thing is real, and it won't need to worry about the water! There's a bridge! We just crossed it!' She strained against Carl's grip to get away.

'Sal, look.'

The creature had slowed and stopped on the far side of the crossing. It was a hideous thing, like some skinless seahorse with finned and powerful legs. Emerging from its back was a skinless human torso with a large lolling head and creepily long, skinny arms, the hands of which dragged along the road. Over all its body the exposed veins showed black against the red flesh, and a single eye stared down at them from its other, horse-like face. All stood motionless, then, assessing its position, the beast placed one foot on the bridge.

Carl and Sally backed away.

A second hoof tested the bridge.

Suddenly a rock kicked off the creature's back, it responded with a shrill wail and spun around. At the bend in the road Old Garrie had reappeared; a remarkable distance to have thrown anything, let alone hit a target. He lobbed another stone, again striking the beast. In his other hand he seemed to be holding a long, bag-like object, but the dog was nowhere to be seen.

'Cummon yoo grut, ugly block head.' He shouted.

The creature's horse-like bulk turned slowly to look back at Carl and Sally, a black, sooty vapour snaked away from its mouth, and was buffeted away by the strengthening breeze.

Garrie continued his taunts, 'Cummon ole black veins, yoo skinless abomination! Rain's cumin, yull wanna be gettin' back to the sea.'

The creature hissed at Carl, then was away at a gallop.

'Run!' Garrie shouted, as he too turned on his heal.

Almost automatically the couple began to run, but Sally suddenly became resistant.

'What are you doing? Let's get the hell out of here!'

'He said to follow the stream, and you were right, it seemed reluctant even to cross a bridge!'

Carl chastised himself, 'Sorry, you're right, come on.'

They headed up a farm track that followed the stream, it curved away from the track so they followed it. They passed another farm opposite and then what looked like an old mill house on their right, but they weren't sightseeing, this was every ounce of flight they could muster. Beyond the mill the main road loomed. 'We'll take a quick breather there.' Carl helped Sally over a low, stone wall. 'Perhaps we can thumb a lift.'

They staggered to a halt on the roadside grass verge, Carl half doubled-over, panting heavily. All the time they were there the road remained silent. All that could be heard was the sloshing and splashing of the rapid little stream as it passed under the road.

'Which way now?'

Carl raised his eyebrows, 'Well, I don't think it's wise to cross back over the stream, so that only leaves this way.'

'Garrie said something about Finstown.'

Carl nodded, 'Once we're there, we'll only be five or six miles from Kirkwall.'

A sudden gust of wind pushed by them, with a hint of rain in it. There was a threatening rumble from the direction they had come and the sky seemed to heave; as it had done when Janet stopped holding it. This time however, it continued to churn.

Sally felt moved, 'Poor Janet, the storm is besting her.'

'Come on, we should get moving.'

They started jogging along the road. Sally was still nervous about the creature and frequently glanced over her shoulder, just in case it was coming. Carl understood, from his research, that the beast could not tolerate fresh water, and as it was now drizzling, he felt confident they were safe.

The landscape trickled slowly by, fields mostly; low rough-topped stone walls penned them in and kept the verges narrow. Eventually they reached a building with "Birsay Outdoor Centre" written above the door. Carl tried the door, but it was locked. 'Where is everyone?'

Sally pointed at the pressing darkness. 'Perhaps this is worse than we think. Perhaps people have been told to stay in their homes. Oh!'

'What?'

'Those people we saw in Kirkwall, when we were waiting outside the shop... what if they were heading for some sort of community shelter?'

'Whatever's coming I guess the staff at this centre didn't feel it worth their while opening today.'

Carl and Sally headed on.

Prompted by the first heavy drops of rain, Carl pulled some thin shower jackets from his backpack. He sighed, 'They won't keep us dry if it really hammers down.'

'Look!' Sally pointed back in the direction they'd come from. The road had been gently ascending, and over the fields they could now see the sea and, jutting out into it, the Brough of Birsay.

'Oh my!' Carl gasped. The headland was writhed in dark streamers of rain. Not the straight curtains, that you might see falling from a heavy summer downpour, but great, twisted, angry lines, raging down then buckling out and away from the land as if painted by some expressive manga artist. 'She's still holding it!'

Sally eased the backpack onto Carl's shoulders. 'She's doing it for us. We'd better make the most of it.'

~

It was becoming clear to the couple that the islanders took such weather events very seriously. They hadn't seen any cars on the road and all of the homes they'd passed were either boarded up or protected around doorways with sandbags. They realised that if Carl had his phone the News and Weather Apps would have moved them into the Tulloch farmhouse that morning, and any thought of island exploring would have been very far from their intentions, not that they'd chosen to be *here*.

The wind was strengthening; the rain was getting heavier. A series of loud thunderclaps echoed behind them. Carl and Sally glanced at each other, both knowing that Janet had done her best, but that now the storm would be bearing down on them. The run, that had become a jog, was now no more than a hurried walk. The movement of the clouds became more forceful and the morning light faded into an eerie, early dusk. Sally drew close to Carl, and he placed an arm around her for support and encouragement. Then, as if in answer to some unspoken prayer, they heard an approaching vehicle.

Chapter sixteen

Carl swung Sally to the roadside verge, the approaching vehicle was a Landrover Defender. Carl waved franticly. The vehicle, its headlights dazzling through the heavy splashes of rain on tarmac, pulled over.

The driver opened his window, 'I donny think yoo two should be oot en what's comin'.' He jumped out of the vehicle and opened the rear door. 'Get en, I'll take yoo to one o' the shelters.'

Carl glanced back down the road, the view had closed down, a wall of cloud draped towards them like a curtain being dragged over the landscape. He bundled Sally into the car and joined her. The driver leapt in. 'Ded yoo no' know the forecast?' He asked.

'We're, er, camping. To be honest we didn't expect to be this far out today.' Carl replied.

'The campsites were notified two days ago.' The driver pulled away. 'Juss how far oot are yoo?'

'Well, firstly, we're camping independently, near Kirkwall, a place called 'Tulloch's Farm'…'

'Ah! Ya the couple that came to the Cathedral?'

'Er, yes.' Carl replied, a little surprised.

'I'm James Sinclair, one o' the guides at St. Magnus. Yoo met my son the other day at the museum.'

'Philly!' Sally replied.

'Aye, Phillip.' James smiled. 'Seems ya good at gettin' ya self ento mischief.'

Both Carl and Sally knew that James must have had a laugh at their expense from Gerald's relation of the ladder incident; they both blushed.

'Have yoo ben thess way o'er night?'

'Er, no, it's a bit of a long story.'

'Well yoo didne get here by bus, they're no' runnin' today.' There was a flash of lightening. 'Yoo should always heed the weather forecasts on the islands…'

'We would have, but we didn't have any means.'

'I'll grant yoo no telly en a tent, but no radio? No mobile phone? The Police posted a warnin' online the same time the campsites were notified.'

'My wife doesn't carry a mobile, I left mine at home by accident…'

James tutted loudly. 'That'll explain why I got voice mail when I tried to call yoo aboot ya enquiries. Oh well, ya lucky I came by when I ded, aye?'

'Er, yes, thank you.'

'Es no mean feat gettin' thess far oot from Kirkwall, ya the triathlon sort are yoo? Iron man? That belly o' yours hidin' some muscle es et?'

Carl was about to say what had happened when Sally piped up, 'Yes it does. He's a very good runner too.' Her eyes told Carl that she didn't want him to try and explain stepping through some sort of portal from Kirkwall to the Brough of Birsay. Or to start on about witches holding back storms, or seals marking causeways, or, indeed, blood red horse monsters from the sea. Tourists practicing triathlon was an adequate explanation and quite mad enough. 'We love running, but we had no idea about the storm. Is it big?' She hugged Carl.

'Beg! Thess es goin' to build ento the evenin', en rage most o' the night.' He stared at Carl perhaps longer than he should for the speed they were travelling. 'Ha, a runner? Who'd o' thought et?'

Carl frowned, he felt a little offended, but then, he wasn't a runner, not at all, and he would have been surprised himself by anyone of his stature making such a claim. He looked at Sally, she shrugged and smiled, whispering, 'We're safe.' She addressed James, 'Thank you for picking us up.'

'Yoo relly are lucky today. I'm no' always oot thess side o' the island; my brother es en hospital an' I was juss checkin' the security o' his livestock…'

Everyone jumped as a wheelie-bin struck the rear wing of the car. Waste paper, card and plastic bottles flew by them, whipped up by the wind. 'Blast et! That well o' damaged the bodywerk.'

James grew quiet and seemed in no mood for conversation; indeed, any driver would have needed to concentrate now as the conditions deteriorated. The rain seemed to wrap around them like a blanket, violent gusts of wind threatened to see them off the road, the windows steamed up too; the vehicles air-con barely able to keep the front screen clear. When Sally wiped her window to see, there was no view beyond the roadside stone walls. She stopped looking. The journey took longer than they thought, and Carl began to appreciate how long it would have taken them on foot.

On entering Kirkwall, James picked his way along the deserted streets turning the car this way and that to avoid debris in the road, mostly upturned wheelie bins but also a shrub in a planter and a toppled moped.

Carl was fascinated, 'This is wild, are storms usually this bad here?'

'They ken be quite severe, often arriving suddenly but I've ne'er known a storm to set en weth such ferocity, an' et hasne relly got goin' yet.'

'Like it had been held back.' Sally offered.

James peered at Sally in his rear-view mirror. Carl nudged her gently, if he wasn't to say anything about the weird things they'd seen, then neither could she. 'Watch out!' Sally called.

They were coming up on a T Junction and something was about to cut across them. James slammed on the breaks and the three watched as a Wind-eze advertising trailer, without a towing vehicle sailed down the road. The little group laughed nervously.

'Et's gonna be a hellish task clearin' up, tha's fer sure.' James sighed.

~

James finally pulled the car to a halt, 'Thess es the St. Magnus Centre. Reckon ya tent'll be flat b'now. Yoo'll have to sit oot the storm here. They'll have food an' blankets, an' they're a friendly bunch. Cummon, I'll introduce yoo.'

Carl and Sally unbuckled, both realising as they watched James exit the vehicle, that it would definitely be safer to stay at the shelter and there was certainly no real reason to risk trying to get back to a tent that was probably wrapped around the apple tree by now. James clung to the vehicle as he made his way around it, inspecting the earlier damage as he went, and the vehicle rocked sharply with each hammering gust.

Carl took Sally's hand, 'Come on then.' He tentatively opened his door. The wind caught it, just as he'd expected, but he was powerless to slow the door's swing, and it dragged him physically from his seat. 'Crickey!'

James reached the couple and offered a steadying hand, although it may have been that he was clinging to them to prevent himself from falling; either way, they stumbled into the building helped by a lady who had seen their arrival and unbolted the door.

James introduced the woman as Dedra, his wife, a woman in her late fifties who seemed very sympathetic. 'Yoo ken slip ya wet jackets off o'er there, would yoo like some hot chocolate, before the power goes oot!' She laughed. They agreed and headed over to the radiator that had been pointed out to them. A room further along seemed a-buzz with people who had clearly gathered together for the duration of the storm.

Carl then made the discovery that would see them all back out into the weather. Glancing admiringly at his wife's curvy shape, as she draped her wet rain mac over a chair by the radiator, he saw something dangling from Sally's cardigan pocket, 'Hey, what's that?'

'What's what?' Sally noted where his attention was and peered down to see for herself.

For a moment they all stood motionless, James out of bemusement towards the continued weirdness of the tourists, Carl in expectation of an answer, and Sally out of sheer disbelief.

Dangling from her pocket was a leather cord. Sally pulled it free and gathered it up in her hands. 'The necklace! The old lady must have dropped it into my pocket when the wall distracted me!' She offered the object to Carl.

Dangling from the cord was a small carved object, he cupped this in his hand and peered at it closely. 'I think it's wood; it's carved into a curled-up seal.'

'Yes.' Sally agreed. 'It's a seal. Oh Carl!' Sally burst into exhausted tears.

'What's wrong?'

'She could have had it, Carl. We could have given it to her on the cliff. The curse would have been broken. We've let her down!'

Carl gathered her into his arms. 'There now, Sal. It's Ok, we'll get it to her…'

'How?'

Carl rested back against the wall, Sally still firmly in his embrace. He pondered the question. 'Old Garrie…'

Sally peered up at him.

'…Old Garrie knows her. He'll know how to find her…'

'If that thing didn't get him!'

They stared at each other for a moment. Sally shuddered.

'I'm sure he's fine. He seemed to know what he was doing…'

Sally shot Carl a bemused stare, 'Throwing stones at a monster?'

James gave them his full attention, 'A monster?'

Carl and Sally looked up at James; for the whole journey they had kept this quiet - disturbing though it had been - because it sounded mad, monsters were the stuff of stories, fantasy films, console role playing games; they had wanted to escape the weather, not to be asked politely to leave the vehicle and watch as the driver sped away from the loonies. James' eyes were now totally fixed on the little seal pendant, 'Tell me now, was et a red monster?'

Carl and Sally both felt a chill up their spines, James lifted his hand to take the necklace.

Carl thrust the seal up into Sally's hand, and Sally, snapping out of her surprise at James' comment, plunged it into the pocket of her jeans.

'It *was* red,' Carl replied. 'What do you know about it?'

Chapter seventeen

It was now James' turn to look perturbed, Carl's frank admission that some strange creature had indeed been seen, seemed genuinely troubling.

'Et's ben spoken aboot fer centuries…' James confirmed.

'A Nuckel…'

James placed the hand that had been reaching for the necklace, firmly over Carl's mouth. 'Dash et man! Yoo ne'er say ets neem!'

Carl pulled away, uncomfortable with the contact, 'Why not?'

'Et encites et, makes et come.'

Sally drew closer to Carl. 'It's Ok Sal, it fled from the rain. Old Garrie suggested it would need to get back to the sea…'

James' eyes widened slightly. 'Es true, fresh water repels et…' He paused, glancing tentatively to the floor then back at them with a smile, 'Ole Garrie, ded yoo say? Yoo've seen hem too?'

Sally rolled her eyes, Garrie was the least strange topic that the old tour guide could be interested in, 'He lives near the Tulloch farmhouse, somewhere along the cliff…' She stated.

'He was preparing the house…' Carl whispered.

'What?' Sally frowned.

'Old Garrie, when we told him we'd seen the little girl, that first time!' He held Sally's gaze, she shrugged. 'As soon as we told him… he stopped what he was doing and went looking for wood. He's preparing the house for Janet!'

'But you said the house was derelict, all fallen-in, no roof…'

Carl smiled, 'And shops don't disappear; back doors in Kirkwall don't lead to stone huts on the Brough of Birsay. Seals don't mark out underwater footpaths…'

'But Kenny; he spoke of old Garrie as if he were just a local.' Sally protested, searching franticly for something *normal*.

'He said that John blamed him for bad weather. If he's linked to Janet that would be an accurate assumption…'

James chipped in, 'Ef ya talkin' aboot Kenny Tulloch, that young pilot from the airfield, he's a pretender - got all his folklore knowledge from that dubious lettle tourist book they sell at the museum, he's barely ben on the islands since school, flies his noisy helicopter en the visitor season, Pah! He e'en puts on a selly southern accent. Oh, nay offense o' course.' James shook his head, clearly agitated. 'Ef he'd e'er listened to his parents or John up at the family farm he'd have made the connection hemself. The young donny seem interested en the history o' the Islands anymore.'

'Oh, I don't think that's true,' Sally replied, in an attempt to calm the man down. 'We heard this lovely local band at the Auld…'

'A band! Ack! Noisy nonsense…'

'No really, they sang beautifully about Orkney folklore, they were called…'

'No' interested.' James interrupted, raising both hands. 'They well have caused untold damage to the accuracy o' the stories by forcin' them ento rhyme, rhymes put together fer rhymes sake!'

Sally fell silent, James' point did make some sense, an existing story probably could lose some accuracy from being altered into Kayleigh's lively style.

Carl too was silent; his hand resting on the little folklore book in his pocket that he'd purchased at the museum.

'One thengs fer sure.' James asserted. 'Yoo've ben entrusted, weth an important task. Janet Forsyth has ben a constant fascination to me since childhood. Workin' at the Cathedral has afforded me a number o' meetin's weth folk who have claimed a sightin' o' her; like yoo.'

'You've seen her?' Sally asked.

'No. Yoo see, those who have, have one theng en common.'

'Which is?' Carl urged.

'They are couples, young an' en love…'

A voice called up the corridor, 'Darlin', es everythin' Ok?' It was

Dedra.

James looked back, 'Aye, dear.'

Carl, knowing Sally would be determined to get the necklace to its rightful owner now that it was found, whispered 'Do you want to try and get back to the farm, to find Garrie?'

'I want to help Janet.' Sally said. 'So, we've got to find Garrie, we can't wait, can we? It'll be too late after the storm, won't it?'

The entrance door shook in its frame, as if some great animal was pummelling it, and great rivulets of rain ran as if gravity had been turned on its side.

Dedra approached. 'Ya no' thinkin' oh goin' oot, are yoo? Yoo've only juss arrived. I've got ya drinks.'

'Et's the girl.' James said, as Dedra offered Carl and Sally their hot chocolates on a tray.

Dedra looked at Sally, her face lightening with understanding. She looked at James. 'Yoo wondered ef yoo'd hear o' any sightin's today.'

'I was hopeful, earlier en the week when I heard that these two had ben makin' enquiries…'

'Yoo've seen her?' Dedra asked.

Sally nodded.

'Et's better than that.' James added. 'They've the charm that binds her. Janet ken be free.'

Dedra's eyes grew wide with surprise.

James took his drink from the tray, quickly slurping it down despite its heat.

'You know that the necklace bears the curse?' Carl enquired. 'The old lady in the shop told us. Going by the museum boards it isn't general knowledge…'

'Et's a story fer the journey.' James hurried, draining his mug. 'Although et's already fierce, the storm's no' yet at ets height. We must go.'

'Oh, do be careful…' Dedra warned.

'The Lord well be our guide an' our protection, my love.'

Carl gave Sally a sideways glance at this comment, but seeing Sally down her drink he realised how determined she was to get on with the job; she believed this man could help them. Carl stared at the wiry but firm looking man, the knowledge he'd already shared did seem to suggest they'd found someone who knew what needed doing.

~

It took Carl a bit longer to finish his hot drink than it had the others, 'I don't know how you gulp down something so hot?' He protested as James and Sally urged him to hurry. He thanked Dedra, handing back to her a quarter full mug after some noisy slurping, insisting it was delicious, but that he'd better get going; all turned their attention to the door.

The rain wasn't just impacting on the glass, the wind was ripping the heavy drops back off again and hurling them down the road. James' resolve seemed to falter slightly, 'Ach! Yoo'll need more protection than yoo've got, car or no; those thin shower macs are wet through already.'

Carl and Sally glanced at the puddles forming under the radiator where the macs were draped, they certainly couldn't go outside again as they were.

'Well I'm no goin' oot untel et's o'er, yoo ken use my storm jacket.' Dedra offered. 'Oh, and I saw somethin' en the charity box, hold on...' She hurried off and returned quickly with an arm full of jackets and a victorious smile.

Carl had sniggered inwardly at the bright yellow sou'wester but as each jacket was rejected due to being too small or inadequate in some other way, he became resigned to the notion that the bright, plastic beacon would end up being his lot for the coming endeavour. So it was that Sally stepped out into the turmoil of the gale in good spirits with an amused grin on her face; Carl following closely behind, firmly holding the hat he'd found in the jacket's pocket.

~

It had been just a few, laboured steps against the wind to reach the vehicle but the whole group, sitting protected inside, looked as if

86

they'd stood face up in a power shower. They glanced at each other, laughing nervously at their purpose as the car rocked in the wind. Carl, adjusting the chin strap on his hat, suggested it was like being a piece of washing in a washing machine.

'Yoo still wanna go on?' James asked.

'I think we're obligated.' Sally replied.

'Aye.' James confirmed, and he cautiously pulled away from the curb.

It wasn't far before James cornered to the left, leaving the route that Carl and Sally knew, the car - side on to the wind - lolled uncomfortably until it reached the relative shelter of screening buildings.

'It's the other way.' Sally pointed out.

'Aye, but thess'll get us to where we *need* to be, local knowledge, yoo understand?'

Sally pondered James' reply, he was local, of course he knew the best route, but it did feel like the opposite direction.

Slowly they continued, James picking his way through debris that heaved and danced unpredictably.

The road began to curve gently right, until Sally was almost convinced that they were heading in the right direction again.

Carl saw an opportunity to hear what James had promised for the journey. 'Have you always known that there was a charm, or artefact involved in Janet's story?'

'Et was a theory o' my ancestor, Grigor Sinclair, a man o' great stature en the Church en Janet's day. When I saw the necklace, an' heard ya concerns et made sense to me; her spirit es restless yoo see, so there's somethin' else en play. A wetch's curse es often placed on an object, en thess case an object o' deep emotional value no longer en the possession o' the cursed.'

Carl nodded, 'Fascinating.' He looked out through the partially cleared windscreen. The tempest seemed to shake everything, the very air had a life to it, the elements so apparent he believed he could actually see the wind.

James glanced back at Sally with jolly eyes, 'Ef yoo donny mind me askin', how was et that yoo came to be en possession o' the necklace?'

Without hesitation, Sally told James about the alley and the shop. She told him of the old lady and how she'd disappeared after explaining the purpose of the necklace.

James' eyes narrowed, 'Tha's remarkable! A curse that has held more than one soul all these years.'

Sally had perceived James' expression in the rear-view mirror; she suddenly felt suspicious of him. Was he keeping them ignorant of something?

Conversely, Carl was in a better place; a witch's curse placed on a love gift; this was gold.

James had noticed a change in Sally's expression, and changed the subject, 'We'll take the Berstane rood, et'll run straight weth the gale, no more dodgin' debris.'

'Are you OK? We're really putting you out...' Sally ventured; perhaps she could gain something regarding his motives for helping them.

'Ha, ha! I've no' felt so alive, en years! Es no' e'ery day yoo get to drive aroond en a tempest weth a pretty girl an' a giant yellow penguin!'

Sally laughed, amused but no less cautious of the man.

A bolt of lightning flashed nearby as they drove into the mouth of the Berstane road. There was an instantaneous crash of thunder, a yellow sort of glow, and the branch of a tree came crashing down behind them. Sally watched as the now uneven crown of the tree was torn apart by the gale, piling branch upon branch across the road.

'Och, shame, that Sycamore's stood fer years. So few decent trees on Mainland.' James lamented.

Sally sighed, 'We'll have to go this way now.'

James smiled, 'Et's fer the best, yoo'll see.'

Chapter eighteen

The Berstane Road took the straight course James had promised, the wind seemed channelled down it, and it was good going until they reached the end of the bungalows. Here the blow seemed more turbulent, a panel van had been blown clean over and there wasn't a way through with the vehicle. James sat momentarily, deep in thought, Carl wondered if he was ready to concede defeat or if his "local knowledge" was being consulted for alternatives. Surely if they headed out over the field to the right they'd at least be heading more in the direction of the farm? You could do that in a Landrover, he felt sure of it. His eyes peered down at the unbroken stone wall that so clearly thwarted his idea, short of desperation.

'We'll haf to walk from here.' James concluded. Pointing to the same stone wall that had frustrated Carl.

Everyone scrambled out of the car, it took quite some effort to close the doors again but as soon as they had they clawed their way to the low wall, crawling along behind James as quickly as they could. The road curved left, again away from where Sally thought they should be heading. Tiles, peeled readily from a low roof ahead of them, clattering and smashing across the tarmac. James crossed himself in a very pious manner, and with a shout of 'Follow me!' He made a dash for it.

Without really thinking about it the couple pursued their determined friend, Sally because she was equally determined, and Carl because he seemed tied to Sally by his heart; he wasn't going to let her down now, shielding her from the tile fragments with his sou'wester armoured bulk.

James cried out ahead of them, he'd made it through but had caught a small piece of slate across his cheek. Carl and Sally caught up. Sally reached for a clean handkerchief for James to hold against the wound, but the wind took it clean out of her hand. In the blink of an eye, it was gone.

'Et's OK, best to let the rain wash et, aye?' A faint line of watery blood trickled to his jawline and flicked away in the gusts. 'Keep to the left.We'll get some protection from the hedgerow.'

His suggestion was partially true, but the tempest seemed to want to use the hedge to swat the comrades.

James urged them on, 'Et's no' far now.' I t was a good thing too, because the hedge got thinner and the going harder, and every effort to speak was a shout torn away into the sky.

The road seemed to end at a white house, but James picked up his pace again down what appeared to be a driveway. Once more they were amongst trees, these creaked under the pressures that churned them, but they were spindly and pliant. Only one lay in their path, and it was easily stepped over. They came to an opening, the storm howling over them, lifted by the trees, but the rain pouring down like a cascade.

'Should we be here? It's someone's back garden.' Sally asked.

James turned to her, the line of bleed rather more prominent. 'There's no one home lassie, et's the perfect short cut.'

Sally, moved by James' cut, queried him no further and followed him across the lawn to a gateway. They headed through and it soon became clear that they were heading towards a cliff top.

'Steady now,' James cautioned. 'We donny want anyone whisked off the edge.'

They approached with much care, fighting the gusts, leaning back against them. James suddenly stopped and crouched low to the ground by a flat rock, Carl and Sally copied him. 'What are we doing?' Carl asked, panting heavily.

James presented an open hand to Sally, 'Give me the necklace.'

Sally hesitated. She gripped the necklace in the pocket of her jeans. 'You said you were taking us back to the farm. I'm not even sure where we are.'

'The necklace, Sally. Et must be destroyed an' cast ento the sea.'

'No!' Sally was horrified. 'It's Janet's love gift. It belongs to her!'

'Et's the seat o' the curse, a curse wrapped en the very poison o' Satan. Et must be destroyed, en order to release Janet.'

There was a moment of tense silence, broken only by a flash and a peel of nearby thunder. Sally glanced at Carl.

'I don't know. He seems to know what he's talking about. It makes sense to destroy the cause of Janet's entrapment.'

'No!' Sally insisted. 'If that was all that needed doing, the old lady would have done it... Wouldn't she?' She turned back to James, 'You were supposed to be taking us back to the farm, to Old Garrie. You kept the truth from us. You wanted to destroy the necklace as soon as you'd made the connection between it and Janet...'

'Kept the truth from YOO?' James snapped. 'Look at ya man here, gaspin' an' suckin' at the air, he's no seasoned ironman competitor. Yoo've ben lyin' to me! Yoo canny be en two places at once, yet yoo claim to be en a shop en Kirkwall early thess mornin' an' I pick yoo up o'er ten miles away near Twatt, juss an hour or so later! Look...' James seemed to calm down. '...I know the dark magic yoo've ben touched by today; destroyin' the necklace es the way to end et. Would yoo have brought the necklace here, knowin' what I intended to do?'

Sally seemed torn now, 'No, the old lady would have done it...' She attempted to move back against the wind to get away, but she quickly faltered, staggering towards James and falling intentionally to prevent herself being forced close to the cliff edge. Attempting to soften her fall she pulled her hand from the pocket, grazing it on the ground, and the necklace fell free from between her clothing.

James saw it immediately. He pushed it across the rough turf towards the rock with the back of his fingertips, seemingly reluctant to pick it up. Sally hadn't noticed at all; she was flat on the ground staring at her torn skin.

Carl saw James clawing beside the rock trying to free something brick shaped from the ground beside it. It was obvious to Carl that James intended to smash the little seal, but Sally's point about the old lady made total sense. He struggled to move in order to snatch up the necklace without succumbing to the gusts, as Sally had, but James was wasting no time, he freed the object beside the rock and lifted it high in the air. Carl could see it now, a rectangular stone, carved ornately with an elaborate cross on its visible side. There was no way Carl could reach the necklace in time!

'Don't!' Carl cried.

James flashed a defiant glance, and committed to the blow just as

91

everything was bathed in brilliant light.

~

Carl shook his head there was a whistling in his ears, he was lying on his face. He pushed himself up. Within hands reach was the necklace, unharmed. He quickly swept it up into his pocket. He looked around. James was strewn on his back a few paces away near the drop, but Sally was nowhere to be seen.

'Sally!' Carl called, staggering to his feet, crouching against the wind but finding it impossible to safely move. 'SAL!!'

'Carl!' Sally's voice seemed distant and faint.

Carl slumped back down to the ground and crawled to the cliff edge. There he saw Sally's pale fingertips, clinging on, knuckles white, a little blood, splashed into faint streams by the rain, trickled down her wrist from the cut palm.

'Oh Carl, thank God you're safe! Help!'

Below them the sea swirled hungrily, and both felt sure they could see something, something churning the water, something red and unnervingly familiar.

'Help!' Sally repeated, urgently.

Carl took a firm grip of Sally's arm and, rolling onto his back, heaved her up onto his chest.

'Lightning strike?' Sally queried.

'No doubt, and I think James is dead…'

'The necklace!' Sally exclaimed, finding it absent from her pocket.

Carl retrieved it from the sou'wester. 'Here, it dropped out of your pocket when you stumbled, James was about to smash it when the lightning struck.' Sally reached out and took the necklace.

'Watch out!' Carl shot, throwing himself across her as a branch rolled and scratched by them.

'The Necklace!' Sally screamed. For in that horrifying moment the cord had snagged on the wind lashed debris, and was flung high into the billowing air. Already clear of them it sailed over the cliff edge and out of sight. Carl and Sally slid on their bellies to the edge in vain hope, but a quick scan of the steep cliff face confirmed that the object was lost to the violent sea.

Sally sobbed openly, Carl too as he held her tightly. Both felt numb to the driving rain, blind to the pummelled landscape and forking streaks of lightning, deaf to the constant, roaring gale and heavy percussion of thunder, all, except a faint, pained groan.

Sally pointed, 'He's moving!'

Sure enough, James' arm was moving. Carl edged towards him…

He found that James was breathing, but although he was moving, and muttering undiscernible words under his breath, he didn't appear to be conscious.

'Look!' Sally had spotted a small bay between the wind-churned clouds; hazily visible at its center was the old familiar wreck.

Carl's eyes widened. 'We're not far from the farm! Come on.' He started to pull himself away along the ground.

'We can't leave him here.' Sally pointed at James. 'Even if we want to!'

Carl breathed a heavy sigh, grabbed James' collar and heaved him along. 'It's a good job he's a wiry man.'

Slowly they picked their way across the sloping landscape, seeking anything that would break the turmoil around them, and eventually, shortly after noon, they neared the gateway in the farm wall.

Carl sighed relief, 'Once we're in the farmhouse we can take a breather and treat our injuries.'

'Do you remember where the spare key is?'

'Yep.'

They reached the Gateway. There, in front of them, was an unexpected scene; a little orange car buried in restless branches. Kayleigh's vehicle was in the yard, pinned beneath the now fallen apple tree.

Sally was filled with sorrow, 'No blossom left! Oh Carl, Kayleigh's trapped inside!'

Slumped at the wheel, a figure was visible through the rivulets of rain and crazed glass of the damaged windscreen.

Carl dropped James and made his way hurriedly to the Micra.

Sally was enthralled, Carl had seemed quite the action hero, carrying her over the causeway and pulling her up from the cliff face; now he seemed to be seeking a way to help Kayleigh too.

Why she had felt the need to drive right into the yard he didn't know, but he had to get her to safety. He placed his back firmly against the tree trunk and pushed as hard as he could, but it had bent the roof down and seemed firmly wedged, the remnant of Sally's bunting flapping in wild tangles.

'This side!' Sally called, able to approach the passenger door with care, thanks to the way the gale was stayed by the wall. She tried the passenger door, it was jammed. Her frustrated cry was closely followed by a chunk of tree branch smashing the door glass, and Carl's arm reaching in for extra purchase. With some effort the door scraped open. Carl peered inside. Staring up at him, in startled shock, was a mascara-streaked Kayleigh.

'I came to get the both o' yoo, to take yoo to my parent's guesthoose, but yoo were no' here. I took doon ya tent an' put et en my boot weth ya bags but then the wend got crazy an' the tree came right doon, I couldne drive away…'

Carl began to ease her out of the car, 'Let's get everyone insid…'

Sally saw Carl's face turn pale. She looked where he was looking.

Where the barns had stood, there was now a pile of splintered, wooden panels; some heaving up and down in the gusts. Others shattering further, sending wooden shards flailing away.

'I'll never find the spare key in that mess…'

'I won't let you up there anyway. It's far too dangerous.'

'Yoo'd best be cumin' weth me.'

Chapter nineteen

Standing in the gateway with a gnarled walking stick, seemingly untroubled by the rising tempest, was Old Garrie. 'Come now, et isne fet to be oot.' He turned and headed towards the cottage on the cliff.

Carl helped Kayleigh out of the car and started to follow, but he had a nagging doubt. 'The cottage is a ruin, where are you taking us?'

Garrie stopped and turned, 'A ruin, yoo say? That tells me yoo've no' entered through the front door. Et's stood more storms than...'

Carl stopped Garrie short, 'Where's James? I put him down here!'

James had vanished.

Sally peered this way and that, 'Perhaps he gained consciousness, and wandered off.'

'He's fine.' Garrie assured. 'I had my boys take hem on ahead. Please, come now.' Again, Old Garrie turned away and the group followed, pushed forcibly forward by the storm.

Carl drew close alongside Sally, 'What do you think he meant by 'boys'?'

Sally looked at him, her expression was one of genuine sorrow - he felt it too. The seal necklace was lost, what else mattered? They'd failed Janet, and, since Garrie had helped them escape the Nuckelavee, they must have failed him as well. Carl decided that the old man should know, so he quickened his pace to catch up.

'Mr. Garrie?'

Old Garrie peered briefly over his shoulder, grunting his clearly begrudging acknowledgement over the constant noise of the wind.

Carl quickly reasoned there'd be a better time and held his position against the buffeting wind until Sally and Kayleigh caught up.

'What did he say?' Sally asked, intuitively aware of his intention to tell.

'I didn't ask; he didn't seem that approachable. Thing is, without him now, we'll have no shelter.'

Sally looked even more low. Carl placed a supportive arm around her. He considered their impromptu quest. They had gone from tourists to some sort of "Indiana Jones" adventure team, collecting a valuable artefact before magical transportation to a different location. They'd been guided by seals and attacked by an incomprehensible monster; had it all been for nothing? Would restoration of the necklace to its rightful owner have freed Janet from her bondage to the curse? Did its loss mean she was eternally bound? Was there nothing that could be done?

Ahead Garrie had reached the cottage. Carl watched with a curious disbelief. He knew the place *was* a ruin, but so much had happened and the day had betrayed a deep magic... Garrie struck the bottom corner of the door three times with his stick, and to Carl's amazement a warm glow of light appeared at the windows and around the edge of the wooden door, indeed more-so as the door was opening slowly, held with diligence against the blustering gusts of wind.

Carl noticed that Garrie was staring at him.

'B'the front door.' He signaled that they hurry inside.

Carl ushered Sally and Kayleigh into the lamp-lit space, he followed them and was followed by Old Garrie. Garrie turned, and with one last, concerned glance out into the storm, closed and secured the door.

Carl let his eyes leave the old man, they came to rest on Sally, whose attention was entirely consumed by three child-like figures clad in grey cloaks, near a fiercely burning fire that warmed the room. One stood gazing at the flames, holding a lump of wood clearly intended as fuel at the right moment, the other two tended James, who was sat up against the wall, still not awake but mumbling something under his breath, supported by a little alcove and wrapped in blankets, his storm jacket, trousers, socks and shoes drying beside the flames.

Sally had instantly assumed that they were children, but now something about them made her uneasy, they were fully covered by their hooded cloaks, but that wasn't the problem, it was their slightness, their heads especially, for they looked in scale with their bodies as if they were fully grown - a child's head was proportionally bigger. For Sally their size begged the question, "How had they brought James to the cottage?" She couldn't see how just three of them would have coped.

Old Garrie clearly aware of Sally's growing concerns spoke up, his voice accompanied by a softness he hadn't expressed before. 'These are my boys...'

All three figures stopped what they were doing and turned to face Garrie, their features still hidden by their hoods. The old man sighed, 'There's much yoo'll hear an' see now, that yoo've no' known before.'

He'd taken off his long coat and was hanging it on a knob fixed to the wall, Sally was still staring at the three stationary little people but Carl had noticed the dryness of Garrie's outer garment, not a drip fell to the floor. Carl looked down at the puddle forming at his feet. He looked at the room, cosy and sparingly furnished, yet a rubble filled ruin yesterday… this was the best holiday he'd ever had, although - with the loss of the seal necklace - it was also the worst.

A nervous scream from Sally snapped him back to attention, one of the short people had pulled a stick from the kindling by the fire and had approached to poke her.

'Deni! Tha's quite enough.'

The diminutive figure stopped, its shoulders sagging in disappointment; it returned to the others, poking one of them with the stick instead.

'Boys, settle doon so I ken entroduce yoo.'

They stopped squabbling and looked up.

'Thess es Deni, Donie an' Dini.' Each cloak bobbed in response to its name.

Kayleigh suddenly gasped, 'They're Trows.'

Carl was amazed and Sally bewildered as Deni, Donie and Dini dropped their hoods. Their faces were pale and a little unpleasant but their smiles were heartening, and infectious.

'Yes,' Garrie nodded. 'Et's as yoo say.'

Sally was the only one without a broad smile, 'What are Trows?'

'The little people… magical people…' Carl replied, as if talking through a slight daze.

Kayleigh clapped her hands together 'I thought they were juss a story… Oh, oh, They love music…'

'I fel sure there'll be music to pass the time later, but now yoo'd be wise to shed ya wet clothes an' dry them by the fire.'

Carl was dry under the Sou'wester, only his shoes, socks and the bottom of his trousers were wet, he rolled up the trouser legs and placed the rest in the hearth. It was here, opposite James, that Carl spotted the little dog, also wrapped in a blanket by the fire…

'Hope they're your new trainers.' Sally teased.

The Trows giggled, and danced in a circle, holding their noses, then holding each other's noses, then falling to the floor as if dead. Sally's smile appeared and she laughed, perhaps these "little people" weren't as disturbing as she'd let herself believe.

Carl's enquiring eye met Garrie's 'Your dog is unwell?'

Garrie looked grim.

'You sent it to delay the creature,' Carl surmised. 'It got hurt.'

Kayleigh knelt down and stroked the animal, there was no response.

'Et's as yoo say, an' now ya here unhurt ya selves.'

Carl nodded, 'Thank you, we would never have...'

'It... it grew.' Sally interrupted.

'Et's a Varden.' Garrie replied, openly.

'A what?'

'A Varden,' Carl repeated. 'Um, it's like a spirit animal, you know, like American Indians.'

Kayleigh now regarded the creature with obvious concern, 'Et's said that Vardens herald impendin' death. They choose their master... faultlessly obedient.'

'He stell obeys his master. Janet's command was that he serve me when she es absent.'

Carl was amazed, 'It belongs to Janet! I wonder how old it is in dog years!'

Sally shrugged; such strangeness had happened now that if a troupe of dancing fairies paraded across the floor, she doubted she'd be surprised. She gave herself a sharp pinch, 'No, definitely awake.'

Carl heard her, 'Pardon?'

'My legs are wet.' She replied, matter-of-factly. Dedra's storm jacket had kept Sally's clothes relatively dry, but her jeans were soaked right up to her thighs. Dini approached with a blanket, he popped it around his waist to show his intention for it, then offered it to Sally.

Kayleigh remained in the fire-place for warmth, she'd had nothing more than a fleece having only expected to pick up the English tourists and their tent, and take them to the guest house. Despite the short, wild walk from her car, she was wet through. She watched as Deni and Donie approached holding a large blanket up as a screen. She undressed, only having to tell Donie to stop peeping once, then let them wrap her gently in the blanket leaving her arms free. She sat beside James and watched wide-eyed as the slate cut on his cheek was healed by some sort of herbal concoction applied by Dini. His work done there he turned his attention to Sally's injured palm without any given knowledge that it had been hurt.

Sally thanked him, acknowledging that the stinging had gone completely.

~

They all sat quietly for a while, the storm continuing to rage outside; Garrie was now watching at a small window.

Carl stated the obvious, 'It's like dusk out there already.'

'Aye, we're a way from the peak as yet though; the cloud's so thick the night es early.' Garrie stepped across the room and brightened a lamp. 'Et'll no' be light again 'tel tomorrow.'

Sally cleared her throat, 'Is she coming here? Janet, I mean...'

Carl and Kayleigh both looked at the old man.

He looked back at them, each in turn. 'Aye.' He crossed back to the window. 'But 'tez a fierce wild oot there, worse than I've e'er seen; she'll be a mere shadow by the end...'

Sally gasped, 'You mean she's still out there? She's not seeking shelter?'

Kayleigh felt a shiver pass through her.

'Et's what she's bound to. At first she's holdin' et back...' Garrie's head sank. 'But then et consumes her.'

Carl and Sally glanced at each other, both knowing the others mind; they'd possessed what could have set Janet free. Carl caught Garrie's eye, Garrie seemed expectant, as if he were ready for Carl to speak, but the moment was soon lost in the wail of the wind. Garrie turned back to the window, how could they tell him now?

Kayleigh broke the brief absence of conversation; to have called it a silence would be inaccurate, for the wind grappled and scratched around the building like a beast clawing to get in. The windows and doors beat in their frames, the fire crackled and hissed as the chimney draw sucked it into fierce hues of molten red, and there was now a constant rumbling. The lightning flickered near and far like flashbulbs at a movie premier.

'Tell us aboot Janet,' Kayleigh requested. 'Yoo knew her from the beginnin', aye?'

Garrie smiled at her, 'Aye, well, no' from the very beginnin', she's told me things that I never knew at the time. Come, let's sit together by the fire, et's a long story.'

Garrie pulled up a ragged chair, Deni fed the fire and the group settled as comfortably as they could before the story-teller. 'There was a farmer neemed Edward Forsyth, on Westray, who married Gwen Davie, the daughter o' a blacksmith from Mainland. They were happy, but nay child came from their unions. Edward, driven by a keen desire to have a son to help hem on the farm, looked to a woman en Pierowall called Erka, feared but renowned fer prophetic werds. Before he'd said a werd, Erka spoke, as ef en a trance, that he would be a father Before the Wenter returned. Erka then sought payment, but times had ben hard fer Edward an' he had very lettle he could offer her…'

Chapter twenty

Erka riled, 'Yoo expect my services fer free Mester Forsyth?'

'No, no, I intended to ask what et was yoo'd require fer payment before I sought ya craft, I didne expect ya words to come tell payment was agreed…'

'Yoo know full well how et werks, man. Well, I'll tell yoo somethin' fer free, she'll suffer…'

'No, dinnie tell me such, I couldne bear et…'

'She'll waste away to a shell, an' the bearin'll come to naught…'

'No, please, neem ya price, I'll pay et… somehow… juss let her live, let me have a child.'

Erka's face changed abruptly, the anger within it twisted into something unfathomable to Edward, something ghoulish, chilling, and yet, in the same instance, deep, appealing and accommodating, her voice softened. 'There es one service yoo could provide me…'

It was late before Edward left Pierowall for home, he excused himself to Gwen, explaining that he'd visited Erka but having no payment for her counsel, had performed some duties instead, a little handiwork. Gwen was upset with her husband for seeking the guidance of such a woman, but on hearing Erka's words regarding a child before the winter, her misgivings seemed to fade quickly; the timeframe required action if it were to be true. Yes, she was put out by Edward sharing their shame but her desire for him was strong and her desire for a babe stronger; without hesitation she took her husband to their bed and so it was that they conceived, in joy, the beginnings of their deepest grief.

Within a few weeks Gwen became sick. A neighbour's wife had been poorly in child-bearing but she had recovered every day by the afternoon - it was all Gwen could do to keep the smallest morsel of food down. Edward, Erka's heated words still fresh in his mind, grew deeply concerned. One afternoon, with his sister Mary tending to Gwen, he marched to Pierowall and hammered on Erka's door.

'I paid ya price, Erka.' He tried the door just as a heavy bolt clunked into place within. 'Yoo said she'd be fine…'

'I said she'd live.' Erka hissed from inside.

Edward's voice faltered, 'An' the child? Yoo said I'd have a child…'

'Yoo well.' Erka snapped. 'Now, leave here, or et well want fer a father.'

Filled with sudden panic, Edward stumbled from the door and beat a hasty retreat towards home.

Weeks turned into months, but where his neighbour's wife had recovered and blossomed, Gwen grew more unwell, weaker, paler, gaunter. Edward felt that she took less space in the bed with her growing tummy than she had without it. Time on the land suffered as Edward found himself unable to pull his mind from his wife's needs, and many a long, Summer afternoon was spent rocking her diminished frame in his arms. A meagre crop failed and his cattle stock wandered onto neighbouring land through neglected boundaries.

If it hadn't been for Mary, rallying volunteers from those families closest to the Forsyth farm, it is certain that Edward would have had no stock left, and no provision for the long Winter ahead. They came at her request, and they repaired walls, brought gifts, wished well and prayed.

Did the prayers work? Edward held reason to believe so, for, as Autumn arrived, Gwen seemed to turn a corner; her nausea calmed and a smile returned, though her weakness did nothing to ease Mary's concerns for the birth to come.

It was one stormy, late Autumn morning that Mary's fears were realised. She had taken to sleeping at Edwards farm and was awoken before daybreak by the anxious farmer.

'Gwen's waters have broken.'

Mary was fully awake in a moment.

'Go fetch me water an' the bundle o' linen I brought weth me when I came to stay; then Deborah, I'll need Deborah, aye, an' yoo oot the way…'

Edward did as he was told, finally collecting his neighbour's mother-in-law, Deborah, who had experience with deliveries. She had been visiting her daughter from Mainland; seeing Gwen's condition, Deborah had promised to stay and help. He felt bad asking her to come out so early, and in such foul weather, but she was clearly excited and her pace at times seemed faster than his.

He spent much time pacing in front of the hearth that morning. Gwen was so weak and progress slow. By mid-afternoon he could bear it no longer. Mary, seeing his anguish suggested he take the air. 'Get ya self o'er to The Point, Edward…'

'But et's blowin' a gale, Mary.'

'Then yoo'll be concentratin' on standin' an' nay frettin' aboot us. Go, I canny worry aboot the both o' yoo.'

'But…'

'GO!'

So, Edward left, and, leaning into the wind, wandered down to the coast, clinging to his coat and constantly brushing his hair from his eyes. It didn't take long to reach The Point from the farm, though perhaps it had taken twice as long as usual against this elemental antagonist. Edward stood on the jutting rocks of the low, rocky cliff, the taste of salt on his lips. Sea spray dashed into the air by the natural groins of rock that reached, like bony fingers, into the tossed surf. Mary had been right, the wildness of the blustering air and the spectacle of nature's strength filled Edward with a heady awe, rendering him momentarily catatonic, motionless yes, but with thoughts - some long quiet - wrestling for his attention. His father had been a devout, God fearing man whose discipline had placed a long, bitter barrier in the way of belief… But no, Edward now saw it for himself, his wilful disobedience, the constant misdemeanours - always his own way, his own impatience. Had his father not loved him he would not have carved from his rotten son a man fitting for Gwen…

Edward's head sank, his hands grew weak for a moment and the gusting, tortured air around him nearly tore his coat from his grasp, 'Oh, Lord God,' he prayed. 'Thess es all my fault. I should ne'er have sought after Erka's advice. Seems fair now to think that Gwen bearin' a child was always possible. I was impatient fer a son. I'll go to the lettle kirk at Pierowall ef yoo let my wife live.' He looked back in the direction of the farm, 'Could et be that all es already done? Have I a son Lord?'

Chapter twenty-one

For all its ferocity, the storm that battered Edward was only a devilishly strong gale, and though the sky told of rain further south over Mainland, here the clouds were shattered fragments, the wetness on his face and clothes had been the ocean below, picked up and hurled. Edward cast a penitent glance at the sky and turned to leave The Point.

At the edge of discernment, a sound stopped him, he stood motionless; had some voice come to him on the wind? Yes, there it was again... But where? Quietly, attentively he listened, slowly moving to fix some direction.

Out to sea, Edward could discern a number of seals, bobbing amongst the waves, gazing at the shore. He smiled to himself, was *that* all it was? He waved a hand dismissively towards them, then frowned. He looked, staring out to them as if something needed to be understood. The sound wasn't coming from the sea, it was coming from the beach! It was like the crying of an infant.

Edward scrambled down the rocks to the wave swept beach, picking his moments to dart from rock to rock over wet sand, making his way along the bay, occasionally listening again then heading on towards the call. It was close now, a baby's anguished cries for sure, but where? He stepped forward, eyes exploring the crevices in the spattered rocks, his legs soaked, his mind unaware of it. There! Edward caught a glimpse of pale flesh as a wave dashed the seaweed about it. He thrust his hand into the swirling water, searching, seizing, pulling the babe from the mouth of the tide. A cold, naked, loud little wretch, kicked the air, but Edward's eyes were back on the waves, something wasn't right; the waves seemed higher here, their movement unnatural. He bundled the child to his chest and started to run up the beach towards a low in the rocks and a path onto the fields beyond. Behind him a blood curdling screech reached after his retreat. Wild-eyed he glanced back, something red in the breakers was chasing a panicked group of seals. Fear girded his pace and he didn't look back again.

~

Sally had to know, 'Was it the creature we saw?'

'The Nuck...' Carl stopped himself from saying its name.

There was a brief pause, Kayleigh mouthed 'Yoo saw one?' to Sally, and she nodded.

Sally looked at Garrie and he nodded also.

Deni pulled a pot from the fire.

'Yoo should eat.' Garrie stepped over to a cupboard to retrieve some bowls, served up a thick broth into each and passed it on to his guests.

Carl was particularly glad to receive it, 'Thank you, that looks great.'

The old man seemed to find Carl's eagerness amusing.

'Did he get away?' Sally asked, but the old man's thoughts weren't with her.

'What?'

'Edward; did he get away?'

'O' course he ded.' Garrie rolled his eyes. 'Wouldne be a story ef all were killed then an' there.' He sat down with a bowl of broth for himself, slurping loudly as he ate it. 'Edward ran, he ran faster than e'er he had as a boy...'

~

Running with the wind, Edward was soon home. Within the boundary of the farm buildings, he finally came to a halt. Sheltered from the storm by the wall of his barn he lifted the rescued infant, staring at it, conflicted as to what to do.

All was quiet in the house, and Edward felt sure that the birth must have concluded, and there would be a child waiting for him in Gwen's arms. The baby in his hands needed a home; clearly the lone survivor from some vessel that had fallen foul of the storm - but he couldn't just walk into the house with another baby. He'd have to explain what happened, yes, that was the right way forward.

Edward stepped into the barn and, finding some cloth, wrapped the baby and nestled it into the hay. The infant, quiet since being lifted from the surf, began to cry. Edward rested a hand on the child's cheek, 'There, there, my lettle one, I'll no' be long.'

The babe, silent once again, stared deeply into his eyes, and he found the parting harder to bear than he imagined.

Inside all was quiet.

'Mary?'

'Edward…'

The reply was leaden.

'What's wrong sester?' He followed her voice.

'Oh, Edward…'

He found her in the kitchen, by the hearth, cradling a wrapped infant in her arms.

'Et's… et's Gwen?' Edward stammered. 'She wasne strong enough!' He sought the kitchen table for support.

'Nay brother,' Mary sobbed. 'Deborah es weth her, she es exhausted an' asleep, et's all taken so much o' her, but no dear brother, et's the bearin'….' Tears dashed down Mary's cheeks as she held the bundle up for Edward to see.

Within the wrapping was an infant's face, as if asleep, but so very pale. Edward knew from the coldness of the babe's skin that all was lost for it…

'Erka said I would have a child before the Wenter: et cost me…'

'Yoo went to *her*, brother?' Mary glared. 'Ded father no' warn yoo to stay away from her?'

Edward gathered himself. Mary was much like his father in her piety, and had welcomed her brother's acceptance of help and prayer over the last weeks and months…

A sudden thought struck Edward, he seized the baby and thrust the wrappings from its face. 'Air!' He exclaimed. 'Aye, air es what et needs!'

Mary gave a stifled scream as Edward turned and ran through the hallway and on outside. The wind hissed around him as he stumbled to the barn. The Christian wants a miracle? He would give her a miracle. Quickly he removed the coverings from the lifeless baby, pushing it

106

with deep remorse under the hay. He would come back, yes, soon; he would see to something proper as soon as he could. He looked to the beach infant - it was gazing straight back at him. He picked it up and, as gently as he could, discarded the old cloth and wrapped the new about it. 'Well yoo cry fer me, lettle one?' Edward stepped back outside, but the infant seemed content so he paced around in front of the farmhouse clutching the bundle to him.

A voice called out from the door, 'Mr. Forsyth, I am so sorry fer ya loss.' It was Deborah. 'Please come en oot o' thess ghastly wend, come to ya wife.'

Edward was desperate to see Gwen, the thought that she had endured so much for so long finally broke him, and his own tears flowed for the loss of his true child and the struggle they had all suffered. He stepped back inside.

'I brought a lettle Whisky to celebrate the birth, Mr. Forsyth, but ef yoo should wish fer a wee dram to settle yoo, I'll happily pour et?'

Edward nodded, heading straight to the bedroom. He stood hesitantly at the bedroom door, observing Mary's care of Gwen before entering, 'Does she know the child es dead?'

Tears returned to Mary's eyes, 'No, Edward, et took all she had to push.'

Deborah arrived with the whisky, 'She's ben as death herself from the moment I pulled the child ento thess world, though she gently breathes.' She gave Edward the whisky and took the bundle from his arm, encouraging him to go to Gwen. He sat beside his wife and wept bitterly for all that had come to pass.

Chapter twenty-two

There was a sudden, startled and concerned cry from Deborah, 'The babe! Es breathin'!'

Edward smiled inwardly, then raised his head from the pillow beside his still sleeping wife, with an expression of confusion. 'What Deborah? What ded yoo say?'

'Breathin' Mr. Forsyth! The lettle one es alive after all!'

'But Mary told me et was dead!'

'I donny understand et, et didne seem to be breathin'.'

'The air!' Mary exclaimed. 'They went ootside, the gale must've filled ets lungs!'

'I ne'er heard o' such a theng! Oh Mr. Forsyth, what sudden joy en all our sorrows!'

Edward stood and approached Deborah as if to take the infant from her, but she kept her hold on it, staring into the baby's eyes and tilting the bundle so that Edward could see. 'I must wash et, Mr. Forsyth; then, when Gwen awakes, she'll have a lovely clean bearin' to nurse.'

Edward nearly protested, he wanted to keep the babe close… No - he calmed himself - it was best that he abide by Deborah's wishes. He didn't want to seem unthankful or cause a scene that might cast questions over this unexpected happiness.

Deborah left the room with the child, Mary flung her arms about her brother, weeping and laughing and praising God. Edward felt uneasy; what had he done? But then, the deceit was set - now he had to live with it…

~

'I always thought that Janet *was* Edward's daughter.' Kayleigh interrupted.

'Et was a well-hidden secret, I ken only tell yoo now because o' what Janet has told me o'er the years.'

Kayleigh seemed deeply excited, 'And she *well* come here, right here weth us?'

'Aye, girl, as she always does.'

Kayleigh stood and went to the window. 'Wow et's the worst I've e'er seen…'

'Fiercer than the '53.' Garrie looked upset, 'That time she came as ef a wraith, I could only hold her as she faded…' A single tear dashed down his cheek.

Kayleigh returned to the fireside, 'Yoo love her deeply, aye?'

Carl could almost imagine the song lyrics Kayleigh was writing in her mind.

~

Edward had stayed with Mary and Gwen, watching for any sign of Gwen's recovery, but it wasn't long before Deborah returned.

'There, she's all clean, such a bonny wee theng.'

Edward had stood to receive the child but Deborah approached Mary instead, handing the infant to her aunt.

Deborah smiled sweetly, 'I'll have to head home now…'

Mary's anxiety rose, 'But Gwen…'

'Es rest she wants, Mary. A quick werd weth yoo, Edward…'

Edward followed Deborah out of the bedroom to the farmhouse door. 'Thanks fer all yoo've done, Deborah. Yoo'll be Ok, oot en thess gale?'

'Es best that yoo stay here. I've ben oot en worse than thess; yoo juss be here when she wakes, aye?'

Edward smiled, 'Aye Deborah, an' thanks again.' He opened the door. The doorway was in the lee of the wind but the roar of the tempest hid Edward and Deborah's voices from Mary.

Deborah shook Edward's hand, but kept hold of it. 'There es one theng…'

Edward frowned, 'Wha's that?'

'I'd juss like to know how et es that ya bearin' should be a girl?'

Edward shrugged, in all the madness he hadn't paused once to acknowledge the sex of the child, and when it was feared dead no-one had volunteered it. 'There's always a hope amongst the farm folk fer a son, but I'm fair sure et's en the Good Lord's hands as to what we're given.'

'Et's juss… I delivered a boy…'

Edward stood speechless, his deception was already exposed! He stepped outside with Deborah, pulling the door closed behind him.

'Where es the dead child, Edward?'

Edward's heart was racing, he found himself pointing at the barn. Deborah started toward it. What was he going to do? He hurried after her.

'Et's under the hay.' Edward informed as they reached the barn, but he needn't have, the wind had been forcing its way in through the door that he hadn't shut properly, and had partially exposed the little, naked body.

Deborah looked understandably shocked, 'Oh! The poor wee theng...' She bent and scooped up the body and the old cloth Edward had used to wrap the baby from the beach.

Edward, his face cast away in absolute shame, caught sight of an old hammer; he looked at Deborah, busy wrapping the corpse respectfully. 'What ef...' Edward thought to himself, '...what ef, whilst she was walkin' home alone... what ef she fell an' hit her head? There'd be no-one aboot t'see et... I wouldne have to carry her far...' He slowly, quietly began to reach for the hammer, hand dropping to his side as Deborah looked back at him.

'Where ded the baby girl come from?'

He told her everything, what did it matter, she wouldn't live to tell another soul. As he spoke, she bound the sorry bundle tight with cords.

'Seems to me that ya God has provided fer yoo an' Gwen...'

Edward had been reaching for the hammer again, he'd edged closer as he'd been speaking, but again he hid his intent as Deborah came towards him.

'Edward...' Deborah's tone held his attention. '...promise me yull no' tell Gwen aboot the beach.'

Edward stared back at Deborah.

'Relly Edward, et would be best, when she wakes, that she knows only o' the birth, an' the lettle girl fer her to nurse an' love.' She held the bundle close to her. 'I'll see that thess one es buried rightly.'

'Yoo'll no' tell anyone what I've done?'

'Ha! What have yoo done? Yoo've rescued a wee baby from certain death, whose parents are no doubt dashed to pieces en the wreck o' their ship at the bottom o' the ocean. Ya her true father now, an' Gwen her rightful mother en ya God's sight. Yoo've ben chosen as guardian fer thess wee bearin'.' Deborah smiled and took Edward's hand in her own. 'Edward, et's no hardship fer me to ferget the sorrow o' days an' give preference to their joys. Yoo take ya gift now an' be the best father yoo ken be. Now... I must be off, go to Gwen.'

'But Mary... she must know that the babe was a boy too!'

'She grew pale as the child's head began to appear, so I asked her to tend Gwen, to mop her brow an' encourage her as she was so tired. There were no cries as the babe came; Mary seemed quite unaware et was o'er untel I'd pulled a linen wrap around the wee body...'

Edward embraced Deborah in thankfulness, then, briefly, he took the bundle, 'I'm so sad I ne'er got to see yoo grow ento a man, my boy. But yoo'll ne'er see hardship where yoo are. Goodbye son.' He bid farewell to Deborah, and returned to Gwen and Mary.

Chapter twenty-three

The baby, none-the-worse for being in the ocean or flung onto the beach by foaming breakers, thrived, and despite Gwen's continuing stupor, Mary was able to offer the child to Gwen's breast for a little milk as need arose. Edward had been putting off the naming of the infant, wanting Gwen to share in the decision but days were becoming weeks and he grew tired of telling visitors that the infant was still nameless.

One afternoon, Edward cast an eye into the bedroom. Mary had sat Gwen up to ease some broth into her, the baby was bundled up on the bed in Gwen's lap, cooing sweetly, as Mary chatted to her silent patient. 'I think yoo should call her Janet, after Edward's mother, she would have liked that.'

'Yoo think, Mary?'

Mary jumped, nearly dropping the bowl of broth and looked up at the doorway. 'Oh brother! Yoo startled me!'

'Yoo think we should neem her after Mother?'

'Et's a good, strong neem, and she's a strong wee theng, do yoo no' think?'

Edward rested a hand on the door frame. 'Aye, that she es… Janet… hmm… es a good neem. So be et.' He stepped into the room, lifting the bundle high above his head then spinning it around into a nurturing embrace, 'Yoo hear that, lettle one? At least until Gwen protests, ya neem es Janet. What do yoo reckon to that?'

Janet gave a beaming smile, Edward couldn't tear his eyes away, an intense sense of protective love flowed right through him. 'Oh Janet, how I wesh ya mother here would open her eyes to see yoo, fer her love would be yet more boundless than my own.

~

'She doesne wake, does she?' Kayleigh interrupted.

Garrie flashed a look of frustration, a brief moment that reminded his listeners what a privilege they were receiving; warm and dry, safe from the storm, fed, and hearing this otherwise sketchy story in a level of detail that could only have been relayed by one of Janet's closest friends. 'Tha's where ya wrong, Miss.'

Sally smiled, 'I'm so glad she wakes up…'

Garrie's downcast face brought an uneasy atmosphere into the room. Dini looked ready to cry, Donie and Deni quietly comforting him. 'Was nigh-on a month before Gwen's eyes opened. Edward an' Mary where standin' close by, babe en Mary's arms, but et was quickly clear that somethin' were amiss.'

~

'Gwen, oh dearest Gwen, ya back weth us!' Edward stooped down to his wife and embraced her.

Mary saw Gwen's confused expression, 'Careful, brother, there's somethin' wrong!'

Edward gently released Gwen, 'Wha's up my love?'

Gwen stared up at them, silently.

'Tell me what I ken do.' Edward pleaded.

Still no response.

He took her by the shoulders, 'Speak to me Gwen, wha's wrong weth yoo?'

Gwen gave a disturbed whimper.

Mary rested a hand on his arm, 'Careful, ya destressin' her.'

'She's broken Mary! I donny know what to do.'

'Let me talk to her, brother, wash her an' dress her. Et's time, that's all, she needs time.'

'What... more!'

'Go, check on the livestock, she'll be en a better place when yoo return, I'm sure.'

With a heavy sigh Edward left the room, threw on his heavy winter coat and stepped outside.

The winter sat like a heavy grey shawl around the island, there'd been no let-up in the thick blanket of fog for over a week, and Edward was fed-up of it. Everything was covered in a skin of ice and the still, cold air seemed to penetrate and gnaw at your bones. Edward began a search for the livestock, calling out to the herd across the obscured land.

It took a fair while that day to account for all his cattle. His anxiety already high because of Gwen, he'd begun to worry. His mind had gone back to the blood curdling screech in the breakers of the bay, the flash of red in the surf... could the beast tolerate fog? Was a certain thing it wouldn't dare leave the sea whilst it rained, that it could not cross a stream of fresh water, but what about fog? A frozen, winter fog?

His animals accounted for, Edward shrugged off his disquiet. What was the creature, other than a story to keep children from the hungry sea and explain the death of livestock or withering of crops in an environment that was frequently harsh? Yes, it was more surprising at times, that stock was still alive.

Edward had wandered along his boundaries and found himself out at The Point again, the first time since finding Janet. The air was still and crisp, the tide out beyond sight in the leaden mist, a marked contrast to when he last stood there - even the waves were silent - if it were not for the debris placed down on the strandline by the tide, it would be easy to imagine that you were standing at the edge of some great rocky waste, not the edge of an islander's world.

'What would yoo have me do, Lord?' Edward tentatively prayed, for he had not done so of his own choosing since that stormy day, neither had he visited the little Kirk in Pierowall. This last fact came back to him now. 'Oh!' He exclaimed aloud, and made straight for home.

On arrival, Edward found Mary with Gwen by the fire. Gwen was staring contentedly at the infant feeding at her breast, she was tidy and dressed, Mary had even combed Gwen's hair and placed it in a neat plaited knot; so long her style. Edward had longed to set his eyes upon his wife again, but somehow, this figure beside his sister stopped short of the whole. There was something lacking from the face, some laxness of the tone, some vacancy of expression.

'Look, Gwen, Edward es returned from the stock.'

Gwen looked up, a simple smile greeting her husband, then an attempt at words...

'She's besotted weth Janet, Edward.' Mary stroked the side of Gwen's face.

Edward crouched at Gwen's side. 'We'll take her up to the Kirk on Sunday, seek a blessin' fer her, Aye?'

To Edward's surprise, Gwen's vocal response was a definite, affirmative expression, her smile notably broader and her free hand now lay upon his arm. He looked up at Mary; her face was a picture of joy caught off-guard. Edward wondered what trials she had had with her sister-in-law whilst he was out. But no, the focus had to be on what was good, and this moment *was* good.

Chapter twenty-four

It was no effort to carry the diminutive form of Gwen - she'd put very little weight on since losing so much during the pregnancy - despite this Edward's breath pierced the late Winter air with sharp fingers of steam that seemed to hang motionless in a trail behind the group as they walked towards Pierowall. Four souls with two sets of footprints in the snow.

Gwen had been a regular at the Kirk; Edward had not, and he was surprised by its condition. The roof leaked in the entranceway though not where the congregation sat, nor where the Minister stood. The windows were glassless openings and there was a hint of decay in the air. That said, the building had clearly been well-constructed, a beautifully crafted example of its kind. Maintenance had failed it. As Edward sat - happy to have Mary, Gwen and Janet with him, and half aware of the Minister's words - he found his mind contemplating repairs.

The Minister had been thoroughly encouraging, although, through concern for Gwen's wellbeing, urged Edward to wait a while on any Kirk restoration projects - 'Perhaps a late Spring start?' he'd suggested, 'Concentrate on Gwen's recovery and stall until fairer weather.'

He also had much to say about Gwen's prayers for her husband, and Edward realised how important it had been to her, how devoted she had been to him. What he had retained of the message that morning, was the guiding of the Lord - that all things worked together, be it good or ill, for the eventual blessing of the believer - Edward contemplated his journey. He had shunned the Kirk, dismissive of it because of his father's strict rules, wilfully ignoring his wife's pleas that he joined her in attendance, angry at God for the lack of a child, seeking the advice of those involved in canny arts, fearful, lost in the overwhelming anxieties of Gwen's ill health, the loss of a son, the discovery of a daughter - God's gift to him - and all this had brought him here, under the word of God, thanks to Gwen's prayers...

Mary interrupted his thoughts. 'Gwen es very tired Edward.'

Edward looked at his wife. She was slumped awkwardly in the chair that the Minister had provided for her, slipping into sleep, a little trail of saliva trailing from the corner of her mouth. Edward swept her up in his arms and began the walk home.

As they approached the cottage where Erka lived, Erka herself appeared from the direction of the shoreline behind the building. For a moment she stood staring at them as they approached, then, as if she had suddenly realised who was coming towards her, she dropped a bundle of beach-combed driftwood in the snow by the road and ran inside, slamming the door behind her. Edward noticed a bundle strapped securely to her back. 'Erka has a child?'

'Yes.' Mary affirmed, gently rocking the sleeping Janet. 'The Kirk ladies were all talkin' aboot her last Spring; said she kept meetin' weth strangers at the Harbour, an' that she "entertained" some o' them…'

'But, she's too old surely?'

'Et's dark brother, dark werk…'

Edward's mind drifted as they left Erka's home behind them, he wondered what she was doing behind that door right now. Was she cursing them again? His blood boiled, but he quickly gathered himself; Gwen was stirring in his arms and he didn't want her to see him angry. She opened her eyes, smiled and held on to him tightly. 'No,' thought Edward, he would leave Erka to God. He looked into Gwen's innocent gaze. He had far more important things for his attention than Erka, for it seemed clear to him now that Gwen would remain like a child all her remaining days. It was just a pity that they had to pass this way to reach the Kirk every Sunday. They passed by the abandoned driftwood and headed for the farm.

If Edward had considered getting to work on repairs before the Minister's suggested time, then he would have been thwarted by that Winter's final throes. Several feet of snow made travel near impossible, it brought the roof of the Kirk down, the rot being more advanced than any had assumed; the collapse turning two walls into rubble. Rumours spread about Erka's activities down on the beach prior to the onset of the storms, and it soon became apparent that she'd been taken into custody at Notland, where she'd be held on a charge of witchcraft until a boat could come from Mainland to take her to trial in Kirkwall.

Edward lamented the collapse of the old Kirk, it had stood for centuries, his parents and Grandparents had always gone there. He wondered if his attendance sooner would have preserved it through diligent maintenance; what was sure, as he stood by the ruin in the thawing landscape, was the fact that the work was beyond him now, both in terms of money and materials. He apologised to the Minister and returned home.

Three weeks later, Edward had converted part of his barn, and the Pierowall congregation started meeting at the farm until funds could be raised to rebuild the Kirk. This suited Edward immensely; not only had he provided for the Church folk but he'd reduced the distance Gwen had to travel each week, however temporary the solution was.

~

'So, what about Janet?' Carl asked, receiving a look of disapproval from Sally.

Old Garrie seemed cross, 'Es as much a part o' Janet's life as anythin' else.' He stood, walking to the window to peer out, but the panes were fogged from the moist air within. He wiped it with his hand and sighed. 'I'll be glad when thess es finally o'er.'

Carl flashed a look at Sally. Sally's eyes urged him to tell Garrie about the loss of the seal necklace. Carl's gaze fell straight into Garrie's concerned face. It was as if he were reading Carl's thoughts. Before Carl could speak, and as if to avoid the subject, Garrie quickly returned to the story. 'I'll tell et from the age yoo first saw her...'

Chapter twenty-five

Janet was a pretty child, her skin pale, her hair a luxuriant, wind tossed veil of purest jet, though none could think of a Forsyth who hadn't had a rosier complexion, or red or fair hair. Edward had discovered that she liked to draw, and had afforded her paper and charcoal sticks. She was full of playful mischief, though some, who gathered on those Sundays at the barn, urged Edward to be firm and exact some discipline before it was too late.

Edward ignored the advice, it put him too much in mind of his father's stern punishments, the very things that had crushed any faith he could possibly have had as a child - not that he could recall having any.

Janet would sit in the hay, sometimes giggling at the Minister's ambling exhortations, or she'd disappear out into the landscape. Twice the congregation had helped Edward to look for her, but now they didn't bother, and Edward didn't fret, for she was never far and would sometimes be back at the farm before him - until one day.

Janet had been sitting in a natural cleft that cut crudely into the slope west of the farm, the ground within the cleft was uneven, but the grass was lusher, and wildflowers seemed to flourish; sheltered from the wind. This place was where Janet went, it was her hiding place, quiet, warm, even welcoming. Sometimes, in the past, folk had found her exploring the nearby rocky beach, but Edward had warned her sternly to stay away from there as she'd nearly drowned there as a babe. The warning was enough to make her shy of the sea, and now she'd play alone in the cleft, or draw the flowers and butterflies.

It was one Sunday, made anxious by the story of a man slaying a giant, that she'd left the service. She'd sat, gazing at the delicate wildflowers and losing track of time, when a shadow danced along the edge of her vision. Certain her father had come looking for her she stood up and looked for his waiting hand to lead her home - only to find herself looking straight into the eyes of a startled boy.

'Oh! Hello.' Janet exclaimed, calming quickly on seeing that the boy was more concerned than herself.

The boy did not answer.

'Yera small boy, I havne seen anyone like...'

'Janet!'

The call had come from beyond the cleft, it was her father's voice, and now the little boy was disappearing, fleet of foot, to the northern end of the cleft.

'No, wait,' Janet cried. 'Wha's ya neem?'

But the boy was gone.

'Are yoo a'right, Janet?' Edward was looking down on her from the edge of the cleft. He crouched and offered his hand to her. 'Yoo've ben oot fer a while thess mornin', I was gettin' worried. I've made some soup, well yoo come?'

'Aye, father.' Janet looked one last time to where the boy had run, then took Edward's hand.

The farmhouse was no more than fifty yards away. Confident of her footing and safely led, Janet gazed up at him admiringly. 'Are there many children who donny come to the Minister's services, Daddy?'

Edward frowned; it seemed a strange question. Could the six-year-old be seeking justification for leaving the congregation each week? 'The Arnot's have their own Holy man at the Castle, but all the common folk join us en the barn. Yoo should relly try an' stay yoo know.'

Janet sat a little while later with her bowl of soup, pondering what her father had said, "...all the common folk join us..." so that made the little boy uncommon... like her.

Most days that week Janet made her way to the cleft, exploring the northern end but finding no evidence of her visitor.

For the next few Sundays Edward insisted that Janet stay in the service, she was fidgety and determined to return to her usual hiding place, but one thing held her to obedience. Mary. Mary had travelled to Mainland after the death of Gwen, some two years before, on the invitation of Gwen's family. It was there that she'd fallen in love with

119

Gwen's youngest brother, William, and with Edward's blessing - and near insistence - had left the family home on Westray. This was her first visit in a while, and Janet was keen to please her.

William and Edward went to survey the boundary walls after
lunch one Sunday, leaving Mary and Janet at the Farmhouse.

Mary watched, as Janet peered out of the window for the seventh time, 'Ya restless thess afternoon, Janet.'

'Sorry.'

'Wha's botherin' yoo? Ya father says ya no' mixin' weth the Kirk children.'

'They donny mix weth me, but I met a boy a few weeks back!'

'Oh? Wha's his neem?'

Janet looked back at Mary from the window. 'I dinny ask.'

'Oh well, perhaps when yoo see hem next? Ya father well be pleased.'

'Oh, donny tell Daddy.'

'Why no', child?'

'The boy dinny go t'Kirk, Daddy wouldne like hem.'

'I donny know aboot that, Janet; he spent much o' his childhood avoidin' the Kirk services. All the same ya father should know…'

'No Mary, I beg yoo.' And such streams of tears wet her cheeks that Mary finally promised not to tell.

Chapter twenty-six

The day had rolled slowly on, Janet finally being afforded time to play outside in the glorious Summer sunshine. Within minutes she was back at the cleft, where, to her surprise she found Deborah.

'Oh, er, hello Janet.'

Janet was disappointed, she'd come down specifically to look for the little boy, but she knew he'd be hiding if adults were about. 'What are *yoo* doin' here? Thess es my father's land.'

Deborah looked cross, 'Es a free land, I prefer the open country to the usual paths, Miss Forsyth...'

Janet glanced past Deborah, a small round face had appeared from behind her ample frame and it was smiling broadly. Deborah looked at Janet with narrowing eyes, she turned to where Janet was staring, then back at Janet. 'Yoo ken see hem ken yoo?'

'O' course, he's right there.'

Deborah sat down in the gently swaying grass fully revealing her hidden companion.

Janet waved, 'Hello.'

There was no reply.

'I've seen yoo here before, are yoo a relative o' Deborah?'

Deborah laughed, 'Nay child, Deni es o' the Island...'

~

'Deni?' Carl turned to the little characters by the fire, but unable to remember which was which, he turned back to Old Garrie and gestured towards them, 'Not...'

'Aye,' Garrie smiled. 'One an' the same. The Trows are an ancient an' cautious race. Yoo ken only see them through their magic or ya own. Ha! An' yoo have none. They have opened ya eyes because they're excited aboot yoo... an' what yoo might have brought?'

Carl's guilt at not possessing the necklace, resurfaced. In that moment he felt that something of that guilt had flashed across his face, for Garrie now frowned a little, shifting uneasily in his chair...

Kayleigh grew unsettled, 'Donny stop there Mr. Garrie.' Her eyes wide with wonder at the story and the great age of these little fellows sitting beside her.

Garrie smiled at her, but the pause in his story had brought the sound of the storm back to his ears, and that seemed to trouble him more deeply than Carl's body language.

~

Deborah introduced Janet to Deni, explaining that he was fully

121

grown, not a boy at all, that as she came to know him better, and it was clear that she would be allowed to, as he'd allowed her to see him, she would be able to understand his thoughts as if they were spoken words - as that was how they conversed - and only a very few have ever been blessed with their company.

Janet's face scrunched up with puzzlement, 'Blessed? But he doesne come to the services at the barn. Es et no' fer God to bless?'

Deborah smiled broadly, 'Es all o' Creation no' a Blessin' o' ya God, Janet?'

'He agrees weth yoo!' Janet exclaimed, aware of Deni's mind.

Deborah nodded.

Janet became excited, 'He heard me, heard me singin' as I played. He watched me as I sang.' She gave a sharp gasp, 'He didne expect me to see hem!'

'Ya special fer sure, Janet.'

'He says yoo were there when I was born.'

'We need no' go ento that now, Deni, she's young to be told o' that day… Do yoo remember ya song?'

'Aye, I made et up, I was watchin' a Kaily Flee en the flowers.'

'Oh, I love Butterflies, Janet.'

'Aye, et was so pretty, so I was singin' to et.'

'Go on…'

Janet Giggled and blushed…

'Kaily Flee, Kaily Flee, flutter now so close to me,
Kaily Flee, Kaily Flee, dance fer me, aye now fer me.
En the meadow grass I see Kaily flee, Kaily Flee,
'Pon my hand et comes to rest, Kaily Flee, Kaily Flee.'

'Janet, are yoo there? Oh, Deborah, how nice to see yoo!'

'Good afternoon, Edward, ya well I trust…'

'Aye Deborah, yoo visitin' ya son?'

'Aye, came en on the same boat as Mary an' her Husband.'

'William, Aye. Fine man.'

With help from Edward, Deborah scrambled out of the cleft, 'I meant to come sooner but my shop's ben doin' good trade, an' weth none else to run et since my husband's passin' all those years ago…'

Deborah was strong minded, sharp tongued and shrewd, she'd not entertained the sale or loss of her husband's shop when he died, and many who had known him and his fairness had supported Deborah in keeping it. None had a problem with the old lady, who supplied their every need - either directly or through helpful direction.

Edward was now staring down at Janet. Janet was staring right at him with startled eyes. Deni was stood between her and her father, with nowhere to hide.

'She's growin' well, Edward.'

'Aye, she is. Proper rascal thou, keeps disappearin' from the Sunday services…'

'Och tha's quite normal, I remember ya father's frustration…'

Edward's gaze fell back onto Deborah, Deni ran, and Janet watched him. She wanted to shout after him, ask him when she could see him again; he'd been so enjoying her song…

'He was a hard man, they're poor memories, I care no' to recall them. I canny be like that to Janet, Deborah.' Edward noticed Janet's stare now fixed on the North end of the cleft. 'Janet, c'mon girl.'

Janet peered up at Deborah, 'Well I see hem soon?'

Deborah laughed, 'Oh, dear child.' She rested a hand on Edward's arm, quietly speaking to him, 'I was tellin' her o' the lettle folk, old island stories, I think she wants to meet one.'

Edward laughed; Deborah quickly gestured for Janet to be quiet. Janet frowned, they'd been blessed by the company of one of God's creations, surely they should celebrate it? But then, her father had not seen him; was his faith not strong enough? Janet remained silent, and after a little more talk of Gwen and Mainland, Deborah made her excuses and headed off.

Arriving back at the farm, Mary scolded Janet as if she had not given her permission to play outside.

Edward laughed, dismissing his sisters challenge, 'Et's her world oot there.' but in that moment, Janet felt that Mary was being unfair; she had told her to run along and play. Janet didn't want her father to think she'd disobeyed his sister…

Janet erupted, 'Yoo told me to go an' play!'

Mary became cross, 'But no' to wander off to God knows where, worryin' ya father. Have yoo no care? Ya Pa's already lost a wife…'

'Now, now…' Edward urged. 'She's always at the cleft these days, et's sheltered an' safe, an' no' far. She likes to imagine lettle people; the local children are no' all that friendly…'

'I donny imagine them, they're real, yoo canny see them cos ya blind to them. They like my singin'…' Janet stopped, her father, aunt and uncle were staring as if they'd been slapped hard across the face.

Edward looked at Mary, Mary flashed back an expression which yelled the need for Edward to take a firm stand. 'To ya room…'

Janet quailed. 'But…'

'To ya room Janet, now!'

Janet left the adults, but on seeing the front door, not yet secured for the coming night, she had a sudden thought. For what it was worth it may have been a good idea, from a child-like perspective, but her father had followed her.

'Janet! Where are yoo goin?'

Tears welling, Janet ran, slamming the door behind her and gaining some distance before Edward gathered himself to give chase, Mary and William not far behind.

As Edward drew close Janet reached the cleft, the day giving way to dusk. She called out, 'Kaily Flee, Kaily Flee, flutter now so close to me…' Edward stopped short of grabbing her.

'…Kaily Flee, Kaily Flee, dance fer me, aye now fer me…' In the gloomy light of the cleft, she could see more than one pair of sad eyes. She smiled, 'En the meadow grass I see Kaily…'

'Enough!' Mary snapped, seizing Janet's arm.

'No! No! They're there...' She resisted Mary's pull.

William stared quizzically into the cleft. Edward stood, shoulders and head downcast, seemingly unable to look at Janet.

'Daddy!' Janet cried, as Mary's pull returned with assertiveness.

'William!' Mary barked, snapping him from his daze and causing him to follow without resistance.

Edward continued to stand for a few moments more, before slowly returning to the farmhouse. By the time he closed and bolted the heavy wooden door, Mary had cast Janet into her bedroom and shut her inside.

Chapter twenty-seven

Janet listened to the adults muffled, sometimes raised voices for what seemed like an age.

She could not fathom why - having been blessed by meeting Deni - she should receive such open hostility *and* be the cause of such debate. She strained to hear the words, catching the odd, disjointed line - Mary would be leaving, and for some reason that would be essential, Edward had left it too late, some darkness was growing, odd incantations shouted at the top of a voice, what next? It was all some delusion that had to be "struck down". It sounded so painful, the next words she caught filling her with nausea.

'Tha's only achievable by takin' her away...'

On hearing her father's footsteps approaching the room, Janet quickly dived into her bed, lying with her back to the door.

'Janet...'

Janet decided not to answer, she'd been so happy that afternoon, but now she was intensely sad, no, she would not talk, she would punish them for the upset they'd caused.

'Janet, are yoo asleep?'

'Leave her Edward. Et's late.'

Janet heard the door close, and cried herself to sleep.

~

'Poor Janet.' Kayleigh lamented.

'It's a long story.' Sally observed. The others looked at her, 'What?

Just saying.'

'Got somethin' else to do?' Garrie laughed, gesturing at a window where the rain ran like a babbling stream, horizontally across the glass.

'They were deciding on what to do with Janet, weren't they?' Carl offered. 'It wasn't just Mary returning early to Mainland, was it? Janet was going with her.'

Garrie sighed, 'Aye, et's how et happened. An' such a scene would break a heart. Janet had to be corrected, before she turned wild, before she got drawn ento darker traditions. Edward, unable to defend against such an argument, due to his own experience weth Erka, buckled to Mary's will. Janet would leave that very next mornin', weth her Aunt an' Uncle. Leave the farm, leave the Island, leave all she'd e'er known, weth the understandin' that her return would depend on her behaviour.'

~

'No! No Pa, I promise I'll be good, I'll no' do anythin' wethoot ya say so.' Janet didn't want to cross the narrow plank over the deep, dark harbour water; it freaked her, tore at her in this moment of unsettling terror. Her screams, as she resisted passage onto the ship, carried far beyond the ears of her father, they clawed at his heart, he wanted to overrule his sister, carry the sobbing but grateful child back to the farm. Surely the threat of being taken away would have been enough? But Mary's gaze stayed his hand. He turned as if to shield himself from Janet's plaintive cries.

Mary half marched half dragged Janet onto the deck of the ship, a few of the sailors shaking their heads disapprovingly. 'Do ya jobs an' donny judge me, the girl es like an animal, thess es fer her own good.'

The sailors did as they were told, but their judgements remained.

Confined to a small, windowless cabin, Janet spent most of the journey in tears on the cabin bench, quietly, repeatedly, fervently cursing her Aunt, feeling beneath her the swell of the ocean, the fear of the very waves her father had warned her to stay away from, the waves that had nearly drowned her as a babe.

'Yoo a'right?'

Janet nearly leapt in surprise. Standing at the door was a small figure. 'Deni?'

'Donny know no-one called Deni. Funny kinda neem that.'

'Who are yoo?'

'I'm Benjamin, I werk on the ship. Why are yoo so sad?'

Janet's eyes, now well accustomed to the dark and aided by the cracked door, could see a boy perhaps a little older than her with dark hair protruding scruffily from a cloth cap. He was rather grubby but his voice was kind and she heard herself answer him. 'My Aunt es takin' me away from home, says I'm wild an' ungodly, she says she's gonna tutor me to behave like a proper girl.'

The boy laughed.

'What yoo laugh at me fer?'

'I'm no'! I'm laughin' cos ya Aunt has spent the last hour throwin' up o'er the side o' the boat.'

For a moment Janet was silent, then she too managed a smile.

'BEN!'

Benjamin turned in the direction of the coarse shout. 'I'm here.'

'Get on wi ya chores, boy, yoo've no business doon by the cabins.'

'Aye.' And with a wink, Benjamin gestured that Janet came with him. 'Queck,' he urged. 'Before Miley comes checkin'.'

Janet leapt up.

'Thess way, or ya Aunt'll see yoo.'

Benjamin led Janet along a dark corridor, to a steep stair at the aft of the boat.

They reached a deck that overlooked the whole vessel from the stern. Hidden by rails they were able to watch Mary, still violently retching.

Janet's eyes flashed around the entire ship, 'Et's beautiful.' There, on the fore-deck, Janet could also see Deborah.

'Et's Miley's Carrack, Victor...' Benjamin was cut short.

'Aye, et's my Carrack!' The booming voice froze Janet in fear, as Benjamin's ear was collected by a tall broad man with a jowly, red face, sunken, bloodshot eyes and purple nose. 'I knew yoo'd be carryin' on wi' thess lettle wetch.'

'She's no harm, Miley. She's juss a scared lettle girl.'

'She's a yon wetch, tha's what she es. She's charmed yoo, used her craft to beguile yoo an' set her free from her cabin. Mrs. Davie came doon t'the harbour an' explained the whole theng. She's payin' handsome to take thess feral child fer care an' correction en Kirkwall.'

'I'm no' feral, an' I'm no' a wetch!'

'Mrs. Davie's ben seck since we shut yoo away. My man here heard yoo cursin' her. She swears she's no' one fer seckness at sea. Tha's wetchery.' Miley turned to the crewmember he'd just mentioned 'Secure the lettle wetch back en her cabin, Drew.'

Janet caught a glimpse of Mary's pale, haggard face staring up from the lower deck before being dragged roughly back down to the cabin.

Out of some malicious game Drew marched her straight into the closed cabin door before opening it and throwing her inside. Janet pitied Benjamin, she would soon be on Mainland, he would have to stay onboard with these awful people.

There were no more escapes on that journey, all that filled her mind after her adventure on deck was Mary's disapproving face. What had she done to earn her Aunt's clear hatred? More worryingly, what would she do now that she was in Mary's stern care, miles away from her Father's trusting liberality?

By the time she heard the noises of a harbour, and the sound of the barrel being dragged from the cabin door, a glimmer of hope had pierced Janet's darkness - she was travelling to Mainland, to Kirkwall, home of her Mother's family; if she behaved, if she did exactly what she was told, they would love her, approve of her and wish her Godspeed back to Westray.

Chapter twenty-eight

It wasn't going to be as straight forward as Janet had hoped, there were only a few members of Gwen's family left on Mainland, her mother, rendered fretful by Mary's assertions of Janet's unruliness, her father, a frail man, distant of mind and erratic of thought, and her busy older sister, Peg, who was more occupied with her father's needs; she had visited, but had quickly accepted Mary's warnings, watched Janet at a distance with little affection and much suspicion, had made some suggestions and departed hurriedly.

Janet, confined to a room in the town house, despaired.

~

'This is such a sad story.' Sally rested against Carl, causing him to rub her back affectionately. 'Was there no one who believed Janet?'

Garrie shook his head, 'Edward had let Mary take her. Fer years he had ascribed Erka's werds - that the "bearin'll come to naught" - to the infant that had ben lost, but as more folk expressed concern aboot Janet's avoidance o' Church at such a young age, Edward had begun to apply the warnin' to Janet. The canny woman had seen hem weth the baby that first day he'd travelled t'the Kirk, before the storm, before her arrest fer wetchcraft. He began to convince hemself that she had renewed curses upon hem from the stake at Gallow Ha; where all wetches were burned. But another concern was growin', Edward began to dwell on the fact that Janet wasne his own, that he didne know her origins, that he didne understand her mind or will. En that moment he forgot the beauty he'd seen en her freedom an' adoration o' nature aroond her, an' weth Mary's werds fillin' his ears he'd agreed to Janet's departure. *Thess* had ben Mary's first werds to others, that her father had despaired, that he couldne cope weth her manipulative craft; an' so, all were poisoned t'wards her, an' none got to meet her wethout Mary's werds en their ears. Other family? There were some but they had moved away some years ago to the south, the mainland that es Scotland, as their father's mind slipped away.'

Sally's eyes welled, and tears dashed down her cheeks. She'd been entrusted with the necklace, but now there could never be a happy ending to the story.

Garrie's eyes were set on Sally, she could almost feel their weight. Surely - if he had indeed hoped that she and Carl had discovered the necklace - surely, he had now figured out that it was no longer in their possession.

'There was a savin' grace fer Janet on Mainland.'

Kayleigh seemed to need this as much Sally, eyes wet from Sally's sorrow as much as her own. 'Please tell.'

'On each Sunday Janet would be taken to the Services at the Cathedral…'

Carl didn't see Garrie's point, 'But she hated that.'

'Aye, the mornin' an' evenin' services, sat between her aunt and uncle, bored her, but durin' the week et was different…'

'Services in the week?' Carl squinted.

'Well, nay as such. The Bishop at the time, George Graeme, was mindful o' the poor, an' maintained facilities created by his predecessor fer orphaned an' displaced children, the provision o' gainful tutorin' an' werk.'

Carl stood and crossed to the fire, picking up a log to place on it. 'I suppose work is a useful…' Before Carl could place the log on the fire Deni had sprung to his side, snatched the log and gestured that he sit down again.

'Hey! I just thought the fire looked low.'

Deni stared at him, shaking his head.

Carl raised his hands, shrugged and sat back down, sharing his blanket with Sally.

Deni placed the log neatly back on the pile next to the hearth and sat between Donie and Dini. Dini nudged him, motioning toward the fire. Deni nodded, stood up, took two logs and nestled them into the glowing embers.

Carl sighed, Kayleigh giggled and Garrie continued with the story.

Chapter twenty-nine

Janet stared at the ragged gathering of youngsters, she knew not one of them that first day, but they, you could be sure, had been fully briefed on their new companion. For many weeks Janet remained the outcast, the one to be treated with watchful caution. Some truly seemed scared of her - a thought that upset Janet deeply - and for the first time ever Janet wished she could make some friends and ease the fears of those whose knowledge had been corrupted.

Bess was different, she had been wary like the others, but Janet quickly intrigued her. Perhaps it was the similarities she saw between herself and the newcomer. She too was a slim girl, albeit on the wrong side of gaunt; she was also the same age and had equally black hair, that straddled her shoulders and stopped shy of her waist. She smiled at Janet. That was all at first, but for Janet it was laced with a warmth she had not felt since Benjamin's company on the Carrack.

Bess was also different, focused and diligent wherever the group of children worked. She would quickly complete her part of any quota, winning the approval of those who employed them. She seemed the model child, but beneath the innocence that her age and public manner portrayed, Bess had a fierce independence, a free will that Janet long desired for herself.

With Mary's vigilance all hope of any freedom had been stripped from Janet. When she was not working with the other children, she was being hand-led to or from them, or she was sitting in her little townhouse room, silent tears in her eyes, fearful of the repercussions of any noise she might make, a fear borne from experiencing her aunt's intolerant wrath; for Mary left no behaviour that she considered a misdemeanour unpunished. Too many times Janet had answered back or cried unfairness. She had learnt - rightly or wrongly - to hold her tongue and her opinion.

The weeks passed by, and Bess drew closer, despite the warnings of some of the other children.

'She's trickin' yoo.' That's what they'd say about Janet's lonely tears, but Bess just laughed at them and sat with Janet anyway, quietly helping her with the fishing net she was mending poorly, too afraid to ask for help in case Mary scolded her for talking when she heard of it.

Bess showed Janet where she was going wrong with few words and great care, and soon the mesh fell correctly into place. Janet thanked Bess but wished that there was more she could do in return.

One evening Mary came to her room with an object wrapped in cloth. Mary's manner was softer than usual; like the Mary she'd known; the one before the aunt who'd taken her from Westray.

'Happy birthday, Janet.'

'Fer me?' Janet looked at the mysterious parcel.

'Aye.'

Janet lifted her hands and received the gift, opening it with a child's lack of hesitation. Inside was a little fabric doll with a blue dress, real chestnut hair like Mary's and a face made of coloured thread.

'I've ben lookin' after yoo Janet, here's someone fer yoo to look after.'

Janet stared at the doll as it sat in her open hand.

Mary grew impatient for a response, the "thank you" that all children should immediately give to the gift giver, 'Yoo donny like et?'

Janet looked up at her Aunt, tears welling in her eyes, 'Oh thank yoo, thank yoo, Aunt Mary, she's beautiful... like yoo!' Without hesitation Janet hugged Mary tightly.

Mary was touched by Janet's response, perhaps even startled, then, recovering, she smiled and returned the hug. Her efforts were paying off, the wild thing was responding to her tough love.

Alone again in her room, Janet held the doll tightly, her aunt - for so long now the dispenser of her suffering - had just performed an unexpected act of kindness.

Janet had feared the immediate loss of the doll when Mary had challenged her about liking it; that's why she had called it and Mary beautiful. Not that she was particularly attractive, but Janet had heard Bess compliment those who employed the children - the results had always been positive - and for some reason the "like you" had seemed fitting to add. Now Janet sat, rocking a little, had she discovered the way to win Mary's approval? Would she soon be able to go home?

Next morning it was as if nothing had happened, Mary was as much the dictator as ever. She pulled her from her bed, harried her as she washed, roughly dressed her, stood over her as she ate some bread and drank some water, then they were out of the door. Janet remained silent all the way to the harbour, guarding her tongue from the usual protests. Mary delivered her to the group and turned to leave, Bess was watching.

'See yoo later, Auntie Mary.'

Mary turned, 'I'll have none o' ya protests... What ded yoo say?'

'See yoo later. Love yoo.' Janet glanced at Bess, who was smiling.

Mary returned to Janet, brushed something from the child's dress, kissed her on the head, said 'Be good' and left. Janet joined Bess, giggling; her unusually happy face catching the eye of some of the other children. That day, to Janet's delight, she had become more approachable, some remained suspicious of her and a boy everyone called "Snotty" always seemed to be staring, but she now sat amongst several of the other girls as she mended her fishing net.

~

'Tha's ironic.' Kayleigh seemed troubled, 'Janet was so innocent, her wildness was juss her youthful energy. En takin' her from her father an' treatin' her the way she ded, Mary actually taught Janet to be deceitful...'

Garrie nodded, 'Janet didne like et either. Even though et made her life more comfortable, an' led to a visit to her father, she didne like bein' dishonest, she felt et contrary to the werds she had heard at the Cathedral an' from the leaders o' the werk group. Et was hard fer Janet to suppress her desire fer fairness; e'en to talk to her aunt an' obey her commands as ef Mary were faultless.'

Sally sat up, 'She got to go home to her father?'

'Aye, an' quickly too. Mary couldne resist showcasin' her success,

Janet's consistent politeness, sweet werds an' guarded tongue were the product o' her commitment. Edward should see the results o' the correct management o' a wayward child, see the value o' firmness.'

~

Miley's Carrack, "Victory Star", was back in the harbour, Janet watched; she was looking for Benjamin. Twice she was told to concentrate on her net, but she continued to glance up frequently, concerned, because she had not seen him. Later in the day Mary appeared, it was earlier than usual, but she hadn't come to pick Janet up. She passed the children without looking at them, and headed to Miley's ship. Janet saw her speaking to Drew, she remembered him. She felt anger welling up inside.

The work leader spotted her, 'Janet, I wellne tell yoo again, keep ya eyes to ya net.'

At that moment the rope holding a crate, that was being off-loaded from Miley's ship, snapped, narrowly missing Drew and Mary, and sending harbour workers diving for safety.

Janet felt a pang of anxiety; many had said unfair things about her, all the stuff about waywardness and witchery. She gasped inwardly, the hate she'd just felt - had it, could it have caused the crate to drop? Janet glanced around at the other children, most were looking over at the settling dust and the activity around it, but one or two had been looking at Janet and had quickly turned away. Bess alone was still observing Janet, and on her face was a perceptive, knowing warmth that instantly calmed the distressed child.

The incident had brought the children's work day to an end. Mary used it as leverage to get free passage to Westray - compensation for the shock of nearly being killed - and the voyage, fitting comfortably with Drew's schedule, was set for the following week.

Chapter thirty

Janet's excitement threatened to be its own end. Many times that week Mary had threatened cancellation if Janet didn't calm down. Janet had forcibly calmed herself each occasion, explaining that she was just so happy, gaining Mary's approval by immediately apologising. She even went to the Cathedral without moaning or fidgeting, and when asked by her uncle about the sermon, was able to relate the Minister's main points on sacrifice for the good of others and that the Son of God's sacrifice was made even as those who would respond to that sacrifice, scoffed and mocked.

Approaching Miley's Carrack Janet felt suddenly perturbed, she'd been dragged onboard last time, over the narrow gangplank and the deep water beneath. In her mind she could hear, afresh, the words of her father warning her to "stay clear o' the sea", and that she had "nearly drowned". She had always sought a position away from the harbour wall as she mended the fishing nets, now she stood on the edge of the gangplank, frozen with inexplicable fear, clutching her doll tightly, with nothing to pull her over.

Mary was approaching behind her. 'Wha's wrong? Get across!'

In that moment Janet realised she could lose the chance of seeing her father. The feat was herculean, though nobody could see the terror in Janet's heart as she padded quickly across the board.

Janet perched herself on the Quarter Deck, behind the main mast, away from the side and the busy loading of goods. This suited Mary well enough, and she too settled there. William had come to see them off, Mary longed for him to join them but he had business to attend to in Scotland. He helped them with their luggage and ensured that Mary had all she needed to hire transport on arrival; this achieved, he bid them safe passage, kissed his wife and left the boat.

Janet had grown a little over the year, but it was obvious that some members of the crew recognised her from her previous crossing. There were whispers and glances that appeared to trouble Mary more than

Janet herself.

A short distance out of the harbour, Mary asked if Janet would like to stretch her legs, but Janet declined saying she would stay with the luggage. Mary huffed 'Suit ya self' and headed in the direction of the forecastle; Janet shivered at the thought of moving, she was clear of the sides of the boat and felt she was the furthest she could be from the dangers of the sea all around her.

Disappearing from view beyond the great, square expanse of the Mainsail, Mary was replaced on the Quarter Deck by an old Sailor. First, his head appeared; his gaze, at first twitchy and widely cast, came to rest on the anxious child, then he climbed the remaining steps to the level Janet was on. He stared for a moment, blinking nervously, his sparse white hair flicking about in the fair wind that drove the boat on. He cautiously approached.

Janet clung anxiously to her doll, heart racing.

The sailor stopped just short of where Janet sat, his head slightly to one side as he regarded the child. She gazed up at him as he craned forward.

The old man addressed her in a whisper, 'Yoo'll no' curse us well yoo?'

Janet shook her head, fearfully.

'Drew's a harsher Captain than Miley.'

Janet felt held by the Sailor's wary tone, asking 'Wh… where's Miley?'

'He's gun, Missy.'

They stared at each other, Janet awaiting more, the Sailor looking compromised, his face ticking and filled with insecurity. He glanced quickly about, then bore down closer still to the now cowering girl. His voice filled with disbelief, 'He fell, o'er the side!'

Janet recoiled from the man's breath, 'Ugh… How? Ded he trip on somethin'?'

'He were stood, then he fell. Dead before he het the sea. Then he was gone… sank like a stone, juss off The Calf o' Eday, as Red Head comes ento view. Et was the day after we took yoo to Mainland.'

'Sank?'

'Like a stone.' The Sailor pulled away purposefully, to check that no one was close, then, drawing nearer than before, he added, 'I think et got hem, no one sinks like that, dead or no'.'

'Et?' Janet turned her head hard against the wall of the Poop Deck to avoid the spittle that was thrown by the old man's words.

He lowered his voice further, 'The Nuckelavee.'

The man's eyes looked crazed; Janet wondered if he was quite sane.

'Et eats the cursed dead…'

Janet gave out a weak cry of pain from her quickly stiffening neck, and the Sailor sprang away, as if stung.

'No, no!' He cried. 'Donny curse me!'

'I wouldne, e'en ef I could!'

Drew was standing behind the old man, he'd come from nowhere, the Sailor backed right into him before he knew. 'Wha's thess, Lang? Yoo shud be below.'

Janet felt her heart would burst through fear.

Drew repeatedly glanced back and forth between her and Lang as the old man garbled some reason for his being on the Quarter Deck.

'Get back to werk!' Drew stared at Janet.

'Captain!' Lang hurried quickly away.

Janet stared back at Drew, barely breathing, what would Mary make of this? A weight of unjustifiable guilt pressed down on her. Miley had died, and some - if not all the crew - blamed her, felt she'd cursed the man, believed she had arcane powers; powers that were unleashed to punish those who had taken her from home.

She was about to plead innocence when Drew burst into laughter and departed, leaving her bewildered and shaking.

Chapter thirty-one

Mary had spent the bulk of the crossing on the Forecastle, standing quite still and looking ahead as if deep in thought. In truth she had been determined not to make a spectacle of herself as she had the previous time; when she had vomited repeatedly. She had begun to feel uneasy behind the Mainsail, and the relief her new position gave her was welcome but dependent on her lack of movement. Rounding Eday, Mary had seen the welcome bulk of Westray. Confident that she would not have too long now to tolerate the swell, she returned to Janet.

Exhausted by the earlier incident, Janet had fallen fast asleep, and this was how Mary found her, as the ship was eased into the harbour, curled up sweetly amidst the luggage.

'Wake up, lazy.'

Janet stirred, seagulls were calling noisily overhead, their shadows flashing across the deck, the sun bright and high, the air warm.

'Janet…'

Janet felt a finger prodding at her shoulder.

'Janet! Get up… or we ken juss sail back straight away…' Mary had no intention of staying on the Victory Star, and its crew had no intention of sailing straight back to mainland, they had supplies to deliver and were heading out from Orkney to Norway for trade as soon as all was done. Janet didn't know this of course, and the thought of not seeing her father snapped her from her malaise.

Most of their luggage was already on its way to the quay, and Mary left Janet briefly to arrange a cart to take them on to the farm.

She returned to find Janet slumped down again on the bags. 'Get up an' help, I'm no' shiftin' all thess on my own. What's wrong weth yoo?''

Janet stood weakly, 'I donny feel well, my tummy aches.'

'Yoo shouldne have slept on the boat, now take thess.' Mary handed Janet a small bag, but it was rather heavier than Janet expected, and she struggled with it. Mary, noting how pale the child looked relented, and instructed her to board the cart and keep out from under her feet.

Before long a rather tired looking horse, led by an equally tired looking man, was pulling them along the cart track that ran from the quay to the village. Mary observed with satisfaction that the old Kirk was being repaired, its fallen walls were up again and roofing timbers had been positioned in readiness for the slates.

At the other end of the village Mary's pleasure was doubled by the fact that Erka's old home was nothing more than a ruin itself, its door hanging on a single hinge, its roof sagging under its own weight. 'Aye,' she thought to herself, 'Et wellne be long before all memory o' that awful woman es gone.'

The cart track ambled its bumpy way through the landscape to Braehead and Janet soon caught sight of her Father's farm. Edward was in the entrance of his barn, repairing an old pew from the Kirk.

He downed his tools and ran to greet them, sweeping Janet up in his arms. 'Oh child, yoo look so pale.'

Mary quickly responded, 'She slumbered on the boat, the nausea well pass.'

'I donny feel seck. My tummy hurts.'

'Now, now, none o' ya old ways child.' Mary's tone was enough to quieten Janet, she'd taught herself not to fight her aunt; she held too much power over her. Besides, she had not an ounce of strength for any altercation.

'Well,' Edward announced, 'I fer one am convinced yoo need carryin' ento the Farmhoose, so tha's what I well do.' And that's what he did, wilfully deaf to Mary's accusations of being too soft.

Janet laid quietly beside the window most of the afternoon. She was intensely happy to be home, but a great sadness robbed her of true euphoria. She had intended to visit the cleft as soon as possible, with the year at its peak it would be full of wildflowers and Kaily Flees, and perhaps Deni would be there? Edward too had expected Janet to run out in the glorious sunshine, even Mary would have allowed it, but Janet remained quietly recumbent, bracing herself for the frequent spasms of pain.

'Yoo've broken my daughter.' Edward jested, attempting to make light of what he felt must be a passing stomach bug. But Mary had become more concerned herself. Even at her best behaved, Janet was not a sedentary child, and a sudden thought came into her mind.

139

~

Carl looked lost, 'What was wrong?'

Sally hugged him, 'Our girl's becoming a woman.'

'She's too young, surely.'

Kayleigh agreed with Sally, 'Et's no' unheard o'… That was et, was et no'?'

'Aye, that night she bled fer the first time; her aunt - fer so long her perceived adversary - drew near to her, comforted her an' explained much that Janet had ne'er known.'

Kayleigh shook her head, 'Et must have ruined the visit.'

'Et made et. Janet had become used to a harsh firmness from Mary, now she saw the deeper affections o' the woman, an' bein' back home was a solace. Her father ded everythin' he could fer her, an' after a few days et was best part through.'

'Did she get to stay with her father?'

'No, she was stell very much a child en all other respects, an' Mary could see that Edward's inexperience weth the bleed was a good excuse to keep hold o' Janet a while longer. Tellin' Edward that he'd be happier ef Janet returned at a later date able to see to her own flow.'

Sally's shoulders slumped, 'Edward sent her away again?'

'Edward, perturbed by the mere thought o' steerin' Janet ento womanhood, took the opportunity his Sister afforded hem. Janet knew thess was juss a visit; the idea o' returnin' to Kirkwall weth Mary wasne anythin' other than expected. Janet respected her more, had ways o' defusin' her wrath, an' she had moved from a spontaneous self-direction to a more obligin' service to others. Tha's where Bess benefitted, their friendship grew an' grew, they were like sesters. Janet was grateful fer her acceptance when the others regarded her weth suspicion, an' at e'ery opportunity Mary ensured her friend's needs were met. As Janet's next birthday away from home approached, she learned that et was Bess's birthday juss days before. Havin' no money o' her own, Janet gave Bess her lettle doll. Mary was initially angry, but Janet sweetly explained that Bess had nothin' an' nobody as lovely as Mary to see to her needs. Days later Mary started to allow Bess to visit Janet fer play, an' Bess promoted the relationship to Mary, weth immaculate behaviour an' a public innocence that fully hid the ideas that she an' Janet explored away from adult ears.'

'Hold on…' Kayleigh had suddenly thought of something else. 'Where was Benjamin? She'd looked oot fer hem on the quayside at Kirkwall, an' he wasne on the boat either.'

'Et was a thought that troubled Janet too.' Garrie admitted. 'Et upset her fer months. E'ery time the Victory Star arrived en Kirkwall she would watch, but no sign o' Benjamin e'er showed. No, she wouldne see hem again fer years.'

'Years!' Sally's exclamation caused the Trows to pull various comic expressions of shock and grief.

'Aye, years. She'd be fourteen by then, an' a handsome young woman too…'

Chapter thirty-two

These were happier times for Janet, she saw her Father more often, travelling not only with Mary but also Deborah when the old lady visited her own kin near to Edward's farm. Chief of her happiness though was the decline in comments that pointed to her being "gifted" with unnatural arts. Janet attributed that to Mary's decreased use of the information, and she was greatly pleased that it seemed to be diminishing quickly without the reminders. When she had turned thirteen the work group let her go, and Deborah offered her work in the shop. She would run stock orders down to the quay when customers brought news that the Victory Star had docked. That's when she heard what had happened to Benjamin.

She was talking to Ewan, the crewmen who usually dealt with Deborah's requests, when her eye was caught by a young boy. He was too young to be Benjamin but he brought the memory of him back quite strongly. 'What happened to the boy who used to be on thess boat?'

Ewan didn't really care, but he didn't want Janet to know; she *was* a pretty young thing... 'Who's that?'

'His neem was Benjamin...'

Ewan raised an eyebrow, 'Oh, hem. Drew sent hem away, he was Miley's.'

'Miley's son? Drew took the boat from hem?'

'Nay. Some friend o' Miley's lost on a game o' chance an' had nothin' to pay Miley weth, accept thess boy who werked fer hem. Some orphan I think.'

'So why ded Drew send hem away?'

Ewan drew Janet away from the busy area they'd been standing in and lowered his voice. 'Story goes Miley had somethin' that belonged to Benjamin, an' the boy wanted et.'

'What?'

'A box; he said Miley had promised et to hem, but Drew reckoned that was no' the boy's concern, that there was nothin' o' worth en et anyway, et's too light, rattles feebly an' the keys messin.' Ewan smiled; his eyes seemed to look right into her. 'You're a good-lookin' gal, why bother aboot a boy when there's men to look after ya needs?'

He stroked her face, she wanted to flinch but smiled back sweetly, saying, 'Where ded Drew send Benjamin?'

Ewan frowned, it wasn't the response he wanted, and yet his touch had not been rejected. 'Drew gave hem to a man on Papa Westray, a fisherman, werks oot o' the Bay o' Moclett.' Ewan rested his hand on a post behind Janet and leaned toward her. Janet squeezed away, laughing to hide her discomfort. She glanced up at the Victory Star, straight at Lang, who sprang out of sight like a disturbed rat. Janet froze.

'I'll breng ya goods to Deborah's, Miss, when we're next en port.'

'Oh, er, Ok.'

Ewan headed back to the boat, amused by the girl's avoidance. Janet headed back to the shop as quickly as she could, imagining Ewan's lustful eyes flicking in her direction.

Deborah seemed quite concerned when Janet spoke of Ewan's behaviour, she even spoke to Mary. Mary seemed to apportion at least some of the blame to Janet, and the decision was made to send her for an extended stay with her father.

All this had come at an inconvenient time for Mary; William and his Sister were in Scotland with family, William's Father was ill and his Mother needed Mary's help. It was not possible for Deborah to leave her shop either and it looked like Janet would have to be trusted to travel alone. Then Mary made an unexpected suggestion.

'Bess… Bess could go weth yoo, she's such a confident girl.'

Within two days the girls stood onboard a small Merchantman, Janet, still nervous of the water, being held tightly by Bess.

Bess seemed thrilled as they waved goodbye to Mary. 'Thess es so great! We'll be home untel the Autumn.'

Bess had many times told Janet that she was also originally from Westray, but had no recollection of the island due to just being a baby. Bess pulled a necklace out of the warmth of her frock, Janet had seen it many times but now Bess informed her that it belonged to her mother, who had placed it around her neck before she disembarked from the boat at Kirkwall, but had - shortly after - died.

'I'm sure some thief wooda had et ef I hadne ben taken en by Bishop Law.'

'I ne'er knew hem, was he kind?'

'Oh, tha's right, yoo joined us after Bishop Graeme arrived. Law, he was very strict, but fair. Et was his wife, Marion who looked after my necklace untcl they left fer Glasgow. I thought et was a geft from her, but she soon put me right.'

'Ken I see?' Janet held out her hand.

Bess wouldn't take it off, neither would she let her touch it, but offered it up for Janet to see. The jewel was a most intense green, that seemed to alter as you moved it. Surrounding the gem was a finely worked filigree of silvery metal, polished by constant caresses.

'Oh Jan, look!' Bess thrust Janet towards the edge of the boat, she had a better view of the water than Janet, and wanted her to see.

Janet screamed, her stomach rolled, what was Bess doing? Then she saw. Just a short way out of the harbour of Kirkwall they had been joined by dolphins! Janet's initial fears fell away, the scream became a laugh. Bess, at first disturbed by Janet's resistance to being ushered to the boat's side, now laughed too, hugging Janet tightly. 'I wellne let yoo go sweet friend, no' now no' e'er.'

~

Sally and Carl had been staring at each other, both had assumed that the necklace worn by Bess was the Seal pendant, the knowledge that it wasn't mattered little to them, their guilt at its loss pressed in. The story seemed to be leading to a point where they should have been able to pass the artefact back; a moment of joyous release.

Now both wondered about the reaction to their news, and its consequences.

~

It was late when the Merchantman finally moored at Pierowall, the dolphins had left them at Egilsay and the girls had settled down. Some sort of magic had worked in Janet's heart, the ominous expanse of the sea, for so long a source of anxiety, had become a showcase of beauty; she had sat in Bess's arms gazing out over the diamond glinting waves and the passing Islands, mulling over this new revelation. Bess had sat, simply smiling at her dearest friend.

Janet and Bess, burdened with their bags but happy and giggling, now walked along the trackway that would see them to the door of the farmhouse, the fully repaired Kirk out of sight behind them and the walls of Erka's home dark and near-roofless ahead.

Bess lamented the condition of the little building, 'How sad. Et must have ben such a sweet cottage en ets day.'

'Et gives me chills when I pass et. Mary said et was a Wetches den…'

'Ha! An' Mary was always right? An' fair?' Bess had been Janet's confidant for years , and knew all the wrongs she'd suffered under her aunt's close supervision.

They stopped on the track outside the building.

'Let's look en.' Bess dropped her bags and quickly disappeared through a doorless opening.

Janet tried to stop her 'Wait!' She knew the sentiment this building was regarded with by Mary and her Father, but she failed to hold Bess back and she now stood frozen and alone on the path. She stared at the doorway; all was quiet... 'Bess? BESS!' There was no reply... Janet edged forward, 'Bess, donny tease...' her hand rested on the door frame, it crumbled beneath her hand and fell to the threshold, she pulled away but the desire to get to Bess was overpowering and she stepped inside.

Bess stood there, silently, like a life-size doll. Janet reached out and touched her. Bess took her hand. 'How long has thess place ben empty?'

'I've ne'er known et no' to be.'

'Look...' Bess wasn't pointing at anything in particular, but motioned to the whole. Janet could see Bess's meaning, for although the roof had tumbled in, the contents of the room was still there; bowls, some broken by a fallen beam, were sitting on a sturdy table, a chair with a rotten throw still draped over it, curtains still held by their last threads at the window, a cupboard slightly ajar full of vessels of many sorts...

Janet pulled her friend's arm. 'We should go, no one's ben en here since the old wetch was taken; we *shouldne* be here...'

Bess's body was reluctant; her mind was pondering something, but Janet eventually manoeuvred her out through the door and back to the bags.

The rest of the walk to the farm had been devoid of the earlier giggles, and Bess didn't regain her animation until Edward appeared from tending to his livestock to find two young women sat with their bags by the farmhouse door; the unexpected return home of his daughter creating a joy that was quite infectious.

'Es thess Bess?' He'd heard of the girl but was unacquainted.

'Aye, Father.'

'Tha's me, Sir.'

He laughed, 'Call me Edward, please. Es Mary en the hoose?'

'Nay, Father. She couldne come, et's juss me an' Bess…'

'Yoo came all that way?'

'Aye.'

'My, my, yoo are all grown up. Erm, Mary *does* know ya here…'

The girls giggled, and Janet explained why they had come.

'Aye, some o' these sailors are a bet notorious weth the girls. Mary's lookin' after ya honour.'

Bess giggled.

'Yoo must be hungry, come en, come en, there's a stew en the pot.' Edward opened the door and headed inside followed closely by Bess. The sun fell beneath the horizon. Janet gazed in the direction of the cleft, there was a stronger desire this visit to get there, but it wouldn't be tonight, not now. The offer of food pulled at her empty stomach, no, this visit would have greater freedom, Mary was not here and Bess was. Something told Janet that these would be wonderful days.

Chapter thirty-three

The night of Janet and Bess's arrival was a restless one; the merry banter of two girls sharing a room for the first time had been interrupted by a surprisingly fierce thunderstorm that shook the house. Edward had allowed the girls into his room, sitting in a large chair, watching over them as they huddled nervously together.

The girls awoke to the sound of Edward bringing them breakfast; some bread and a sliver of cold meat. Through the window the day looked overcast, droplets from the night's deluge still clinging to the pane.

Outside it was unwelcomingly cold and unseasonably blustery. Seeing that a stroll would be unpleasant, Janet decided to stay and clean the house; a task that her father had only lightly performed. She and Bess spent the day dusting, sweeping, sneezing and laughing, and Edward returned from the land to find his home clean, a welcome fire in the hearth and a hot pie on the table.

He was delighted, 'I fel I need to wrestle yoo back from ya aunt soon, or I'll be missin' oot.'

Sunday saw all three attending the Kirk in Pierowall, Edward had been heavily involved in its restoration, there was even glass in its windows. Janet felt totally welcome, the congregation warm and friendly, many asking after Mary and her husband. Bess was welcomed too, she thrived on social interaction anyway, and all who spoke of her later gave a good report. Edward happily accepted his daughter's praise on the quality of the restoration. Janet was left in little doubt of her Father's ongoing strength of faith as he repeated praise for his Saviour, the source of his skills with wood and stone. Erka's old cottage was hardly acknowledged in either direction, be it for the morning or evening service, and it seemed to Janet as if the absence of its mention was preparation for its final collapse and ultimate replacement with rough, tussocky grass, swaying anonymous in the wind.

Next morning the sun streamed into the bedroom. Janet opened the window and drank in the sweet breeze. Today she'd visit the cleft again, maybe introduce Bess to Deni, oh how she longed to see him, if only to prove he wasn't some dream or childlike fantasy. She seemed to recall Deborah indicating that the little fellow was part of God's Creation, his presence a blessing… She frowned, or was that the Kaily Flees? Her heart missed a beat… had she made Deni up? No, surely he was a part of the reason she'd been taken to Mainland? Mary had repeatedly cautioned her on her overactive imagination, punished her for it, corrected her. Even though she tried, she couldn't picture Deni's face; was that proof that he wasn't real?

Bess, perturbed by Janet's not-too-well-hidden anxieties, was reluctant to leave the farmhouse; Edward's kindness and fatherliness had touched her and she didn't want to displease him. Her friend now wanted to go somewhere that she hadn't discussed with him, and now couldn't, because he'd left earlier to tend to his animals. It seemed out-of-character. Her Janet was more subdued, easier led.

Janet was surprised by Bess's hesitancy, her Bess was so spontaneous, so adventurous. How ironic that on mainland Bess had been such a free spirit, and she herself had been so controlled and suppressed, yet here, where her own freedom was so apparent, Bess had become so staid.

Troubled that Bess might be ill, Janet tried one last time to ease her out of the house. 'Dad would want yoo to get some fresh air, et was so dusty en the hoose the other day. Come on Bess, come see more o' the place where yoo were born.' Janet still just wanted to see the cleft, but if it took more effort on her part, well, so be it; she'd certainly grown used to it pacifying Mary.

Bess, accepting that Edward would want her to stay in good health and seeing that, beneath the anxiety, Janet clearly felt freer here with her Father, started to contemplate the broader opportunities such a turn might afford her. Grabbing her shawl, she was first to the door.

Bess moaned as she sat, staring down at Janet from atop the rise of the cleft. 'Es thess all yoo brought me oot to see?' Janet had been up and down, waist deep in flowers, searching every fold of the cleft for somewhere a Trow might hide. Perhaps he didn't recognise her and was scared? How she hated the thought of being the cause of fear - she didn't want to be like Mary.

Once or twice, away from Bess, she had quietly called Deni's name.

'I'm bored!' Bess called.

'Donny yoo like the pretty flowers? Look at the flutterin' Kaily Flees...' Her voice trailed off as she tested a piece of the clefts face to see if it hid a doorway.

'They're much the same as the flowers an' butterflies roond the bay at Scapa. They're lovely Jan, but yoo donny seem interested en them ya self. Why *are* we here?'

Janet, returned to Bess, scooped up a bunch of wildflowers in her hand and offered them up to her, 'Fer fresh air, drink en the air Bess...'

Bess stood, 'I'm off.' She wandered out of Janet's line of sight. 'Are yoo comin'?'

Janet felt deeply upset, no Deni, a disapproving friend... it was a horrid day. She started to climb out of the cleft, flowers still held determinedly in hand, then - as she glanced one last time into the cleft, she caught sight of a small figure. 'Deni!'

Bess heard, but misunderstood, 'Et's too early fer dinner.'

Deni, with a finger held tightly to his lips, gestured that Janet be quiet. She heard his voice clearly in her mind, 'Dangerous.'

Frowning at Deni, Janet called, 'Oh, ya right, et es too early.' Janet, not content to leave her friend unaware of Deni, called her back to help her out of the cleft, but Deni darted out of sight.

'Wha's wrong weth yoo, Jan? Yoo seem all distracted an' cross...' Bess was staring into the cleft where Janet was still looking.

Janet, allowing herself to be pulled up, replied, 'Lettle people used to live here, I used to play weth them when I was small.'

Bess stared at her.

Janet heard an assertive 'SHHH!' in her mind, and instantly felt guilty for betraying Deni's wish to remain unknown.

Bess laughed, 'Do yoo believe en Fairies?'

'Well, I...' It wasn't fairies she'd been talking of, but knowing that Trows were real certainly meant that Faery Folk could be, she'd never considered it... and now she didn't know what to say.

Bess continued to laugh.

'How dare yoo!' Janet could see only one way to kill the ridicule and protect Deni's anonymity. She began to walk purposely up the slope back to the farmhouse. 'I juss shared weth yoo how I used to play, I didne have the children yoo had aboot yoo, *I* was aloon...'

Janet's distress was convincing and Bess chased after her apologising for teasing her, 'Let's no' go back to the farm yet. The lettle cottage en Pierowall, let's go back there...'

'No, I wellne, I donny like et.'

'Juss cos ya dad an' aunt donny like et…'

'No one likes et! No one's ben en et until us! What does that tell yoo?'

Bess huffed, 'Where then?'

Janet had a sudden idea; Ewan had told her that Benjamin had gone to Papa Westray to work for a fisherman. You could see Papa Westray from the Bay of Brough, maybe the fishermen would be out of Moclett? Maybe she would see him? 'Come on, we'll go to the beach.'

Bess rolled her eyes, but held her tongue, convinced she had offended Janet.

They linked arms and headed off along the track, Janet still holding her flowers.

It was better than Janet hoped, even Bess seemed brighter as they approached the bay on the track that overlooked it. Several small boats bobbed out in the shallows and the men were hauling in the nets.

The tide was on the ebb, and although this was the very place her Father had cautioned her about the dangers of the sea, Janet saw only the gentle lap of negligible waves; all sense of danger had evaporated. Bess and Janet stepped out along the wet sand, the voices of the fishermen carrying clearly over the water. It was apparently a good catch and the head man was keen that they spread it evenly between the boats. One young man was told to pay attention to the nets rather than the ladies on the beach, making the girls giggle. They waved at the fishermen and continued walking, stopping only when they reached the Point of Cott at the bay's far end. The girls watched as the men reset the nets and heaved on their oars to deliver the fish to Pierowall.

Although Bess knew little of Benjamin, other than Janet's first meeting with him on the Victory Star - a story Janet had shared soon after their friendship had begun - Bess perceived some more focused interest towards the fishermen than she'd seen in Janet before. 'Let's follow them, Jan…'

'Oh, Lord no…'

'Why no'?'

Janet pulled her gaze from the boats. 'Et's no' the done theng, Bess. Et's awful forward; are yoo fergettin' why I'm here?'

They stared at each other momentarily before collapsing into the coarse tussocks of grass on the Point, laughing. Suddenly Bess was on her feet, hand outstretched to Janet. Janet took it and they hurried off towards Pierowall.

Chapter thirty-four

As they headed along the coast to Pierowall, Janet told Bess what Ewan had said about Benjamin working for a fisherman out of the Bay of Moclett.

'Ded yoo see hem on the boats?'

'I'm no' sure, they were all men…'

'From what yoo've told me, he must be a young man by now. There were a few.'

Janet stopped, breaking Bess's grip. 'I think we should go home.' Janet pointed up the slope where the roof of her Father's barn was visible.

Bess took Janet's hand again and urged her forward. 'We're juss gonna look…'

It was much closer to lunch by the time they neared the quay; Bess had taken an interest in Erka's cottage again, its far side being easily approached from the beach of Pierowall Bay. Strangely the cottage seemed less dark, less imposing to Janet since they had entered it before and she followed Bess without the familiar foreboding. Despite this both girls had been sent running and screaming when Bess had peered through the glassless back window only to disturb a resting crow, its shrill cry and percussion of wings instantly robbing Janet and Bess of their bravado.

151

'Oh Lor', et was juss a bird!' Bess gasped. 'See what ya wetch stories do?'

Janet laughed, 'I find ya more easily frightened when ya caught en somethin' yoo shouldne be at.'

'Well I like the lettle cottage, an' when I come back to Westray proper I'm gonna get et repaired an' live there.'

Janet's laughter faltered, 'Good luck weth that, I donny think yoo'll find any local craftsman who'll touch the place.'

They'd headed on towards the quay with Bess saying she'd do the work herself if she had to, and Janet stating plainly that she'd not visit ever. Now they sat on the beach by the quay, perhaps a little closer than Janet had wanted, but the sand had looked drier there and so Bess had dragged her to it and they'd settled, delving into a bag for a small piece of pie that Janet had wrapped in a cloth for them.

A voice came from the wall of the quay above them, 'Are yoo followin' us?' A tall, slim man stood there, arms folded, his unkempt hair blowing about his face, his attention divided between the girls and his Master.

Bess smiled, 'We're lookin' fer Benjamin.'

Janet urged her to hush, but of course it was too late.

'Who shall I say's lookin'?'

Janet stood up and hurried away, stumbling up the foreshore towards the cart track, dropping her flowers but too anxious to stop for them as she heard Bess's trademark confidence. 'Juss heard that he was a good catch... fer a fisherman!'

Janet's embarrassment had marched her all the way home, if only she could have figured out who Benjamin was from a distance, seen that he was well treated and healthy, it would have been enough. She'd never wanted to talk to strangers, certainly not after being seen to have followed them; what message did that send? And why was Bess taking so long getting back? Janet stood at the farmhouse gate staring down the track for signs of her coming.

Bess took such a long time to return that Janet feared her Father would get home before her, a situation that would require explanation, and Janet didn't know how she'd cope with that.

She was just about to go looking for Bess, feeling that it would be best if both of them were absent should Edward come home, when a laden figure appeared on the track.

Initially Janet thought it was someone else, she'd been carrying the bag with their lunch in, Bess had been carrying nothing. The lone figure was carrying something, a bundle, hastily wrapped.

Realising that it was Bess, Janet ran to her.

'Oh Bess! I was gettin' so worried fer yoo. I'm so sorry I left yoo but…'

'No need fer explanations, Jan, ya like a sester to me, et was I that made yoo go to Pierowall. I made yoo uncomfortable, I realise that. The young fisherman was quite insistent that I follow after yoo. He was so gorgeous. Then his Master appeared an' he thought I was such a lovey theng that he gave me some fish.'

'Bess, yoo donny know them, yoo should have declined the fish…'

Bess opened the top of her bundle revealing two large fish, 'I couldne turn them down, look how good an' fresh they are.'

Janet had to admit they looked good, but they would mean confessing to Edward the unladylike conduct their day had included.

'Nonsense. We juss tell hem we bought some fish.'

Janet didn't like lying to her Father, but it certainly seemed better than telling the truth and being sent back to Mary early.

Janet looked again at the bundle Bess carried, 'What else have yoo got Bess? Yoo've more than fish en there…'

'I learned somethin'.' Bess started walking towards the Farm again. 'That head Fisherman… he saw my necklace…' Bess was beaming, Janet could tell that Bess was overflowing with excitement. 'He recognised et Jan! Et was my Mother's, yoo remember me tellin' yoo?'

'Aye.' Janet's attention was no longer fixed on the bundle.

'He'd last seen the necklace around my Mother's neck! Turns oot she was one o' the first people he met when he came to the islands, there on the beach o' Pierowall bay; e'en helped her collect driftwood along the shore. Jan, yoo know the lettle tumble-doon cottage?'

153

Janet's mind was suddenly ahead of Bess's story. 'Oh! No. Oh Bess…'

'What? Jan, et's great news. The cottage es mine, et belonged to my Mother, et's mine by right…'

Janet was silent, her eyes back on the bundle.

'Et's where I've ben, yoo seemed reluctant weth all the stories yoo've grown up weth. Et seemed a good opportunity to look o'er et properly.'

They reached the Farmhouse door and entered.

'Yoo should see what I found.'

A strange curiosity filled Janet's head, she took Bess's arm and led her to their bedroom, it would buy them time to stow the bundle should her father return, for she knew how he'd react if he found out where it had come from.

Bess had spent some considerable time exploring the two rooms of the cottage. Janet had seen the first, with its completely fallen roof, but Bess, looking harder, had found that part of the old roof obscured a doorway. The second room still possessed part of its roof and, compromised though this was, it afforded a dry corner, and in the corner was a box with a lid, lit by the light spilling through the glassless window.

Sitting by the foot of the bed, Janet watched nervously as Bess unpacked her loot.

'Look.' Bess's voice flowed with a luxuriant, almost seductive tone, as she pulled a beautiful piece of fabric from a fish free fold in the bundle. 'Feel et.'

Janet found herself experiencing the soft kiss of the silk before Bess swept it up around her neck. 'Oh, Bess…'

'Shhh, look at thess.' Another fine fabric emerged, lace this time, exquisitely worked. 'I canny imagine any man resistin' me ef he catch a glimpse o' thess…'

'Bess!'

'Oh, donny be so cold to the thought o' love, Jan…'

'I could ne'er be cold to love, I desire et's warmth, but Bess, beware o' lust, fer men are inflamed weth et fer the sight o' so allurin' a theng.'

Bess giggled and Janet joined in, but Janet realised that Bess's take on love was starkly different to her own.

Next out of the bundle, depleting it almost entirely was the immaculate pelt of a seal pup. Janet felt deeply attracted to it but there was another thing troubling her. 'Dear Bess, all these thengs, fer all the years they've sat undamaged en that decayin' place, does et no' strike yoo as unlikely?'

Bess frowned, 'What do yoo mean?'

'Bess, they feel new, they smell fresh… Ken we be sure they donny belong to someone else?'

'How so?'

'Perhaps hidden?'

Bess's eyes glinted warmly, 'Feel the pelt, Jan.'

Before Janet could protest, she felt her fingertips collide with the skin, she gasped, 'Et's so warm.'

Bess frowned; she had expected "soft".

'Et's like ya holdin' a live seal pup.' Janet felt a strong desire to take it, to place it around her shoulders… she tore her fingers away, 'How? How es et so well kept, so clean, so untouched by decay. Such fine thengs, Bess. How?'

The door of the Farmhouse opened and closed, 'Girls? Are yoo here?'

Bess, eyes wide, quickly dropped the pup skin onto the bundle and started to push it under the bed. To Bess's annoyance Janet stopped her abruptly, pulling the bundle back and opening the fold on top to reveal the fish. Bess's distress turned to mirth at her oversight as Janet retrieved the food and headed to the door. 'We're juss back ourselves Dad,' She opened the bedroom door and peered down the stairs. 'Oh!'

Bess, puzzled by Janet's exclamation, shoved the bundle firmly under the bed and joined her friend who was now giggling and holding up the fish.

At the bottom of the stairs Edward stood, also holding up some fish. 'I had to go to Pierowall. When I saw the Fishermen, I thought et would be nice t'have some fish tonight.'

Janet started walking down the stairs, 'We saw them at midday, an' thought exactly the same.'

'My treat, to say thanks fer bein' so kind.' Bess added.

Edward smiled warmly, touched by Bess's apparent thoughtfulness. He laughed, 'Why ded yoo take them upstairs?'

'Oh, et wasne intentional, we're only juss back an' we were puttin' our bags away, an'… well, et was earlier that we'd got them. We'd had such a lovely afternoon we'd almost forgotten they were en the bag.'

Edward looked at Bess, Bess nodded affirmation and smiled. 'Well, what shall we do weth five Trout?'

Two of the fish made their way into a stew of herbs and a pleasant meal ensued. They exchanged their surprise at having not bumped into each other, but it turned out that Edward had approached Pierowall over land, not along the coastal trackway. The girls learnt that Edward knew the fishermen well, and that the Head Fisherman had asked him to come back at the end of the week, as he had a surprise for him.

Janet noticed Bess frown. Bess had been very attentive to Edward, almost uncomfortably so; this was a notable change. Janet was about to ask what was wrong when there came a knock on the door.

Chapter thirty-five

It was Edward's near neighbour. 'Evenin' Edward. There's goods washin' ashore at Grobust. Yoo best come or yoo'll soon miss oot.'

It was not uncommon for goods to be washed ashore, either from a wreck or from the lightening of cargo during a storm, but it was hard to tell which had caused the objects washed ashore at Grobust, for although there had been a storm a few nights before, no one had seen a vessel in distress, and there was no actual wreckage washed up. By the time Edward and the girls arrived with a small handcart, most of the items worth having had been claimed by other Islanders, many already leaving, and Edward estimated that they had about a half hour before returning home to beat the fall of night.

What little they did get was grabbed from the waves, items that had only just arrived too, a keg of rum, a linen sheet, a length of rope…

Janet, although certainly more confident that the sea didn't pose as immediate a threat as she'd grown up fearing, had still chosen to stay clear of the breakers, weaving her way up and down the ribs of bedrock that jutted out from the west end of the bay.

Janet's search looked like being totally fruitless, a passing Islander informing her that most of the spoils had been washed up as far as Scaun, near a mile further North. Never-the-less Janet continued a little longer, finally discovering a child's shoe. Cradling the object in her hand, Janet stared first at it then out to sea. It seemed certain to her that lives had been lost, that the vessel from which these objects had come had been swallowed up and now sat with its ghosts on the sea floor. A wave crashed heavily on the rocks nearby and Janet hurried back up the beach to the others.

Bess was already at the handcart; Edward had sent her there whilst he made one final sweep of the decreasing shore. 'Anythin'?'

'Juss thess.' Janet opened her hand to show the tiny shoe.

'Oh, that's sad.'

Janet scratched a shallow hole in the sand, placed the shoe in it and buried it. 'Bess…'

'Yes, Jan.'

'Yoo seemed to be troubled when Dad told us aboot the Head Fisherman's promise o' a surprise at the end o' the week.'

Bess responded with a long silence.

'Bess? Wha's wrong?'

Bess sighed, 'I was goin' to tell yoo at the end o' the week. The Fisherman didne juss know my mother, he said he knew my father too. He said he'd be at the quay Friday afternoon.'

'Tha's good; we ken walk to Pierowall weth my father, to meet…'

'Oh Jan! Donny yoo see? Ya father es my father. I'm *his* surprise!'

Janet stared. 'I donny see how; I'm my father's only child.'

Bess giggled, 'His an' Gwen's only child, but ya father an' my mother must have…'

'Oh… but I donny think he'd…'

'Oh Jan, es et no' good news, we're sesters!' Bess saw that Edward was returning to them, another length of rope coiled and slung over his shoulder. 'Hush now Jan, I stell wan' et to be a surprise fer hem.'

Janet noticed how Bess stared longingly at her father, but despite understanding Bess's suggestion, she still could not believe he'd be untrue to Gwen.

They'd headed quickly off towards home, Janet gazing - deep in thought - out across the rocks she'd scrambled over, out where the breakers still smashed heavily as they reclaimed the beach. There amidst the seaweed stood a small, bedraggled animal, like an ugly seal pup with gangly legs. It stared back at her.

'Father.'

Edward looked where Janet was pointing. 'Seems the wreck has a survivor after all.' Edward left them on the trackway and attempted to collect the dog from the rocks, but it ran away from him. He tried a couple more times, but with the day fading he gave up and returned to the girls. 'We've got to go, before we lose the light. Either et well follow or go ets own way. Come on.'

As Edward and Bess headed away, Janet stared down the beach to where the animal had run. She saw it looking again. 'Come on!' but it held fast and Janet, prompted by the fading light, felt obliged not to tarry.

Despite turning many times to look for the creature, Janet didn't see it. They stowed the handcart in the barn and headed inside.

There was some talk about the evening's unexpected activity, but all were soon in their beds and ready for sleep. Janet remained awake for some time, troubled by the little shoe, the little dog and Bess's bold beliefs. But there was something more; the room seemed to have a faint luminescence to it, an indistinct, barely perceptible glow - usually it was pitch black - Janet lay open-eyed for a long time, focused on the sleeping shape of the girl who claimed to be her Sister; why didn't she feel excited by the prospect of her best friend being related? No, that was wrong, deep inside she was hopeful of some truth in Bess's presumption, it further sealed their love for each other. No, there was something else troubling her, was it her father's silence over the years or was it the connection Bess had with the little crumbling cottage and its previous owner?

Janet turned her attention to the room, was there a full moon outside causing the eerie absence of complete darkness? She quietly crossed the room to reach the window. No, it was impenetrably black beyond the glass. She turned, expecting some light to be entering the room from a neglected candle on the landing; to her surprise the source was beneath the bed!

Now she was a bit frightened, but she approached the bed and crouched down to look closer. A faint, green glow was escaping from the bundle that Bess had pushed hurriedly beneath. Janet's first response was to fully close the bundle returning the room to darkness, but then she felt an uncontrollable curiosity and pulled the bundle towards her.

She opened the bundle allowing the green light to return. She glanced up. Bess was sound asleep, her back to Janet. Janet peered nervously into the bundle. Beneath the hastily stowed fabrics was another object, a leather-bound collection of papers. Had Bess kept the existence of this from her, or had her Father's return interrupted Bess's presentation?

The green glow was coming from a small gem, not dissimilar to the one in Bess's necklace, elaborately worked into the leather cover with a silver thread, suddenly Janet felt scared, the pup skin seemed to touch her of its own accord. She nearly screamed but pulled the bundle tightly shut instead. It would all have to go; Bess would have to take it away. None of this belonged in the Farmhouse, and certainly not in the bedroom. Janet pushed the bundle back where Bess had placed it and returned herself to the bed, the rooms welcome darkness easing her mind.

Come morning though, all memory of the light, even of the bundle, was gone from Janet's recollection.

Chapter thirty-six

The rest of the week fell away, all three now stood on the quay, the head fisherman approaching them, arms wide. A weathered Merchantman was moored nearby, a number of cattle on its deck.

Edward accepted a hearty hug and slap on the back. 'Edward, Edward, I have somethin' fer yoo.'

Several members of the community, most of whom Janet knew from the Kirk, were suddenly appearing from buildings beside the quay.

Bess, who had practically skipped to Pierowall, now began to doubt her interpretation of the fisherman's intentions, this was some local celebration, a civic event, a presentation for something deserved, recognition of efforts made that benefitted all, not the presentation of a long-lost daughter. She somehow diminished into Janet's shadow.

Edward seemed confused, 'Wha's all thess, Daniel?'

Janet began to realise that Bess's expectations had been dashed.

'Edward, yoo have given the local community e'ery moment spare to yoo, to rebuild the Kirk. Ya craftsmanship has ensured the future o' the buildin'. Ya sacrifice has ben an example to young an' old alike. Et's fer thess reason we'd like yoo to accept our geft as a thank yoo.' Daniel gestured to the animals on the ship at the quayside.

'Fer me?' Edward shook his head. 'No, et's too much, I...'

'Six heifers, Edward. Accept them or we'll think the less o' yoo!'

Those gathered laughed and clapped, Edward accepted, and the animals were led ashore. He thanked his neighbours, but they insisted that it was the least they could do in return for his selfless hard work.

Janet was drawn into conversation with a group of the womenfolk, and learnt that her father had been losing animals over the previous few months - at least four older cows - down at Tuquoy Bay, the southmost point of her Father's land; this was where he had been going every day since the girls had been on the island, for there he was constructing a stone wall to keep his stock away from the sea.

Bess had withdrawn herself from the crowd, and was sitting on the low wall at the far end of the quay, staring out towards Papa Westray.

Daniel gave a little cough as he approached so as not to startle her, but she'd already noticed him coming, a wiry, unappealing man at his side. Bess already knew that this was her Father and that her invitation to the quay at the same time as Edward was coincidental; the man with Daniel being associated with the vessel that had brought the livestock.

'Bess, I'd like yoo to meet Finulf Skebister...'

Bess sighed.

'Thess es the man I told yoo aboot.'

Bess turned, giving Finulf the briefest of glances. He was as smartly dressed as a man in his role could have been, he had clearly made an effort. He was older than Edward and not so upright with more grey about his hair, but for all his wiriness he looked strong... 'Where were yoo?' She'd been willing to totally forgive Edward for his absence in her life, she recognised the complications - a new-born of his own, a poorly wife, other family members present - but this sailor... Why hadn't he come for her, why hadn't he looked after her?

'Beggin' ya forgiveness miss, I knew nothin' o' yoo 'tel I were told that a wee bearin' had ben shipped weth Erka to Mainland.'

Daniel excused himself and headed away. Finulf continued, 'I would help her, see, collectin' driftwood, she fascinated me. Others... they teased me, said I were playin' weth fire, fer she had a reputation. I juss saw her as a knowin' creature... gifted. At times she could influence the weather, fair winds to set to sea by...'

'So, what? Yoo brought her fine fabrics from o'er the sea to charm her? To bed her?' Bess accused.

'Et was quite the other way, she ded charm me. She asked me to find rare spices, powders, herbs that were no' native to the islands. I found them all. T'was then that she let me to her bed...'

Bess juddered, visibly disapproving.

'Nay, please, donny judge me as an opportunist, fer my part I loved her...'

'Yoo didne stop them when they came fer her...'

'I was away… at sea, ets my life… Et suited ya mother, she was a solitary creature, wild, rare. Et would have crazed her to have another always there, always en her way… Ken I see et?'

Bess was caught off guard by Finulf's last words. 'What? See what?'

'The necklace…' Finulf's eyes flicked from Bess's eyes to her neck and back again, the chain of her mother's necklace just visible. '…Daniel said yoo stell have et.'

Bess instinctively protected the jewel, her hand clutching it through her clothing, but Finulf's eyes looked so sad, so lost, that she relented and drew the necklace into sight.

Finulf licked his lips, his sad eyes had rounded with an intensity that Bess didn't understand. Had he wanted to meet her, or had he just wanted to see this thing he'd once seen about the neck of his lover and had now learnt adorned her? She thrust it back out of sight, fearing he might try and grab it from her, but his reaction surprised her.

Finulf clapped his hands, laughed and danced, 'I feel good! After all thess time I find et's true, I am so happy to find yoo Bess, please fergive me. I ded go to mainland when I heard a wee one was weth Erka, but by the time I came…' he hung his head, 'Erka had already received the penalty they'd laid upon her. I had no clue as to where a lettle one might be an', o'er time, the truth faded ento a hopeful story.'

Bess noticed something else, Finulf's whole manner seemed lighter, younger, even his hair seemed less grey somehow. Her hand gripped the pendant about her neck once more, did it possess power? Had something of her Mother's art been passed on to her?

Finulf offered his hand, 'Come. Yoo've stayed away from the gatherin' too long. Let us add to the joy an' celebration.'

And so it was, and those who'd gathered to thank Edward rejoiced also in Finulf's joy. Bess was warming to the idea of him, learning more as folk filled the gaps. He was Captain of his Merchantman, "Seabird", and had many times shared with those he knew in Pierowall of his visits to Mainland, and his searching of the crowds in hope of seeing Erka's eyes in a child.

One Islander was not so happy. Mrs. Dooney had been the one who first spotted Erka was pregnant, she knew that Finulf, and possibly other sailors, had visited Erka in the nights leading up to her being with child. This innocent looking girl was the daughter of a known witch, conceived in unholy union. Mrs. Dooney was convinced that Bess should be treated with utmost caution. She approached Bess, leant close to her and whispered, 'I know what Yoo are, I'm watchin' yoo, yoo'll get nothin' by me.' Then she disappeared off through the crowd, heading home without talking to anyone else.

The gathering had lasted into the evening, the appearance of Daniel's younger fishermen with food, ale and instruments had led to dancing and singing. Bess had been roused to hatred by Mrs. Dooney, but now her heart was as light as those of the revellers around her, for Dooney had not returned and some plan had come to mind that satisfied and excited her. Benjamin had been there too. Janet now recognised him, for he was dressed in smarter clothes with his long hair tied back from his face, and she realised he had been the one who had challenged them from the harbour wall. Both girls thought him a fine young man; he had danced with Bess and spoken quietly to Janet.

As Edward and the girls headed home, aided by the flickering light of torches, Bess had spoken openly of how much Ben must like her, but Janet remained silent about the looks she'd received from him and the brief conversation they'd had.

Chapter thirty-seven

All had retired by candlelight, Bess had talked Janet to sleep, but something caused Janet to stir later.

Allowing her eyes to open, Janet was not prepared for what was happening. The room was bathed in a soft, green light. A quiet, melodic voice was repeating undiscernible words, and Bess was absent from the bed. Where was Bess? Janet rolled, sitting herself on the edge of the bed, her answer immediately apparent.

163

Kneeling with her back to Janet, Bess was a dark silhouette against the emerald glow, nightdress discarded, the smooth line of her naked shoulders broken by her cascading, black hair.

Seeing the garment close behind her friend, Janet stepped quickly from the bed, picked it up and began to restore it to its rightful place.

'Oh, no, my lettle one, my lettle pup. Mother has some werk to do, return to ya slumber…'

Janet frowned, it wasn't Bess's voice, but the very thought was swept aside by a heavy wave of drowsiness. Her eyes flicking between the glowing, green gem around Bess's neck and the open leather-bound tome as all else grew quickly dark.

'Aye, sleep my lettle pup, heavy ya eyes, vacant ya dreams, seared ya memory…'

Janet's eyes already closed, she felt the warmth of a body close, assisting her back into the welcoming oblivion of the bed.

'Sleep…'

Janet was woken at first light by a whimpering noise coming from outside. She stepped quickly from the bed and crossed the room to the window. Out on the track sat the strange little dog, it was sitting, staring straight up at her.

'Bess, Bess…'

Bess stirred and grunted, pulling the covers tightly around her.

'…et's that lettle dog.'

'Mmm.' Bess acknowledged.

Janet looked back at Bess. Something troubled her… Had Bess been up in the night? Was she unwell? No, everything was fine, it was just early, best to let her sleep. Janet looked back through the window. 'Oh! the dog's gone again…'

'Shhh.'

Janet smiled and headed downstairs for something to eat; this might serve her purposes.

'I juss saw that dog, Father.'

Edward was preparing some porridge, 'Aye, I heard et, but couldne see anythin'.'

'Et was on the track the other side o' the yard wall.'

Edward laughed, 'Daft lettle theng.'

'I think I'll have a lettle to eat an' go see ef I ken find et.'

'Ha, good luck weth that, et's way too timid, yoo saw how et was on the beach, et'll run a mile from yoo an' Bess.'

'Oh, Bess es fast asleep, I think I'll go alone - less frightenin' fer the wee creature.'

Edward nodded, 'Well, ef anyone's gonna friend et, yoo've got the best chance.'

Half an hour later, and with Bess still sound, Janet was heading off down the track towards the Bay of Brough. The dog had been a convenient excuse, Benjamin had told her that he'd be tending a damaged net in the bay if she wished to be passing. Janet very much wished so, and it seemed very provident to her that Bess was so dopey after the late night. She asked herself again if there wasn't also some disturbance in the night, had Bess been out of sorts? She stopped walking, should she return to see after her friend? Looking back, she found that she was already a fair distance from the farm, but more surprisingly just seven steps behind her was the dog.

Janet stepped towards it, 'Hello.'

The dog barked and shot away.

Janet shrugged, and continued her journey to the bay.

In sight of the beach Janet heard a padding sound behind her, she glanced briefly to confirm her suspicion that the animal had returned. On seeing Janet's eyes, it made to run away again, but when Janet carried on walking it checked its flight and continued to follow. Janet smiled and began to sing a Kirk song quietly as she picked her route through the tussocky grass.

'O' the Father's love begott'n,
Ere the worlds began to be,
He es Alpha an' Omega,
He the source, the endin' He,
O' the thengs that are, that have ben,

An' that future years shall see.

At His Werd the worlds were framèd;
He commanded; et was done:
Heaven an' Earth an' depths o' the sea
En their threefold order one;
All that grows beneath the shinin'
O' the moon an' burnin' sun…'

There was no sign of Benjamin on the beach but Janet knew it was still early and Benjamin was coming from Moclett not Pierowall. A local waved from their cottage at the northmost end of the beach and Janet returned the pleasantry. She was too far away to speak to and Janet considered visiting to kill time, but seeing the dog had now appeared at the edge of the sand, Janet sat down quietly on a flat rock.

'Ef yoo wanna stay weth me, ya welcome.' Janet made momentary eye contact.

The dog yapped unthreateningly, it was thin, its fur matted and, in some places, missing.

'Are yoo hungry?' Janet lifted her bag and reached inside; the dog tensed. 'Et's Ok, I've brought a lettle food to share weth Benjamin, ya welcome to a piece o' meat…' Janet revealed a thin sliver of beef, the dog tilted its head. 'Come on then.' She waved the slice; the dog edged a couple of steps forward before shying and backing off again. Janet relented and threw the meat to the animal. Staring at Janet it sidled towards the food, snatched it up, swallowed it whole and glanced down at the bag.

Janet giggled, 'Oh! No… I'll have nothin' fer Benjamin ef I give et all to ya self.'

The dog came two steps closer and sat down.

Chapter thirty-eight

Several minutes passed, Janet talking, sometimes singing, until the dog jumped to its feet again. Its attention was beyond Janet and towards the sea. Janet turned to see a small boat, its owner pulling on oars and heading for a marker buoy. She stood, awaiting the moment that Benjamin would gaze her way, allowing her to wave.

Benjamin, clearly focused on his work, dealt with the collection of a net from the marker first, then turning and waving he headed in to the beach.

Driving his boat purposely onto the sand nearby, the young fisherman leapt from it and greeted Janet. 'So good to see yoo.'

His advance towards Janet was suddenly halted by the dog as it bolted between them, barking furiously.

Janet didn't want this at all, 'Stop et!'

Benjamin returned to the boat and approached again with a fish. 'Et's fine, he's hungry es all. Here yoo go fella.'

The dog had been giving ground again, seeing that Benjamin lacked a fear of him, but the fish was a good size and had been thrown just feet away. He darted to it, picked it up and ran up the beach to the cover afforded by the tussocks of grass.

'He's a yappy lettle theng, very protective o' yoo…'

'Oh, et's no' mine, well er… I donny think ets anyone's, et appeared earlier en the week up at Grobust, there were goods washed ashore…'

'Was he washed ashore too?'

'I think so, no' relly sure, seems no' to have any owner here though, donny know anythin' aboot et. Yoo reckon et's a he dog?'

'Aye, I could see his testicles when he ran away from me.'

Janet blushed.

'Oh, what I meant to say was "Aye, I'm sure on et." Sorry.'

Both stood awkwardly for a moment, Janet finally breaking the silence, 'Yoo've brought ya net ashore, does et need attention?'

'Aye. Daniel noticed et was torn the other day; when we saw yoo an'

Bess on the beach.'

Another silence.

'Ken I help yoo weth et? I used to mend them on the quayside at Kirkwall...'

'Sure.' Benjamin returned to the boat to get it.

'I used to look fer yoo...' Janet succumbed to her own nerves and fell silent, but there was nothing wrong with Benjamin's hearing, He returned with the net...

'Wha's that, yoo used to look fer me? When?'

'When the Victory Star was en, though I now know yoo were no longer on et.'

'Even ef I had ben, I rarely got to the deck; Miley used to gev me chores below when we were at harbour...'

'One o' the crew told me that Miley fell o'erboard.'

Benjamin sat on the flat rock and pulled the net close to inspect the scale of the tear; it was big. 'Everythin' changed that day.' He seemed troubled and thoughtful.

Janet sat next to him and lifted the net to afford Benjamin better access to the damage. 'Well yoo tell me aboot et?'

Benjamin looked at her, then back at the net. 'Miley wasne the wellest o' men, he drank an' ate too much. A crew member called Lang protested aboot carryin' yoo to Mainland when he heard what yoo were accused o'. Miley had yoo restricted to a cabin to appease hem, but e'en after yoo'd left, he kept on at Miley, said he'd cursed the ship, 'specially as et came to wider knowledge that yoo'd ben on deck...'

'Why ded yoo let me oot?' Janet asked.

'Saw yoo boardin', yoo were so scared... I took pity on yoo.'

'I dedne wanna leave my Father an' I was scared o' the water.'

'Miley didne seem right that evenin', nor when we set off the next day, he looked pale, he juss stood at the side watchin' the sea. I saw hem. By the Calf o' Eday he glazed o'er an' tumbled forward; I reckon the weight o' his clothes dragged hem doon, fer he often wore many layers fer sake o' warmth. Lang got all uptight, kept goin' on aboot thess curse, but Drew scolded hem an' had hem flogged fer such talk on the ship. Theng es, well... Drew... he didne much like that I'd let yoo on deck. Maybe he thought yoo *had* charmed me, I donny know but he sought to part me from the crew at his earliest opportunity...' Benjamin seemed quite agitated now.

'P'haps we should talk o' somethin' else, yoo seem upset.'

'Drew took somethin' that rightly belonged to me; Miley had said I should have et when he died.

'The box...'

'Yoo know aboot my box?' Benjamin stated, looking into her eyes, obviously surprised.

Janet blushed again, 'Et was when I looked fer yoo, a crewman called Ewan said there'd ben some dispute between Drew an' ya self aboot who owned a box that Miley had.'

'That box was mine, *es* mine, an' I'll get et back one day.'

'What was en et?'

'I donny know, but Miley said et was what few belongin's I'd ben found weth.'

'Ewan said yoo were an orphan...'

'Yoo know more aboot me than I know aboot yoo.' Benjamin looked up from the net, regarding Janet studiously.

'What yoo up to?' Janet laughed nervously.

'Was et true?'

'What?'

'The reason they took yoo from here to Mainland.'

Janet stopped laughing, she frowned, did he have to ask that? Did he not know the answer already?

Chapter thirty-nine

Suddenly the dog barked and headed off at pace towards the source of his displeasure. Bess appeared from where she'd been sitting, she'd clearly been there for a while because her skirt was creased, but the little dog had only just become aware of her.

As before, it stopped short. 'Oh, Janet, yoo found et, Edward said yoo'd gone to look fer et.' Bess walked towards the animal, forcing it to give ground, but it didn't do so for long. Without warning the bark became a growl and the dog stood firm. Bess froze. 'Call et away Janet, I donny wesh to be bitten.'

Janet noticed that Bess's necklace was not tucked away as it usually was, and that the green gem was catching the morning sunlight and flashing into the dog's eyes, 'Et's ya jewel, Bess, tuck et away…'

Bess looked cross, but the animal looked ready to advance, so she did as she was told. Immediately the dog calmed and retreated to the couple on the beach. Janet crouched down, it was the closest she'd got and she gently stroked it. 'Oh Bess, he's shakin'…'

'He's shakin'? *I'm shakin'!*' Bess turned to Benjamin. 'Yoo saw et, et was aboot to bite me!'

'I think yoo surprised hem, he was just bein' protective. How long were yoo there anyway?'

Bess realised she'd displeased Benjamin, 'No' long, I er, didne want to interrupt yoo.'

Benjamin leant close to Janet's ear. 'I've no idea what came o'er me…' He whispered. 'O' course ya nay wetch, though I think yoo've cast a love spell on the dog.'

The animal was sitting quietly at Janet's feet, staring up at her with big eyes and full acceptance, as if awaiting her command.

Bess remained stationary.

'Come an' make friends.' Janet urged.

Bess dismissed any idea of befriending the creature, 'Et's juss a stupid dog. Et hasne e'en got a neem.'

'His neem's Boy.' Janet informed.

The dogs stumpy tail thumped the beach rapidly.

Bess had a thought, 'Ef yoo like I'll go an' get us somethin' to eat…'

'No need.' Janet replied. 'I've got a lettle, but et's only enough fer two.'

Bess then realised that Janet had intended to meet Benjamin; hearing that her provisions were only for two left Bess with little doubt that *she* wasn't part of Janet's plan for the day. That riled her so she attempted to break the couple's tryst. 'Do yoo wanna collect shells?' She knew Janet loved shells.

'We're workin' on thess net.' Benjamin pointed out.

'Sorry.' Janet added.

'Fine.' Bess headed off towards the rocks.

Benjamin and Janet continued with the net until Bess was a good distance off.

'Now I feel bad.' Janet admitted.

'Yoo shouldne; she was listenin' en. What friend does that?'

'She's ben so kind; I was so alone en Kirkwall 'til she drew close to me.'

'The local folks talk darkly o' her mother.'

'I dedne know her. There was much talk as I was growin' up, mostly when we passed the old cottage...' Janet paused thoughtfully. 'But folk do accuse, an' there's often nothin' en et.'

Benjamin nodded. 'No' sure I trust her.'

'She's Ok, honest... She likes yoo.'

Benjamin remained silent.

Janet looked back at the net, 'What causes these gashes? We didne mend anythin' like thess en Kirkwall.'

'Daniel talks aboot a creature that robs nets, but et's only e'er an outward lyin' net, the rocks are rougher oot there an' the current strong.'

'No' much frayin' fer rock wear. Es Daniel's creature the one I've heard aboot?'

'Daniel says we shouldne...'

'I know,' Janet interrupted. 'We shouldne say ets neem... so et *es* that one?'

Benjamin stopped mending the net; he looked out towards Papa Westray. 'I've only e'er heard stories. Some o' the crew on the Victory Star mentioned et when Miley died, but usually the talk es o' how et spreads disease or takes livestock.'

Janet pondered the creature taking livestock, was that how her father had lost some of his cattle? Why he was building a wall to keep his stock away from the shore?

'Et's all a bit of an answer-all to me. Ef somethin's lost, or sick, or damaged, et's thess one cause.'

'Has Daniel said what et looks like?'

'Yes, he calls et a bloodied horse weth two heads an' long skinny arms, but et's only what he's ben told, he's no' seen et either.'

'I've seen et.' Bess called loudly. Janet and Benjamin had thought her too far away to hear; they now wondered how much she *had* heard. She started moving towards them again. The dog, which had been lying by Janet's feet, was growling quietly.

'Hush now, Boy.' Janet whispered. The animal stopped, sat, stared up at Janet and waited for further instruction.

Bess was still a little way away when she continued. 'I was en Kirkwall when the trouble came. Robert Stewart, illegitimate son o' Earl Patrick rose up against them that had imprisoned his black hearted father. He seized control, but an army under the authority o' Keng James came, dividin', trappin' an' siegin' Robert an' his men en the Earl's Palace, the Castle an' Cathedral. They brought en cannon on the Palace an' Castle, but the Castle was too strong. En the end one o' Robert's men betrayed them all. Et was a bloody endin' an' late en the day...'

'Wha's thess got to do weth the creature?' Benjamin interrupted.

Bess stopped just feet away, 'The bodies.'

Benjamin and Janet sat silently awaiting Bess's elaboration. Bess stared back at them.

'The bodies...' Benjamin prompted.

'Yes, en the night. No one had counted them. They'd juss ben pulled together fer the 'morrow, but there were one less by mornin'.'

Benjamin wasn't convinced, 'So... some relative came an' spirited their kin away to protect the family neem?'

'No, I saw et...'

'Yoo must have ben a wee child, what were yoo doin' to see anythin' so late en the day?'

'I was told to stay en. Bishop Law had to appease the army leader who was ready to tear doon the Cathedral as some sort o' punishment to the Islanders fer harbourin' rebellion. He'd already started demolishin' the castle. I had a way to creep oot - I always have - an' I followed. Law saved the Cathedral, he visited the dead, prayed en tears an' headed home. I had to hide as he passed, I was juss aboot to leave too when...' Bess paused again, staring back at the sea.

'What?'

Bess looked into Janet's eyes, 'I heard et... comin' up from the harbour. I froze. Et came ento view sniffin' an' breathin' loud. Et quickly crossed to the bodies, looked around, grabbed one up en et's gnarly fengers an' left. I ran home an' hid en my room.'

Benjamin returned to mending the net. Bess frowned, had she not just helped him to know for sure about the reality of the beast?

He looked back up, 'There are much better shells to be found on the Grobust.'

'Jan, es Benjamin tryin' to get rid o' me?' Bess had asked in jest but Janet's awkwardness seemed to hint that there was truth in the observation. 'Fine!' She headed up the beach towards Pierowall, the most direct route to Grobust.

Janet called after her, 'Oh Bess, donny be like that!' But Bess just kept on walking.

Janet stood but Benjamin took her hand, 'Let her go, Janet... Let her go.'

Janet smiled at Benjamin and turned her attention back to the net, but her heart was troubled and she felt it would remain so until she made peace with Bess.

Chapter forty

The net had been repaired quickly with Janet's help, giving Benjamin a short time to talk with her and share the food she had brought. Both instinctively knew they were close of heart and desire, but Benjamin was here to work. 'I have other duties I must attend to; Daniel well no' be pleased ef they're no' fulfilled.' Benjamin kissed Janet's hand, heaved the net over his shoulder and started for his boat.

'I'll see yoo 'gain soon?'

'Aye, at the Kirk tomorrow.'

Janet blushed, 'O' course.' She watched as Benjamin set out and restored the net to its position, then, with a last wave he focused on his boat and the waves. Janet, still troubled by Bess's departure, headed home for some bread.

Bess knew Janet was coming, but had wilfully ignored her calls.

Janet thought it strange that Bess had not heard her, seeing as she'd heard the much quieter conversation between Ben and herself earlier. She approached, admiring the oddly ornate patterns Bess had scratched into the sand at the water's edge. Bess was now standing motionless on the beach looking out at the swell, clutching her necklace in one hand. The sea seemed different here, wilder, less sheltered, and Bess somehow fitted the scene. Although she had not yet looked at Janet, Janet felt that her bearing was sad.

'Oh, dear Bess, I'm so…'

'Donny be apologisin', he's a fine man, yoo beat me es all.' Bess's gaze remained fixed on the choppy waves; her voice tinged with buried spite.

'I brought yoo a lettle bread, yoo must be hungry.'

Bess looked at her crossly, 'Yoo said yoo only had enough fer two!'

'I came by the Farm.'

The idea that Janet had considered her needs seemed to wash Bess's barriers down, 'Oh Jan, none well separate us, we are so close. We may no' be sesters by blood, but we may as well be, aye?' She took the bread, consuming it hungrily.

'Aye.' Janet looked anxiously at the horizon; the waves were biting into Bess's patterns and a squall could be seen to be rising out to sea. 'We best head home Bess, the weather's gettin' ill.'

'So et es.' They started to head up the beach towards home, Bess releasing her necklace, but not tucking it out of sight.

'Et's no' usual that yoo wear ya jewel openly…'

'Oh, et's a source O' joy to me now Jan, let et see the light I…' Bess stopped: She was looking at the low part of the cliff, where the path was.

'Wha's up?'

Bess pointed. The little dog was waiting there.

'Et's Ok Bess, he's very obedient, I told hem to stay there so that yoo wouldne be troubled when I came doon to yoo.'

Bess started walking again, reluctantly sliding the pendant out of sight, for she perceived that the animal had some genuine dislike of it. She looked back out to sea, 'Oh dear, Looks like we're all gonna get wet.' The downpour was racing up off the sea. 'I do hope ya Benjamin found shelter or made good progress home.'

To Janet there was a puzzling lightness, almost dismissiveness to Bess's comment, but before she could challenge her, Bess shot off, running in the direction of home, laughing and screaming with delight as the first heavy drops began to fall. The dog barked, cowering as she passed him and Janet gave chase.

Janet reached the Farmhouse first, Bess staggered up, panting heavily and the dog sat at the gate; all were wet through.

'Come on Boy.' Janet called. The dog approached.

Bess instantly protested, 'Oh, no, I'll no' put up weth et en the hoose.'

'Et's no' ya decision.'

Bess shrugged, 'Sure, but yoo donny know the creature yet, no' properly, what ef et starts smashin' ya Father's pots or bitin' the furniture. What would Edward say?'

Janet looked at the dog. She sighed; Bess was probably right. She looked up at the barn, 'Come on Boy, we'll get yoo en the dry at least.'

Janet had dried the dog as best she could with some old rags, then left him sitting obediently in some hay. 'I'll come back weth my father when he's home, to introduce yoo. Now I've got to get dry too.'

Janet walked into the kitchen to find Bess naked by the hearth, her clothes hung to dry in front of the flames. 'Bess! Fer decency go put somethin' on; my father could come home at any moment weth the weather turned as et es!'

Bess giggled lightly, 'I hadne thought o' that, Jan.' She headed for the bedroom.

Edward did return soon after, he'd finished his wall out by the bay and his stock seemed settled, so, seeing no likelihood of a let-up in the rain, he'd headed home. Janet introduced him to the dog, though he too was happier that it stayed in the barn. Seeing that the creature had settled nicely Janet agreed and so it was that Boy joined the family.

~

Garrie had crossed the dimly lit room at this point in his story, crouched down and stroked the little dog, the others watched in silence, readily accepting the old man's tale and the age it ascribed to the animal.

Garrie heaved himself back to his feet, placed a kettle by the fire and returned to the story.

~

Next day was bright and fresh, the sea was calm and gulls danced high above the shore. Rising early, Janet, Edward and Bess had made the short journey to the Kirk. They had stopped at Erka's cottage and to Janet's surprise Edward had offered to help in its restoration. Bess glanced at Janet, smiled and thanked him; his only stipulation was that it be stripped back to the walls and all the rot within burned. Bess had suggested that Benjamin could help them, but Janet didn't want to commit him without asking.

The Kirk had been restored well, although the night's rain had shown up a small leak in the roof. Edward offered to patch it but the Minister said he'd already spoken to a man from the town and that the repair would soon be done.

There was sad news that morning, for old Mrs. Dooney had passed away, quite unexpectedly, the night Edward had received the heifers. The Minister listed her many attributes and shared the nature of her pious and tireless work for the Island's community, ending with a request for individuals to step forward and take on some of the important elements of her work; Janet saw Bess disappear briefly with the Minister after the service, both returning light of mood and smiling as she and her father were preparing to head home.

Chapter forty-one

'Wo, wo, hold on!' Carl looked around at his startled companions. The Trows looked like three owl chicks staring out of the gloom, barely lit by the low flames of the fire, with unnaturally wide eyes. 'We keep hearing it in the story…'

Sally, hand on heart through the shock of Carl's outburst, tutted loudly, 'Hearing what?'

'Bess.'

The faces wanted more clarification.

'She's manipulating everything.'

'Well that's obvious,' Sally laughed, 'I've known that since Bess tucked Janet back into bed and Janet remembered nothing of the revelations of the night.'

'Ya both wrong.' Kayleigh interrupted.

Carl and Sally looked at her, how could anyone not see…

Garrie waited expectantly, the Trows pretended to whistle, but none of them could.

'Et's Erka's spirit…'

'Huh?' Carl managed.

'I'm right aren' I Mr. Garrie?'

Garrie acknowledged Kayleigh's interpretation with a nod.

'This is getting confusing.' Sally rested back against Carl.

He grunted again, 'Huh?'

'Bess had her mother's necklace, somethin' she'd always hedden away, she also had some profoundly well-preserved artefacts from her mother's cottage. Whilst Bess slept, Janet had found Erka's parchments en amongst the fabrics, an' e'en without Bess's intervention she fergot all aboot findin' them. At some point Erka's magic was awoken, some connection between the papers an' the necklace, perhaps e'en at the moment she discovered the documents en their bindin's en the cottage. But that moment o' connection allowed Erka to express her will through Bess. Oh, es dark magic fer sure.'

Carl ran his fingers through his hair, 'But if that's how it was, how was it that Janet ended up with the reputation of witchcraft? Why was she tried, and not Bess?'

Sally offered a thought, 'I guess Mary had seen to that opinion years before. Dragging Janet off Westray, shutting her away on the Victory Star, and all the trouble *that* caused. I'm guessing that crewmember, Lang... I guess he never let the idea go...'

Carl huffed, 'Lot of fuss over a lively child...'

'En line weth attitudes,' Kayleigh shrugged. 'The Kirk *was* the community then; any absentee would have ben doubted morally. The talk o' lettle people would have stirred memories o' pagan times, retuals an' rites. Et was the time o' King James en Janet's youth. James blamed wetches fer the loss o' one o' his ships en a storm as he returned from Denmark weth his new wife Anne. His ideas aboot wetches had ben born en Denmark where they hunted them. He became paranoid that they were actively tryin' to kill hem, so he instigated repeated wetch hunts an' trials, an' wrote a book "Daemonologie" to help others see the give-away signs. So, Mary was relly tryin' to protect Janet.'

Sally sat forward again, 'But she wasn't evil. Even as a child she attributed seeing Deni to God's Blessing, as a young woman she was attending the Kirk, she found love... What went wrong?'

Carl drove his point home, 'Like I said, Bess was manipulating everything, she wanted Benjamin...'

Kayleigh corrected him again, 'Erka was manipulatin'...

Carl shut up, the thought of witchcraft was becoming starkly real to him, but it wasn't just the use of herbs to heal or a quiet supplication for safe travel, this was frightening stuff. A woman long dead, waiting for connection between her magic and an artefact worn by her daughter, to possess her and... 'Hold on. Was there some feud between Erka and Janet's family?'

Kayleigh shook her head, 'We donny know Janet's family... Edward found her.'

Sally juddered, 'That's worse. If it's a feud with Edward then Janet shouldn't have been...'

Garrie interrupted the speculation, 'All thess well oot, Erka had her reasons to harm Janet...' He was standing again, back by the window although nothing could be discerned through it due to weight of lashing rain and darkness; the lightning merely illuminating the torrent rather than giving any hint of a landscape beyond. The very stones of the cottage seemed to vibrate with the roar of the billows without.

The debates that had flurried within were now silent, the Trows had made hot drinks and were distributing them. Everyone settled again for Garrie's continuation, although he seemed distracted by weighty thoughts at the window, and the words would be a little while coming.

Carl and Sally huddled together again, resting their backs against a wall, Kayleigh felt her fleece half-heartedly, aware it would still be wet. The Trows tended the fire, the dog and James.

Sally whispered to Carl, 'I need to talk to you, when this is all over.'

Carl nodded assurance, though he had no idea what she wished to say.

'Aye, Bess's deeds...' Garrie sighed. 'So diligent was she, that o'er the next few weeks she had become indispensable an' would, et turned oot, be stayin' on Westray when Janet returned to Mainland. The thought that one day, perhaps soon, Mary would send werd fer her to return, left Janet cold. She weshed to stay weth her father an' Benjamin.

'Weth Bess so busy, Janet began to spend more time weth Benjamin, an' weth her fear o' the water much subsided, he used his spare time to teach her how to handle sail an' oar.

'By Summer's decline, Bess was movin' en to her mother's cottage, ets once dark face now transformed by collected flowers, new glass an' fabric at the windows. Island life tecked on, an' Bess spoke to those she helped an' those she helped spoke to visitors... an' word got back to Mary that Janet spent much o' her time weth a course an' beguilin' fisherman.'

Sally recognised the complications, 'Oh dear.'

'Aye, "Oh dear" et was, but Mary was subtle, she came a few weeks later on the Victory Star, to see fer herself an' talk to Edward aboot what should be done.'

Chapter forty-two

Janet was out with Benjamin on Daniel's own praam. Daniel, becoming aware of Benjamin's connection to Janet, had encouraged it by giving him more work that could be quickly finished, affording him more time with his young lady. The small sailing praam was a further effort to strengthen the bond between the two youngsters, especially as Benjamin had no real family of his own. The boat was small and fast; Janet, growing in confidence on the water, loved it, because they sat closer and the little launch was cleaner than Benjamin's fishing boat.

Benjamin had taken Janet to the north of Westray, looking at some of the shallows that caused ships to wreck. Noup Head seemed particularly dangerous, a sheet of rock sat just out of sight and could easily hole the underside of a laden vessel, even at high tide if the weather was heavy; the cliffs too, large and vertical, offered no escape for a ship driven against them by a storm. The only mercy here were a few caves, where a survivor might seek shelter until help arrived.

Returning home, the couple were greeted by the sight of the Victory Star, freshly arrived and moored at Pierowall.

Benjamin grinned, 'Well, well, thess es a rare opportunity.'

Janet knew instantly what he was thinking, for he'd often lamented being too busy with his work when the ship was docked. She turned to him assertively, 'Now Ben, donny do anythin' daft.'

'O' Jan, I'm at my leisure, I canny miss thess.'

'Yoo've no place on that ship, Benjamin Garrioch…'

Benjamin laughed at Janet's use of his full name, 'Nor has what belongs to me.' He swung the boat flat against the harbour wall, and making it secure he leapt up the stone steps.

'Ben!'

'Shh!' He peered over the top of the wall. 'Och, et's fine Jan, Daniel es there; they're loadin' fish fer Kirkwall. The Victory Star well be settin' oot wethin the hour fer tide's sake, et's now or ne'er. I'm gonna help load the fish.'

Janet watched Benjamin disappear from sight, then, feeling somewhat impotent to help, she sat with a heavy sigh and struck the side of the praam in frustration. Almost despairingly, she began topray, 'O' Lord, keep hem safe, help hem find wha's his…'

'No, I'll have that here.'

The owner of the voice was out of sight, but Janet knew who it belonged to, she quickly ascended the harbour steps and peeped. There receiving a bag from a sailor was Mary, looking particularly well dressed and in robust form. Janet looked at the ship, the last of the cargo was being loaded but there was no sign of Benjamin.

'Finally.'

Janet looked towards some barrels sitting on the harbour wall, straight into the eyes of Ewan. 'Oh, Hello.' She had hoped to stay out of sight and head off with Benjamin in the praam when he returned, now she knew she had to cover for him so he could slip away. She raised her hand for Ewan to help her up the last steps; an act he quickly stepped to. 'I've juss ben oot on the water, are yoo here long?'

'No Miss Forsyth, we've gotta make good weth the tide today, an we've got perishable goods to deliver.'

'Oh, what a shame.'

'Aye et es, I'd heard yoo've ben weth ya father here on Westray, but I hadne seen yoo 'tell now…'

'Ewan! What are yoo doin' man! Get the rest O' those barrels onto the quay, yoo know we're pressed fer time.'

'Aye Drew!'

'Oh, deliverin' too.' Janet's spirits rose for she could see that Benjamin still had time and Drew was out of the way.

Ewan headed off apologetically, Janet dismissed him with a smile of relief and on turning away realised that Mary was now aware of her presence.

'Janet; an' to think *that* sailor was the reason we sent yoo to ya father, have yoo nay shame...'

'He spoke to me first Aunt Mary, et would have ben rude to...'

'I'll have none o' ya backchat girl, or I'll think ya behaviour's slippin' fer my absence.'

Janet swung her arms about Mary's neck. 'Oh dear, dear Aunt, I'm so happy to see yoo.' Looking over Mary's shoulder she saw the startled face of Lang as he recognised her and stumbled to give as wide a space as he could between them. She continued to hold Mary as she watched Lang ascending the gangplank. He had misjudged his ascent; turning to step onto the boat, he stepped instead into the air beside the plank, plummeting with a frustrated cuss, into the water below. There was a chorus of laughter from his fellow sailors; two of whom offered down a pole to collect him. Finally, Janet felt Mary recover from the suddenness of her embrace, better still she was returning it!

'Och, Janet, yoo've ben away so long, I've missed yoo, but that Ewan has a reputation...'

'As long as I live, I'll no' talk to hem again, Auntie.'

'Juss as well, fer I hear news that might give yoo a worse reputation ef ya seen fraternisin' weth such as Ewan Cedigan too.'

Janet's mind was about to touch on what that news might be when she noticed a commotion on the deck of the ship. It was Benjamin! A crew member had thrust him out of a door beneath the poop deck and was marching him towards the gangplank. Lang, dripping wet and spitting salty water, scurried by him with a black look of disdain.

Drew appeared on the quayside as Benjamin was bundled down it, 'Wha's thess?' He prevented Benjamin from walking away.

The sailor at the top of the gangplank claimed he'd found the fisherman in Drew's cabin.

Janet turned to Mary, 'Have yoo got all ya belongings Auntie?' She picked up two of Mary's bags and pointed herself in the direction of home.

Mary lingered, held by the Captain's manner.

'Well now, lettle Benjamin, yoo've grown...' Drew turned to the sailor who'd brought him off the ship. '...had he got a small box on hem when yoo found hem?'

'No Cap'n, he was juss stood en the middle o' the cabin lookin' dumb.'

Several sailors laughed.

Drew squared-up to Benjamin, 'What were yoo doin' en my cabin?'

'I was juss helpin' Daniel load the fish en time, the tide bein' well on the turn. I slipped, es all, on the juices o' the fish...'

Some laughed again, but Drew struck him and a silence fell over the crowd.

Janet, desperate to get her aunt away noticed Daniel, he was approaching Drew and Benjamin, flashing her an apologetic look as he came by.

Drew was about to apply another blow as Daniel reached them. By far the bigger man Daniel restrained Drew's arm. 'Es quite enough Captain, ef yoo want our fish yoo'll see fit to stop. He's sorry he slipped through ya doorway, an' I know he'll take ya punishment wethout retaliatin' fer as long as yoo dish et oot, but I asked hem to help because o' the fleetness o' the tide today, an' yoo relly shouldne be wastin' ya time.'

There was a brief exchange of glances, frustration from Drew, disappointment from Daniel and disbelief from Benjamin that Daniel would pretend he'd been part of the scheduled loading team. Drew pulled his arm free of Daniel's thick hand and, pushing Benjamin deliberately out of the way, called for the crew to make haste.

'Thank yoo...' Benjamin whispered.

'Hush an get my praam back to Moclett, we'll have to talk Ben, we need thess ship way more than they need us...'

'But Daniel...'

'I know, the box, sort oot my praam sonny an' wait fer us at home.'

Benjamin glanced up to see Janet urging her aunt to travel home with her. Mary looked him up and down, turned to Janet and then back again with a sideways glance.

Blood dripped from Benjamin's cut lip, he wiped it from his chin and headed for the praam with no further dispute.

Daniel watched him go then gazed up the track to check on Janet, just in time to witness her last turn and gesture of gratitude. He nodded and headed towards the fishing boats with the other fishermen who had clearly been ready to act had the scene developed differently.

Chapter forty-three

Mary almost fell on the track when she saw Erka's old cottage restored. To hear that Edward had been involved, and that the whole community had rallied around Bess, did little to reconcile her angst. On hearing the connection to Erka, Mary was ready to take Janet back to Mainland then and there, and she would have done had the Victory Star not already set sail.

Janet told her of the work Bess had been doing for the community, visiting the sick and assisting the Minister all over the island and Papa Westray. Hearing this, Mary finally found strength to carry on towards the Farm.

When Edward returned from his work, Bess and the cottage were the sole point of conversation for much of the evening. Mary wanted reports on Bess's behaviour during her stay, her manner around the neighbours and wider community, and when, exactly, the sense of dread had left the stones of the cottage…

Edward had laughed at that suggestion, but Mary had insisted that the place had been covered by a darkness that prevented entry, and challenged Edward regarding when he'd felt comfortable to pass its threshold. Edward simply replied that it wasn't his cottage to enter, he'd had no desire to, but that the place had a happier feel since Bess had taken it on and much of the rear of the property was still fairly sound thanks to roof repairs he had put in place as payment for counsel all those years ago.

Mary did not wish to talk about the past, she was far more concerned about the here and now, and to Janet's despair the conversation changed its focus to the reason for Mary's arrival; reports of Janet being involved with a fisherman.

Edward defended Janet's choice, 'Benjamin's a fine young man, Mary.'

'Well, that's no' true ef thess Benjamin es the same as got involved en fightin' doon by the quay when I arrived…'

Janet felt the need to correct her aunt, 'He was only the recipient o' Captain Drew's fury…'

'Hush child, Captain Drew es beyond doubt...'

'He had Ben's property.'

Mary grew cross, 'No more, Janet!'

'But…'

Edward intervened, he knew an argument would not help Janet's cause, and if Mary intended to take her from him again, he wanted some say in when she would return if he couldn't delay it. Firmly he instructed Janet to feed the dog, a statement that caused Mary to raise an eyebrow for she was not keen on any animals; helping with the cattle when Gwen was ill had been her greatest feat of suffering for others, and she actively sought to avoid any contact with beasts on Mainland.

Janet wanted desperately to defend Benjamin, but her father's wink convinced her that he had her interests at heart. She headed out to the barn.

'Hello Boy…'

The little dog wagged its stumpy tail, he'd been curled up in the hay dozing, as was his usual routine after food, his tummy was indeed full and Janet realised that her father had simply given her space from her aunt, time to calm down and think. She slumped down next to the animal, hugging him close, 'I donny wanna go back to Mainland, Boy, inevitable though et es.' Janet burst into tears, she caught herself envying Bess's freedom, then chastised herself. Bess had at least rediscovered family here. Finulf may be absent most of the time, but he was still her father, solace to a child brought up as an orphan. Janet sobbed again, Bess would be staying on Westray and she knew she'd miss her terribly.

Janet delayed her return to the house as long as she could. Her father would seek greater access, she felt sure of it, and this end would be better achieved without her pleading to Mary or arguing with her.

As Janet left the barn, she was surprised to see Mary heading out of the gate, her father welcomed her back inside and apologised for sending her out on a false errand.

'I understand Father but where es Mary goin'?'

'She promised Deborah she'd visit her kin an' report back ef they had any needs.'

Janet looked sad.

'Wha's up, Janet?'

'Ef she cannot wait 'tell tomorrow to visit, et must mean she's en a hurry to return, an' I wellne be here much longer.' Tears welled in Janet's eyes.

'No' so, my darlin' child; the Victory Star es goin' to Ireland an' then roond to Norway. Et was lucrative fer Drew et seems. He's organised other captains to fulfil the usual schedules but none have the space to carry two passengers back to Mainland fer three weeks…'

Janet tears flowed, 'Then tha's all I have…'

Her father embraced her, 'Now, now sweet girl, Deborah es keen to have yoo return, an there's greater opportunities fer yoo en Kirkwall…'

'But I wanna be here, weth yoo Daddy, an' Ben, an' Bess, an' Boy.' She held him tightly.

'And yoo ken be. Mary agrees she has no right, at ya age, to stop yoo spendin' time weth ya family. When Deborah affords yoo leave, yoo ken come.'

Janet coped much better after her father's news, even if three weeks slipped by all too quickly. Mary hadn't been restrictive, although she clearly didn't approve of Janet being allowed to see Benjamin before the day of departure.

Benjamin had been on land duties as punishment for the fray at

Pierowall, but Daniel had heard of Mary's plan to move Janet back to Mainland, and played his part in ensuring the couple could meet.

So it was that they lay, hands held in the praam, anchor set, just beyond the Bay of Swartmill, south of Spo Ness, Boy curled up at their feet.

'Oh Ben, why ded yoo have to board Drew's ship?'

'Juss had to, Jan.'

'We could have had more time, I leave tomorrow, an' the bordin' gained yoo nothin'.'

'Den et?'

Janet sat up. 'I didne think yoo got the box.'

'Before Miley stood oot on the deck the day he died, he gave me a lettle key, et was as ef he knew. Told me et opened my box, an' that the box was iron-bound an' too strong to break open. I'd gone to find the box after Miley had gone, but Drew found me en Miley's cabin an' threw me oot sayin' everythin' was his now. I kept the key safe...' Benjamin revealed the key. '...always weth me untel an opportune time, though I must admit I didne think et would e'er come.'

'But yoo didne have the box when they threw yoo off the ship.'

'No need, I quickly found et, opened et, stuffed the contents en my tunic, relocked the box an' returned et to et's place. Ef Drew e'er manages to open et he'll be sorely disappointed.'

Janet giggled and lay back down, 'So what *was* en the box?'

'Well, I'm no rich man from et, fer there was very lettle, but et's *my* very lettle, an' now et's back weth et's rightful owner.'

'What?' Janet repeated impatiently.

'A seal pup pelt, an' thess...' Benjamin pulled something from a pouch on his belt. It was a hand carved seal, threaded onto a leather cord to make a necklace. '...I added the cord so that yoo could wear et.'

Janet gasped in delight as she cupped the creature in her hand, then sitting quickly, she lifted her hair to allow Benjamin to place it. He sat up and did so.

'But yoo didne gain much from the box, should yoo no' keep close what belongs to yoo?'

Benjamin smiled, 'Et's what I'm doin' Jan. I have no rings, no great

187

horde o' jewels, I'm no rich man, but what I have es yours.' He paused briefly, 'Ef yoo'll commit to me… well, the seal es yours an' yoo mine.'

Janet sat staring at Benjamin as she gently fondled the little carving.

'Have I an answer, Jan?'

'Oh Ben, ef et means I'm yours; I'll ne'er let et go.'

Ben lay back, pulled Janet into his arms and they kissed.

Janet giggled, 'So ya parents were seals.'

Benjamin laughed, a seal pelt and carved seal were not what he'd expected to find in a box that had been handed to Miley when he'd taken Benjamin into his care, a box that he'd grown up believing would reveal something of his past. 'Always wondered why I like seals so much, Jan.'

'Me too, I love seals…'

'And that pelt actually feels warm, as ef et's a livin' theng.'

Janet was momentarily reminded of Bess's collection of fabrics, gathered from a box in Erka's cottage. The seal pelt there had felt warm to her, 'I suppose they're warm by necessity, et bein' so cold en the water.'

Benjamin went on to explain how no pelt he'd ever handled felt so warm and that he put it down to the connection with his family, but Janet didn't catch everything he was saying - her mind was suddenly trying to recall something, something about Bess, something about parchment in leather binding beneath the pelt in the bundle… ach, but it was all long gone now, back with Bess in what was now *her* little cottage. Janet's focus went back to her lover and she returned to his lips.

Chapter forty-four

Two days later, Janet was aboard Finulf's Merchantman with Mary. As expected, Mary had refused to let Janet take her dog to Mainland;

Janet had hugged him tightly and asked him to look after her father. Her aunt's face was a picture of surprise when the creature walked over to Edward and sat at his feet. Mary's astonishment did not end at the reaction of a little dog, for not only did her niece, who had once feared water, seek a position by the side, she was also leaning over it looking out to Papa Westray for any sign of the fishing boats.

'Careful Janet, ya confidence weth the water may have grown - Edward said as much - but yoo shouldne resk fallin' en.'

Janet sighed with disappointment, Daniel's fleet had already set out and there wasn't a single boat in the Bay of Moclett.

If it hadn't been for a whale, the journey back to Mainland would have been uneventful; Finulf seemed too busy to spend a moment in conversation with his daughter's friend, and the crew could only be described as indifferent. The passage already paid, Janet and Mary felt like little more than cargo for delivery. It had been a relief to disembark.

Janet pulled her bags off the cart that had brought them up from the Harbour, and headed up the steps of the townhouse. William opened the door and welcomed her back. 'I believe yoo've grown thess Summer, Janet.'

Janet would have answered affirming his observation, indeed, she felt she'd grown in many ways, stature, confidence and emotionally, but William had quickly darted down the steps to assist Mary.

William was just another example of Mary's hold over people, she'd moan about how long he'd spend in Scotland, just enough to make him uneasy and keen to please her when he was home, but never any more than that, for she didn't want him to stop going. Janet never really knew what William's business was, but it gave Mary a standard of living she did not wish to lose.

Janet rolled her eyes and was about to head up to her room.

'Er, hello… Janet.' The voice came from the doorway to William's study. A man stood there, looking anxious.

'Oh, hello…' Janet was at a loss, he knew her name and had the advantage, for although he had a familiar face, she certainly hadn't seen it for a while and could not put a name to it.

The visitor remained looking at her, as if it were her part to speak. Janet lowered her bags, which were becoming heavy for the waiting.

Mary entered, 'Ah! Grigor.' She noticed the vacancy in Janet's eyes. 'Yoo remember Grigor Sinclair, Janet… He used to werk weth yoo…'

Janet remembered; this man had been amongst the orphans working on the nets, he'd been very quiet, but he *had* been there. 'They used to call yoo "Snotty"… "Snotty Sinclair".'

The man acknowledged the nickname, adding that he was allergic to fish and the nets always set him off. Then Mary insisted that it was most definitely "Grigor" now, that he'd been away from the islands and was now back - all grown up - that he was a fine young man and would be joining the Deacon, 'Supportin' hem en his ministry to the poor an' needy. Grigor well be o'erseein' the very group yoo both werked en.'

Mary took Janet's bags and headed upstairs. William entered, looking pink from his efforts up the townhouse steps. He nodded politely to Grigor before passing by.

Janet and Grigor stood silently for a moment, both choosing the same moment to speak and apologising profusely before Grigor insisted Janet speak first.

'I was juss curious as to where yoo'd ben. Yoo left the werk group two Wenters before me… Mary said yoo'd ben away?'

'Aye, I was fifteen, et was the agreement. When I was six. I was pulled from a wreckin' ship, but my parents were lost. I was known by one o' the rescuers - he knew I had a relative en Scotland an' sent werd to hem.

'My mother's brother was the Minister at St. Peter's Kirk en Thurso - he stell es - Alexander Urquhart es his neem, but he had no time to care fer a child. He knew o' the provision fer orphans here an' had me enrolled en the werk group stipulatin' I go to hem when I turned fifteen.'

Janet was glad that some relative had finally taken Grigor in; but for some reason she couldn't get interested, perhaps it was due to not being as emotionally invested as she had been for Bess. In all honesty,

Janet was looking for a way to leave Grigor to whatever he had visited William and Mary to achieve.

'Mary said that yoo've ben werkin' weth Mrs. Finney at the store…'

'Aye, Deborah has known me since birth.' A sudden thought dawned on her, 'I relly must see her. Et was good to see yoo…' Janet called upstairs, 'I'm off to see Deborah, Auntie!'

'Very well, Janet…' Mary appeared at the top of the stairs. 'Perhaps yoo'll see Janet safely there Grigor?'

'Oh… aye Mrs. Davie, et would be a pleasure.'

Janet's heart sank, but she resolved to get there quickly and give him no alternative but to part company.

Grigor was quite breathless and Janet looked rather pink as they arrived at the store.

Janet offered her hand to shake, 'Thank yoo fer seein' me to the store, Grigor, I hope yoo enjoy ya werk weth the orphans.'

Grigor smiled knowingly. 'Aye, I'll see yoo soon Miss Forsyth.'

With that Grigor headed down to the harbour and Janet, puzzled by his tone, entered the shop.

Deborah greeted Janet with open arms, but she looked grave.

'What's wrong?'

'Et's ya aunt child, she heard yoo'd met a man on Westray that doesne meet weth her standards fer yoo. She intends to find yoo a suitor o' greater means…'

'Benjamin es wonderful, he may have his own fishin' fleet one day, he's young es all.' Janet's defence of Benjamin suddenly faltered as she realised what had already happened. Mary had removed her from Westray and had wasted no time in introducing her to Grigor. 'Oh Deborah! I've got to get back to Ben, we have an understanding. I know he's no' rich, that his prospects are wholly dependent on the roughness o' his hands an' hard, dangerous werk, but we belong together. He's given me one o' his most precious possessions as a witness o' his love.'

Janet showed Deborah the carved seal, spilling her feelings and Benjamin's words.

Deborah remained strong, 'Do nothin' rash, my dear, Mary told me that she wished to keep yoo on Mainland, donny give her any reason that would urge ya father to allow et. Any hysteria or runnin' away would merely resurrect the old excuses that ya wild or dark. Oh Janet, since the death o' the King's wife, Anne o' Denmark, there's ben a rise en the hunting o' wetches…'

'I'm no' a wetch, Deborah!'

'Thess I know, but Mary ded damage weth her accusations en ya youth. Yoo'll be wise to be the model woman.'

'Oh Deborah. I donny wish fer any other man, what do I do?'

'Bide ya time my darlin' girl, be obligin', I'll be sure to afford yoo leave to travel home to visit ya own.'

Janet held Deborah tightly.

'We'll get through thess my dear.'

Within just a few months King James died, replaced by King Charles, and Deborah quietly rejoiced that her sweet Janet might now be safe.

Chapter forty-five

Mary continued to seek out *appropriate* men in her attempts to impress Janet. If she turned the girl's head for just a moment, she'd surely have sown doubt about any relationship with that "lesser man", but the continued negativity towards Benjamin just fed Janet's resolve to love him.

Janet would chat obligingly with her *visitors*, even laugh at their jokes and anecdotes, but when the meetings ended, when Mary asked her what she thought of what's-his-name or so-an-so, Janet merely smiled sweetly and remarked what nice friends Mary had. It was as if Janet had no interest in relationships at all.

On her seventeenth birthday, Janet was subjected to a "gathering", she had expected family members to attend, but she knew very few of the guests, mostly men from William's business circles. Their interest in her was suffocating and she'd had to retreat, claiming light-headedness.

Gradually the interactions with Mary's *friends* began to change, Janet found herself suddenly alone, especially when William was away. Mary would make some thin excuse, leave the room and it would become quickly clear why. Almost all the invited men would start to spout their interest in Janet, how, if she would accept them, they would desire her as a wife. Initially Janet sought time to decide, unwilling to upset her aunt by straight rejections, but as the incidents increased and began to oppress her, she soon began to turn her aunt's *matches* away. Unsatisfied, they rarely returned, much to Mary's displeasure.

Janet was confused by Mary's actions, wasn't this why Mary had sent her back to Westray in the Summer? To escape the attention of men? No, she knew why, it was to escape the attention of the men Mary didn't deem appropriate.

Only one man remained incapable of expressing the desires the others so easily articulated, Janet began to like him for that. Their interactions gradually moved towards friendship, and there was nothing Grigor wouldn't do for her.

Grigor had seemed to be Mary's favourite at first, but she soon realised that his uncle had not provided him with any sizable financial means, and her attention moved to other options. Despite Mary's coolness he continued to visit. Mary, crippled by his presence being at her own initial invitation, felt unable to stop him; Janet, well aware of the situation, took great pleasure in that. Occasionally Grigor's appearance would frustrate the advances of another from her aunt's menagerie, and this was Janet's greatest amusement.

The pressure to accept one of Mary's matches went on for some months, and certain hints began to surface in Janet's interactions with her, but Deborah had suggested she'd help and she was about to honour her word.

Mary huffed as she blundered into Janet's room one morning. 'Get your thengs together.'

'Wha's up?' Janet hardly moved.

'Deborah's daughter-en-law es unwell.'

Janet clung to her pillow, 'Wha's that got to do weth me?'

'Deborah cannot leave the shop, there are deliveries ya well no' be able to deal weth.'

Janet had dealt with *all* the deliveries since returning to Mainland; Deborah had even trusted her with the shop whilst she visited a frail relative on Hoy… suddenly Janet realised that this was Deborah's way of getting her back to Westray, back to Benjamin. 'Then I must go.' she exclaimed, and quickly rose.

'Yoo wellne need much, I want yoo back quickly, et's time yoo chose a husband.'

The statement was clearly aimed to upset Janet - perhaps anger her so that Mary had reason to keep her home - but Janet kept calm, even managing a reply. 'Oh? Yoo think I'm ready to marry, Aunt Mary?' She busied herself at the bedroom cupboard.

'I feel et would help ground yoo, give yoo some stability… But donny be worryin' aboot et until ya home again, then we'll find the *right* man together, he's got to improve yoo. Perhaps yoo'll consider one o' the fine young men who've visited lately…'

Janet didn't wish to be grounded or stable, and pretended she'd been busy selecting clothes, 'What was that Auntie?'

'Juss hurry ya self; Deborah was quite plain that yoo travel today.' Mary left the room, Janet listening quietly until Mary's footsteps disappeared, then she danced around the room, lifting the little carved seal from its warm hiding place and kissing it.

Soon after breakfast, Janet was standing on the Kirkwall harbour wall, she kissed her aunt and took a bundle from Deborah, thanking her with a quiet whisper.

Deborah simply smiled knowingly, waving goodbye as Janet boarded Finulf's Merchantman.

Finulf stood motionless at the helm, gazing at the sky, he looked thoughtful, his crew hurriedly preparing the ship. Janet's eyes became locked on him. She was sure that the man had carried a little grey in

194

his hair and beard, and that his stance had been bowed, but here his dark locks possessed not one strand of silver and he stood as upright as any younger man. His eyes met her own; eyes as bright as Benjamin's. Janet had to look away. She turned to the harbour mouth, observing the pale tops of the waves beyond, and loose, broken clouds above.

They were soon out onto open water. The wind was well for a fast crossing, but the swell was harsh, Janet felt a hint of her old anxieties about the water, and sat down close to the main mast.

A crewman noticed her troubled expression, 'Ye'll be fine, Finulf has sailed en worse than thess.'

'Thank yoo.'

The sailor paused, 'Ye Bess's friend, aye?'

Janet nodded.

'Reckon we'll be en Pierowall fer some time while thess weather passes through, I'll have time on my hands ef yoo know what I mean?'

Janet shrugged.

'We could... get together?'

'Oh... My Ben well have all my spare time...'

Finulf shouted an order from behind them; the crewman smiled, nodded and headed away to fulfil it.

A driving rain setting in, Janet sought another place to sit, somewhere more secluded, more sheltered amongst the crates and barrels, and here she stayed for the rest of the crossing, keeping her head down and wondering how Finulf would bring the vessel safely into the harbour.

Finulf seemed less troubled by the deteriorating conditions and it became apparent to Janet that the Seaman's confidence was founded in experience, he swung the Merchantman into Pierowall bay and the churning swell quickly stilled within the protection of the Point of Brough. Finulf hadn't needed much sail for the journey, but what he had used was now tidied away, it seemed too soon but the momentum of the ship remained, its captain skilfully steering it towards the quay. Janet looked out at the approaching harbour. On one arm of the harbour wall stood a single figure, a young woman with black hair swirling in the wind. It was unmistakably Bess, and Janet's heart was glad. Both young women waved as the ship entered the harbour mouth, its speed now checked and manageable.

Janet, feeling much safer now as the ship was moored, gave Finulf an admiring smile, her relief acknowledged with a nod and knowing eyes.

Chapter forty-six

Janet had not been able to stop herself spilling her cares out to her friend. Bess listened intently about Mary's attempts to tempt Janet from Benjamin with suitors of *her* choosing. In her heart, Bess loathed that Janet had not succumbed to her aunt's plan, leaving Benjamin available; he'd remained steadfastly faithful to Janet over the months of her absence, despite Bess's attempts to turn his head.

Bess, moved by her longstanding friendship, promised to help.

Janet thanked her, it mattered little that Mary was too far away for Bess to do anything, her friend's care was enough.

Bess kissed Janet when they reached her cottage, insisting that Janet visited her properly before she left. Janet promised, then headed off towards the home of Deborah's kin.

Janet wasn't surprised when Deborah's daughter-in-law, Sarah, appeared at the door of the Finney farmhouse. She was not surprised when the bundle was unpacked and contained nothing more than new, linen bed sheets; neither was she surprised when Sarah said 'Och, I'd no' expected these so queckly.'

Janet made a brief comment on the deteriorating weather, and her father's neighbour thanked her and suggested she headed home.

The farmhouse was quiet and empty, Janet set about tidying, tutting her father's lack of discernment regarding the appropriateness of cobwebs and mud in a kitchen, but her disapproval was soon replaced by concern. The light was fading outside, Janet had lit the lamps and started a stew in a pot over the fire, but there was no sign of Edward.

Janet glanced out the door, a stiff wind was now driving bands of persistent rain off the sea; she ran to the barn for a better view across her father's land, but there was no sign of him. On discovering that Boy was absent too, she decided that they must be together; with some solace in the thought, she returned to the farmhouse.

Her relief came as darkness arrived; there was a noise at the door - a scuffling sound - then a click of the latch...

Janet, already in the hallway of the farmhouse, edged towards the door, 'Father?' Her relief was quickly faltering as the door swung open with nothing but the wind to urge it. She stared out into the early fallen blackness of the storm, her eyes widening at the discernment of a moving bulk.

The little dog bolted into the house, yapping joyfully at Janet's feet, its fur matted and bloodied; she swept him up into her arms and backed hastily away from the door but the animal pulled itself from her arms and returned to the opening. It looked back at Janet and barked at her.

The bulk was now at the threshold, lit by the lamps.

'Ben!'

Benjamin stepped into the house something large over his shoulder, 'Thank God ya here! Help me Jan.'

Janet realised that Benjamin's burden was Edward. 'Father! Oh Ben! Thess way...' She led Benjamin to her father's room and had him place Edward on the bed. The dog curled up at his feet, exhausted. There was a great deal of spattered, clotted blood. '...what... what happened?'

'Et's bad Jan, the weather forced me to shelter at Tuquoy Bay before I could make good fer Moclett. The wind driven waves had started to flood my fishin' boat, an' I thought et prudent to wait oot the squall en the fishin' hut off the beach.'

Janet shot out of the room to get water, 'Keep talkin', I ken stell hear yoo.'

Ben followed Janet to the door, 'Well, I wasne there long before ya wee dog appeared, scratchin' at the door. When I opened the door et

197

ran off around the hut; I was en half a mind to leave et but et called fer me, yappin', an' I felt I should go after et. Et started to take me up to the wall ya father built to keep his stock away from the sea. I could see that et was damaged as I approached, an' bloodied entrails lay o'er the disturbed stones. Concerned I started to run...'

Janet returned with a bowl of water and immediately started to bathe her father.

'I reached the wall an' heard thess moanin' comin' from the other side, I peered o'er an' there he was, covered en blood but I knew hem instantly, knew I had to get hem back t'the farm. My eyes fell on the gore strewn stones o' the wall, an' I realised that the guts belonged to a larger animal. The trail was now visible to me, dashed doon to the further end o' the beach an' to the hungry waves. The dog was standin' on a rock lookin' oot at the choppy water, growlin'...' Benjamin paused until Janet looked up.

'Ben?'

'Et was starin' right at me, et had clearly ben the cause o' the blood, a heifer, dragged off to where'er ets den es. Now et was sittin' en the breakers, like some red granite boulder, waves splittin' violently on ets back...'

Janet frowned.

Benjamin drew close and lowered his voice to a whisper. 'The Nuckelavee...'

Janet dropped the wet cloth into the bowl and placed her fingers on Benjamin's lips. 'Hush!'

Benjamin's eyes were frozen open, staring at the window, out into the darkness of night. 'Et started to move towards the beach. I had one chance; I threw ya father o'er my shoulder, grabbed up ya dog by the scruff o' ets neck, he protested an' writhed, I almost lost my grip but I wasne leavin' et outside to the mercy o' that beast...' Benjamin caught his breath, 'Then I ran, ran fer the fisherman's hut. The beast was quick but I had the ground, I had time to place ya father doon, to slam the door, an' brace et. The creature tested that brace, I feared et would give but et held. Et hadne seen the small openin' that served as a window on the side o' the hut, so I queckly placed the table against et,

198

an' one o' the benches to pin et there. I dragged ya father to the furthest corner, sittin' next to hem an' holdin' the dog again. Et felt so long, Jan; I could hear et movin' ootside, scratchin' at the door, pacin', circlin' the stone hut, lookin' fer a weakness. Ya father renewed that door an ets frame last winter; et saved our lives today. Finally, the beast tried the window. The table started to sheft, so I threw my weight against et. I could feel the creature's strength weth e'ery blow. I stayed et fer what felt an age, untel I could hold et no longer an' scrambled to the far wall. The table flew across the room behind me an' a long, raw-fleshed arm followed et; the fingers explored where they could reach, then the arm disappeared ootside again. An eye peered en, I could smell ets breath, et turned my stomach. The hand returned, ets long gnarled fingers strainin' to reach the length o' the room. I felt a glad sense o' relief, fer there was no way those fingertips could touch us. Again, the arm left. There was a frenzied scratchin' ootside, then silence, then a crash. I didne realise what was happenin' at first, then weth subsequent crashes the chillin' truth dawned on me. One o' the stones around the window fell ento the hut, the hand scrambled en again but et was still no' enough, further batterin' at the openin' resumed; et was tryin' to smash a hole beg enough to reach us through.'

'How ded ya get away?'

'Et was almost through; blindly the arm returned to test ets progress. Boy tore hemself from my grip, I couldne hold hem, he bit the creature's wrist an' the beast retreated. Then the rain came, Jan, the blessed rain, an' the creature screamed oot, et ran back to the sea. Ef et hadne ben fer the rain I donny think I could have fought et off, e'en weth ya brave lettle dog. Weth the beast gone I took up my pack, threw an oiled skin aboot ya father, bore hem up upon my shoulders an' made my way through the rain to the farm.'

Janet cupped Benjamin's cheek. 'Well, ya my hero fer brengin' hem home; there's some ale en the pantry ef yoo need et?'

'Aye, that would be good, I'm shakin'!'

'I'll join yoo when I've seen to my father's wounds.'

Janet found no wound on her father, puzzled she finished undressing him and drew the bedcoverings about him for warmth before heading to the kitchen. There she found Benjamin, he had cleaned the dog and rescued the stew. She fell shivering into his arms.

'Et's ok Jan, et's o'er, ya father's strong he'll pull through.'

'But what to do, Ben?'

'Fer now we stay away from Tuquoy…'

'But Father's stock, et must have ben the creature that's ben takin' them.'

'I'll see Daniel tomorrow at Pierowall. When I tell him what happened, he'll help me move the stock to the Knucker Hill fields. He'll want his boat back from Tuquoy bay; weth the whole fleet together the creature well stay away.'

Chapter forty-seven

Janet invited Benjamin to stay close to her that night, he kissed her and accepted but insisted on sleeping in the barn out of respect for her and her father. This was the outcome, despite Janet's plea that he stayed and held her.

'What would people say o' ya character Jan, ef they came to learn that I'd shared ya bed whilst ya father was ill?'

'I donny care, I love yoo.'

'Come to me en the mornin' there es somethin' I must show yoo.'

Janet protested, but seeing that Benjamin was set on his decision, she finally yielded.

Janet spent a good deal of the night watching her father, and it was the small hours before she finally convinced herself that he was breathing more comfortably. She retired to bed, remaining dressed in case her father should wake and need her.

Janet stood on the beach at the edge of the tideline gazing out to sea, the waves kissing her toes. Benjamin had risen early, his promise of sharing something in the morning had left with him, Janet was confused, he'd never failed to fulfil his word before. The flotilla of fishing boats had disappeared from sight some hours before, but she couldn't tear her eyes from the horizon. The swell through Papa Sound was giddying, just watching it left Janet queasy; the sand shifted beneath her feet and she was forced to look down and step to the side for balance. Around her the water was laced with blood, she froze. The movement of the waves suddenly seemed unnatural, a breaker, larger than the others by a considerable degree seemed to turn and come straight at her, lashing towards her throat…

Janet sat up, her breath laboured, the light of dawn outlining the bedroom; she stepped quickly to the window. There was no sign of life in the barn, and the thought that Benjamin could have left without word played so heavily on her mind that she rushed hastily down the stairs and out through the door.

Janet flung the barn door open, the early morning light hardly penetrated it, 'Ben!'

Benjamin leapt up from the hay and stumbled into sight; partially clad he swept his hair from his face. 'Jan? Wha's up? Es et ya father?'

'Oh Ben, I thought yoo'd gone!' Janet told Benjamin her nightmarish dream. 'Donny go to sea today…'

'Et was juss a bad dream, Jan. I've got to get my boat back…'

Janet objected, she had a bad feeling, an inner grief, a fear of losing…

Benjamin covered her mouth gently with his hand, 'Hush now, the whole fleet well be at my side, we look oot fer each other.'

'But!'

Benjamin pulled her into his arms, his warm skin pacifying her, warm like the pelt of the seal pup. She looked up at him, running her fingers up his chest.

'There's somethin' I must show yoo. Come an' see.'

Janet let herself be led back to the hay, she crouched gently down, expectant, but her assumption that Benjamin meant to make love to her was quickly corrected.

201

Benjamin flung his shirt on and reached for his pack, 'Come.' He took her hand and pulled her up.

Boy began to follow but Janet bid him to stay.

They left the farm and headed across the island, passing the gully where Janet had played as a child. She hadn't seen the Trows for a long time. Ben had become her sole focus, …little people? The stuff of childhood. 'Where are we goin'?'

'Come.'

Janet kept to Benjamin's pace, passing Saintear Loch and Knucker Hill. She glanced back to the farm, visible from the rising ground, and wondered how her father was, her only comfort being the fact that it was still very early, the sun barely grazing the misty horizon over Papa Westray.

As they approached the cliffs beyond Knucker Hill, overlooking Red Nev, Benjamin bid Janet to be quiet and keep low as they approached the cliff edge. He smiled, pointing down to the rocky beach.

Janet frowned at what she was seeing, 'Why have yoo brought me here to look at naked folk, Ben? Who are they? I've no' seen them before.'

Below, just sixty or so yards away, were six young people, completely naked skipping around on the rocks with a startling agility.

'Watch, they're no' what yoo think.' He picked up a stone and flung it some thirty feet along the cliff. It rattled and clicked down the steep face, the youngsters froze then quickly grabbed up their grey-coloured garments. Janet's eyes widened as they slipped swiftly into these sack-like clothes, each instantly becoming a familiar, sleek animal.

'Selkies…' Benjamin whispered.

Janet had been longing to return to the farm, now she let her strength slip from her, and she lay motionless on the edge of the cliff. The Selkies were circling in the water, glancing up at the cliff for signs of danger.

Then Benjamin said something strange, 'One day I'll join them.'

Janet's heart faltered, 'Ben?' She looked at him, he'd pulled the seal pup pelt from his pack.

'I ne'er knew my parents, Jan; I was brought up as an orphan, passed from one guardian to another...' Benjamin had placed his hand into the pelt, bringing the diminutive front limb to life. '...who knows perhaps my true family are stell waitin' fer me oot there?'

Janet began to edge away from the cliff, she didn't know what to do with this revelation, this man was her Benjamin, nothing could change that, but he was no longer the Benjamin she'd believed him to be.

'Wait Jan.' Benjamin stood, the Selkies saw him and dived. 'I'm stell the same guy yoo met all those years back...'

Janet was shaking her head and backing away, a tear dashing down her cheek...

'Jan, ya special too. Yoo ken see the lettle folk, yoo told me o' the pelt yoo'd touched that was warm, et isne normal, Jan, to feel the warmth, et's a sign o' who yoo are...'

Janet shook her head, 'That belonged to Bess, et was her mother's pelt; I know my father Ben... he's no Selkie.' Janet turned for home.

'Wait Jan, let's talk...'

'I must go home to father, we'll talk later. Donny go to sea today, promise me...' Jan started to run.

'I canny promise that, Jan, wait!'

'I must go to my father.'

Chapter forty-eight

'Did Ben follow after her?' Sally had to know.

'He returned to the barn, gathered his remainin' belongin's, told the dog to have werds on his behalf an' headed to Pierowall to meet Daniel.'

Sally huffed, 'He should have chased her, held her, promised never to leave...'

Garrie looked uncomfortable. 'Janet needed time; she'd ben through so much since Benjamin had arrived the night before. He knew she needed that time. Et was only his love for her that held hem to human life. Would he no' have dived ento Selkie ways otherwise, left all to find his true family? Besides, he knew no' what was comin', any better than the next man.'

Sally nuzzled into Carl's ample frame, quietly whispering, 'I would have wanted to be chased.'

Kayleigh wasn't ready to accept a long pause in the story anymore, even a dull tale would have helped to deaden the anxieties brought on by the raging gale outside, but this story was alive to her! She had walked the self-same streets of Kirkwall, even the very stones that Janet's feet had touched. 'What o' the dream, Garrie? Ded et come to naught as Ben said?'

Garrie was wringing his hands, he hadn't seemed to hear the question, he seemed in a daze; eyes fixed on the flickering lightning through the window.

'Ben told Daniel what had happened an' Daniel agreed to shelve the plans he'd had fer the mornin'. His men crossed the island to move Edward's stock to the Knucker Hill fields. On seein' the damage to the wall from a distance Daniel quailed, he'd heard too many stories to travel doon to the beach an' risk entanglement weth the creature should et return there. Daniel agreed to take the whole fleet around by sea to retrieve the fishin' boat, there'd be safety en numbers; the decision was made.'

Garrie turned to his audience. 'Ben had expected to see Janet as they returned to Pierowall, passin' the farm he had expected to see her at the gate to thank Daniel. Edward's herd was large, ets movement to the hillside would have been visible from the farmhoose, but Janet wasne there. Ben hadne wanted to leave the island wethout havin' made some more positive contact. A smile or wave from her would have eased his mind. He sighed deeply, perhaps et *had* been too soon to tell her his news, an' now he had to leave wethout knowledge o' Janet's understandin', fer Daniel was behind schedule an' there was still the boat to retrieve.'

Garrie gestured to Dini to top up the mugs, Deni to tend the fire and Donie to fetch some more blankets, the cold of the night creeping into the house as the storm sucked the fire's heat up the chimney.

'Thess es too much, I canny bear et!' Kayleigh cried, 'Please tell us that he was Ok, that he saw her again.'

Donie gave Garrie a folded blanket, he returned to his seat leaving the blanket folded on his lap. 'Weth necessity forcin' hem to leave weth the rest of Daniel's fleet, Ben had sent a boy from the quayside to the farm to let Janet know the cattle had ben moved an' that he would return as soon as he could.'

~

The boy received a less than warm reception and left the farm feeling that Janet cared little for Benjamin. The truth was different, Edward had woken moments before the child's arrival, Janet had flown down the stairs, hopeful that Benjamin had returned, hopeful that he'd heeded her concern and not gone to sea. Confronted by a small boy, Janet's disappointment was great; if Benjamin was so deeply in love with her, he would surely have come in person.

Janet acknowledged that the cows were safely away from Tuquoy Bay, closing the door on the disclosure that Ben intended to return as soon as his duties would allow.

Janet hurried back to her father, seeing diligently to his needs, but she couldn't hide her upset from him. He saw the moisture in her eyes, and his enquiry led to her sobbing in his arms as she told him of her dream and Benjamin's indifference.

Edward managed a smile 'Ach, he's a yon man, Janet. He likely knows little o' how to deal weth a woman's...' He paused.

'Devotion?' Janet ventured.

Edward nodded quickly. 'Reckon I owe hem; the last I recall I was neither here nor safe.'

Janet slumped to the bed and spilled the whole story; exactly how Benjamin had told it. Edward could see that there was more, 'Go on my love.'

Janet heard her lips speak of the Selkies, but it troubled her, a wave of intense guilt rose within; surely, she had just betrayed what Benjamin had given her in confidence, and she collapsed in floods of tears, 'Oh, I've ben so unkind to hem, Father. Do not tell a soul aboot his secrets. I am surer now than e'er o' his love fer me...'

Edward let her cry, more for time to resolve his own conflict than to offer advice, for Janet had mentioned the warmth of the pup skin and a seed of revelation was growing deep in his mind. After a while he began to gently stroke her hair saying, 'Now, now my child, hold steady, he es weth the fleet, the day es fair an' still. Yoo well see hem again soon, aye?'

Janet raised her head and let him wipe her tears away, 'Aye, Father... Do yoo have need o' anythin'?'

The thoughts inside Edward wrestled with him. 'Er, no...'

Janet got up and headed to the door to perform some duties elsewhere in the house. 'Wait!' Edward called.

Janet stood still at the door.

'There's somethin' yoo should know.'

Janet slowly turned, 'Father?'

'Come, sit. None who hear such should be standin'...'

Janet sat on the bed, 'What es et Father, what es wrong?'

Edward could not keep it from her anymore. Had he been killed by the creature Janet would have never known the truth; she deserved to know the truth. As the story of what happened unfolded it was Janet's turn for amazement.

'Then ya no' my father?'

'I have ben ya father,' Edward continued. 'I've ben all a father could be, my sweet girl, juss no' blood. I found yoo en the breakers, the seals were there, I realise now that Benjamin may be right, yoo may well be a Selkie...'

'Ben!' Janet quickly stood. She looked at Edward, 'I must go before he leaves Pierowall.' She was nearly out of the door when she stopped, 'Thank yoo, Daddy, I'll be home soon. Oh, the dog! Shall I put hem oot?' Boy was curled up on the bed.

'No, he's fine, let hem sleep. Go now my child, hurry.'

Chapter Forty-nine

Of course, she *was* too late, she knew she would be. The boy Benjamin had sent, worked at the quay. Her continued pace was maintained both through desperation and a last hope that he'd heeded her plea not to go.

On her arrival the quay was unusually quiet. Janet desperately searched over the edge of the sea wall, but any hope that a small boat was moored out of sight, Ben waiting patiently, soon died and she slumped down on the far leg of the harbour wall, tears raining down into the dark water below. She felt abandoned, totally alone but for a small group of seals staring blankly up at her from the still waters of the bay. She gasped and jumped to her feet, screaming, 'Go!' she gestured out to sea with her arms. 'Go an' rescue Ben, quickly, go.'

The seals, startled by the sudden movement and noise, bolted for deep water. To Janet it was clear that she'd merely scared them, distraught she turned, half blinded by her tears, intending to run home to her father but stumbling over the same boy who had come earlier to the farmhouse instead.

The boy had witnessed her call out to the seals, he'd seen them dive quickly out to sea, as if responding to her command, now Janet had turned and knocked him to the ground.

'Donny hurt me!' He shielded himself with his arms, 'I'll no tella soul.'

Janet, thinking he understood that the contact was an accident, pulled him to his feet, brushed him down and apologised. With no further discernment of the boy's anxious expression, Janet headed for home.

The boy watched, motionless, as Janet seemed to walk calmly away. The sound of his own breathing loud in his ears, he tried to make sense of what had come to pass that day. The fisherman asking him to take a message to Janet, her lack of warmth on receipt of the message, her sudden arrival and animation on the quayside, and now the picture of peace as she walked away. She didn't even look back at him - but for that he was relieved.

Janet was not calm, she was embarrassed, what had she been thinking shouting out like that? What had she thought seals could do? Had she lost her senses? 'Not all seals are Selkies…' She heard herself mutter. 'Oh Ben, how dare yoo do thess to me now…'

'It's good to see you back on Westray Miss Forsyth, but tell me are you alright?'

With her head downcast, Janet hadn't seen the Minister who was standing at the Kirk gate with Bess. 'O! Hello Minister, Hello Bess. I was, erm…' Janet had no excuse for her state, she felt sure that her manner must appear lost and loaded with concerns to be so unobservant, the Minister was a large, rotund man after all and Bess was becoming a creature of flamboyantly coloured fabrics; their presence in the landscape demanded the eye to snare.

Bess intervened, 'Es somethin' wrong? I saw yoo runnin' thess way by the cottage an' followed after, but…' She turned to the Minister and laughed, 'I was juss tellin' the Minister, yoo must be possessed, fer I could run no further an' had to stop!'

'Dear Bess, et's all horrible, an' I was so excited to be home!'

'Come inside dear girl.' The Minister pointed to the Kirk.

'No, no, I muss get back to Father, he was attacked yesterday at Tuquoy by that creature, the one yoo saw as a child Bess, I'm sure, fer Ben's description ded match ya own!'

Bess looked shocked, 'The creature es on Westray?'

'Aye, yesterday, Father saw et draggin' a cow o'er the wall by the bay…'

'But tha's terrible! Et attacked hem?'

'Well, no, Father tried to drive et off weth a rod he uses to drive the herd…'

'A brave man your father, but foolish in this instance I fear.' The Minister lamented.

'Et ded beat hem to the ground, an' there he lay 'tell Ben found hem an' rescued hem, fer the beast returned an' would have taken hem were et no' fer Ben's swift deeds.'

Bess seemed impressed, 'Benjamin fought et?'

'He dedne, he sought hidin' 'tell the rain fell an' drove the monster back to the sea.'

The Minister nodded, 'A wise young man; but why the haste to the quay and the shouts? Ha! We could hear you from here!'

Janet felt a fresh wave of embarrassment, and the words came; well… to what ill before a friend and a Minister? 'I had thess silly dream, an' I'd missed sayin' goodbye to Ben, an' I was so afeared, but et's so foolish, I donny know what came o'er me?'

Bess was intrigued, 'What was thess dream?'

'Et was naught, juss a dream, but relly I must get home to Father.'

'You're a good daughter, Janet. Go, I'll drop in tomorrow and you'll let me know what you need.'

'Thank yoo Minister, thank yoo Bess…'

'I'll step weth yoo Jan, an' see yoo best part home.'

Janet acknowledged Bess's offer and they headed off down the track.

It was not far-gone noon when they reached the cottage and Bess bid Janet better for the rest of her stay, assuring her of better news to come from Mainland. This made little sense to Janet, her present cares were all here, but she accepted the well-meant words of her friend, bid her farewell and continued on.

Janet wasn't a great deal closer to the farm when she first noticed the chill of the wind and the milky hue of the sun. What was this change in the feel of the day? Low cloud had hidden the top of Knucker Hill - more the norm in Winter than now - and the feeling of dread, notably absent whilst in converse with Bess, was rising again. She quickened her stride.

'Ded yoo catch hem?' Edward called down as she entered.

'No Father, he was long gone…'

Silence.

'But the Minister said he'd attend on yoo tomorrow.'

'He's a good man. I'll look forward to that.'

'The weather's changin'…'

'Oh?'

Janet cut some meat and put it on a plate, she didn't wish for their conversations to be awkward now that Edward had revealed the truth;

not since he had fulfilled the role of father so admirably.

She took the food and some ale up to him, 'Et's turned cold oot.'

'Hmm, Autumn's fer an early appearance thess year. Reckon Mary'll want yoo back before the weather gets too unpredictable.'

'I donny need to do her biddin' anymore.' Janet stated plainly.

'Wha's that child?'

'Mary's no' my aunt, she has no say en what I do…'

'Now, now, Janet…'

'Et's true; I was found, an' though I love yoo as a father, I need no' do as *she* says.'

Edward looked very grim indeed. 'Janet, et would kill her to know. Please, fer my sake donny tell her, I beg yoo!'

An intense feeling of compassion seemed to smother her resolve, any sense that she may have an answer to Mary's demands that she acquired a husband other than Ben, seemed to dissolve, she couldn't drop Edward's revelation on his sister, his only living, blood relative; she just couldn't. 'I'm sorry Father, I wellne, but please, well yoo speak fer Ben? Mary intends I take a husband when I return.'

'Ya too young! Et's folly. I'll write her a letter that yoo ken take weth yoo, detailin' what Ben has done fer us en savin' my life, an' that I have agreed yoo shall wed when the time es right.'

Janet could not stop her tears, 'Oh, thank yoo Father.'

Boy sought a place in their embrace and they spoke of little else but plans of marriage for the rest of the day.

As light faded, so Janet rose to pull the curtain closed. 'Et's the thickest o' fog oot Father.'

'Hmm, Daniel well have held to Westray ef he didne set a course fer Moclett.' Edward could see Janet's concern. 'Donny be afeared my love. Daniel knows these waters too well, he's as sound a decision maker as any man I know. Reckon they're more 'an safe; yoo'll see. Ow!' Edward had been straining up to talk to Janet and was now clutching his side.

'Dear Father, rest, yoo've much to heal that canny be seen.' She eased him back under the covers. 'I'm sure ya right aboot Daniel. I expect my dream was naught more that the upset o' yesterday.'

Chapter Fifty

'Her dream was real though, was et no'!' Kaleigh read Garrie's downcast expression giving her all she needed by way of an answer. 'Damn! I knew et, she lost her true love!'

'The song we heard, Sal. It was a lament for Benjamin.'

Sally looked at Garrie.

Garrie nodded affirmation 'The fishing boats were found empty, run aground on the rocks beneath the eastern cliffs o' Red Head, no trace o' a man en sight.'

'Poor Janet.' Kayleigh sniffed, 'They were so right fer each other.'

Sally was frowning.

Garrie continued, 'Et hadne taken long fer news to reach Pierowall. A relative from Moclett, concerned by the fog o' the previous afternoon an' evenin', had arrived seekin' news o' the fleet. Findin' that et hadne returned to Pierowall to await safe conditions, the relative raised the alarm, an' a number o' sailin' vessels headed fer the fleet's last known destination. On the way they met another fisherman from Calfsound, who had chanced upon the fleet boats early en the mornin' an' was headin' to Pierowall to report them.

'Janet had no' slept well, an' so rose at the first sign o' light. She had figured a plan to ease her concern aboot Benjamin's safety, an' felt sure that ef his boat had ben recovered from the bay then all would be well. Et would take juss ten minutes on the cart track to reach the bay an' ease her fears, an', seein' her father sound, she headed fer the barn.

'The mornin' was chill an' fresh but clear, an' although the sun had no' yet topped the horizon an' the stars were stell visible en the west, the dawn was bright.

'Boy was glad to see her as she opened the barn door. He stood expectant o' his breakfast, but quickly padded to her as she bid hem. He was her only consolation as she observed Benjamin's boat from the rise atop the bay, unclaimed. Briefly she crumpled to her knees, gatherin' the animal en her arms an' sobbin'.

'Distraught, Janet was aboot to head home, but Boy's attention was fixed on the beach, a low growl en his throat. Janet froze, what had he seen?

'The beach was fully exposed by an exceptionally low tide, Tuquoy's beautiful, pale sand stretched oot to the distant water, an' a lone figure was knelt at the water's edge. Boy barked. Janet bid hem hush an' watched as the figure looked back at them, stood an' headed quickly to the further side o' the bay. Janet leapt to her feet an' called oot fer news o' the fleet but the figure seemed en full retreat, as ef disturbed from an unlawful deed. Boy sprang forward as ef to give chase but Janet called hem to heel. There was a sharp disturbance en the breakers that took Janet straight back to her dream. Why had she come? She stepped away, turned an' wethout lookin' back, hurried en the direction o' home.

'As she reached the main track that would see her to her door, Janet came across a herd o' cows, at first she thought them to be her father's, but they were loose ef that were the case. Then she saw Mr. Mullan, who kept a herd on the fields from the Point o' Cott to Skelwick. He was movin' them.

'He greeted her, notin' that she was up early, but Janet, stell anxious from what she had seen an' the fact that Benjamin's boat had no' ben collected, simply acknowledged hem weth a nod an' weaved her path through the herd en the direction o' the farmhoose.

'On arrival home, Boy seemed anxious, he was whimperin'; et was no' like hem, so Janet allowed hem en. She checked on her father, he looked peaceful, so she let hem sleep. She tended the fire then sought oot Edwards's store o' rum. She hovered beside the keg, fingers poised to free Edward's tankard from ets hook on the wall. Boy stared up at her. He was whimperin' again. Janet told herself to get a grip, but moments later she was settin' beside the hearth, comfortin' the lettle dog curled up on her lap, the warmth o' the fire on her feet an' the heat o' the rum en her throat.'

'Janet awoke to a thumpin' on the door. The Minister had come, juss as he'd said he would. Janet hurriedly let hem en, dismissed his concern aboot her dishevelled appearance an', leavin' hem to stroke Boy, headed upstairs to rouse her father fer his visitor.'

Garrie's audience all witnessed the tears welling in his eyes.

Kayleigh, most sensitive to her host's emotions, also cried, as she acknowledged the tale's revelation of Edward's death. He had succumbed to internal wounds, passing in his sleep.

~

Janet was distraught, inconsolable. The Minister, concerned by the empty tankard with its familiar scent of rum, insisted that the Kirk folk would deal with all the necessary arrangements, and that Janet should stay for a while with her friend Bess.

'Get what you need Miss Forsyth, I will walk you, Bess was so concerned for you yesterday, she certainly will not turn you away in your time of need.'

Janet had become like an automaton, following the Minister's instructions without protest, allowing him to carry her hurriedly gathered belongings and using him for support along the path, Boy trailing behind them.

Bess quickly answered the Minister's knock, arriving at the doorway voice filled with sympathy. 'Oh, sweet Jan, bless yoo, come en.'

Boy growled.

'Oh dear, no' you, dog.' Bess glanced at the Minister, who, with Janet's agreement headed back to Pierowall with Boy, the little animal glancing frequently back.

At mid-day the news of the lost fishing fleet arrived. Bess had seen folk heading to Pierowall in unusually high numbers, some obviously troubled. She had challenged one passer-by from the doorway of the cottage. 'Wha's up? Where are yoo all goin'?'

'The Moclett fishin' fleet es lost…'

Overhearing the reply, Janet collapsed.

Chapter Fifty-one

The grief of the island community was great. Not one person on Westray lacked a relational connection with at least one of Daniel's men, the suggestion was made that a day of mourning encompass both the memorial for the fleet and the burial of Edward as both had been so important to the Islanders, and Janet agreed.

Janet had word sent to Mary regarding her brother's death, her aunt had to know, even if it did mean that she would take Janet away from Westray, even if it did mean she would discover that Benjamin was no longer a threat to her intentions for her niece. Indeed, Janet felt sure that Mary's grief for the loss of Edward would somehow be softened by Benjamin's demise, and amongst all those present she would be less the mourner for it.

The days passed quickly, but Janet received no reply to her message.

One morning Bess had gone out before Janet was awake. Janet's nights at the cottage had been fraught with nightmares and restlessness, but that morning she rose rested from a few hours peace. Observing the arrival of a Merchantman through the window, Janet decided to head along the beach from the cottage to the quay to ascertain whether it would be heading back to Kirkwall that day, and whether an urgent message might be sent.

The vessel looked like the one that belonged to Finulf, and the closer she got to it, the more convinced she became. Seeing Bess at the far end of the harbour wall was confirmation that it was the ship of her father and a great wave of disappointment flooded her heart, not because of any dislike for the man, but for the knowledge that every time he arrived at Pierowall he always stayed the night. By morning it would be too late for a message to travel to Kirkwall and for Mary to make arrangements to arrive in time.

Janet was about to give up her cause and return to the cottage when a familiar voice called to her softly, from nearby.

Janet was surprised to see Deborah, she couldn't imagine how she could have overlooked her plump, motherly frame, but now, observing her warm smile and sympathetic eyes, her tears erupted. Deborah hurried to her, consoling her and holding her, gently turning her away from the quay, gently urging her away from the attentions of a man who stood by the gangplank.

'Oh Deborah, my father es gone an' I sent word to his sester an' she has no' responded an' I fear the message es lost an' Mary well blame me...'

'Now, now, dear girl, peace,' She glanced briefly back to the ship. 'The message was received, but Mary es bitter ill since the night o' ya departure. William asked me to come, represent the family, an' breng yoo home weth me afterwards.'

Janet's tears grew more intense, 'He's gone Deborah. Lost to the sea...'

'I know dear child, I heard. I am so sorry. Come, let us go to ya father's hoose...' Deborah, holding Janet tightly, directed her more forcibly away from the quayside towards home, weaving through those who had arrived and those who were assisting with cargo, evading the enquiring eyes behind them.

As they walked, Janet began to feel a comfort in the motherly old shopkeeper that none of Bess's silky words had yet achieved, and she was glad of it, for she knew that her father would be laid-out in his coffin at the farm... that she would have to look on death again. Deborah's presence would be very welcome. Despite her desire to attend to him, Bess had repeatedly persuaded her to let the Kirk folk see to the needs of his body, that she should concentrate on her best memories of him and see to her own healing. Janet had not seen him since that dreadful morning, and a great fear of attending him had begun to grow.

Mrs. Mullan was at the farmhouse, watching over Edward in her turn. Deborah thanked her and relieved her, saying that it was fine to go, and that Janet would see to her father's needs for the rest of the morning. Mrs. Mullan reluctantly left, staring suspiciously at Janet as she passed her in the hall.

'Come now my girl,' Deborah bid. 'Come, say goodbye to ya father properly.'

The Kirk faithful had looked after Edward well, Janet had become convinced that death would look ugly, but here was her father, dressed in his best, looking as if in peaceful sleep in an open, woven casket on the kitchen table.

Janet's tears flowed again, Deborah insisting that she let them. 'He loved yoo so dearly…'

'Oh Deborah, he was no' my true father. I know yoo know that.'

'He told yoo how he found yoo… Et es good that yoo know.'

'But et's no easier…'

'I know. By blood or no' he has ben a true father to yoo.' Deborah drew alongside, rubbing Janet's back and paying her own respects.

~

Deborah was anxious, but she hadn't shown it. She had been approached just days before, in Kirkwall, by the man who had been on the Merchantman. He'd arrived at her shop soon after William had asked her to represent the family at Edward's funeral. He had addressed her by name and sought information on a woman in her employment. Deborah had sung Janet's praises, denying any knowledge of unusual behaviour when the man had made inference to it. He acknowledged Janet's absence due to her assistance with getting goods to a needy member of Deborah's family, and had asked when she would return. Smiling, Deborah had said she wasn't sure and requested that he gave her some means to contact him when she did. He'd written down his name, Mr. May, and an address in the town, insisting, in an urgent tone, that Deborah ensured the girl attended him.

On travelling to Westray, Deborah had hoped to encourage Janet to stay there, hoped to warn her about the enquiries of Mr. May, hoped to figure out how Janet might evade the man should he actively seek her. But Deborah's intentions were abruptly thwarted when Mr. May appeared alongside her on the ship.

~

'Off to pay your respects to the dead, Mrs. Finney?'

'Oh! Mr. May, er, yes, et es a sad time.'

'Strange that you didn't tell me of the funeral…'

Deborah stared.

'Perfect place to be sure of meeting Janet…'

Deborah wanted to snap at the man, wanted to challenge him on his reasons for seeking the girl. But she knew why, she knew there'd been another panic about witches through England since King Charles had married Henrietta Maria, the French King's daughter, this had only been made worse by Charles' dismissal of parliament. Agents, claiming royal authority, had been seeking stories and following leads. She didn't want to give him the pleasure of discovering any concern regarding Janet's safety upon the realisation that a witch hunter was pursuing her. She snorted dismissively, 'Doubt the girl well attend the funeral, they were no' close, tha's why she was workin' fer me en Kirkwall, an' livin' weth her aunt.'

'Why *is* she on Westray then?'

'She has friends there, ded yoo no' know? Et's where she grew up…'

The inference of ignorance seemed to bother him, he stated plainly "of course he knew that she had grown up on Westray!" then he stomped away with a parting order, that Deborah take him to Janet when they reach Pierowall.

'I well look oot fer yoo by the quay.' Deborah called back, smiling inwardly as his reaction had shown him to be moody and shallow, and his parting now had afforded her an opportunity to disappear.

Deborah had not smiled for long; Janet was in real danger. May was a bloodhound, and witch hunters were not known for their compassion. She hurried to the aft of the merchantman, where there was some seclusion afforded by bulky cargo, and where a seagull was sitting minding its own business, perhaps hopeful of some scraps when the ship was docked and offloaded.

If a search had been set for Deborah now, however meticulous, she would not have been found, for the words she chose to use could render a soul invisible in plain sight. May ducked as a gull swooped closely by him, disappearing ahead of the ship.

Chapter Fifty-two

May had waited for Deborah until a sailor insisted that all passengers had disembarked. Unconvinced that she could have passed him without being intercepted, he demanded that a search be made. The sailor resisted him but May bundled him off the gangplank into the water as he made his way back onboard. He was quickly discharged from the deck by other sailors who'd witnessed their ship-mates dive. Flustered, May stalked off to find a local tavern, and intelligence regarding the whereabouts of the Forsyth home.

Deborah glanced quickly out of the kitchen window. The track to Pierowall was empty but she didn't know how much time they had.

'Oh, dearest child do yoo have any belongin's, we have to get yoo away.'

Thinking that Deborah was talking about a return to Kirkwall, Janet was dismissive. 'I think I'll stay, the farm needs runnin', I…'

'No, dear girl, yoo must flee…' Deborah's tone froze Janet. 'Ya en grave danger. I've no enklin' o' who's cast suspicion on yoo, but there's a man after findin' yoo… a witch hunter…'

Janet became pale, Deborah quickly supporting her.

'My thengs are stell at Bess's cottage, I must go fer them…' Janet turned, but Deborah's arms resisted her.

'No, yoo canny resk et, yoo must go ento hidin', until thess man es gone.'

'But where?'

Deborah checked the Pierowall track again, it was still clear. A gull was sitting on the gatepost. 'Come, I sent word to some friends.'

Janet's condition was like that of a shocked child, so Deborah led her out of the farm. She nodded to the gull, who, freed from its duty, called out and flew, heading back to the ship with a fading hope that any scraps of edible cargo would remain there.

In a short while the two women were stood beside the cleft. 'Yoo well be safe here.'

Janet gestured at the clouds, 'But et looks like rain.'

'Have yoo truly fergotten where yoo are?' Deborah asked, pointing down. Janet's eyes followed, meeting the gaze and broad smile of Deni.

Janet was thrilled to see him again, but her emotions overpowered her and she was unable to do anything for herself. Deborah and Deni helped her down into the cleft and to the hidden door. She would not have found it for it was magically concealed, enchantment, ancient like the very bones of the land. Janet felt the cold kiss of bedrock around her body, an icy caress akin to passage into a place of death, but with any fear stripped away as eyes met with a lit, warm, subterranean world.

'I must go.' Deborah said.

'No Deborah, please…'

'I must keep watch. I must divert the man. Deni well send some o' the others fer ya thengs when the coast es clear.' She gently propelled Janet away from the entrance. '…Go enjoy the hospitality o' the Trows.'

Mr. May had made enquiries; he'd discovered how to reach the Forsyth family home but also that Janet had been staying with a Miss Skebister at the other end of the bay. May was soon at the cottage door, knocking impatiently. There was no answer. He tried the door and found it open. 'Anyone here?' he called, stepping onto the threshold.

'Ken we help yoo?'

May pitched around, he hadn't heard Bess and Finulf approaching, a couple of burly sailors in tow; sailors aware of May's antics on the gangplank. Roughly, they pulled May out of the doorway, but he was no weakling and he quickly freed himself from their grasp, pushing them away and taking his stand. A small number of islanders had been passing on the track and had stopped to witness the altercation; an unusual event that might be quite entertaining and certainly worth discussion over some ale later. Deborah was in their midst, though no eye could perceive her.

May looked at Bess with calculating eyes, this woman certainly matched the descriptions, 'I'm looking for Janet Forsyth, is that you?'

'I'm Bess. Es Jan no' home?' She stepped to the open door, 'Jan! Jan… What do yoo want o' her?'

'I'm investigating allegations of Witchcraft.'

Bess's reaction was swift, and unexpected, 'Jan? A wetch. Oh my! An' to think I've allowed her under my roof! Yoo must take her belongings! Wait here, I well get them.'

Deborah scowled.

There was a tense wait, one sailor suggesting they give May a sound beating, but Finulf refused to allow him, warning him that May was a representative of the King and that any violence might well be regretted.

May smirked, although the girl was taking a considerable time.

Bess returned with a bag, 'Thess es hers; I've put all that belongs to her en et, there's nothin' left en the cottage.'

'Never-the-less, I should like to look, there may be some hidden marks…'

Finulf and the sailors all moved as one to stall May's mobilised attempt to enter the cottage and he backed down. He looked first at Bess then at the sailors and snorted, 'Far be it from me to delay your whoring any longer…'

This was too far for Finulf, he grabbed May by the collar of his coat and marched him away from the cottage leaving him flailing across the track. 'Tha's my daughter! Go, I'll no' tolerate yoo!'

May shocked by the man's strength, gathered up the bag and headed off towards the Forsyth farm, straight by Deborah whose whispered incantation still rendered her as naught more than a nameless form amongst the gathered onlookers.

Deborah glanced at the bag as May stumbled passed; she had provided Janet with her holdalls from old stock in the shop. This bag was not Janet's. She took a deep breath and, renewing the words that hid her, followed May.

~

'Bess had framed her, hadn't she!'

Sally corrected Carl, 'Erka.'

'Aye. But no' so much framin' as self-preservation. She knew that ef May entered, he would quickly find all manner o' relics that would place her en the flames.'

Kayleigh thought framing was still the best summary, 'She let Janet take the blame, but she also incriminated her further. Yoo said the bag wasne hers.'

Garrie nodded, 'May had found the Farmhoose empty, he'd entered an' searched, he'd found some lightly scratched marks on the floor boards o' Janet's bedroom. Findin' nothin' else he'd entered the kitchen, weth the corpse o' Edward en ets casket.'

'Weth no room on the table, May emptied the bag on the stone floor. Crouchin', he picked through the clothes; Deborah, watchin' through the wendow. The clothes ded belong to Janet, she recognised them, but there was also a doll.'

Sally thought it strange, 'The doll that Janet had given to Bess?'

'The very one. Deborah saw, as May lifted et from the mess o' clothes, that the dolls hair - indeed Mary's own - was tied around et's neck, tightly holdin' a lead shard deeply cut weth runes. What May would define as a Poppet.'

Carl felt this needed elaboration for Sally, 'Like a voodoo doll, meant to harm the individual it depicted.'

Garrie shrugged, he knew nothing of voodoo, but acknowledged the link to harming another. 'May took a knife from his jacket an' cut the hair short, loosin' the shard, slippin' et an' the severed locks ento his pocket. Deborah knew that et was no' good to cut a curse from a poppet wethout healin' werds, the shock o' seein' May do et took her

221

concentration juss as May looked up, an' Deborah found herself discovered by his gaze. Knowin' any disappearance now, even oot o' sight from the window, would cast suspicion on herself, Deborah smiled, waved, an' headed to the Farmhoose door.'

~

May stepped quickly to the door to detain her but found her willingly entering.

'Sorry Sir, I fell asleep on board the boat. Yoo'd left before I could meet weth yoo.'

Something of Deborah's confidence, and willingness to come to him, impressed May, perhaps she was going to help him to his goal after all.

'She's not here.'

'I didne think she would be...'

'And yet you are here...'

May's observation felt incriminating. 'I'm here because I knew yoo'd come here first, no' because I'm lookin' fer the child... excuse me please, I wesh to pay my respects to the departed.'

May felt obliged to let Deborah pass.

'Och dear!' She pretended that she was seeing the clothes scattered across the floor for the first time. 'What a mess, how disrespectful! She has clearly ben here Mr. May, fer these *are* her garments, but why on earth would she breng them here and dump them by Edward's casket?'

'That was me, the woman she was lodging with gave me her bag, I was examining the contents...' He shook his head, why was he explaining himself to this old nag?

'Oh, how easy et es to point the finger at someone, to jump to a conclusion based on such small evidence.' It was the boldest defence of Janet she dared to give, but May was too dismissive.

'Perhaps to the untrained eye, but I assure you, *my* skills in investigation are exemplary.'

Deborah picked a path through the clothes to reach Edward's side, she rested a hand on his chest, sighing deeply, 'Dear man. How desperately sad he would have ben to hear thess news o' Janet.'

A cold smile cut across May's face, 'You said they didn't get on, why would he be sad?'

Deborah's heart raced, 'No, I said they were no' close, but that was Janet, like many young people, such free spirits. Edward was a devoted father. He would quickly have swept her up ento his arms - had she allowed et - but she's an independent girl...'

'And if she is rarely here, why are there so many of her belongings upstairs?'

Deborah feigned puzzlement, 'Relly? Show me.'

May was very happy to do so; he'd caught the old woman out and was moments away from exposing her falsehood, perhaps less than a moment more from gaining intelligence of Janet's whereabouts. He threw open the simple trunk in the girl's bedroom.

'Oh dear, yoo've gone wrong... as I ded doonstairs...'

May seemed highly annoyed, 'These are a woman's clothes, are you suggesting they belonged to the man!'

'No, no, Mr. May, these are neither Edward's nor Janet's.' She pulled Janet's long dress from the box, this would be her biggest lie so far, she took a deep breath. 'I havne seen these fer so long, I guess he could no' breng hemself to throw them away. These are Gwen's dresses, they belonged to Edward's wife. Thess was her wedding dress, no' as grand as ya used to, no doubt, but we Orcadians are no' so grand as mainland folk. Oh, happy thought! They are now reunited en Heaven.'

'Ha!' May retorted, rendering Deborah anxious. 'Edward's room is obviously the one across the hall, such happy folk sleep in separate rooms *do they*?'

Deborah drew closer to May; this would be a pleasure and she didn't want to miss the slightest twitch of frustration on his face. 'Gwen was very poorly. Ah, but yoo couldne have known that. She nearly died en childbirth, et left her weak o' mind an' body. At night she would drool an' gurgle. Though he stell loved her, he slept apart, he had a farm to run. Sleep es important...'

'And this?' May snapped, pointing at the floor.

Deborah was still masking her joy at thwarting May's investigation, when her eyes perceived what the man was indicating.

Chapter Fifty-three

Carl's investigative mind had jumped ahead, 'Deborah saw meaning in the scratches on the floorboards.'

'She had to suppress very strong emotions; she knew exactly what she was lookin' at. T'be seen t'recognise et would've cast doubt on her own ennocence…'

'Wetches marks!' Kayleigh gasped.

Garrie nodded. 'They were light an' difficult to see, so she seized the chance May's ignorance afforded her. She apologised fer the weakness o' her eyes, an' asked what he was tryin' to show her. He huffed, an' walked oot, convinced that the old crone could contribute nothin' to his search. Deborah steadied herself on the door frame as she confirmed his departure. Cautiously she returned to the marks. Weth protective werds on her lips she stared at them, fixated on them, occupied them. Discoverin' their utter darkness, she recoiled. Their origin was en night, the trappin's o' day cast aside. Deborah had felt nothin' as evil since Erka lived, fer the interpretation o' the whole was stoppin' an ennocent heart, that o' Mrs. Dooney, one held by the protection o' the true God, an impossible theng, but here concluded. An' the worst - that which disturbed Deborah most - a simple mark, one stroke through which she could see another ennocent held to forgetfulness. These marks represented a cold, callous murder an' Janet had ben a witness. Deborah sobbed; the scratches that May believed confirmed Janet's identity as a Wetch, actually proved her virtue - the revealin' o' thess to May would condemn the interpreter, an' although Deborah wanted so much to clear Janet's neem, she feared the flames too much herself. She had t'find another wey.'

Garrie's eyes were set on Carl, sending such a chill through him that he felt the need to change the subject. 'Did May leave Westray?'

'No' straight away; he stayed fer the funeral an' memorial, but although Deborah was there, his quarry was nowhere t'be found. Deborah had warned Janet to stay away, an' although et caused her great distress, she heeded her friend. Werd o' his castin' a locally known sailor ento the dock 'twixt ship an' harbour wall had travelled ahead o' hem, an' few felt hem a savoury man to discuss the whereaboots o' a daughter o' the island.'

'Janet was safe.'

'Aye, he left empty handed, on the next tide.'

Sally sighed relief.

'How old was Janet now?'

'Nineteen, a score before the Wenter.'

Kayleigh smiled. 'Ken yoo tell us o' her time weth the Trows?'

'Et was a happier time... The halls o' the Trows were infused weth joy, a bright luminescence gave light as day, an' as Janet stood there - Deborah gone that first time - she could feel her mind filled weth song.'

Kayleigh's eyes grew bright, 'The Trow chorus.' But her excitement quickly faltered. The Trow chorus was thought to be a constant, ever changing refrain, Deni, Donie and Dini had been silent of song the whole time. 'Wha's wrong?'

'There es a sorrow.' He turned to the downcast trio, 'Boys, we need a break, would no' a line or two o' the Old Song warm ya hearts again?'

Deni, Donie and Dini looked up slowly, the others observed a wetness to their eyes, but Donie stood, pulling something like a clarinet from his tunic, the size of which should never have fitted without protruding somewhere. The other two rose.

'Aye, tha's good boys.' Garrie started to tap a rhythm on the flags with his stick. Donie began a floral melody that filled the room beyond the means of a single instrument and the visitors felt their spirits rise in an instant.

Dini stepped forward, Deni clapping a complimentary beat to Garrie's, and the group heard a rich, deep voice in their minds.

'Goes the old song, mirth all hail, rhythm keeps a tappin',
Tellin' o' a time as gone, that made the halls o' Tal-a-non.

Freedom won through secret ways, under noses nosin',
Tellin' o' the clever plan, set liberty en Tal-a-non.

Born o' craft, born o' love, all o' life's a lesson,
Tellin' o' a truth tha's strong, that made the heart en Tal-a-non.

Life es rich as life ken be, walls resound we sing on,
Tellin' o' a precious throng that richly guarded Tal-a-non...'

Garrie's guests listened, ten verses, twenty; they seemed to know the words before they came, a rich understanding of the Trow kingdom of Talanon growing in their minds. An awareness of the magical origin of their kind grew, the realisation that they were created for servitude but had escaped to a hidden and joyous sanctuary unseen by all but loving eyes.

~

'Carl? Carl?'
'Sal? What's up? I think I must have drifted off to sleep...'
'Yes, me too, I think the song just sent me.'
A quick glance around confirmed that all, bar the old man, were soundly snoozing. It seemed lighter outside, like dawn, but the wind still roared and the rain still streamed across the window where Old Garrie stood gazing out despite the impossibility of discerning anything through the misted, water-streaked panes.
'Did I miss the end of the story?'
'I don't think there was one.' Carl stretched, 'I think the song was meant to bring rest.'
Garrie gave an affirmative chuckle.
Sally quickly joined him, also trying to see what could not be seen

through the glass. 'Is she coming?'

Garrie looked sad, 'She should be here, but the storm es stell ragin'. I fear she'll be spent, an' well no' be long weth us.'

Sally rubbed his arm compassionately. 'She'll be fine with you here to look after her...'

A tear trickled from the man's eye. 'Yoo donny have the seal necklace, do yoo?'

Sally seemed to sense that he would rather hear that they knew nothing of any such object than to hear that it was lost, to hear the words "What necklace is that?" rather than a simple but revealing "No."

'No.' She replied.

'Oh Lord! I fell asleep, I canny believe et! What ded I miss?'

Garrie regarded Kayleigh stoically, 'Nothin', we all took the opportunity to rest.'

The Trows stirred, performing an elaborate synchronised stretch and yawn, followed by bright eyed smiles.

Kayleigh stroked Dini's cheek, 'Thank yoo fer the song.'

Dini blushed and received a well-meant jostle from the other two.

Garrie stared soberly at the door.

Sally felt dreadful.

Chapter fifty-four

After some breakfast, and despite his openly growing anxiety over Janet's failure to arrive, Garrie continued to speak of Janet's time with the Trows; how Deborah had urged her to stay with them until she could arrange somewhere safer. How the little folk spirited her belongings from the farmhouse and Boy from the fireside of the Minister's home. How the Trows loved her and ceremonially adopted her when weeks turned into months. How, amongst the belongings the Trows had returned to her, she found a seal pup skin that felt warm,

227

and how she believed it must be Benjamin's; a precious thing she would treasure forever in memory of her lost love. How there was a letter, written in Edward's rustic hand, that defended Benjamin, outlined the family's debt to him and upheld his right to marry Janet. How her tears flowed for days on end the little people constant in their care and service. He pointed out the reaction of the islanders to Janet's apparent disappearance, and Bess's part in weaving a story that Janet had fled due to her implicit part in the presence of the Nuckelavee.

Carl needed confirmation, 'Was Bess responsible for the Nuck... er, the creature's appearances? I mean Janet saw a person on the beach that time. Was it Bess?'

'Aye, et was. Erka's jewel enabled her to direct the energies o' the beast's huntin' ento a focus on Janet herself, an' - to the islanders - et seemed to disappear.'

Sally shivered, 'It hunted Janet?'

'Aye, but et had lettle to go on, fer the Trows had no' only spirited Janet's belongin's from the farm, e'en her scent was gone. A sight o' Janet though...'

'But we know she was tried for witchcraft, so the beast never found her.' Carl seemed quite convinced by his assumption.

'No' so. Yoo see, as Janet started to explore the tunnels an' caverns o' her new home, she found a way to the caves at Noup Head. Et was here, weth Boy, that Janet stumbled across the creature. Crazed weth unsated hunger et saw her an' gave chase. Janet, stell no' wholly attuned to seein' the hidden portals o' Talanon, passed the doorway an' was trapped weth the lettle dog at the deepest end o' the cave.'

~

'So thess es my end.' Janet crossed herself piously. 'But so be et, fer all I loved es dead; an' be et quick fer by such a way I'll join both my dear love an' my guardian en heaven.'

Boy looked at Janet and snorted. Stepping forward he held his ground between the Nuckelavee and Janet, his fierce yapping causing exaggerated caution in the beast.

'Run Boy, there's no chance fer yoo here…'

Boy slowly glanced back at Janet and she noticed a change in his face. His eyes seemed to bulge with a fiery glow, his jawline was becoming broader, then his shoulders.

The Nuckelavee made its move, attempting to beat the distracted dog against the wall of the cave, but Boy's reaction was sudden and explosively violent. He wrapped himself about the sweeping arm, tearing at the flesh with tooth and claw, both of which had grown beyond the size of a man's hand, his body already the bulk of a bull and still growing, his yaps becoming deep barks and fearsome growls.

Janet screamed, terrified for Boy's wellbeing, despite the manifestation of his hidden powers. 'Oh, Boy, Boy, be careful, Oh!'

The beast tore its arm from boy's jaws and rapidly retreated, shielding itself from Boy's chasing aggression.

Steeling herself, Janet followed, feeling along the wall for the entry to Talanon… where was it? She knew the vicinity but it eluded her. Boy and the creature were near the cliff face entrance to the cave, out of Janet's sight; their struggling shadows flickering the light around Janet's frantic search.

Suddenly a shrill bark echoed around the cave walls, and Janet could see Boy fleeing back towards her, limping heavily, his size and form back to normal. 'I canny find et Boy! I canny find the door!'

The creature, still out of sight gave a chilling scream and Janet knew it was coming back. She swept Boy into her arms. 'I'm so sorry Boy, I fergot yoo are my livin' love, an' so brave. Ded yoo protect father en the same way b'the wall? Ah, but thess es surely the end.'

A noise behind her swung her around. Seeing a Trow hurriedly beckoning, she obeyed, following him with great relief into the song filled paradise.

The Trow gestured they remain motionless and for the first time since Janet's arrival, the Trow Chorus fell silent. She could hear her own breathing, heavy, laboured, anxious. Perceiving the approach of the monster, she held her breath. Initially the creature bustled passed. Janet sighed relief but the Trow insisted she remain silent and still.

The Nuckelavee, finding his prey absent from the back of the cave, whined in confusion. An eerie silence followed, and Janet understood the Trow's order. The beast was now hunting again, returning down the cave, sniffing, feeling for hiding places. Janet's heart began to race uncontrollably, she felt sick and lightheaded, she wanted to run, and would have if a group of Trows, lightly armoured and carrying ornate, crafted spears, hadn't silently appeared in the tunnel. The soldiers held their position in silence and it was clear to Janet, that if the creature didn't find the Trow tunnel, there would be no engagement.

There was a snort very close to Janet's shoulder, she closed her eyes, praying inwardly, tightly clutching Boy and becoming aware of the sticky trickle from a cut on his flank. Silence.

It was clear that the beast had stopped, was listening and drinking in the air through its nostrils quietly. Finger tips appeared, exploring what looked, from the creature's standpoint, like a crevice. Those horrible fingers, gnarled and arthritic, their ends deeply cut, bloodied from the melee with Boy, the nails ugly, ridged and pale.

Suddenly the whole of one hand was through, finding the crevice magically wider than it seemed. It almost had Janet but a fleet spear pinned it to the rock beside her. The creature, wailing, tried to pull its hand away but the weapon held fast. The Trow that had brought Janet back into the tunnels, now grabbed her hand and, with urgency, led her away.

With a deep, throaty growl the Nuckelavee entered the passage, the cold glare from its single eye tested the steel of the Trows. The eyes of its horse-like head assessed the spear that pinned it to the wall. A smile chilled the resolve of the soldiers and with a sharp, forceful thrust it slid the hand quickly down the length of the spear shaft. With hardly a pause it began to approach the spearmen, who readily gave ground, following Janet and her guardian.

Janet was already lost; this was not the way she'd taken to reach the Noup Head caves. She clung grimly to her rescuer's trailing hand; Boy now limp under her arm. The noise of pursuit seemed to be closing in on them but the sound of Trow boots, echoing down the tunnel behind them, had diminished to none. Her guide led her into a narrow, torch-lit room, the iridescence of the walls absent, the ceiling draped in black darkness due to its height. They crossed a broad plank over a cut in the stone floor, then another before stopping, Janet's guide quickly pulling the wood from the gully. Janet could hear her companion's mind-song begin again, but her horror that the room had no apparent exit left her in despair.

> 'Daro an' Diel, we'll catch et today,
> Daro an' Diel, we'll catch et today.'
> 'We'll net et an' pin et an' gut et today
> Vengeance well come an' yoo'll rest en ya grave.'

The refrain repeated, but its words disturbed Janet. They were dark, and cold, with a tune quite unlike the other songs she'd heard in this bright and beautiful place.

A second voice joined the first, they were not alone, a third and fourth as the Nuckelavee flailed into the room. It stopped, eyes unaccustomed to the flickering light, staring into the shadows above. The Trow with Janet started to wave and clap bringing the creatures focus back to Janet. With its desire for her flesh emboldening it again, the beast stepped quickly over the first plank, its bulk dancing between silhouette and spot-lit horror, a green, malignant glow at the level of its unfeeling heart.

Janet backed away until she felt the chill of the wall against her back, the fingers of her free hand frantically exploring the crevices for another hidden way. Her rescuer held his ground, arms high in the air, waiting as the monster drew closer, closer.

Suddenly the Trow dropped one arm, with a look of excitement on his face that brought the Nuckelavee to a halt. Movement behind caused the beast to turn its single eyed head back to the entrance. Here, two small, unarmed Trows, dragged the first plank from the gully. The creature seemed torn but the burning eyes of its horse-like head remained fixed on Janet. Again, it stepped forward, each step quickening. Janet's guide lowered his other arm. A heavy thud echoed down the chamber, followed by a roar, Janet was sobbing, crouched now on the floor, holding Boy tightly, watching her rescuer as the beast seemed ready to strike. Suddenly, a great curtain of water

231

obscured the view of the Nuckelavee. The creature, already partly aware of the descending sheet of fresh water, had attempted to stop, but its committed attack had left it skidding into the icy shield. Its long, startled, equine face pierced the barrier, sending it convulsing onto unready back legs. Stumbling and tripping, the monster attempted to retreat, but the water, governed skilfully in this purposely prepared trap, ran quickly around the room in its gully, preventing the Nuckelavee's escape. Its driven focus gone, the beast paced like a caged animal, clearly distressed.

The waterfall's reservoir was spent, its volume swirled and rippled in the gully, Janet's terror refusing to accept the containment of the pursuer. It took many comforters appearing now from hidden ways, to turn the chill in her heart to a hint of acceptance. Boy was quickly taken into care and Janet's guide urged her to her feet, encouraging her to raise her arms. The beast was becoming more and more agitated; could it hear the Trow song?

'Daro an' Diel, we'll catch et today,
Daro an' Diel, we'll catch et today.
We'll net et an' pin et an' gut et today
Vengeance well come an' yoo'll rest en ya grave.'

Janet's guide broke from the chorus, his voice crystal clear to her above the chanting. 'Daro an' Diel, were the heroes who slew the other two Nucks, back when they bit us to kill us. We drenched ourselves en poison an' faced them. Mine realised what was happenin' an' tore my chest weth ets hoof.' The Trow pulled up its shirt revealing an ugly scar. 'Et has tormented me to know that I failed, but today I well put et right. I knew et would find Talanon one day. That's why I made thess room. Now yoo well trap et, an' we well end et. Lower ya arms.'

Janet lowered her arms. The chant stopped. A great mechanical noise, clunked above them in the darkness beyond the torchlight, and a heavy net, woven to boulders, crashed down on the beast. A pall of dust shrouded the room and there was silence.

Chapter Fifty-five

Old Garrie gave another deep sigh, his attention wavering. It was clear to his guests that Janet should be safely home, but the storm still swirled and she was strictly bound to it; the curse would not let her go until the end.

Garrie forced his attention back to his audience. 'When the dust cleared the beast was motionless…'

Carl was lost, 'Hold on, how many of these creatures were there?'

'There were three, shaped by those that had created the Trows as slaves. They were intended to hold the Trows to slavery through fear; fer all who tried to escape were brutally slain.'

'So, if two of them were killed by Daro and Deil's self-sacrifice and this one was trapped and killed in Talanon, where did the one we saw come from?'

Garrie huffed, 'One an' the same.'

'It escaped?'

'Janet had them set et free…'

Carl, Sally and Kayleigh looked at each other in disbelief. Sally turned to Deni, Donie and Dini. Dini took up the story, his voice clear in their minds.

'I was there. Dorn had trapped the Nuck, pinned tight under boulders an' net. We cheered hem, an' our song found new werds. He'd taken great efforts o'er thess day, toiled o'er the chamber, ets mechanisms, ets reservoir, the carvin' o' the anchor stones woven ento the net. Et had werked! The beast was ours! The last o' the three, at our mercy! Oh, the thrill, fer et had long ben the other way roond. The creature had always ben a night terror fer young an' old alike.

'Dorn rushed fer a spear. Thess was his kill, et always had ben. Now he would be a hero o' Talanon, now they would carve statues en his honour! He raised the spear but Janet bid hem to wait. Et seemed that *she* wished to slay et. Dorn hesitated; Our song grew quiet, unsure

233

where our werds should go. He handed the spear to her, the creature's hate-filled eyes watchin'. She placed the point o' the weapon onto the Nuck's chest, causin' et to growl menacin'ly. She twested the spear-point superficially, as ef torturin' her attacker. Young Trows hid their faces. There was an unbearable tension. Then there was a clatter, the sound o' some small, metal object hittin' the stone floor. Dorn picked et up, but quickly dropped et an' stepped away, eyes filled weth terror.

'Janet picked up the object, screamed, dropped et an' smashed et weth the butt o' the spear. Fer a moment she stood there, wide eyed. All attention was off the beast; our song fell silent.

'Janet stared at the twested metal an' cracked, green jewel that had ben a part o' the shattered pendant. She looked at the shallow wound she had inflicted on the creature's chest, an' she knew. She knew that the gem had controlled et, ets desires, ets will. Havin' touched that charm, she now knew many thengs that she couldne understand, but one theng was clear to her. She fell upon the beast's side, strokin' et, tellin' et no' to be afraid. We were amazed. The animal's voice was no longer a cause o' fear fer us; now et expressed the distress o' the snare.

'Janet urged us to free et. Well, we were bewildered, we had intended immediate death fer our ancient adversary. Dorn insisted et should die, fer who knew; perhaps ets will may be twested again to hunt on behalf o' those who would control et; a thought made worse, fer now et knew a way ento the corridors o' Talanon.

'Janet's werds brought home to us the decision we had to make. Touchin' the jewel had shown her the origin o' the three, that they had each ben a rider an' his steed, great an' good, twested an' corrupted ento a bestial form to do the biddin' o' the true evil. E'en Dorn's head sank, fer he knew Janet was right. We had sought our freedom, why too should thess creature, once so noble, no' also be free?

'A number o' us, emboldened by what was clearly right, gathered around Janet an' the beast, an', though some quailed, we cut the mesh. The Nuck stood slowly, the remnant o' the weave slippin' from ets back. Et genuinely looked puzzled, like an animal boxed an' placed en an unknown space. Dorn wondered ef et e'en knew us, ef et e'en recalled the horrible thengs et had done. I pointed oot that et was lost, that et had no recollection o' the route by which et had arrived, that et had ben driven by ets lust fer flesh an' now needed to be taken back to the sea.'

Carl shook his head, 'That's nothing like the monster we saw. Dorn was right to fear its return to evil purposes.'

'No' so,' Garrie replied

'But it attacked…'

Sally understood, 'It loved Janet.'

'Huh?'

Sally pulled him close, whispering in his ear, 'It was after what we had; Janet's necklace.' She looked to Garrie, who had turned away, tears welling in his eyes. Even though he was old, there was nothing wrong with his ears, and Sally's whisper had reached him. He'd known they didn't have the necklace, now he knew they'd had it. Was it something to do with James Sinclair? Destroyed or lost? Sally continued, 'The creature is still alive because it loved Janet for releasing it.'

Garrie nodded affirmation, 'Et stayed by the caves at the cliff, an' Janet would visit et. One mornin' she found that et had brought Benjamin's rowin' boat. Her tears flowed that day, fer she stell believed that the beast had played a part en the loss o' the fleet.'

Carl had fixed his eyes on Dini, making the Trow very uncomfortable. 'You said she'd learned much from touching the thing she'd cut from the creature's chest…'

Garrie coughed and wiped his eyes with a handkerchief from his pocket. 'She learned a great deal, perhaps the whole history o' the Trows an' those who had made them from the very stones o' Westray. But et es no' a part o' Janet's own story. What she found o' her own predicament ded lettle to appease her sorrows. Her contact weth the jewel had given her somethin' she could hardly bear. Et had restored her memory o' Bess's night-time incantations, the knowledge that Erka resided en the green gem aboot her friend's neck, controllin' her. Et told her o' Erka's pure hatred fer the Selkies; how she would trap them, skin them an' throw them back ento the waves to drown. That Deborah was Erka's sester, one o' the three who had once enslaved the hearts o' three noble horsemen an' turned them ento twested beasts.'

235

'Poor Janet, was there nothing for her at all? No comfort?'

'A lettle. But et ded no' start as such. Et had taken some weeks fer much o' all thess to clarify en Janet's mind - as long indeed as et had taken fer Boy to recover from his wound - an' when she heard Deborah's voice, she became wary…'

Carl was stumped, 'Heard Deborah's voice?'

'Oh aye, as ef she were stood en the room weth her. Deborah claimed she had felt the creature's spirit bein' set free, that she had felt Janet's touch on the jewel an' that the gem's destruction had aged her.'

~

Janet was unsure, 'I donny trust yoo. I know who yoo are an' what yoo ded.'

'Then yoo'll know what I ded fer the Trows.'

Janet searched her mind, finding what Deborah had done and what it had cost her. The innate goodness of Deborah's heart was apparent to Janet, but she had been gone so long and she had promised to find a place of safety for her. 'Why have yoo ben away so long?'

'Oh, sweet child, so much has happened an' I so wish I could have come to yoo, but May watches me; ef no' hem, the eyes o' one o' his men es always upon me. Everyone I talk to es interrogated, but my craft has ben deep-hidden fer so long that my life es as normal as et ken be, an' my customers speak so well o' me that e'en May's suspicions o' my involvement en ya disappearance have dwindled. Yet he still watches, my love, so I am tied to Kirkwall…'

Janet picked up on Deborah's faltering voice. 'What es et, Deborah?'

'Oh Janet, yoo should know, an' I'm so sorry I couldne get word to yoo, but ya Aunt… when I returned to Kirkwall… I found that she had died. There was a doll, May found et en belongin's that Bess had called yours, an' much o' et was, but thess doll was a poppet, an' May dismantled et wethout the proper actions an' werds. He ended her illness an' misery, but had I discovered the device I could have rectified et an' brought ya Aunt through. Oh Janet, I'm so sorry!'

'Deborah, ets… ets fine, there was nothin' yoo could do.'

'Oh, dear girl, ya friend Bess es bein' controlled by Erka's pendant, ef there were some way we could destroy et she could be free again.'

'I've let her doon…'

'Erka's kept yoo blind, et's part o' her craft.'

'I should have seen et. Look at Finulf, he was no more than a bent old man, grayin' hair an' wiry. The last I saw hem his hair was as raven as Bess's, an' I'd fair say he could give any younger man a sound hidin' en a fight. An' Boy. Boy saw Erka en Bess; he ded growl an' try many times to tell me - why, he even knew et was the necklace!'

Deborah could feel Janet's unrest. 'Calm, my dear, there es nothin' we ken do now, we must be patient, do nothin' to resk discovery. Promise me.'

Janet promised and the conversation came to an end, but she found herself able to reach Deborah many times over the following days, indeed, any time she needed her, for although Mary had treated her so badly at times, Janet had still loved her.

Chapter Fifty-six

It had been some time since Mr. May had seen Deborah. He had left others to watch - as she had suspected - but now their reports caused him to come in person; the smile on his face upon seeing her, chilled her blood.

'Ah, Deborah, it would appear that you have lost much of your former power since I last saw you…'

Deborah, aware that he had already linked her more aged appearance to the use of arcane abilities, responded quickly. 'Et es yoo has aged me Mr. May…'

He mocked an expression of shock.

'…Yoo follow me, yoo watch me, yoo challenge my customers. An' now others have become my shadow too, do yoo think me blind?'

May was staring at the far end of the shop. 'Where does that door lead?'

'More questions, Mr. May?'

'Hardly trying ones; just, you have a door that makes little sense, for your shop abuts another and is not so deep as to spare room for further storage.'

Deborah stared at him, she didn't even look at the door, 'Yoo know the answer.'

May frowned.

'Et *was* a back door, but the shop es very old. The neighbouring shop was built tween thess an' the next as Kirkwall prospered. The door es a relic…'

'And yet not blocked off; the shelves do not cross it, Deborah. Where does it go?'

Seeing two stocky men standing at the entrance of the shop, turning a customer away, Deborah headed towards May's bone of contention, mumbling.

May followed closely, 'What's that you're saying?'

'I said that I liked et, et's a lovely old door.' She flung it open to reveal a rough stone wall.

May examined it. 'You are a mad old woman Mrs. Finney…' He turned to address her more but found her absent. 'Mrs. Finney?' May left the doorway to seek her, but the shop appeared empty. He approached the men at the door but they swore that no one had left. He gazed back into the shop, thoughtfully rubbing his chin. Finally, he closed the door. 'That door is to remain shut, no one in, no one out. I'll be back within the hour.'

Invisible to her captor's eyes, Deborah watched though it tired her immensely to maintain the illusion she'd begun. She stepped out of sight behind the racks and rested.

Returning to her previous mumblings, the stones behind the old door faded away, revealing the clifftop fields of the Brough of Birsay.

~

Sally looked at Carl, 'That's the door *we* passed through!'

Carl nodded, 'That's when the shop got walled in.'

'Could he do that!'

'He bore the authority of the King; he could do anything.'

'Et es so. He confirmed that the entrance had remained closed, entered, an' looked around the shop one last time. Findin' the old, false door closed again, he laughed, exclaimin' that he knew she was hidin', that he judged her guilty o' collusion weth a known wetch, indeed, that he believed she was integral en Janet's escape, an' that fer thess reason he was permanently closin' the shop.

'Silence greeted each statement, so he declared that ef she didne come oot, et would look like her shop was empty, an' she would be sealed en. Then he looked again at the old door, a curiosity grabbed hem. En a moment his hand was on the handle, he swung the door open an' ran his fingers doon the cold ungivin' stone behind. He punched et weth his fist, an' cussed Deborah, sayin' that he had her either way. That death through starvation or death at the stake were fittin' ways fer a wetch to die.

'Weth that May left the shop an' stood watchin' as stone clad the old shop wall. All the while the blocks were raised, Deborah chanted. An incantation that would afford access fer right hearts.'

'That's us,' Sally whispered, hugging Carl's arm.

Carl's shoulders sank, 'Hundreds of years for someone with a right heart to arrive and what did we do?'

Sally could see the upset in his eyes, she felt his despair, she shared it.

Old Garrie continued, 'The way o' Birsay afforded Deborah ample distance to avoid bein' seen by May, an' she was finally able to return to Westray, payin' a local Crofter to row her to Pierowall one evenin', when the storms o' Winter had given way to Spring.'

Kayleigh smiled broadly, 'Janet must have ben so relieved to see her.' But her smile soon faded, for Garrie's face spoke of no happy reunion.

~

'Oh sester, back weth us are yoo?'

Deborah's heart faltered. Why had she just walked so openly along the cartway? Had she assumed the fading light would hide her from unfriendly eyes? Why choose to pass Erka's cottage at all? She'd been careless! Not all her problems were called May, 'Juss visitin' my son, Bess.' She laughed nervously, remaining motionless, unwilling to turn and face the voice. 'Strange, that yoo call me sester...'

'Bess isne here anymore, Deborah.' A number of male voices now struck Deborah's ears, most from within the cottage but at least two, clearly observing the awkward encounter, chuckling at Deborah's predicament, aware of her angst.

Deborah glanced back furtively. Gasping at the sight of Bess, for she too had been aged by the liberation of the Nuckelavee. A bold streak of white invaded her raven hair, lines of malice creased her brow. 'Oh Bess, dear Bess, remove ya mother's necklace, et's too powerful!'

'Bess es gone, Deborah.'

Deborah scowled. 'Then ya appearance must cast suspicion on yoo, Erka.'

Bess laughed, girlishly, 'Oh no, I've seen to et that et gains me sympathy.'

'Yoo've told the community that Janet has cursed yoo!'

'Aye, ded lay me doon fer weeks. I let no one visit. My boys saw to spreadin' preparin' werds, how the illness had robbed me o' my youth. An' all those long weeks have I 'venged myself; cast curses on the Islanders so that their grain donny sate them an' their calves starve fer want o' fat en their mother's melk. All bar the Forsyth herd o' course.'

'I well tell...'

'Yoo'll no tell... ya caught.'

The men laughed.

Deborah began to step away, an incantation for fleetness already spilling from her lips. She had expected to be grabbed by Bess's goons, but they just stood and laughed. She turned and ran - straight into a rack of baskets! The rack fell casting baskets across a flagstone floor. Deborah flailed around; she was back in her shop! The thought of Erka's power, that she was strong enough to have done this, made

Deborah vomit. She ran to the old door, screaming the words to open the way, but behind the wood the stone remained. 'Pah! Yoo have me sester, but I'll no' give up!'

Chapter Fifty-seven

Garrie continued, 'Deborah set to work undoin' the lock on the way o' Birsay. Drawin' on all the knowledge o' her old arts she managed to negate the cold barrier o' stone, but there was another layer to Erka's enchantment, fer Deborah could still no' pass.'

'Had Janet expected her to arrive?' Sally asked.

'Aye, but et was late now; Janet had retired an' was asleep when Deborah called oot to her. She informed Janet o' Erka's consumption o' Bess an' the troublin' rise en her power. How Finulf an' his crew were more like henchmen now than sailors, but how all suspicions, had ben redirected to Janet herself. E'en the more frequent storms o' the Wenter juss gone, had ben blamed on the missin' girl.

'Deborah admitted that she was now incarcerated en her shop by May's physical, and Erka's arcane interventions, but that there was a way fer others to pass.'

~

'I well come now, under cover o' night.' Janet cast her bedcovers aside.

'No, stay safe en Talanon. May es stell on Mainland an' Erka's eyes are everywhere on Westray. Send those I send to yoo.' Deborah fell silent and Janet realised that the whole experience that day, had taken Deborah to a point of exhaustion. What had she meant though 'Send those I send yoo'? Janet didn't have to wonder for long, for three Trows came running into her room. She smiled, their song was different to the general song which always filled the kingdom, but it complimented it, bouncing off the rhythm like some tangent narrative.

'Called we rescuers
Rescuers three,
Called we heroes, me, me, an' me;
Deborah calls
Oot, oot 'cross the sea,
Help us to find what help we ken be.'

Janet knew what to do, she led the rescuers, and Boy, down through the tunnels to the caves at Noup Head, and, with their assistance, lowered Benjamin's boat into the calm sea.

Janet turned to Boy, 'I have a special job fer yoo, dear Boy, ya to go weth them an' protect them. The Kengdom es a hidden place, but oot here, though they are filled weth their own kind o' magic, they well be vulnerable.'

Boy jumped into the boat without hesitation, and with a Trow on each oar and one regarding the stars, Janet watched them until they escaped the light that had followed them from within Talanon.

All became quiet as the splashing oars grew indiscernible against the gently lapping waves that kissed the cave-mouth rocks.

'Janet, are yoo there my friend?'

The voice had called down from the cliff top. Janet recognised it as Bess's, and, heeding Deborah's warning of Erka's power over her, Janet slid quickly and quietly back into the darkening cave.

'I've ben blind.'

Janet headed for the safety of the tunnel entrance.

'I couldne find yoo; two years an' I ded no' recall yoo talk o' lettle people en the cleft on ya father's land when we were children. Such ways are well hidden from the dull eyes o' the normal, an' malice such as mine cannot physically pass…' Bess paused. 'Jan? Well yoo no' talk to me?'

Janet was tempted to speak, to tell Bess to cast Erka's necklace into the sea, but she hesitated.

'So be et, Jan, but when the Trows are gone their magic well fade away. Yoo'll no' be hedden anymore. The three an' ya mutt are easy pickin's.'

A sharp wind cut across the cave mouth and breakers flooded into the opening. Janet's heart grew heavy as she fled into Talanon.

~

Kayleigh burst into tears, 'I canna bear et! There es no hope. An' Janet stell locked ento thess curse, all these years on...'

'There es hope.' Garrie sounded confident but his eyes met with Carl's and he sighed, his voice quietened, '...there es stell hope.'

Sally crossed to Kayleigh and place an arm around her, 'The Trows and Boy made it to Deborah.'

Deni, Dini and Donie came closer.

'O' course, fer they are here.'

Sally returned to Carl; the Trows hugged Kayleigh and her mind filled with their affirmation. 'Et's all so sad.'

'Why don't they sing without being told to? They only stopped when necessary; when Janet was being hunted... why not now?'

Everyone looked at Carl despairingly, as if a pursuit of the reason might break them all. Deni openly sobbed; so recently Kayleigh's comforter, he now needed her comfort.

'Es true,' Garrie admitted. 'There must be motive or request now fer song, fer much has gone that cannot be restored.'

'Bess, no, Erka? Ah! Whoever it was talking! They said their malice couldn't pass into Talanon physically. But something did pass, didn't it? Something to break the magic of the Trows?'

Garrie looked at his diminutive companions, now lamenting together. 'Aye.'

A silence filled the space, and Carl realised he had uncovered the bitterest of pain. 'I... I'm so sorry...'

Donie crossed to Carl and hugged him.

'Can I ask what happened? Should I ask?'

'Werds.' Garrie's ton was matter-of-fact. 'Erka had recalled Janet's talk o' lettle people, through Bess's memories. She had chastised herself fer no' being attentive to Janet's openness to Bess that first

243

time they returned to Westray together. But the location o' that conversation was clear; the cleft near the Forsyth farmhoose.

'Weth her male guests sleepin' off their lusts, an' under cover o' night, Erka hurried up the track to the farm an' was soon standin' en the cleft, chantin'; watchin' the way her werds fell. She had longed fer thess day fer so long. To find the illusive entrance to Talanon.

'Et wasne straight forward, Erka had to werk fer her prize, changin' the timin' an' pitch o' her invocation, but she was no' one to let go an' the way finally gave up et's place. Approachin' the doorway Erka found et protected by layers o' Trow-craft. She felt a buildin' heat, like one would feel before a blazin' fire, until et became impassable an' she found et impossible to concentrate on counterin' the charm. So, she stepped back an' gathered herself. She laughed, an' the Trow guards, hidden wethin the portal, trembled. The werds she spoke tainted them, e'ery one o' them, an' they fled ento the Kengdom.'

Sally frowned, 'Tainted?'

'Poison, delivered through speech, a plague born en dark phrases. Sensin' Janet was no longer wethin the concealment o' the secret halls, she casually used more o' her power to pass sweftly to Noup Head where, prevented again from comin' closer, she saw a lettle row-boat pass oot o' golden light ento the blackness. Failin' to get a response from Janet, hidden from view by the cliff edge, Erka grew angry, drivin' the breeze up ento a squall; weth the intent to tease the sea ento a forest o' boat drownin' rollers.'

Carl rubbed Donie's back, purposely pulling the positive from Garrie's words. 'She failed!'

'Aye, en that moment she was spent, et would take time now to build her power again, an', although et frustrated her no' to kill the three Trows en the boat, she was content, fer her deeds would undo their kin an' their realm. By the time Janet had made her way back, the Trow song had already faltered, the guards from the cleft already ill an' the first to meet them, already ailin'.'

'Couldn't Janet help them?'

'No, she carried the sickness herself. Then, alone en her room, callin' oot to Deborah, fadin' ento her own oblivion. Feelin' her flesh grow cold an' hard like stone.'

Carl was feeling the oppression of the story now, 'But it's not the end, Janet survives.'

'Aye, but her awakenin' was to silent halls an' a hungry belly.'

'All gone!'

'Nay, but there were none that would come near her.'

'There were survivors?'

'They've no' ben seen, but the portal at the cleft ken stell be o'erlooked by all bar the most persistent seeker.'

Kayleigh expressed some relief at this statement but the devastation of Erka's act was clear for all to see.

Chapter Fifty-eight

Janet walked the corridors of Talanon like a ghost. She didn't know what day it was, but lest it be Sunday she sought out and knelt in the Trow chapel hall, and prayed for her diminutive guardians.

'Oh Lord, thess tragedy has o'ertaken us, save them tha's left Lord. The craft that claims them es o' the dark. We look to ya light. There's some would say the Trows are creations o' magic an' no' a part o' thess world an' ya creative act; but they are made o' the very stones o' the earth, an' the earth es ya creation. They have demonstrated their love to me fer years, protected me an' fed me; they are the very embodiment o' ya great love, protection an' provision. Save an' heal Lord, I pray, Amen.'

For a while Janet remained there, singing songs of worship out into the silence and weeping often.

Over the following days Janet continued to visit the chapel and pray. She visited the homes of those she had been closest to, but found them empty; where once there had been smiling welcome and music, there was now an earth muffled silence and scattered stones. Stones. Janet stroked them, sobbing, for each one's magic had left them and they were again what they had been. Despite this Janet would occasionally hear a distant noise or perhaps a sound like someone hurrying away, and she let herself believe that the Trows, keeping their distance, still watched over her.

One morning she saw Benjamin's boat returned, the wet footprints of the Nuckelavee nearby. She stood by the breakers, calling for him but he did not come. Fear of who might hear her drove her back to the boat and she spent the day curled up, lamenting her losses. It was here she first sang her lament for the loss of her love.

In the kitchens there was ample food for many months, but as the days became weeks her mind convinced her that she may be consuming all that the frightened remnant had left. Convinced that she must leave, Janet collected her belongings and made her way to the portal at the cleft. Not once looking back, she headed purposely across the field to the farmhouse. The sky was dark and heavy with the likelihood of rain; the air, reluctant to abandon Winter, was cold and unwelcoming.

Janet had expected to find her home in justifiable disarray, and it came as no surprise to find it so, the door left to swing in the breeze, dust thick on the surfaces, cobwebs, like torn curtains at the windows and hanging like phantom tapestries about the walls. There was a dank smell of decay, and evidence that some wild animal must have used the place like a glorified burrow.

Although Janet had no expectation of finding something to eat on the shelves in the kitchen, she peered in anyway. Moulds, long spent, added their own aroma to the mix, discoloured liquids defied recognition, their scent promising a bitter stomach and retching. Janet headed to bed unsated.

~

'Is that when she was found?' Sally asked. 'When she was taken and tried?'

'The museum boards spoke of a ship in a storm that Janet brought safe to harbour,' Carl pointed out. 'Or is that just a romanticised addition for the tourists?'

'Erka made sure that Janet's return to the farmhoose became generally known. She knew et would only be a matter o' time before the news would spread and her schemes facilitated.'

Kayleigh was surprised, 'She dedne go after her herself?'

'Nay, she knew what she wanted fer Janet. There was a lust en her fer et. She'd burned, an' she blamed Edward's family fer et. She'd poisoned Janet's neem on the tongues o' the Islanders, an' was content to see what played oot. Wetches burned, an' the Islanders considered her to be one.'

'So is the ship in the storm true, did she rescue...' Carl stopped, he sensed he was running ahead of the old man's story.

'Janet begged fer food by the side o' the cartway from those who'd pass that way, but all shunned her, an' she was forced to wander an' gather what lettle herbs an' shellfish she could find to keep the pain from her belly; daily wanderin's en all weathers...'

'What of her father's cows?' Carl queried.

'Claimed by the neighbour, Mr. Mullan. Compensation, he maintained, fer an illness his sesters endured after eatin' meat from a pig he asserted had ben cursed by Janet. None had prevented hem, but perhaps et was fer the best, seein' as no one was there to see to the needs o' the herd. O' course, there were other reasons why folk wouldne share food weth Janet, the harvest had ben poor an' the Wenter long, the supply o' provisions from Mainland had ben broken by the storms. People were short themselves. On seein' Janet mysteriously appear again, an' her bein' pale an' gaunt after the sickness en Talanon... Well, they were fearful to approach. Nay, many Islanders were juss as desperate fer some respite from their growlin' guts...' Garrie rested back en his chair; not as one does to relax, but as one exhausted, tired of the story, tired of waiting, tired of this continued cycle that, convinced of the loss of the seal necklace, must now be the lot of all who loved Janet, forever. He looked at Carl. '...There *was* a ship, Janet had seen et one day whilst collectin' winkles an' some fish from a net that had belonged to Benjamin. Et was at anchor aboot two hundred yards off Noup Head. The wind had fallen canny that afternoon, an' so the Captain had elected to wait et oot, rather than resk the dangers o' the route. Janet, an Islander all her life, knew the message o' the wind an' was aware o' the danger that now faced the crew an' any passengers. Rememberin' the lettle baby shoe from the beach en her childhood, she decided to watch. Ef thengs took a bad turn she would try an' help.'

~

The skies darkened in the West even as Janet sat watching, a perceivable decay in light and temperature, the wave-tops foamed ominously and the swell began to test the hold of the anchors. Janet pulled her shawl tightly about her.

'Keepin' the news to ya self, Jan?'

Janet turned to see Bess. Knowing Erka's control of the girl Janet stood and started to back away.

'Oh, I'll do yoo nay harm, I'll let others do that fer me an' keep my hands an' reputation clean. But here's yoo now, levin' up to the rumours, hexin' that ship an' waitin' fer the spoils to wash ashore at ya very feet...'

'Tha's no' true! I well help them ef they need et...'

'How? They wellne hear ya calls above the wend, an' by the time that anchor breaks the water well be too treacherous e'en fer one skilled by the teachin's o' Benjamin Garrioch.'

Janet glanced down at the waves, they were already dangerous, the anchors already dragging. 'Thank yoo, Bess,' Janet praised. 'Yoo have made up my mind en time.' And with that Janet turned and ran in the direction of Benjamin's boat; Erka's laughter ringing in her ears. Bess had begun to saunter in the direction that Janet had fled, initially wishing to watch the drama, but Janet had disappeared, aware of the hidden ways of the Trows she had already passed into the tunnels of Talanon heading for the caves at the foot of Noup Head. Bess cussed, then another thought struck her; if there was going to be a wreck the Islanders should know about it, if not, well - then they should witness who had robbed them of the salvage.

Chapter Fifty-nine

Janet tied a rope around her waist and, after fixing it to the rowing boat, dragged it into the swirling breakers. More than once she lost her footing on the slippery rocks but the tether held and she climbed onboard, setting the oars and pulling against the waves. The sea threw her about mercilessly but she was praying earnestly through gritted teeth and the resolve it gave her carried her on to her goal.

~

Sally admitted that she wouldn't be able to row even on a still day. 'Was it all her own strength or was Erka ensuring Janet made it so she could help the ship and make the Islanders hate her more?'

'Bess had left to gather Islanders to the impendin' wreck, but Janet wasne alone. Beneath an' ahead o' the boat, hauling on the rope that hung from the fishin' vessel's bow, was the Creature.'

'Did she know?'

'She would realise ets help later, but fer now she attributed her progress to determined effort. A Sailor on the merchantman saw her final approach, had he no' she would likely have ben dashed to pieces on the side o' the pitchin' ship. He threw down a rope an' Janet grabbed et. Abandonin' the rowin' an' the tether she wrapped the rope around her waist an' let the Sailor pull her up.'

~

The Sailor shouted above the roar of the waves and wind. 'Vhat are you doing?' He was tall and strong, with fair, wavy hair and piercing, pale grey eyes.

Janet was firm, 'Are yoo no' familiar weth the coastline here-a-boots? Thess storm esney risen a patch yet, ya anchors well either drag ya bow under the waves or they'll sheer an' yoo'll be driven onto the

249

rock shelf under the Noup an' smashed to splinters on the Head.'

The Sailor understood and took her quickly to the Captain.

Janet was surprised, almost all the sailors she knew in this position were older men, strong of frame and weathered by the salt. This man was a pale youth, sitting limply in a chair and looking fit to vomit. Within moments Janet knew she had to act on his behalf.

She turned to the sailor, 'Get the anchors up an' heave to.'

The Sailor glanced half-heartedly at his Captain and headed off to instruct his fellow men.

Janet addressed the captain, 'Where, yoo headin'?'

'Bergen, Hordaland.'

'I well try an' see yoo to the shelter o' the Bay at Pierowall, Yoo ken ride the storm oot there.'

The man looked as though he might acknowledge the help, but suddenly spewed across his own lap. Janet left him to see what she could do on deck.

One anchor was clear but a second had clearly snagged. The chain became taut in the swell, pitching the ship like a toy, and the wind threw the bow across the ungiving metal, tearing at the wood and decapitating the figurehead before violently snapping and sending all flailing to the floor. The great wooden head crashed to the deck narrowly missing a member of the crew, who, wits intact, quickly lashed it down.

Recovering their feet, the sailors heaved to, but it was soon clear that the ship was heading for the shallows.

Janet felt inadequate to the task, had it just been sentiment that had driven her to the vessel, the thought of a little, child's shoe? The hull scraped suddenly on the edge of the rock shelf. There were no children here, just an inexperienced Captain buckling to fear instead of pushing on to safety whilst it was still in reach. How many wrecks owed their fate to an amateur, but then, what was she?

A cheer broke her from her self-doubt. Looking, Janet realised the ship was holding to some sort of current that was driving them along the side of the hidden ledge. It defied all she knew of the way of the sea here, but she was glad of it. Curious, she peered over the side at the churning waves, they were alive with seals, the chain from the broken anchor, that had dangled limply against the hull, now stretched tightly in the direction of their travel and the flash of a red fin caused her to seek a way of keeping the sailors from copying her observations.

She drew those nearest to her together, amongst them was the man who had brought her on-board. 'Your vorters here are strange ant treacherous.'

'Aye, but roond the Head the water well be calmer an' Pierowall en reach.'

'I believe you've saved our lives. Vater's father vill be grateful to you.'

'Vater?'

The Sailor tipped his head to the cabins and Janet understood that he was speaking of the Captain. 'He is the son off a vealthy German merchant who has settled in Bergen. His father is the very reason he is here. The boy is totally useless, guess his father vas trying to make a man off him. He vill not like my report, but he vill be glad off the intervention that allowed it to reach him. Ah look, the path is open. I vill steer; vill you stay at the bow ant guide us safely through any remaining snares?'

Their eye contact lingered, Janet blushed, 'Aye, I'll, I'll guide yoo.'

They both laughed, 'I'm Harolt by the vay.'

'Janet.'

Janet returned to the side, smiling as the Sailor brought the ship about and the chain became slack again, 'Thank yoo my friend.' Janet glanced down at the water, acknowledging the departing seals with a nod.

As they rounded Noup Head, small gatherings of locals could be seen on the clifftops making their way along cliff paths within curtains of pouring rain, their demeanour downcast from being wet to the bone and seeing the reason for their journey safely pass in the deeper water. Janet was happy that it would take them time to trudge back to Pierowall, and that she would be safely home long before.

Chapter Sixty

A safe haven in a storm, Pierowall's quay was full, and two unfamiliar, naval ships were at anchor in the bay. The calmer swell had given Vater time to recover, and he now appeared on deck, albeit spattered in his own vomit.

He seemed angry, 'You!'

Janet, Harolt and some others looked up, and Janet sensed this was a common method Vater used to address crewmembers.

'Yes you, girl.'

Janet rounded to his approach.

'Vhat right have you to overrule my orders! I should have you flogged…'

Harolt barred Vater's approach, 'She saved your life, ve ver all dead, but she…'

'Ve ver not dead! My provision vas above exemplary. It vas the crews choppy sailing. You all panicked ant took the orders off a voman, I'm amazed ve are still alive at…' His voice faded, his face losing the faint colour it had begun to regain. His eyes drew him forward Pushing by Harolt and Janet his stumbling became a run. '…My… My figurehet! My beautiful Lady!'

'Ripped off by the very anchor you had us tethered to. Further vaves vould have had that chain rip us to pieces.'

Vater pointed wildly at Janet, 'No! it is her fault, I vant her off my ship! GET HER OFF MY SHIP!' He returned his attention to the figure head, stroking the splintered remains.

Harolt, clearly respected by the other crew and possessing some authority amongst them, organised a boat to take Janet ashore. He accompanied her, shielding her from the rain with his long coat and walking her home to the farm, finding out all he could of his crew's rescuer. Upon reaching the farmhouse, there was very little he didn't know of Janet's family and her current situation. The loss of her

Father, Aunt, and Benjamin, framed her sufferings. His experience of her actions and selflessness, touched him. He felt genuinely attracted to this brave young woman. They stood by the door, briefly silent, gazing into each other's eyes. The weather wasn't letting up, it was time for a decision.

'May I visit you ven I can?'

Janet nodded. She felt like the tide was turning on her misfortune.

Harolt cupped her rain moistened cheek and bent down to kiss her. Their lips drew close, Janet could feel his breath.

'Jan?'

Startled the couple fell apart, Janet's eyes falling upon a dark figure in the gateway. Recognition exploded into her mind, 'Ben? Ben!'

Harolt, immediately understanding that this was the fisherman Janet had thought lost, excused himself. Janet could read the disappointment on his face, she was flattered but compromised - here was Ben, the love of her life, safe, alive!

Harolt's gaze drifted into Benjamin's as he passed him in the gateway, Benjamin stepping back to let him by. Both men nodded. Harolt's eyes flicked down to the seal pelt over Benjamin's arm, he glanced back at Janet, then headed away.

It seemed like an age before anything happened, both stood motionless, rain lashing down.

'Fer heaven's sake, Ben, where have yoo ben? I thought yoo dead!'

'Was that one o' ya Aunt's suitors? Seems to me yoo no' so unwellin' to come to some agreement.'

'Oh Ben, come enside, et's ben so long.'

Ben looked down the track towards Pierowall. Harolt was gone. He closed the gate and approached the house.

Janet opened the door and stepped inside, unable to take her eyes from Benjamin lest he disappear again, some ghost of her conscience for contemplating the lips of another.

He stopped inside the doorway, his face gaunt, weathered, tormented. Janet reached out to stroke his face, to comfort him, but he stepped back.

'Ben, where were yoo?'

'Seein' yoo again has ben the only theng tha's kept me together.

E'ery day I've carried the image o' ya face en my mind, the memory o' ya sweet innocence en my heart.'

'Ben, nothin's changed, Harolt was…'

'He was en the place yoo promised was mine aloon…'

'Ben, et stell es…'

'No… no longer.'

'Ben, no! Nothin' happened weth hem…'

'Looked to be happenin' to me.'

'Ben, please understand, I thought yoo dead.'

Benjamin shook his head. 'E'ery day I've longed only fer yoo. Strived to claw my way back.' He pointed towards Pierowall Bay. 'Now I'm a deserter. Ef they catch me I'll be flayed. I wouldne have resked that ef I'd thought yoo'd given ya heart to another…' He stepped back out into the rain; Janet took hold of his arm to restrain him but her finger tips slipped on the pelt. 'I must hide, I must think.'

Janet let him leave, her protest stalled by what he had seen, and the deep desire that, in his time of thought, he might understand what she had believed all these years.

~

'So, where *had* he been?' Carl asked.

'He an' the men o' the fishin' fleet had lost their freedom; they'd found themselves en the midst o' naval ships an' were pressed ento the service o' the Keng, by a ruthless Captain.'

Kayleigh nodded, 'The other ships en the bay.'

'First time he'd ben back to Westray since bein' taken. Entirely provident too, fer the ship's Captain had en no way entended to stop, bein' forced to shelter en the bay because o' the storm. Et gave Benjamin an irresistible opportunity. The Fishermen had ben relieved o' anythin' resemblin' a weapon, an' were held to menial tasks onboard, but Benjamin had ben allowed to keep his seal skin, fer none understood et's power to transform hem, thinkin' et some sort o' vest or garment…'

'I thought Janet had that.'

Sally laughed at Carl., 'No, she had the one that had been in Bess's bundle of treasures…'

Carl looked blank.

'You remember? Before Erka's cottage was restored for Bess. Bess had visited, claimed things. Janet had found it warm to the touch. Benjamin got his pelt from a box on Miley's ship later on; different pelt. Erka's Selkie skin belonged to Janet.'

Garrie grunted affirmation, 'She'd found a pup Selkie washed ashore en a storm. She'd striped the infant from her coverin's an' threw her ento the sea to die. Et was her way, she hated Selkies, they'd assisted the Trows to escape her thrall all those years before.'

'That's why she'd targeted Janet and her family, she'd recognised the baby in Edward's arms as the Selkie child!' Carl nodded his head, agreeing to his own summary. He smiled, 'Benjamin used his pelt to escape the anchored ship.'

'Endeed fer the landin' boats were guarded an' none expected a man to survive the storm tossed, icy swim to shore.'

Sally seemed thrown, 'So, Janet just let him go? She should have cried out to him, followed after him.'

'She realised he needed time. He knew how the fleet's disappearance must have looked that day. He understood the tone o' her voice, the reaction o' Harolt. Aye, he knew Janet must have spoken o' hem fer that Seaman to wethdraw the way he ded.'

Sally saw the opportunity to test an assumption. 'So, he came back? You came back…'

'No' soon enough.'

Carl picked up on Sally's idea. 'You're Benjamin?'

'Of course he's Benjamin! I'd figured that out when Janet used his full name to tell him not to board Miley's ship to retrieve his precious box, Benjamin *Garrioch*, Old Garrie. And he is old…'

'Och, steady on!' Garrie protested.

'…like the shopkeeper we met, that must have been Deborah, and the dog…' She pointed at Boy. '… and our other friends…' She stroked the cheek of the nearest Trow. Deni blushed. 'Wait!' The colour drained from Sally's face. 'What do you mean 'Not soon enough'?'

Chapter Sixty-one

Janet hadn't left the house for several days. She'd run through the events of that evening in her mind so many times that she was now just like a vapour hanging in the room, dependent on some change or sudden thing to move her again; letting Harolt walk her home, that had been her error - what a reunion she would have had with Benjamin if the sailor hadn't been there.

Tears would have welled for the umpteenth time had there been moisture left in her to spill. She'd seen the seal skin in Benjamin's hands, she'd thought the one the Trows had found had been his. That pelt now sat on her lap, her hand within it transformed, and she stared at it contemplating the truth of her origins.

The change came suddenly and saw her to her guard, first a knock - had it been the first? Or was it the last of numerous knocks? - then a splintering of wood and a bustle of bodies into the hall off the kitchen.

'En here!' The voice belonged to a man that Janet recognised, a ropemaker from Pierowall.

'What are yoo doin'?' Janet's tone was devoid of emotion through days of lament.

'Take her!' another islander shouted, and she was quickly held, her seal pelt falling to the floor.

Janet struggled, 'Leave go, what es thess?'

A stranger entered, 'My name is May. It's a pleasure to finally see you face to face, Miss Forsyth.'

Janet almost laughed - it was the only emotional reaction left to her after such long mourning - 'What right have yoo t'storm ento my home like thess?'

'Oh, every right, it's my job to flush out the likes of you.'

'And what es that?' She knew how he would answer, but for some unfathomable reason she wished to hear it, to have it confirmed.

'You my dear are a practicing witch, who has caused the suffering of the godly folk of this island. You are accused of summoning foul weather at your whim, of sickening folk, animals and crops, of rousing infernal beasts with intent to kill, of the creation of poppets to inflict suffering and prolong death…'

This was enough for Janet and she collapsed, only to be quickly revived by the bowl of cold water that sat on the kitchen table.

Janet opened her eyes to the unpleasant Mr. May, hauling her head up by her hair.

'You will appear before Bishop Graeme, where my witnesses will have you condemned for your devilry.'

A sudden desire to flee gripped Janet, she flayed about in the unyielding grip of her captors like a small bird in mist netting, launching to the horizon but locked fast in the maw of death.

May rocked back on his heels, standing above her, gloating. 'Take her away, gag and secure her, let no one speak to her lest she beguile them. I will go to the harbour and secure the earliest transport to Kirkwall.'

With that Janet was roughly hauled away, her efforts to find freedom soon forsaken through futility and abruptly administered pain.

Ben saw her torn from the house, yes, he did want to step in, to rescue her, but the numbers involved were large. He recognised many of the islanders, but why were they so angry? What could have changed since he'd been taken? Why treat Janet so brutally? He followed at a safe distance, fearing discovery and a return to the ship that would surely end any chance he had to save her.

Janet was taken to Noltland Castle, overlooking Pierowall's wide bay. This was home to the Sheriff of Orkney Sir John Arnot. The building was imposing, Janet had always given it a wide birth, and now, as if it were some great dark cage, she gave a last effort of resistance, falling to her knees to prevent passing through the stone arched entrance into the courtyard beyond. It was, of course, a pointless gesture; the men that had marched her stumbling up the road, now dragged her forward until she struck the wall. Her eyes glanced up wildly, focusing on words purposely hewn into unyielding stone

"When I see the blood, I will pass over you in the night". She recognised the words from the Minister's sermons. The Israelites, under tyrannical Egyptian servitude were instructed by Moses to smear the blood of a lamb on their door frame so that the angel of death would see it, recognise that a sacrifice had already been made, and pass on to the homes of those who had enslaved them. Was there justice here then? Would this Sheriff see how ordinary she was and overrule May's accusations? Janet put up no further resistance and was led inside.

Bound and gagged Janet was set to one corner of the vaulted lower storey, there were no windows but a roaring fire cast shadow flecked light towards her. Two men sat watching her carefully. Janet could see how they saw her, a feral creature sprawled awkwardly, staring back with wide eyes. No, this wouldn't do, she had to be a woman, a fine example, gentle and fair. When he came, the Sheriff would find a girl in her right mind, wrongly accused. She corrected her posture, sitting upright, her tightly bound wrists nursed protectively in her lap.

The younger guard became uneasy, 'Here, wha's shey doin'?'

The reply threatened to turn Janet's nerve; it was from a woman tending laundry by the fire. 'Shey's preparin' t'enthral yoo. I've seen et all before.'

Janet's eyes remained fixed on the approaching servant.

'I'm wonderin' ef they removed all the charms she uses fer enchantment. Yoo should search her.'

The older guard stood instantly. Fetching a torch from the wall he approached Janet directly, ordering the other man to search her.

'I'm no' touchin' her, what ef she ded curse…'

'Hold thess then!' The older man thrust the flame towards his reluctant companion, casting light on the housemaid's face. Janet somehow knew it would be her, she had no place at the castle, she wasn't one of Sir Arnot's staff, but her powers could take her anywhere. Janet simply stared at Bess's amused face as the first man rudely searched her body, until she felt the leather cord snap; her eyes falling despairingly on the little seal pendant as it departed.

Defeat settled upon Janet, her clothes ripped, her flesh showing, she slumped to the cold cobbles the gag choking her sobs as Bess negotiated possession of the necklace with the guard. Janet glanced sorrowfully up at the man who'd refused to touch her. Clearly at odds with what his companion had just done he took a blanket, that had been for his own use through the coming night, and wrapped it about her. 'Please donny hold thess against me Miss…'

Janet shook her head.

His companion quickly chastised him, 'Leave her, yoo soft fool.'

~

Kayleigh stood, 'I need a break.' She investigated her clothing and, finding it dry, excused herself to get dressed in the back room.

In the pause Carl and Sally took the opportunity to restore their own attire; it was then that Sally made an observation, she pointed to the window, 'The rain's easing.'

The glass was no longer streaked with streams of wind-danced rain; indeed, it was partially clear and the quality of light stronger. Garrie quickly stood and peered out. He gasped and headed to the door.

Chapter Sixty-two

Garrie swung the door open. There, for all to see was a blackened body. Blades of flame, small but obvious, licked up legs, torso and arms alarmingly.

'She's here.'

The figure rested a hand on Garrie's shoulder before stepping passed him into the cottage. Garrie stepped out into the buffeting gale.

Carl and Sally gazed at the new arrival, it was clearly the form of a woman, defiled by extensive burns.

'I thought you had escaped the fire.' Sally words had been a barely audible whisper, filled with horror.

Carl held Sally, who looked dangerously pale.

Kayleigh, returning and discovering Garrie's guest, stood motionless. This was not what she'd expected.

'Nay.' The figure declared; her voice hoarse through its smoke damaged larynx. 'I didne escape, but Janet ded.'

At that moment Garrie returned carrying someone else. The body was almost limp, the frame frail and old. Long, white hair flowed almost to the flags, knotted and twisted by the wind.

The Trows quickly pulled a straw mattress to the fireside and Garrie gently placed his burden down upon it.

Carl and Sally watched as Janet was attended to, the Trows respectful and tender in their service, and Garrie whispering quietly, emotionally. Kayleigh continued to stare at the tongues of flame that flickered around the unexpected guest. 'Bess?'

The glazed eyes of the figure moved from Janet to Kayleigh. 'Aye, I'm Bess.'

Carl stepped in front of Sally protectively.

Kayleigh's interest in Bess evaporated, 'Auch, she's nay harm.' She looked to the fireplace for the one who had lived the torment she'd just been told of.

'No harm!'

Kayleigh regarded Carl. 'Nay harm. She's here. To be held by the curse was fer those that loved Janet.' She pointed to the charred remains of clothing about Bess's neckline.

Sally understood, 'No green-jewelled pendant.'

'Gone,' Bess rasped. 'So now I bear the curse o' my own lips.'

'Erka's werds.' Kayleigh corrected.

Bess turned to Garrie, 'An' stell nay end discovered?'

Carl saw Garrie's eyes almost meet his own before the old man closed them. 'Nay, dear Bess, nay end.'

'What happens now?' Kayleigh asked tearfully. 'I mean weth the storm easin'?'

'We fade again.'

'Oblivion,' Bess added. 'But another storm well come.'

Garrie nodded, 'Et es a cruel hex.'

Kayleigh huffed indignantly, 'Where ded yoo take the seal pendant?'

Garrie quickly defended Bess, 'Et's nay her fault.'

'I'll tell yoo all I know,' Bess offered. 'But then I'm leavin', the last o' the rain soothes me…'

~

Sensing impending victory over her Selkie victim, Erka hatched her dire strategy. So many had aided her quarry over the years, this object in her possession, this gift given in love, *this* gave her power over all of them. Too late for her Father, her Mother, her Aunt (that last thought amused her) but she had played a part in all their deaths, yes, true satisfaction. The curse she was about to weave was timely, for all found in Janet's heart who outlived her, would be bound to it; distressed for ever by their loved one's torment. And Janet would die, strangled and burned within days, a few weeks at most!

She bound the curse to the seal necklace, then, elated at her prowess, decided to visit Janet again before her execution, tell her the fate awaiting her, then hide the necklace somewhere it would never be found.

May had returned early the next morning, he had secured a vessel for the crossing to Kirkwall, but Janet's state annoyed him, she looked like an abused girl in her torn dress. No, that wouldn't do at all, the Bishop was known for leniency, any possibility that sympathy might be provoked, had to be removed, and his eye fell on the very thing.

'You will wear this for your modesty.' He pulled a slightly damp, black gown from the laundry beside the fireplace.

Janet, feeling only the embarrassment of partial nudity, and nothing of how such a dark garment might lead her to be perceived, gladly donned it when May freed her hands.

Janet recognised the men who arrived to take them to the ship - members of Finulf's crew - and she wondered if Erka's hand was once more at play. Never-the-less, Sir Arnot had not come to her, justice had not been served. If trial in Kirkwall was her last hope, then to trial she would willingly go.

May was impressed with her resignation, it made his life easier. 'Yes, this one will be no trouble to me now,' He thought to himself as he locked the cabin door. 'She is broken and impotent.'

The crossing reminded her of a similar journey some thirteen years before, she remembered her visitor that day, the young boy who would grow to catch her heart, but there was no visitor today, just the feel of the swell and the pacing of a guard.

Benjamin had tried to stow away, employing his old technique of acquiring goods to take onboard. He'd been just feet from the gangplank when an officious voice called out to him to wait. Seeing a small group of officers approaching from the now moored ship he'd spent the last five years on, he dropped his crate and ran. In his bag the seal pelt seemed to call for him. Yes, there was another way to follow Janet. Perhaps a way to rescue her would present itself in Kirkwall.

Soon Janet was back on the quayside where she'd mended nets all those years before. Was there a chance here, here being so close to Deborah? Could she reach her in her mind?

'Deborah? Deborah?'

'Auch, child, I have let yoo doon. Erka es stronger…'

Janet's relief was great. 'Yoo've let none doon, Deborah.'

'I canny break thess prison she's raised aboot me. The Trows pass en an' oot as ef nothin' was there, they breng me food an' Boy comforts me, but I canny send them to help yoo fer they would incriminate yoo further.'

'Et's fine Deborah, I well be set free, fer I have done nothin' that May say's I have. Bishop Graeme es a good man who'll see through the lies. He's the man who provided werk fer the orphans when I was a child. He's a fair judge, I am sure…' Janet faltered.

'Oh, dear child, I well no gev up. I well find a way.'

'Bess took my seal necklace back on Westray…'

'Erka intends ill I am sure; I must counter her…'

'Deborah… should fairness fail… Look after Boy for me.'

At that moment Janet was bundled into a holding cell in one of the stone buildings by the quay. Deborah's power, weak from seeking passage from Erka's prison, was not enough to reach her. Janet's mind fell silent, and the terror of her last instruction to Deborah, filled her loneliness.

~

Kayleigh gently brushed Janet's hair as she rested. 'What awful thengs yoo have endured.'

Garrie stood and approached a wooden box in the corner of the room. Opening it he pulled out two seal pelts.

'Is that what you do now?' Sally asked. 'Put on the skins and become Selkies?'

Garrie's tone was depressed, 'Nay, I am tied to thess action by the curse.'

'Erka's curse demanded most from Janet,' Bess added. 'Et punished her fer her desire to help folk, required her to stand before storms such as the one yoo've seen, ne'er endin' untel reunited weth the seal necklace. Then the curse went further, those she loved would rise first, perhaps days before. Initially oblivious to the repeatin' events they would gradually remember, an', as the storm approached an' arrived, their anxiety would grow…'

Carl gestured to the pelts, 'And these?'

'Erka's last cruel twest,' Garrie responded. 'Remindin' us o' her hatred towards Selkies. Janet has ne'er returned to her kin, taken from her home by May, she'd ben separated from her pelt. Erka knew I would find et, she knew I would look after Janet's precious thengs; prevent their theft when the cracklin' o' wood fell silent on Gallow Ha. She knew I was a Selkie, so she stipulated that one o' her kind would present her weth her coverin's but that Janet would be bound to refuse, held as she was to the curse.'

Kayleigh acknowledged the cruelty, and asked how it was that the Seal pendant's whereabouts had been forgotten, for surely Bess would know if Erka had hidden it.

'E'en Erka didne know what became o' the necklace.' Bess replied. 'She went to the trial an' on her return, changed as she was, et was gone.'

Sally looked about to spill how the necklace was now lost forever, so Carl quickly comforted her and asked how Erka had "changed".

Bess stared vacantly into the fire, 'Et was some days after Janet had arrived en Kirkwall. May had spent the time attemptin' to extract a confession from her weth violence. A cruel man indeed, he left her weth bruises oot o' sight; leavin' each time, only when she fell unconscious. He consoled hemself that he had all the evidence he needed, an' so pursued a date fer the trial. Bishop Graeme afforded hem an afternoon the followin' week, an' et was widely publicised. Erka was thrilled, but on her arrival shey soon noticed a threat to her plan en the crowd on the quayside as she came ashore.'

'Benjamin had come?' Carl guessed.

'Aye, but Erka wasne goin' to let that stop her now.'

Chapter Sixty-three

Benjamin strode purposefully towards the Cathedral, he was not afraid here, he'd left the naval ships behind, swimming as a Selkie with his clothes and pack wrapped tightly in Janet's pelt. The hope that he might get here sooner had been dashed by the focused efforts of the Captain he'd been serving under. There had been eyes everywhere. It was only the provision of a hiding place by Deborah's son that had stowed him long enough to make the watchers weary; Benjamin escaping the island at night from the shallows of Grobust.

He had made shore at Quanter Ness, donned his dry clothes and headed along the shore to the harbour, keen to find the safety of a crowd.

The sky looked heavy of rain by the time he found the holding rooms empty, Janet already on her way to the trial. He would only have one chance now; a rescue from Marwick's Hole, the notorious pit-like cell in the Cathedral itself.

It was half way to the trial that his eyes met hers. Beaming, bright eyes that stopped him dead in his tracks; the sound of distant thunder pricking at his discernment.

'Jan?!'

'Oh Ben, dearest Ben, I am set free!'

Benjamin stepped closer, struggling to believe his eyes. He ran his fingers across her cheek then swept her up in his arms, spinning her around. 'But how? I saw yoo taken. Heard the opinions o' May from the shadows. How are yoo free?'

'Bess had ben controllin' them all along, May's men came across her here on Mainland juss last night en full incantation, naked an' smeared weth blood. Her own werds have condemned her before witnesses, Oh Ben I'm free!'

Ben happily accepted her thrown embrace, the hurried kisses.

'Come Ben, let us watch the trial, let us hear the verdict on one who hates our kind, the final victory fallin' to the Selkies!'

Ben felt an elation rising within, and he was soon allowing himself to be led by the hand by this vision of joy, towards the sun-lit, imposing, red stone bulk of St. Magnus Cathedral, backdropped by the blackest sky.

Upon arrival he could see that the proceedings were underway. The crowd was thick and he could not get far forward. He tried to see Bess, but where he knew she'd be was perpetually obscured.

His companion had a suggestion, 'Use ya ears. Save ya eyes fer me.'

Benjamin smiled, this was a great day, he'd reconciled his fears about Harolt the moment Janet had been taken. He loved her and would do anything to save her, anything. Now he and his love had a future. With his eyes ensnared, he swore never to lose sight of her again.

Janet had been staring out into the angry crowd, wondering how and when she could put forward her plea of innocence. From the word go, May had dominated the proceedings, his opening accusations had left the crowd baying and calling for "justice against the witch!" His performance seemed to play to the noise, somehow it served his purpose. Each time Janet tried to protest about some point that May put forward, May would have the guard at Janet's side subdue her.

She felt a sense of despair rising, then she saw him; he had come! Her Benjamin, working his way along the back of the crowd. Her heart lifted, a smile almost made her face, but something was wrong. He seemed to be elated and light of mood, a manner starkly contrasted by the sea of anger between them. He was being led, yes, his focus was on something… someone leading him by the hand… BESS! She gazed up into his eyes, furtively glancing at Janet with a disdain that landed a blow far greater than her guard had yet administered.

Bess took Benjamin into her arms, his back to the court, then the pair were obscured by the jostling mob. Janet slumped down but was brutally hauled to her feet by her bound wrists.

'I call on the witness of Mr. Mullan, neighbour of the Forsyth family.' In calling his first witness, May had denied Janet any opportunity to claim innocence at all.

The hall fell quiet.

What had Mr. Mullan to say of witchcraft? Janet wondered, surprised by how the herdsman cowered as she looked at him.

'Fear her not,' May assured. 'I hold the right to execute sentence immediately in the event of the manifestation of devilry.'

Janet wanted to protest, she wanted to speak of the little Kirk on Westray and the dear Minister and the love of the Kirk folk who looked after the needs of her departed father when she could not. But her lips seemed held…

Suddenly Janet knew; Erka was using Bess, she'd captivated her dear Ben, and now, now she was holding Janet's tongue.

'I ded see Mess Forsyth one day, early t'was, hurryin' from Tuquoy Bay. She gave me the merest o' nods t'acknowledge my greetin' o' her. She seemed evasive an' wild…'

'You headed to pasture that lay alongside the east shore of the bay,' May prompted. '…a slope that lay next to Forsyth land. What did you see in the bay?'

'I saw blood. There was blood en the breakers an' on the sand.'

'Your conclusion?'

'She were callin' the beast.'

'What beast?'

Mr. Mullan paled, clearly pained to say.

'Come now man, are you not within the walls of God's house? The Devil's menagerie cannot touch you here. See…' May waved a dismissive hand towards Janet, '…even the witch is powerless to defer judgement. Spit it out man!'

'The Nuckelavee…' At the gasps of those gathered, Mr. Mullen slapped his hands over his mouth.

'And your further evidence?' May demanded, unwilling to lose it to rising anxiety.

Fingers trailing through his beard, Mr. Mullan claimed to have lost animals from his herd through wasting, and that it was clearly the devil's work as those that ate the flesh of the butchered animals, became ill. Mullan faltered, he felt the mobs disgust that anyone would eat an animal deemed cursed, 'Et was a time o' need.'

'What time of need?'

'That caused b'the storms, they caused the crops to fail, Sir, aye, and we couldne get provisions by sea fer weeks on end.'

'And what do *you* say is Miss Forsyth's part in all this?'

'Sir, she twests the weather to her will, they say she argued weth Benjamin Garrioch…'

'Who?'

'A fisherman who were courtin' her. When he left her to go to sea weth the fishin' fleet from Moclett, she ded breng doon such a fog that et could be touched, an' she ded open the mouth o' the sea an' swallow up the whole fleet. None left t'tell the tale…'

Janet's eyes looked frantically for Benjamin, if she could just point him out in the crowd, call out his name - she could render Mr. Mullan's claim void. But she could not speak and though she tried to point her guard instantly restrained her. Bess's eyes bored into Janet's. Ben locked in that enchanted embrace. She draped her hair around his neck and in a blink they both vanished from sight. Janet gasped, what could be done against such power?

There was a boy standing where Mr. Mullan had stood. Janet had not even noticed the Herder leave. She knew the boy as a son of the Harbour Master on Westray, the boy she'd stumbled into the day Benjamin disappeared. He seemed greatly troubled by Janet's gaze. What could she have done to terrify this child?

May probed, 'What did you see, boy?'

'I dess see a woman enstructin' seals to find Ben Garrioch, I saw them dive away to do her biddin'.'

'What woman?'

The boy pointed a trembling finger at Janet. 'Her, Mester, she jumped at me, knocked me to the groond. I begged fer my life an' she let me go.'

May dismissed the boy, 'Minister, please come forth.'

Janet's heart lifted, could the Minister of the little Kirk say anything bad about her?

'Your observations Minister?'

'I have known the accused all her life, she always was a wilful child, skipping Kirk attendance; her father had to hand her into the care of her aunt here on Mainland.' The Minister turned to the Bishop. 'Mary did a good job and was able to place the child into the work party your predecessor created for orphans and the children of the poor.'

The Bishop acknowledged the detail and regarded Janet with searching eyes. Janet noticed the light of recognition and hoped it might aid her better than the Minister's words; each of which had pointed to waywardness. The storm outside drew closer.

'When Janet returned to Westray, she seemed a model child, quite remarkable for such a short time. Coming of age, Mary had tried to seek a suitable match for her niece, but on returning again to Westray after further time here on Mainland, she became enamoured of a local fisherman, a course fellow with no family locally, who was known to become embroiled in rowdy behaviour. I fear this was the turning point. Mary was not pleased, and I think this drove Janet back to her old ways. I have myself seen her quite possessed of spirit, I have seen her screaming at the sea, and she was under the influence of alcohol the very morning I found her father had died. Most mysterious of all has been her disappearance until now, though the possession of otherworldly craft observed by others who have brought this case before Bishop Graeme, goes someway to an explanation.'

Janet now knew how she was seen, her heart laboured in her chest. What hope of freedom remained? Her eyes fell on the black dress and she closed them in despair; May had dressed her for the part, she was her own living poppet, waiting for her own hair to be tied about her neck.

'Is this yours?'

Janet glanced up, in front of her face was the fabric doll her aunt had given her all those years ago. She knew she had given it to Bess, but unable to deny that it had been gifted to her, she nodded.

'This doll was made by Mary Davie, nee Forsyth, Edward Forsyth's sister, Janet's aunt. Her widowed husband could not face attendance this day, but he confirmed my suspicion that the hair of this doll had been his wife's hair, cut as an act of loving kindness to grace this child's toy. He also spoke of the accused seeking communion with 'little people'...' May stepped up to the Bishop, holding up the doll and the lead shard embossed with unfathomable runic symbols. 'Before us is a witch your reverence...' Lightning flashed outside, '...and she must be dealt with.'

Chapter Sixty-four

The Bishop turned to Janet, 'Do you have anything to say Miss Forsyth?' His tone was soft, sensitive. If she could have spoken, she would have thrown herself on the warmth of his manner for mercy; but Erka still held her tongue. Hot tears found the fastest path down her cheeks. Thunder rolled around the building.

The Bishop sighed heavily, 'Very well. From the evidence I have seen and heard presented to me on this day, it is my conclusion that you are indeed a practitioner of arcane and malevolent arts.' Again, the thunder roared. 'A Storm Witch, yes.' He nodded at his own invention. 'It is therefore my due responsibility to sentence you according to the guidance of King James and approval of his successor. Tomorrow morning you will be taken, bound again as you are, to the top of the Clay Loan, to Gallow Ha, where you will be tethered to a stake, strangled and burned. You will spend the night in Marwick's hole, there, in the wall of this great house of God, to plead for your soul before His great mercy. This is my righteous judgement in the sight of The Most-High. This trial is over.' The Bishop rose and the crowd erupted, their volume drowning the storm outside.

Forcibly the guard took her by an arm already black with the bruises of those violent days. She screamed. Her voice regained she cried Benjamin's name, 'Save me Ben!' but the clamour drowned her calls, and the briefest glimpse of him amongst the jostling shadows, lit sharply by lightning flashes, seemed only to confirm his indifference, his face twisted in contempt. The guard pulled her harshly forward, stumbling her towards the baying crush. Lang, from the Victory Star, was there, he levelled his aim and spat at her, shouting 'Wetch! Wetch!'

Forced away towards the pit Janet's eyes sought out Bess and found her visible, mocking face. For a moment, their eyes were locked in mutual venom as the guard cut her bindings and pushed her down into the Cathedral's notorious cell.

The hole reeked of stale urine, the walls slippery and cold beneath her searching, recoiling fingers. The floor littered with tattered rags - the torn cloth of garments once worn by other tortured minds faced with a night to contemplate impending death. A voice above her, most likely that of the guard, said something she did not catch. Something like spital spattered down the wall beside her, she shrank from it, crouching fearfully against the opposite wall. The volatility of those above echoed around her, then a heavy grate rang closed across the opening, and Janet abandoned hope.

Despite the anxiety and fear - or perhaps because of it - exhaustion had claimed Janet's senses. As she slept, she dreamt. Deborah was standing with her.

'Hello child, I'm so sorry I couldne protect yoo, I have sent hem fer yoo, he'll come soon. Yoo must go weth hem an' no' return, fer there'll be nowhere fer yoo here. Nowhere safe.'

It was much later that the chill and nausea broke the oblivion of her slumber. The storm still rolled distantly, noticeable once more in the deep silence. She vomited in the corner before perceiving the green glow that bathed the stone walls. She did not look up at the source poking through the grate of the metal hatch above.

Janet rebuked her observer, 'Have yoo no' done enough?'

Bess replied, 'Auch, lor' no! Yoo have forever t'suffer, an' all ya pets an' lovers.'

'Why, juss why?'

'Fer my pleasure. Ya kind ded take what was mine.'

'The Selkies?'

'Yoo see! Yoo know! I canny fathom why yoo asked at all!'

'Does Bess know what yoo do through her?'

The answer was a shrill laugh.

Janet's head rolled back, bringing her eyes up to meet what was undeniably Erka's glare, the green jewelled necklace dangling down through the bars of the grate. 'I am no' afraid.'

'Oh? Yoo well be. As they draw that cord aboot ya throat yoo well fear.'

'No, I well find yoo en the crowd an' I well stare at yoo weth a smile on my face, untel all wonder who I'm starin' at; an' they well look an' they well see the source o' my joy, an' May well suspect yoo.'

'Oh Jan, ya so dim to tell me. I may lack power now from a busy day, but I promise yoo I'll have adequate that yoo wellne find me when yoo look fer me. Yoo'll juss hear my laughter on the wend.'

'Yoo have shared too much too, ef ya spent now then yoo ken be spent again, then yoo should fear, fer Ben well come an' kill yoo weth juss bare hands.'

'Dear Benjamin? Auch, I have more than enough power fer hem, I well enjoy usin' his strength tell I bore o' hem. Then weth yoo burned t'dust I'll send hem t'his part en ya future, e'er seein' e'er despairin' o' hope.'

Another noise came from above, the approach of footsteps. 'Damn, I paid well fer hem to be kept away. Goodbye, little pup.'

Rising hastily to leave, Erka gasped as the pendant about Bess's neck snagged on the grate, snapping the chain.

Bess stood, staring down confused, bathed in the flickering light of the distant storm.

A green light struck the floor beside Janet, her eyes cast quickly from its glare, then with an assertive motion she flung a rag from the floor over it, wrapped it tightly and gripped it in her hand, 'Go Bess, hurry, do no' be found here, be free, Erka well burn weth me tomorrow!'

A voice came from above, 'Anyone there?' A face appeared, glaring down through the grate. It was a guard.

'Where have yoo ben?' Janet asked.

'Wha's et to yoo?'

'Yoo should be guardin' me.'

'I donny guard fer your sake, I guard fer the sake o' others. Besides yoo were oot cold an' there were thess... hold on! I'm no' answerable to yoo! Shut up, wetch!'

'Or what?'

'Or, or I'll...'

For a moment the guard disappeared, then he returned with a burning torch, not that Janet was bothered, for she felt Bess had now had time to slip away. '...I'll burn yoo before daybreak.'

Another voice joined the conversation, 'Tha's no' ya place.' The voice was familiar.

'Stop there!' The guard freed an axe from his belt. 'Announce ya self.'

'Juss one o' the Bishop's men. He asked me to breng thess food to the prisoner when she woke. From ya converse I assume she's awake, or are yoo talkin' to ya self?'

A flash of lightning aided the flickering flame of the torch, 'Auch, et's yoo.' The visitor obviously presented little threat as the guard immediately put down the axe. He demanded that the visitor show him the food, and stepped away from the grate to view it. 'Tha's too good fer the likes o' her.'

'Yoo think?'

'Aye. Look, I'll take et off ya hands an' yoo ken get off home; et es late.'

'Hmm, et es. Ok, here yoo go.'

Soon the guard was back at the grate, stuffing his face with a crusty pie, 'Delicious.'

'Ya'ra pig.' Janet scorned.

The guard feigned terror, 'Yoo gonna turn me ento a pig, wetch...' The statement was followed by a high-pitched grunt, the guard stared incredulously down at Janet, clutching his throat, he gave a throaty squeal.

Janet gazed up in disbelief, was he really turning into a pig?

Suddenly the guard's eyes glazed over and within moments Janet was staring up at the man's face pressed unconscious against the bars above her. It was shocking, she almost screamed but her voice was lost to the fact that the face was now sliding away, someone else was above, perhaps the one who'd delivered the food. The latch above clicked across.

'Ben?'

A familiar face appeared in the opening.

'Grigor!'

'Hello dear girl.'

Chapter Sixty-five

Sally was amazed, 'Grigor?'

Carl shrugged, 'Who else was left? Deborah was bound by Erka and, with May labelling her as a witch, she could hardly show her face even if she could escape the shop, everyone would have known her. The Trows, well that's a no brainer. Send the dog and you've got a problem opening grate locks, not to mention the risk of him swelling up like a giant wolf and gobbling up bystanders. Benjamin's bewitched. Harolt's in Bergen most likely, and Bess has just shed all of Erka's powers.'

Bess protested, 'I woulda gone. I was scared ez all, such necromancy had come from me as to have me burned a thousand times o'er.'

'Why *did* you burn?'

Bess stared at him, he felt uncomfortable. 'Erka had popularised me; anythin' that anyone needed was supplied them. No werk was too much, fer et was achieved through Erka's art. Weth Erka gone I couldne maintain the regard o' the islanders, thengs remained undone. People started to grumble. Then, after a lettle time, May returned to Westray. No longer protected by Erka's thugs, the cottage proved to be o' great interest to the man. Once a wetches den, he might gain from ets study. He asked questions, got too close, tried to force hemself on me. Wethin days o' refusin' his advances I was taken to Kirkwall fer trial as a wetch. I had burned all that belonged to Erka, but somehow the most mundane o' thengs, items I had o'erlooked: bowls, light markin's on wooden utensils, May had gathered them all, an' I was burned.'

Silence filled the room, Bess accepting the quiet acknowledgement of her torment at the hands of such a wicked man.

Sally turned back to Garrie, 'So, Deborah *sent* Grigor?'

Carl explained that Deborah's words were a dream.

'Weth magic, does et all no' bleed ento one reality?' Kayleigh offered.

Sally turned to Garrie, '*Did* Deborah send Grigor?'

'Aye, she ded, though to hem et was juss his desire to set her free. His knowledge o' Janet defied the verdict. He werked from the Cathedral, he had access an' a fine reputation, no one would have suspected an unlawful motive en hem.'

Carl chuckled, 'Ha, the guard certainly didn't.' He pulled himself up, 'Hold on! Had Grigor killed him?'

'Nay, a herbal concoction, he were fine; et was chiefly due to hem that no one gave chase.'

'But he'd seen Grigor.'

'Tez so, but that wasne his reasonin'; he'd ben tricked, drugged - his reputation would be en tatters, he'd lose his job. Nay, on comin' too, the guard hid the remainin' pie, closed an' locked the grate o'er Marwick's Hole an' stood guard o'er an empty cell untel he was relieved en the mornin'. His replacement, seein' the cell empty raised the alarm. Janet's guard was questioned but held fast to his story that he had neither seen nor heard anythin'; that Janet had simply vanished. Mr. May approved, et fed the hysteria aboot wetches an' had many more poor souls fed to the flames.' Garrie raised a hand to Bess's arm in comfort. 'Grigor knew none o' thess o' course. En his mind he was a wanted man as much as Janet was a condemned woman. He had a praam waitin' on the shore en the Bay o' Weyland juss north o' the harbour wall. Janet fought hem then, the waves were great after the storm an' the wend stell fierce. Janet claimed et suicide. Grigor corrected her determinedly, sayin' that she had to come. That her chances were better runnin' weth the wend, than stayin' an' chokin' before the fire.

'Janet clung to a nearby rock, lamentin' that all she had was on Westray, an', rememberin' Deborah, Benjamin, the Trows an' Boy, she claimed the islands were her very life, an' that to go was as sure a death as flames.

'Grigor, patience all but spent, drew close to Janet, statin' plainly that they were already gone, as ef the fire had already consumed them. They were as good as ded to her.

'Janet contemplated Grigor's werds, the wend wheppin' her hair aboot her face. By stayin' she might see her loved ones again, but she also risked puttin' them en terrible danger by association.

'She could hear Deborah en her mind, urgin' her to go. Pale an' sullen as she was, she lay her hands upon the lettle boat an' awaited Grigor's added strength to drive et doon ento the frothin' waves.'

'She actually left everything?'

'Aye, et was all she could do.'

Kayleigh had to know, 'Where ded she go? Et's ben a mystery all these years.'

'Mainland Scotland, an' doon towards the border. Grigor figured none would know them, and he hoped to win her affection fer his part en her rescue, but et quickly became apparent that her heart had ben broken by Benjamin's indifference.' Garrie sighed deeply. 'Further an' further they travelled an' weth e'ery mile Janet faded, untel, cradled en Grigor's arms a year later, she breathed her last en mortal life.'

'And when storms hit the islands her restless soul would be found in a futile attempt to protect those she had loved.' Carl glanced with pity at the prone figure by the fire.

'Et es so. Et es only then that she learned I'd ben bewitched, that my behaviour at the trial had no' ben o' my own will.'

Bess sighed, 'Had she lev'd oot her life, I would have burned an' ben gone fer good, but the agony o' burnin' es a fittin' punishment fer my part…'

Garrie seemed distressed, 'Yoo had nay armour against ya mother's arts.'

Bess turned away.

Sally changed the subject, 'What did Janet do with Erka's necklace?'

'She told me she ne'er destroyed et.'

'Why not!'

'She found she couldne.'

'A protective incantation?'

'Aye, I fear so. But et es lost to knowledge now.'

Suddenly Janet sat up, 'Deborah!'

Everyone stared at the frail, yet spellbinding figure.

Janet tried to stand. Bess was first to react, Garrie nearly fell as they helped her up.

'Deborah es sending the seal necklace!' She exclaimed. 'Et es comin', we are finally saved.'

'Deborah had et?' Garrie shook his head in disbelief, staring at the Trows. 'I could have gone there, could have reclaimed et…'

Deni stepped forward, 'No' so.'

Donie continued, 'Only innocent love could cross that threshold. Deborah knew she could only hold et open fer us to cross untel Janet's life was gone, after which her power would diminish further. She had us come to yoo, had us promise silence fer fear yoo would try an' break the wall that May had built, incriminate ya self an' be tried.'

'My love fer Janet *was* innocent!'

Dini took Garrie's hand, 'Yoo, like us, are under Erka's curse. None under a curse are pure.'

Garrie looked up at Carl and Sally, then back at the Trows, 'How ded she find et?'

'She sent a gull to rob Erka before she could hide the Seal.' Deni said. 'No' the brightest o' birds, et brought et back to Deborah instead o' takin' et to Janet. We tried to bring et, but et always returned to the draw.'

'Deborah says thess es the right time.' Janet interrupted.

Garrie's attention was wholly back with her, 'The right time fer what?'

'She senses the green stone.' Janet said. 'We ken defeat Erka an' her curse forever... Oh Ben! She says we ken dwell weth our Kin!'

Sally could bear it no longer, 'I'm so sorry.' She fell into Carl's arms sobbing violently.

Carl continued. 'It was us Deborah entrusted with the pendant.' He pointed to James, who was still resting beside the fire under a blanket. 'James intended to destroy it, we rescued it, only for the storm to snatch it away from us and hurl it into the sea.'

'The storm es almost o'er.' Bess pointed to Janet's ghost-like appearance. 'Ef I hurry to the sea... oh but es et the most unlikely chance that et es washed up where I look first?' Despite the futility, Bess left with focused intent, leaving the door swinging in the wind.

Carl looked back at Janet, she had crossed the room like a phantom and was peering at Sally.

'Sal.'

Sally emerged from Carl's embrace.

'Et's O'right my dear, none o' thess angst well help ya wee baby.' She patted Sally's belly.

Sally seemed caught off guard, she looked at Janet's hand, then up at Carl with an expression of complete guilt.

Carl's eyes spoke of revelation. 'You're... pregnant?'

'I've let everyone down!' Sally bolted for the open door.

277

Chapter Sixty-six

Janet beamed at Carl, 'Best that yoo go to her, Yoo are the father after all.'

'Yes, Er, yes.' He hastily stomped outside, but what stood before him almost shattered his already compromised nerves.

Sally was laying in the wet, wind buffeted grass. Ahead of her, hands raised and screaming defiance was Bess and in front of her, climbing up over the cliff edge, was the Nuckelavee.

Carl swept Sally up off the ground and brought her back to the wall of the cottage, eyes fixed on the creature.

The beast seemed genuinely perturbed by the flames that swirled about Bess's frame. It raised a great fist away from her.

Everyone was now outside.

Janet called out, 'Stop!' and though she seemed to be just the faintest of vapours her chest clearly heaved with an excitement lost on the rest. 'Let hem come.'

Bess backed away, recoiling from a wet snort that was clearly aimed at her.

As the creature approached, Janet moved forward until they were together. She stroked his slippery, vein-streaked neck.

The Nuckelavee swung its clenched fist down towards her, Garrie cried out in dismay, but the blow didn't land.

'What have yoo got fer me, my friend?'

A throaty rumble emanated from the creature's chest and its fingers unravelled. Dangling from one digit, by its leather cord, was the seal necklace. Janet laughed like a child, seizing the necklace she skipped and danced, the clarity of her form returning, her great age dropping away into youthfulness.

Carl looked down at Sally, she was recovering from her Nuckelavee induced faint, and regarding him with sorrowful eyes.

'I'm so sorry about getting pregnant, I hoped to tell you at some point during the holiday, but everything got so busy. I know you didn't want...'

Carl smiled, 'Hush Sal, I'm so happy...'

'But we said...'

'I can't think of anything I want more, besides, it takes two, so the blame...' Carl watched as Sally was snatched from his supportive arms, straight into the air, arms flailing.

No one had noticed James' waking and pulling an object from its hiding place.

'Hah, ha, es a pretty picture o' joy.' James was standing in the door of the cottage, dressed only in his shirt, vest and Y-fronts, Erka's necklace around his neck, a hideous grin across his face.

On sight of the jewel, the Nuckelavee took a few steps back.

Garrie acted on instinct, he was nearly on the man when he froze; held by some invisible force.

'Back!' James ordered. 'All o' yoo, or I'll drop her.'

'When yoo said he'd tried to destroy the necklace et didne make sense to me. Why would a man o' ya time wesh to destroy the seal?' Janet started to walk towards James. 'Now I understand. Et were no hem, but Erka.'

Erka let Sally drop a little, then thrust her higher into the air, screaming and clawing for purchase. 'I said back!'

Janet stopped, 'But I canny give ya the seal ef I stay here, Erka.' The situation seemed to have reached an impasse. 'Besides, how ded yoo find ya way back? I bore yoo to the border o' England.'

'Grigor kept me after ya death. He'd listened to ya stories o' the seal an' the green gem, but juss as I'd stayed ya hand when yoo weshed to dash et on the granite bones o' Scotland, so I stayed Grigor's hand too. Grigor found solace en marriage after ya demise, an' the necklace was passed doon through his family. I let some o' them wear me so that I could *encourage* their return to the islands an' twest the story. Et's ben a fine race to find the Seal, Janet, an' I've enjoyed watchin' yoo suffer, but now yoo have et I must be merciful an' breng aboot ya end.'

'Merciful! I have et, the curse es o'er; what exactly do yoo hope to end?'

The seal necklace vanished from Janet's hand and reappeared in that of James. James instantly dropped it to the ground and raised his foot.

Carl was closest and attempted a rescue, but found himself flat on his back some distance away. Seeing Sally's distress at his flight he quickly shot her a thumbs up. 'I'm OK!'

Erka laughed, 'There es somethin' yoo donny know aboot the curse. Sure, et held until yoo regained the artefact - all curses must end, but I was so confident that yoo'd ne'er find et where I would hide et, that I wove a joke ento the curse. I laughed loud as I declared yoo an' the giver-o'-the-gift could live a life weth their kind fer all the days they stell possessed the token o' love. When I heard these two claim that they had et, I couldne believe my luck. Destroyin' the seal abruptly would end any chance o' freedom from the curse.'

'But et's done!' Deni protested.

'The curse es lifted!' Dini pointed out.

Donie stepped forward. 'Leave her aloon!'

'Och, nay, tha's the beauty o' thess moment. Fer as long as they have et they ken be weth their detestable Selkie kin. Yoo see? I win, robed o' my beautiful plan, I am compensated by my joke. I ken prevent the clause from e'er bein' possible. Just as yoo die - so well they.' And with that all three Trows became the boulders from which they were made.

Sally nearly dropped as Erka laughed dismissively, foot poised to strike, when a great bulk appeared at speed through the cottage door behind James, it was Boy, and Erka was completely unaware of him.

The blow was powerful. James was pounded to the ground well clear of the seal. Instantly Garrie was free to move and Sally began her descent.

Carl, having seen Erka's power falter at the undoing of the Trows, knew he had to help Sally, but he'd barely got to his feet as the Varden burst from the doorway of the cottage. Sally was falling now, and there was no way he could get there in time.

Kayleigh, could have done nothing for Sally, even if she'd thought to; she was too slight a frame. Her eyes were on something else.

Garrie bent down and retrieved the Seal necklace.

'Sally!' Carl cried, as he realised his faltering, limping run was not enough to save her. He stopped, shielding his eyes from the horrific sight of his wife's impact on the rocky teeth of the cliff edge.

At the absence of the sickening sound of cracking bones and spattering blood, Carl let his hand drop. Sally was descending softly towards him, arms open, tears of relief streaming from her eyes; for the Nuckelavee's great, webbed hands had plucked her from the air. In the next moment they were reunited, the embrace of thankful lovers; almost unbreakable - but Sally let go of Carl and swung around. She flung her arms about the Nuckelavee's wide chest, the scar where Janet had freed the beast of its controlling amulet, was there before her eyes. She praised the creature without hesitation, 'You are truly a noble creature.' She looked up at its two, blood flushed faces, and quickly retreated to Carl.

A chilling whimper filled the swirling air. Boy was standing, bull-like beside the stunned James, looking out to sea at the clouds of the passing storm. They were churning, twisting, arching back.

Garrie shifted uneasily, 'A death.'

Janet stepped quickly to him, taking his arm. 'But who?'

Chapter Sixty-seven

All eyes fell on Kayleigh, her back was to them her Auburn hair billowing in the changed direction of the wind. She turned, finger tips clutching the chain of the necklace, eyes fixed on the glowing gem in its lattice of filigree silver strands. Was she thinking she could save everyone from the returning tempest if she just placed that chain about her neck? No one could tell, and no one would ever know, for as the pause of expectation began to stale, another figure stepped in and the jewel was smothered by a handkerchief.

'Deborah!' Janet exclaimed.

'Nay time fer pleasantries my darlin' child. Do what I say an' do et quickly.'

'What must we do?'

'Erka cannot possess at whim, someone must succumb to the jewel's invitation an' set et aboot their own neck. She has cast her spirit ento the storm en order to destroy the Seal an' end ya happiness. She es angry an' her power es no' yet spent. Et's time to flee, no' stand. Ya flight seals ya future. All storms end, ef the green gem es destroyed Erka es vanquished. Benjamin, get ya Selkie pelts an' go; immediately!'

Filled with urgency, Garrie ran, but Janet protested, 'Yoo are all en deadly peril, I wellne abandon yoo now.'

'Nay, I'm sure yoo well no'. But now Jan, right now, yoo must fly an' secure the necklace where et belongs!'

Boy bounded up to her, still in his bulky form. Janet received him with open arms. 'Oh, my sweet Boy, well done yoo!' She ruffled his fur and he immediately returned to his normal size, Janet sweeping him up to her breast 'Yoo canny come where we are goin'.'

Garrie disappeared into the cottage.

'Yoo must stay weth Deborah an' do what she bids.'

Boy's whimper returned with increased vigour.

'Es et so?' Janet asked looking up at all who'd helped her. 'Or es thess juss sorrow at partin'?'

Boy barked.

'Do yoo understand? Yoo canny come weth us.'

Boy stared. Garrie returned from the cottage with the skins, the white of his hair all but gone.

'Go to Deborah, Boy.'

Janet marvelled at the appearance of a broad smile on Boy's face. She looked to the others again, 'Thank yoo all!' and, pelts in hand, they headed down the cliff path to the sea. 'They well smash the amulet, an' Erka well be the one to die.'

Garrie nodded, 'Long o'erdue.'

Deborah surveyed those remaining, her eyes falling with pity on Bess. 'Dear, dear Bess. Ye've suffered so long…'

'I canny rest untel Jan's safe...'

'Et's o'er, Bess. We have only to destroy the amulet at the stone. There es nothin' more yoo ken do. I give yoo permission; the curse es o'er. Janet es safe now. Rest from ya pain es here, well yoo let go?'

Bess stepped up to Deborah, tears flowing down her scarred face. 'Ef Jan's safe, I'll go weth joy.'

Deborah raised her hands, Bess's skin knit together, the flames died, her youth and beauty returned. Deborah's hands rested gently upon her, then, in a tender embrace, Bess blew away in the buffeting breeze, like the smoke she had once become.

Deborah turned to the Nuckelavee, and it began to retreat from her. Try as it might, its efforts came to nothing, scuffing up the turf as Deborah drew it to her. Desperate, it reared up to strike her.

'Steady now, Niall, too long have yoo endured thess form, ya insatiable hunger, ya need to be en the brine, the drownin', burstin' agony o' ya lungs beneath those waves. Nay, yoo must become two again. Yoo were the noblest, the thinker o' the three, ya mount, the finest o' steeds...'

The Nuckelavee's rearing stopped, on all fours it shook its heads as if fighting malaise.

'...be Niall again, return an' desmount.'

The surface of the creature's body seemed to twist and shift; an obviously painful process. Within moments the beast's form became two separate bodies, still fleshy and raw. The torso fell from the mount's broad back, then, appearing in spasms of change, came skin, hair, cloth, and metal. Carl and Sally stared in wonder, for before them now, pushing himself up from the ground as if embarrassed about being decked, was a fully armoured knight and a magnificent, grey horse dressed in heraldry of red and gold. The man quickly drew his sword and ran up to Deborah.

Kayleigh screamed a warning but Deborah's demeanour of calm didn't flinch.

The knight dropped to one knee before her, the point of the weapon thrust into the shallow turf. 'My sword es yours my Lady.'

'Ya service es complete, bar one small deed, Niall.'

'Neem et my Queen.'

'Take thess girl safely home weth the hound an' the man who bore Erka, he well need attention.'

Niall's eyes flashed to the Varden with a hint of caution.

'No!' Kayleigh cried. 'I wesh to stay an' help…'

'Ya help well be to prepare shelter at ya home. Our two friends well need a hot drink an' rest very soon.'

Boy looked quizzically at Deborah.

'Es a time o' choosin' again, Boy. Ya master has passed where yoo canny follow. I know yoo would guard us ef yoo could, but ya power fer thess day was well spent - as et was the day yoo kept the Nuckelavee from killin' Edward at the wall, buyin' time fer Benjamin to arrive - All these years Erka's control o'er my imprisonment was through her will alone. Such was her strength she was able to hold that incarceration o'er distances I couldne imagine. But I've grown too, I charmed May's wall to open to pure hearts. I could e'en open the Way o' Birsay fer such, but Erka's power prevented me from passin' through either path. Ya action today broke her conscious hold long enough fer me to be free, an' so I came, resolved to bring her doon. She who was my Sester by blood, well I help cast ento the pit o' hell. Ya role en that es fully played dear hound. Go. Find ya new master. Yoo well know who, yoo always do.'

Niall had placed James over the saddle of his horse and was now standing with Kayleigh, waiting for Boy. Boy looked at them.

Kayleigh smiled, 'Yoo look hungry. Come on.'

Boy glanced back at Deborah, whimpered, then turned and trotted slowly away.

Kayleigh gave a parting call, 'Come to the guest hoose when all's done.'

'They'll bey weth yoo shortly.' Deborah promised, turning to Carl and Sally. 'I'm askin' yoo to take a dangerous path.'

Carl shrugged, 'We've come this far, I feel we need to make up for our earlier short-falls.'

Deborah turned to lead the couple away, 'Come on we've go' a wee step to get to where we need to be.'

'But the Trows…' Sally protested.

'What aboot them dear?'

'Aren't you going to return them to their true form too?'

'But they *are* en their true form.'

Sally found that she understood. She smiled weakly, 'Ha! Just seems so sad.'

'Aye, their kind were so wonderful, full o' joy despite adversity.' Deborah looked up at the great arching claw of cloud. 'Today es an end o' many thengs. Come, we must go before our journey es made e'en more uncomfortable.'

Chapter Sixty-eight

Carl watched the face of the storm as they made their way along the clifftop. He knew where they were going. James' ancestors had been led to believe the wrong story; it wasn't the seal that had to be destroyed on the stone, it was the green gem. 'The storm's coming in fast.' He observed, pointing to the great curtains of rain sweeping across the sea.

'Her eyes are en the rain. She knows only where we were, she well have to search from there. Et'll afford us time.' Deborah increased her pace.

Sally noticed, 'Not much time then.'

'I fear she'll be close enough when she realises what's happenin'.'

'Close enough?'

The clifftop grew suddenly dark. Deborah stopped and swung around. To Sally and Carl it was obvious that she had reached her goal.

'Here?' Carl remarked.

'Aye, fer me.' She held her hand out to Sally. 'Take et.'

'Where?' Sally willingly received the necklace wrapped in Deborah's handkerchief.

'To the stone,' Carl replied. 'Where we were with James.' He took

Sally's free hand. 'Come on Sal, the rain's about to reach the old cottage. Deborah's going to shield us.'

'Go! An' donny look at et!'

Carl and Sally pounded up the slope. It didn't seem so far without a blinding gale in your face, or the fight to hold each step that they'd experienced the day before. Suddenly there was a great flash of light and an instant peel of thunder. The retort caused Carl to glance back. Seeing Garrie's cottage splitting apart in flames gave him access to energy reserves he didn't know he had, 'Guess she knows her jewel isn't there.'

'Carl, I'm scared.'

'We can do this Sal, look, there's the stone.'

All about them was illuminated with a constant flickering brilliance, Carl and Sally dropped to the ground by the flat rock.

Curiosity too pricked to resist, they looked back together. Lightning was spewing upwards from the ruin of the cottage, Deborah silhouetted, standing like some gunslinger awaiting the command to draw, and beyond her the curtain of rain, pulsating and contorting, twisting this way and that, like some great head looking, searching, then it locked on Carl and Sally's position. The need for light gone, all fell dark again.

'She's coming! Quick Sal, smash it.'

Sally wasn't hesitating, she'd already acquired a rough stone and rapidly brought it down on the cotton parcel.

Carl looked for confirmation that it was over. Rain lashed into him, followed by a fearsome gust that threatened to push him from his hands and knees, 'I don't think its broken... hit it again!'

Sally raised the stone with both hands, a great bolt of lightning was caught and dissipated by Deborah. 'THE CROSS STONE!' She called, sweeping the curtain of rain aside with a swipe of her hand.

Sally brought the rock down on the hidden necklace, again nothing!

'James had a brick shaped stone, carved with a cross!' Carl frantically explored the hole beside the flat rock. 'He dug it up from here! Agh, of course it won't be back, he had it in his hands when the lightning struck.'

The couple anxiously glanced around, aided by the sporadic, electric flickering of Erka and Deborah's fight.

Sally pointing to the cliff edge. 'There!'

Carl sprang up between gusts, edging his way towards the Cross Stone. A dreadful hiss sprang up in the wind. Carl grabbed the stone and turned to come back. Sally was reaching towards him in an attempt to help bridge the gap he had to cross. Deborah was on her knees, clearly at the end of her resources.

Sally seized the stone and raised it to strike. Deborah fell, Erka sending down rain dense enough to drown her, then such a blast of wind cut up towards Carl and Sally that the jewel's covering was blown clean away. Sally's eyes fell into the heart of the stone.

'Look away!' Carl knew it was already too late.

Sally's raised arm faltered, 'The necklace is frightened, it's clinging to the rock. The wind isn't moving it at all.'

Carl fought the desire to seek the source of the green glow that highlighted the rain, he took the Cross Stone and knelt down, feeling for the necklace.

'I can't destroy it.' Sally was clearly unaware that she no longer had the means to do so.

Carl's fingers found the chain and he brought the stone down sharply. Nothing happened, 'Grr, missed!' He raised the stone again, feeling for the amulet. His fingertips grazed the gem and lightning fell. Carl was thrown back. The Cross Stone, snatched clean from his hand, was cast once more to the lip of the cliff. Carl glanced frantically between it and Sally.

'I must put on the necklace.' Sally stood, unmolested by the gale.

Carl thrust himself from the ground towards her, 'No Sal! Fight it!'

The air hissed and cackled.

'Without a body she is just wind and rain.'

'AN' THAT ES NO' T'BE FEARED?' Erka's voice was in Carl's ears, howling around him. He flailed his arms as if trying to beat it away.

Sally's eyes met his own as she glanced back at him, and his heart sank, for they were glowing with the same eerie hue of the gem. For a moment he thought she'd put the necklace on but there was nothing around her neck. He pushed against the air to reach her. Sally bent down towards the amulet, hand outstretched, rivulets of rain pouring from her fingertips.

Further gusts knocked Carl sideways, but he saw a last desperate opportunity, and put his full weight behind a kick to her wet trainers with his size twelve boots. 'Sorry Sal.'

As she fell, Carl twisted around and was able to catch her. She screamed at him in frustration, but as she opened her eyes, he noticed a welcome absence of green. He dragged her away from temptation, desperately trying to form a plan.

The wind seemed to hiss 'Loser!'

But something new occurred to Carl. 'Forget it! Help yourself!' and he sat with his back to the cliff edge, holding Sally protectively in his arms.

The rain and wind seemed to coalesce above the flat rock, the electricity that crackled menacingly around them, arced down like claws, scratching at the necklace, reaching with futility, powerless to grip the artefact.

As Erka's infuriation grew Carl slid his hand back towards the Cross Stone. He'd thought it closer but it was further than he expected and, with Sally's weight also upon him he overreached and slipped on the wet turf, knocking the stone clean off the edge of the cliff. He stared incredulously, perplexed by his own clumsiness, but the sudden stillness of the air sent a foreboding panic through his chest.

'Carl.' Sally's tone did nothing to ease his concern.

Carl pushed himself back up, the landscape floodlit with forking sparks of light that seemed to originate from two sharp, waist height points. He blinked, they appeared hand-like and part of a woman's form. A resplendent figure of crazily swirling, dancing droplets.

Carl smiled. 'Can't get it?'

There was definitely a look of absolute rage in the elemental face. 'PUT ET ON!' Erka demanded.

Sally reached out towards the temptation but Carl held her tightly, fighting his own confused thoughts.

He grabbed a nearby rock, 'Now who's the loser!' he mocked, and flung the missile with adrenalin fuelled accuracy straight through the figure's head. Sweeping Sally up with him, he had intended to hurl them both as far off the cliff as he possibly could, in a bid for deep water, a last insane bid to escape and remove Sally from any risk of possession. He couldn't. As Carl turned, his path was blocked by an unyielding, naked body, bigger than his own. Carl nearly fell down again as he collided with it. The arms of the body caught the couple and steadied them.

Carl found himself staring into the noble, understanding face of a bearded man with a long, crystal tipped staff. Behind him, others were appearing, one ran up to the bearded man and handed him the Cross Stone. Carl's eyes grew wide with astonishment at its retrieval, and fascination as the great man offered the bottom of his staff to a hole in one end of the stone, slowly screwing it into what was obviously its proper place!

A deafening roar now pervaded Carl's consciousness, Sally's grip on his arm was painful, and he fought his desire to remain ignorant of what was coming. He flicked his eyes towards it. The great mass of the storm had gained altitude and was now falling towards the gathering. The Nobleman stepped softly forwards; despite the imminent storm tsunami, he seemed in no rush at all.

Carl swallowed hard, for it was obvious he wouldn't get half way to the flat rock and necklace before being dislodged from the cliff like dust being blown from a long shelf-bound tome. Carl braced himself swinging Sally tightly into his arms. Then... nothing!

Chapter Sixty-nine

Another distinct figure had stepped forward... Janet; clothed now, only in a thin, gown-like undergarment that was enslaved to the promiscuous wind, she was holding back the storm whilst the bearded man continued his slow procession, a chant now audible above the deadened gusts!

'But she isn't a witch.' Sally whispered.

'She was holding the storm back on Birsay, remember? She showed us. Erka's own curse has given Janet the chance to defeat her!'

The rain and lightning tore and wrenched for a way to prick through Janet's protection.

'This is it Sal, Erka's power is weakening, she's spent!'

The man raised the staff over the flat rock and, without glancing down, with a distinct gruff bark from the back of his throat - a final syllable to his chant - he brought the Cross Stone down on the green gem.

Green sparks flew in all directions, every droplet that had been kept aloft by the swirling tempest now fell like a blanket, and a single intense light sucked the static from the air and threw it at Janet.

As if the last throe of Erka had been expected, the bearded man, in one fluid movement from his shattering of the jewel, had flung the staff high into the air. It sailed up, and with an elegant arc its crystal tip brought it firmly into the ground at Janet's feet, the lightning bolt absorbed by the Cross Stone. Janet's eyes betraying shock and adulation, equal in their measures.

Everyone stood still as the billowed clouds began to disintegrate, pulled once again by forces of nature opposed to the arcane will of Erka. Sally didn't know where to look, for there were at least thirty individuals standing around the clifftop and only Carl, Janet and herself were wearing anything at all.

'Selkies.' Carl whispered. 'A fitting end to one who caught and skinned their young.'

'Och no! No!'

Carl turned to see Janet hurrying to Deborah's prone body. 'Deborah!' The couple quickly followed Janet.

Deborah looked up at them, Janet's knees buckled and she quickly drew Deborah's head and shoulders across her lap. 'Oh Deborah, stay weth me.'

'My time es long gone, child. Ded yoo no' hear the Varden whimper?'

'I prayed et were fer Erka.'

'Erka passed when yoo were a babe, a stone locked malevolence dependent on innocent flesh.'

Janet held Deborah tightly.

'Es fittin' I depart; my sesters are gone, an' all our kind, an' all magic, nothin' o' supernatural art es left openly en the isles, save the greater werk o' the Creator.'

Janet sobbed.

Deborah looked at Carl and Sally, smiled warmly and breathed her last. As the couple looked down on Janet and Deborah, they noticed flakes, like petals, dropping away from the old lady's form. Janet too seemed aware of the change, she lowered her friend to the rough turf, stood and stepped back, marveling, as a swirl of butterflies lifted off into the air, and with the tears still wet on her face, Janet danced amongst them. 'She well always be here!'

Sally and Carl held each other, kissed by the delicate wings of the dancing creatures. They looked back up to the crest of the slope to see how the Selkies were responding, but all bar one had slipped away. Carl wandered back up to the flat rock and addressed the man. 'Was this some place of significance to the Selkies?'

'Et es now, et's where the last o' the sesters that bore them malice, was defeated.'

'But why here, the Cross Stone buried, ready?'

'Deborah's choice. Yoo see, the flat stone marks where She buried Edward Forsyth's son. Erka said that the Forsyth child would come to naught, but Deborah had woven a deal o' her own power ento the burial. T'was the fate o' the child's spirit to defeat the spite that had rendered the body void.'

Carl finally recognised the man. He was young now, like Janet, but there was something about the eyes and line of his jaw.

'We owe thanks to yoo an' ya wife,' Garrie declared.

'But we, we lost the necklace…'

Sally and Janet joined them, Janet leading Sally by the hand and taking hold of Carl's.

'Yoo were part o' the greater story,' Janet affirmed. 'Ya love fer each other afforded access to the shop an' the Seal. Against that kind

291

o' love, darkness canny prevail. Weth et y'efforts are ne'er made aloon.' She joined Carl and Sally's hands before returning to Garrie. 'Yoo intend to leave the islands very soon, I feel et, but yoo well no' be leavin' our hearts. Yoo'll receive a Selkie blessin' to shield yoo from the dark. Expect a geft.'

'Such gefts are no' given lightly.' Garrie added.

'Come, Ben. We must go to the others; I hear them callin'.'

They'd almost reached the cliff edge when Garrie paused. He turned; his eyes wet with tears. His lips shaping his thanks, voice lost in emotion. Janet eased him back, smiled one last time and led the way down the cliff.

Carl treasured Sally's hand as they made their way down the slope towards the remains of Garrie's cottage. 'They'll just call it a lightning strike.'

Sally nodded.

It wasn't long before the couple were standing at the front door of the guest house belonging to Kayleigh's parents. It was on the North-East boundary of the airfield. To one side was a stable block where two chestnut mares were observing a newcomer with keen interest. Niall was there, exploring the tack room. On finding a brush that took his liking he returned to his steed and began grooming the grey stallion. Glancing up, he saw Carl and Sally, and paused briefly to acknowledge them.

Kayleigh suddenly appeared at the door. 'A fine beast ain' he? I'm gonna make e'ery effort to keep hem here.' Her eyes came back to Carl and Sally. 'Oh, sorry, yoo must be exhausted, Lord knows I am. Come on en; tea's brewin'.'

Carl paused, 'Don't the planes worry the horses?'

'What? Er, no, they're used to them.' Kayleigh laughed.

'What's funny?'

'First time I saw yoo, yoo were fascinated by the folklore o' the islands. Yoo've now lived et, an' the first theng yoo wesh to know es ef my parent's horses are spooked by planes!'

'All folklored out I guess. It'll take me ages to get my head around

292

what just happened.'

'Come en. Mum an' Dad are preparin' a room fer yoo.'

'Oh, er, that's ok, we'll just set up the tent again at the Tulloch...'

'I'll no' hear o' et, ya my guests now, wellne ask a penny o' yoo, come on. Oh my, ya both soaked again! There are bath robes upstairs, I'll dry ya thengs en the dryer.'

Carl read Sally's keen, bright eyes. A little comfort for the last of their stay. Was it a couple of nights? He'd lost all track of time. They followed Kayleigh inside, thanking her profusely.

Chapter Seventy

Carl and Sally's last days on Orkney were spent in a community spirit. They helped with the recovery of Kayleigh's Nissan and rolled up their sleeves in Kirkwall, assisting with the storm clean up. Kayleigh's parents seemed to know the whole story by the end of the first day, their esteem of the couple expressed in fine food and great wine.

Kayleigh's rescue of Carl and Sally's tent had been timely, safely stowed in the car boot on top of the couple's large suitcase and cool box, it only needed drying in the stable block out of the more seasonal spells of drizzle, before being packed away ready for the homeward journey.

Their last night was spent back at the Auld Motor Hoose, Kayleigh soon persuaded by the locals to sing a few songs with the backing of a single guitarist. Carl and Sally felt very emotional, it didn't feel like a week anymore, and it felt too much like home, too familiar, too welcoming.

'Not sure I want to go.' Sally admitted.

'Me neither, I'm dreading work.'

'Oh, yes, I'd forgotten about that.' She ran her hand down his cheek and flicked his beard. 'You really gonna shave it off?'

'Don't s'pose I've got much choice.'

'Perhaps just a tidy up…'

'It is tidy!'

'Well, perhaps…' Sally took hold of Carl's beard and pretended to trim it back with scissor-like finger movements.

'Get off! Anyway, I'm still on Orkney, young Mr. Chambers doesn't dictate my appearance here.'

'I asked the bar staff what yoo were drenkin', hope yoo donny mind.'

The couple looked up to find James and Dedra, with drinks for the table. 'Ken we join yoo? Donny want to cramp ya style!'

'That's fine, how are you?'

'Recoverin', et was quite alarmin' relly. Heard an' saw everythin', but lacked the will to break free o' et.'

'Same as Bess.' Sally acknowledged.

James was truly a knowledgeable man regarding Orcadian folklore and culture over the centuries, and Carl sought contact details from him so that he could follow up on themes for his column.

'Yoo wellne be er… mentionin' that I was possessed by a wetch, well yoo? Only I'm no' sure how folk would react.'

Carl had already considered this. 'I'm not telling Janet's story at all.'

James looked surprised, 'Relly?'

'But isn't it exactly what you wanted?' Sally pointed out.

'It's more than I wanted, and the media wouldn't leave James or Kayleigh alone. Huh! Imagine what they'd make of Niall! No, I'm not that sort of journalist. I've got quite enough to be getting on with, just keeping to the traditional stuff, Trows, Nuckelavees, Selkies, witches. This one week's been a gold mine.'

James shook Carl's hand. 'To my shame tha's all I relly sort fer. I rang the guest house an' enquired after yoo, an' when they said that Kayleigh had brought yoo here, well, I juss had t'be sure.'

'Perfectly understandable, but we'll all stay in touch, yes?'

Kayleigh re-joined them having finished a third song. 'Stay en touch?' She laughed. 'We're family. I'm gonna visit yoo an' ya gonna tell me all the folklore doon ya wey. P'haps we'll get to watch Black Chuck runnin' 'cross a field…'

'Shuck…' Carl corrected.

'Chuck, Shuck, whate'er; hope yoo've got a spare room.' She looked over at Niall, who seemed to prefer the company of Boy at the end of the bar, and sighed. 'Kinda hopin' I ken persuade hem to give me a ride doon on his big horse.'

'How's he doing?'

'Well Sally, et's gonna bey interestin', he got rather excited aboot a light switch last night, an' yoo saw how he was en Dad's car earlier. Spends loads o' time weth his horse…'

'I suppose that's understandable though?'

'Sure, but look at hem, worth the wait I reckon.'

~

As Carl rose for work on Monday morning, Kayleigh's keenness for Niall still amused him. As did her story to other locals about where he'd come from; her flat mate at university.

Carl's mood was light as he stood examining his beardless chin. 'Huh,' he chuckled 'That's taken years off!'

He put on one of the few buttoned shirts he possessed but, deciding a tie was still too big a step, left the top button defiantly undone. He regarded his over-all look in the mirror.

'Very dashing,' Sally teased.

Carl grabbed her up in his arms and kissed her.

'Ew! That's weird!'

'What?'

'You not having a beard. It's like kissing another man!'

'I'll grow it back…'

Sally drew him back, 'Perhaps, or… maybe… not?'

Carl kissed her again.

'You're going to be late…'

~

The car had started on the third turn of the key and only cut out once at its usual junction. Carl made a mental note to tweak the idling. Then

295

thought to himself, 'I'm going to be a Dad. I need to take control of my life.' He'd had offers and contacts in the broader journalistic world. Perhaps that was it? Give Chambers his notice? Yes. He was convinced. But then… should he discuss it with Sally?

He was still debating the idea as he swung open the door to the office. He was greeted by Chris's Cheshire cat smile.

'What?'

'Nice chin, Mr. Ree.'

'Alright, just doing my bit to steady the boat…'

'Storms over.' Henry chuckled.

A young woman appeared from Mr. Chambers' office.

'Janet?' Carl gasped.

The young woman smiled. 'No, sweetie, I'm Liz, Mr. Chambers' new PA.'

'Is that Carl?'

Liz glanced at Chris, who nodded affirmation, then back through the office door. 'Yes, Mr. Chambers.'

'Send him in. He's half an hour late!'

'Here we go.' Carl thought to himself, as he headed towards Mr. Chambers' office, briefly glancing at an envelope on his desk. 'You're sure your name isn't Janet?'

Liz laughed and shook her head.

'Ah Carl, welcome back.' It was by far a warmer greeting than he'd expected, and he turned towards the man at the mahogany desk. There was a whoop behind him from Mark, who'd been waiting just for this moment of discovery. 'Clive?'

'After chatting with Chris last Friday week, I thought it prudent to relieve my son Alfie of his responsibilities here and come back with someone young and bright enough to support me with all the interweb stuff. Love the Herald, didn't love that it was declining through my ineptitude, must admit I got a bit scared, staff to pay and what-not.'

'We'd have helped if you'd wanted us to…'

'Nonsense! You boys do too much as it is. Acquiring content and engaging in research. No, I couldn't see my way forward and I panicked. It won't happen again now Liz is on board. We were long overdue a woman's touch around here. I was running the place like a dinosaur, blast it, and we know what happened to them...'

'Alive and kicking and thriving in the Congo.'

'Ha! That's the stuff! I remember that article, riveting, splendid. So, you, Henry, Mark and Chris, I'm upping your pay. Best team in the industry and I'm going to keep you all, you hear! Anyone who can put up with my boy's demands eh? Salt of the ruddy Earth! Now, my boy, fruitful trip?'

'Absolutely, but no spoilers...'

'Ha! Quite right. Quite right!'

The conversation over, Carl edged back out to the others, Henry gesturing that the old boss was clearly bats! Carl crossed to his work station and looked down at the envelope.

Mark looked up at him 'You alright Carl?' There was a note of mischief in his voice. 'Your holiday sun tan's completely vanished.'

'I didn't get a tan.'

'Your usual paleness is paler.'

Carl picked up the envelope, there were some small objects sliding around inside. 'When did this arrive?' The handwritten address was a thing of beauty.

'On the door mat this morning, must have come Saturday. That's the fanciest way I've ever seen a name written. Another mystery?'

Carl broke the wax seal and opened it. Before he could peer inside a number of butterflies appeared from within. The whole office was now watching Carl's smiling wonderment. Infused with intrigue Carl looked down into the envelope...

Mr. Chambers appeared at his door, 'What's going on?'

Mark laughed, 'Carl's got butterflies, and something else.'

Carl tipped the remaining contents into his free hand, turning to show the others two beautifully made, sea glass, seal necklaces strung with leather cord.

Henry laughed nervously, 'What are they?'

'Gifts.' Carl beamed. 'Reminders that our efforts are a part of something greater, that the purposes of life are never achieved in isolation... that we are never, need never be, alone. That security is found in love...' He laughed, recalling the news he hadn't yet shared,

"Oh, just so you all know, I'll be a dad by the Winter!'

Thankyou for reading JANET: Storm Witch.
If you enjoyed your read, please give a few minutes of
your time to review it.

Find out more on The Earth Cries Hub website:
http://theearthcrieshub.wixsite.com/homeworld
or search 'The Earth Cries Hub' on Facebook.

Very Best Regards
Christopher J. Reeve

Printed in Great Britain
by Amazon